Praise for the No~~vels of Brad Taylor~~

Ring of Fire

"With Taylor's latest Taskforce novel featuring Pike Logan and Jennifer Cahill, he has further established himself as an elite military-thriller author. At this point, nobody is better at tackling hard-core action mixed with timely themes. . . . Fine work from a thriller writer at the very top of his game." —*Booklist* (starred review)

"Taylor's meticulous research brings that sense of chilling believability to his Pike Logan thrillers. . . . While intense action is a hallmark of Taylor's series, the well-developed characters are realistically explored. . . . A high-energy thriller." —Oline Cogdill, *Sun Sentinel* (Florida)

"Brad Taylor's aptly titled *Ring of Fire* continues his ambitious evolution from master of the military thriller to more of an American John le Carré, with just enough Robert Ludlum sprinkled in for good measure."
—*Providence Journal*

Ghosts of War

"*Ghosts of War* might not just be Brad Taylor's best novel but the best thriller of the year."
—ConservativeBookClub.com

"Brad Taylor will have your heart pounding and your pulse racing out of control." —*Suspense*

"*Ghosts of War* uses a bigger canvas than Taylor has employed previously, yet it is every bit as suspenseful, exciting, and believable." —Bookreporter.com

The Forgotten Soldier

"This exploration of the human side of war should quickly be recognized as one of Taylor's best efforts. Comparisons to Vince Flynn and Brad Thor are expected . . . but Taylor is now in a class by himself."
—*Booklist* (starred review)

"A realistic page-turner that fills a need for thrills while questioning the complicated process of statecraft."

—*Kirkus Reviews*

The Insider Threat

"The alternating first- and third-person viewpoints offer up a splendidly intense plot peeled back layer by layer in the best tradition of Jack Higgins and Frederick Forsyth." —*Providence Journal*

"Through well-defined characters and dialogue, this novel is a page-turner that is a must read."

—*Military Press*

No Fortunate Son

"With his latest, Taylor firmly entrenches himself on the level of James Rollins, Vince Flynn, and Brad Thor as the modern master of the military thriller."

—*Providence Journal*

"Logan and Cahill are a dream team, and military-thriller fans who seek realistic scenarios should consider Taylor mandatory reading." —*Booklist*

"A chilling novel for our time, with a frighteningly realistic plot." —*The Huffington Post*

Days of Rage

"A Pike Logan thriller filled with heart-thumping action and insane heroics. . . . A fun, satisfying adventure."

—*Kirkus Reviews* (starred review)

"Combines up-to-the-minute spy craft with musings about the morality of murder, even when justified, and shows that the latest gadgetry still can't replace human intuition and skill." —*Booklist*

The Polaris Protocol

"A great premise, nonstop action, and one of the baddest villains in the genre . . . make this a winner."

—*Publishers Weekly*

"Taylor continues to tell exciting action stories with the authenticity of someone who knows the world of special ops. He also has the chops to create terrific characters whom readers will root for. This series just gets better and better." —*Booklist*

The Widow's Strike

"Clever plotting and solid prose set this above many similar military action novels." —*Publishers Weekly*

"Taylor, whose background in Special Forces gives his work undeniable authenticity, delivers another exciting thriller that the covert-ops crowd will relish. Get this one into the hands of Vince Flynn fans." —*Booklist*

Enemy of Mine

"The story moves along at a rapid clip. . . . Satisfies from start to finish." —*Kirkus Reviews* (starred review)

"Few authors write about espionage, terrorism, and clandestine hit squads as well as Taylor does, and with good reason. . . . His boots-on-the-ground insight into the situation in the Middle East and special skills in 'irregular warfare' and 'asymmetric threats' give his writing a realistic, graphic tone." —*Houston Press*

All Necessary Force

"Fresh plot, great action, and Taylor clearly knows what he is writing about. . . . When it comes to tactics and hardware, he is spot-on."
—#1 *New York Times* bestselling author Vince Flynn

"The first few pages alone . . . should come with a Surgeon General's warning if you have a weak heart."
—*Bookreporter*

"Well written, edgy, and a damn good yarn."
—*Kirkus Reviews*

Also by Brad Taylor

Short Works

RING

★ OF ★

FIRE

★★★★★★★★★

BRAD TAYLOR

A Pike Logan Thriller

DUTTON

DUTTON

An imprint of Penguin Random House LLC
375 Hudson Street
New York, New York 10014

First Dutton premium mass market printing, 2017

ISBN 9781101984789

Printed in the United States of America
2 4 6 8 10 9 7 5 3 1

For Tom Greer, an Operator, a warrior, and a friend.
See you on the other side.

Saudi Arabia has long been considered the primary source of al Qaeda funding, but we have found no evidence that the Saudi government as an institution or senior Saudi officials individually funded the organization. . . . Our investigation has uncovered no credible evidence that any person in the United States gave the hijackers substantial financial assistance.

The 9/11 Commission Report

Finding: While in the United States, some of the September 11 hijackers were in contact with, and received support or assistance from, individuals who may be connected to the Saudi Government. . . . Neither CIA nor FBI witnesses were able to identify definitively the extent of Saudi support for terrorist activity globally or within the United States.

Report of the Congressional Joint Inquiry into the Terrorist Attacks of September 11, 2001—Redacted Pages

(U) (SECRET) Derived From G-3
Declassify On: X1

(U) Details: (S) Pursuant to the investigation into the 09/11/01 terrorist attacks, the Federal Bureau of Investigation in Tampa Division became aware of _____ is allegedly a wealthy and successful international businessman. _____ and his family resided in a $530,000.00 in an affluent section of Sarasota, Florida. On or about 08/27/2001, the _____ fled their home.

(U) (S) Based upon repeated citizen calls following September 11, the FBI and the Southwest Florida Domestic Security Task Force became aware of the _____ family. Following an inspection of their home by agents of the Southwest Florida Domestic Security Task Force, it was discovered that the _____ left their residence quickly and suddenly. They left behind valuable items, clothing, jewelry, and food in a manner that indicated they fled unexpectedly without prior preparation or knowledge.

(U) (S) Further investigation of the _____ family revealed many connections between the _____ and individuals associated with the terrorist attacks on 09/11/2001. More specifically, a _____ family member, _____ also

Declassified FBI report detailing the fleeing from Florida of a wealthy Saudi family with ties to the 9/11 terrorists, courtesy of the Florida Bulldog (FloridaBulldog.org)

★ RING OF FIRE ★

1

One day in September 2001

Dexter Worthington didn't set out to murder anyone. Nobody in his position would. He was an up-and-coming small businessman, and killing another human being would definitely be counterproductive to his goals. All he was doing was trying to ensure the growth of his company.

But he killed nonetheless.

Holding the positions of president, CEO, CFO, and every other slot on the board of his firm—which is to say it was barely large enough to be called a *firm*—he hoped today was the day when he finally broke out. When he caught the whale of a contract that would allow him to quit groveling for scraps at the military industrial complex's table and start throwing out scraps of his own.

The owner of a small aircraft maintenance firm called Icarus Solutions—a name Dexter thought incredibly clever—he had struggled to survive for years, barely earning enough to pay the rent for his hangar at the Sarasota airport. He had lived hand to mouth for so long he was no longer sure what the opposite would be, his privileged upbringing a thing of the past. The pressure had destroyed his marriage—although that had probably been preordained with his choice of bride, who was used to the better things in life. He cursed the misfortune that arrived time and time again, convinced it wasn't his abilities but unseen forces conspiring to drive him into the grave.

That all changed the day he met the prince.

Seven months earlier, an aircraft from Saudi Arabia had landed in Sarasota, Florida, and a pompous delegation had exited, running through a spring shower to a caravan of limousines. They'd raced out of the airport without talking to anyone, and then one of the pilots had approached his hangar. He was an Aussie or Kiwi from his accent, and Dexter could tell he was upset, even if he tried not to show it. It turned out the aircraft had a maintenance issue, and nobody within the Sarasota Manatee Airport Authority was willing to help him in the timeline required. The pilot said the "prince" would be in the area for only about four hours, and he wouldn't be pleased if his plane wasn't airworthy when he returned.

Dexter had agreed to help, and one thing led to another, until a crown prince of the house of al-Saud was personally thanking him. The entourage then left in the same flurry in which it had arrived, and Dexter found himself standing next to the one Saudi Arabian who'd remained behind. His name was Tariq bin Abdul-Aziz, and he was the reason for the prince's visit. The son of an incredibly influential Saudi financier, Tariq lived in Sarasota and wanted to learn to fly.

Strangely enough, they'd bonded through that mutual love of aviation, with Tariq showing up for coffee each morning just to watch the airplanes come and go. Somewhere in the conversations, Dexter had mentioned that he had failed to secure a single government contract in the entire time he'd been in business and that Icarus Solutions was on its last legs. Tariq had smiled knowingly, explaining that Dexter didn't understand how such things worked, and took the time to show in detail the slimy underbelly of government deal making.

And now Dexter was committed. Driving up to the access control point for Tariq's neighborhood, he wondered if he'd made a mistake. Didn't matter, because it was too late to do anything about it now. He gave his name and identification to the guard manning the gate. The guard looked at it, compared it to a board in the shack, then handed him a pass. Dexter put it on the dash, then drove his Honda Civic through the gates of Tariq's posh neighborhood, hoping the darkness would hide the dents and gouges on the Civic's battered frame.

Ogling the ostentatious McMansions that lined the road, most garishly illuminated with lighting that should be reserved for the Vegas strip, he felt giddy and more than a little scared.

Either the prince had come through, or he hadn't. If he had, Dexter would build a McMansion of his own, perhaps in this same neighborhood. If he hadn't, well, Dexter was finished. His entire business—not to mention every other asset he owned—would be forfeited for the two million dollars he'd borrowed to make the "donation."

At least he'd never have to pay another blood cent to his shrew of an ex-wife.

Small consolations.

Two blocks from Tariq bin Abdul-Aziz's house, he unconsciously slowed, not wanting to hear the decision. Reflecting on what had brought him to this point. Without even realizing it, he drove past the house, seeing one of the four garage doors open, an SUV with the rear hatch raised in front of it, the lights on inside.

He backed up and swung into the driveway, his headlights sweeping across someone with a suitcase. He squinted and saw it was Tariq.

He parked and got out, now considerably worried. "Tariq, hey, what's up?"

Startled, Tariq whirled around, then grinned sheepishly. "Dexter, you scared the shit out of me." No sooner had the curse word slipped from his mouth than he was glancing around, looking for his wife.

A small man with an olive complexion and a pencil-thin black mustache, Tariq had initially surprised Dexter with his Western habits, but Dexter had learned he'd spent the majority of his life outside of Saudi Arabia, having attended boarding school in England before college in America. His wife, on the other hand, was devoutly religious and didn't take kindly to his Western affectations.

When she didn't appear, Tariq loaded the suitcase into the rear of the SUV. Dexter noticed it was crammed to the windows with all manner of items, increasing his alarm.

He said, "What's all this? What's happening?"

Tariq smiled, saying, "I received some wonderful news. I made it into a prestigious graduate program in my home country, but I have to be there the day after tomorrow. We're flying home."

Dexter saw Tariq's wife coming toward them from inside the garage, carrying a baby and wearing a black abaya, her head covered in a colorful hijab.

Confused, Dexter said, "You're all leaving? For good?"

"Yes. We have tickets for tonight, but I hope to come back in a year or two."

"What about the house? Your cars? The furniture?"

"It's my father's house, actually, and he will deal with it. It's nothing."

Finally, Dexter asked the question that mattered the most: "What about me?"

He saw confusion flit across Tariq's face and realized

that two million dollars to this man was the same as a five-dollar bill to Dexter. Something that didn't really matter.

Dexter said, "We had a deal, right? I created the shell company and provided the required 'donation.' I know it's already been withdrawn. Don't tell me you guys screwed me over two million dollars. It's nothing to you, but everything to me."

Dexter finally saw recognition. Tariq said, "Yes, yes, I'm sorry. I've been so preoccupied with packing I forgot." He placed another suitcase in the back, then turned around, formally straightening up and extending his right hand. Dexter hesitantly took it, waiting.

Tariq said, "Congratulations. After fierce competition and extensive vetting, you beat out thirteen other international companies." He winked, then said, "Based on my father's recommendation, the royal family has selected you for the maintenance contract."

And like that, all the fear was washed away. Once a beggar of scraps, Dexter was now a player. The owner of a multimillion-dollar contract that would guarantee his rise.

Dazed, he started to reply when Tariq said, "I'm happy for you, my friend, but we're late for our flight. I'm sorry, but I have to go."

He reached into the SUV and retrieved a briefcase. He pulled out a folder and said, "All of your contacts are in there. Remember, you can't mention either my father or me. Just contact the people in there and they will do the rest."

Dexter nodded dumbly. Tariq hugged him, kissing both of his cheeks, then climbed into the driver's seat. He checked to ensure his wife and baby were settled, then gave Dexter a two-finger salute before driving away.

Dexter turned to watch him go, slowly winding in a circle as the car's taillights receded around a corner. Dexter was left reflecting on his new fortune. He gripped the folder hard enough to bend it, thinking one thought: *Need a new shell company.*

He drove his old Civic out of the land of milk and honey, pulling out his cell phone as he did so. He clicked on the speed dial for a contact labeled CHIP SAVOY.

There was no way he would let his money-grubbing ex-wife know about his newfound largesse, and to make that happen, he needed Chip.

A fraternity brother from college, Chip had done much, much better than Dexter up until now. Currently a hedge fund manager on Wall Street, Chip had been the one to walk him through the establishment of the shell company in the Bahamas for the Saudis, and also the one who had fronted the "donation" inside that shell company.

They had been as close as brothers in school, and whenever they were together, the income disparity between the two men disappeared. Chip treated Dexter as he always had—as his own blood—but Dexter knew that at the end of the day, money mattered. Chip was smart and had done the research on the contract. When he'd seen the companies vying for it—all of them the biggest names in the industry— he'd realized the potential for massive profits, given Dexter's light footprint. He'd fronted Dexter the means for success because he expected a return. And Dexter had no illusions about what would have happened if it had gone south: His "brother" would have taken everything he owned.

But that was water under the proverbial bridge, because it had worked. Now all Dexter needed to do was protect his investment.

The phone rang and rang, then went to voice mail. He

left a message, fantasizing about the Playboy Bunny Chip was probably sleeping with at that very moment.

He turned onto Highway 41, going home, and was hit with a logjam of cars. Traffic was always a pain, but not at nine o'clock at night. And then he remembered: The president was visiting Sarasota, doing some goodwill thing at a local elementary school the next day. He'd arrived thirty minutes ago, and his security team had jammed up every major artery.

Dexter muttered in aggravation, then settled in to wait, his twenty-minute drive to a beer now drawn out to at least an hour.

Chip Savoy exited the subway, fighting his way through the great unwashed mass of people also striving to leave. One man bumped into him, spilling Chip's morning coffee and eliciting some choice words.

The daily morning commute was becoming very trying, but it was the price he would have to pay if he wanted to live in Greenwich, Connecticut, instead of Manhattan. The city had been cool and new when he was scraping by for a living, but that had been years ago. He hadn't had to scrape for anything in a long time, and he had eventually decided it would be prudent to move to the upscale landscape of Greenwich. Nothing makes money like more money, and acting rich was half the battle.

Fine suits, fine dining, and fine cars—all a show for his clients. Well, mostly a show. There was no denying he enjoyed it, with the exception of the commute.

He'd taken to leaving his house earlier and earlier in an effort to beat the rush, but as far as he could tell, the rush started sometime around five in the morning, and there was no way he was getting up in the dead of night to arrive at work hours before any other executive. He had appearances to keep up, after all.

He reached the street and entered the flow of people swirling about, all headed purposefully somewhere, moving faster and faster, as if the time spent on the sidewalk was dangerous. He stopped, glancing into a cloudless blue sky, taking a moment to simply savor the day. Once inside the office, he knew this simple pleasure of doing nothing but breathing would be overshadowed by the dog-eat-dog world of making money.

Eventually, he crossed the street and entered his building's plaza, showing his badge to the security man and walking through a small turnstile. After a short wait, he walked into the elevator and rode to the ninety-fifth floor, with others getting off before him, stealing glances at him as they left. The higher one went, the more money was spent on the space, and he was going very high.

The company he worked for had the entire floor, and the elevator spilled right into the middle of it. He exited, seeing the young guns already at work, slaving away in a cubicle farm that stretched throughout the office, all striving to reach Chip's level.

In the not-too-distant past, Chip had been one of them. Now he had an office. Not a corner one, to be sure, but at least one with a view of Manhattan. The corner office would come soon enough.

He said a few pleasantries as he went through, leaving the cube farm behind on the way to his coveted space away from the chaos. He passed by his secretary's desk—she wouldn't be in for another hour—and unlocked his office. He swung open the door, and the reams of folders sitting on his desk gave him a spasm of regret. It was like a continual gushing of paper and electrons, all of them deals staggering in their monotony, with little inspiration and certainly no joy.

Was this how his life was to end? Working day after day cloistered in an office, slaving to make a profit for a company that didn't even know his name?

Lately, he had taken to fantasizing about doing something else. Something in the outdoors, where the money didn't matter. Maybe something in Alaska or . . . Borneo. Someplace that would allow him to flex his muscles instead of his ability to read numbers. A life he had always wanted to live but never had the courage to attempt.

In exactly one hour and forty-six minutes, in the brief second before his life was extinguished, he would dearly wish he'd made that choice.

He sat down to work, pulling the first folder to him. When his personal phone began buzzing over an hour later, he realized he'd lost track of time in the mind-numbing tedium. He glanced at his ridiculously ostentatious Hublot chronograph and saw it was eight forty-five in the morning. Too early for a business call from one of the partners.

He recognized the number and relaxed, punching the answer button and saying, "Dexter, tell me the good news."

"How do you know it's good?"

"Because if it were bad, you'd wait until I had to track you down."

He heard laughter on the other end, then, "Yeah, it's good. I got the contract. I have all the POCs and I've already talked to one. It's real. I'm in."

Chip stood, gazing out at the Manhattan skyline. "I'm glad to hear it, bud. Last thing I wanted to do was answer for a two-mil loss. When do you leave?"

"I haven't figured that out yet. Hey, Chip, the reason I'm calling is I want to set up my own shell company in the Bahamas. With that law office in Panama like we did with the Saudis."

"Mossack Fonseca? Why? You doing something illegal?"

"I thought you said it was perfectly legal."

Chip laughed and said, "It is, but it's never used that way. It's used to hide assets from taxes."

"Well, that's exactly what I want to do, except hide it from that bitch of an ex-wife."

Chip saw a speck in the distance, growing larger. He put up a hand to shield his eyes and said, "Ahhh . . . I see. Yeah, I can set that up. Actually, it'll work for taxes, too."

He paused, watching the speck grow impossibly large in the span of a second. He managed to get out "Holy shit," before a Boeing 767, last known as American Airlines Flight 11, slammed into the side of the North Tower, tearing through the heart of the building with the force of an avalanche and bringing with it 350,000 pounds of steel and jet fuel that incinerated all in its path.

Sitting in the den of his house, Dexter heard Chip shout, then silence. He said, "Chip? Chip, you still there?" He got nothing.

He redialed the phone, but Chip's line went straight to voice mail. He stood up and went to his Rolodex in his makeshift office, digging through until he found Chip's landline. It was no better. He went back into the den, thinking about whom he could call next, when he saw a breaking news story on his television.

He sat down heavily, not believing the grainy image of an airplane smashing into the World Trade Center.

He remained glued to the television the rest of the day, numb to the carnage. He spent hours on the phone with other fraternity brothers, trying to confirm what he already knew in his heart. Initially, like many, he felt outrage and anger. It wasn't until later that he would feel fear, when he saw a picture of Mohamed Atta, the ringleader of the hijackers.

A man he'd once seen at Tariq bin Abdul-Aziz's house.

3

One day in September 2016

I wiped the sweat from my eyes, the oppressive Charleston humidity making it feel like I was breathing water, even at seven in the morning. I waited for Jennifer to arrive, keeping track of her time and eyeing the eight-foot wood wall in front of me.

This was it. The cutline for winning the bet, and Jennifer knew it. I could smoke her on flat runs, swimming, and everything else, but I would be lucky to beat her on an obstacle course—especially after she modified each obstacle to suit her strengths. But I had some leveling of my own planned.

She ran up, sprinting the last hundred meters, looked at her time, then put her hands on her hips, breathing deeply. She said, "You want to do double or nothing? Before we go?"

Standing there in her Nike shorts, ponytail askew, after losing all three of the first legs of the triad, she was making a pretty bold pronouncement. She had a lot to lose.

I said, "What's the 'double,' since we aren't talking money?"

She'd apparently been thinking about it, because she said without hesitation, "You clean the cat box and do the dishes for a solid month. No bitching about how you cooked or that the cat hates you. You just do it."

A pretty strict bet. We shared the duties in our house—which meant I let her do them when she couldn't stand the filth building up—but if I lost, I'd be on her timeline. Which meant I'd actually have to clean.

On the other hand, if I won, I'd get . . . well, something more.

Choices, choices.

Two weeks before, we'd started talking about the differences in physical abilities between men and women, a conversation born from the fact that women were now allowed into all combat positions in the military. I was against it for some select specialties, and—of course—she was for it all the way. One thing led to another, and we'd made a bet. A race, so to speak, with winner take all. To make it fair, we'd debated the rules and the course. We'd already completed 90 percent of the events, and I'd won handily on most—the swim being the only one that was pretty much a draw. But now we had the obstacle course on the grounds of the Citadel, the military college of South Carolina.

As obstacle courses go, it wasn't that big a deal—the usual log-walk-rope-drop chain of events—but after surveying the thing, Jennifer had made a modification for every single obstacle. For one, we couldn't just climb the rope, touch the top, and come down. We had to climb the rope, get on top of the beam holding it, and traverse it to the far side.

I knew why. She was a damn monkey, and she knew that while I could win on pure strength, I couldn't match her climbing skills. I'd agreed because I knew I'd be so far ahead on points when we reached the obstacle course I'd be able to coast.

Only I wasn't that far ahead. Not nearly as far ahead in our agreed point structure as I thought I would be. She'd proven to be in better shape than I expected—especially on the mental side. The ruck march should have crushed her mentally, but she finished the damn thing only eighteen minutes behind me, slogging over the Ravenel Bridge on willpower alone, the sixty-pound ruck looking like a giant tick on her back, making me wish I'd run the entire twelve miles instead of keeping Jennifer in sight, toying with her. I *really* wished I hadn't agreed to the point spread on the obstacle course. Because I was in danger of losing.

But there's no way I would admit that.

I said, "Okay. You're on. But if I win, I get twice as much."

She scowled and said, "I can't believe you think that's appropriate. I was assuming I'd just clean for a month."

I grinned. "You're sure you'll win. What's the risk?"

Still not agreeing, she kicked the body armor I'd managed to scrounge from a buddy at a National Guard armory near our office in Mount Pleasant. She said, "This is a handicap that I shouldn't have to wear. We don't do big army."

"No, we don't, but it's a handicap for every single male on the battlefield. You want to prove your point, put it on."

She did so, now wearing about thirty pounds of ceramic plates ensconced in a vest that would alter her ability to navigate the obstacles. I put on my own armor, looked at my watch, and said, "Ready?"

She nodded, staring at the wall so intensely it was almost comical. I said, "Five, four, three, two, one."

On the utterance of "Whuu—" she took off, hitting the eight-foot wall in front of us and leaping over. I shouted, "Hey!" but she wasn't stopping. I sprinted to the wall, getting over it and seeing her on the obstacle called the "belly buster."

Basically, all you had to do was leap up onto a fat horizontal tree trunk about four feet off the ground, then jump out and catch another, higher pole and pull yourself over. Simple. Except Jennifer had dictated that you had to go over the top pole, then back around, then fling yourself to the lower pole again. If you couldn't maintain your balance, you started over.

I saw her leap, then swing her body in a circle around the log, like some Neanderthal gymnast on bars. She made it completely around, but her armor caught on something, threatening to cause her to fall. She clamped on with her legs just as I leapt up on the belly buster next to her. I swung my arms once, then launched myself into the air for the high log. I slammed into it, got around about half as gracefully as she had, and saw her fling herself back to the lower log. I did the same, smiling that I'd caught her. If she was slowed down by the armor on this obstacle, it would even it up for me the rest of the way.

She balanced on the lower log, then leapt back to the high one, scrambling to get over it and on with the course. I hit the lower log, windmilled my arms, and fell off.

Shit.

By the time I was through it, she was already on the ropes, two obstacles ahead of me, climbing like a demented spider monkey even with the armor on. She scrambled to the top of the frame holding the ropes, then began *running* down the four-by-four to the far side. No way would I be able to match that.

The course was two miles long, and I'd have to pray that the armor wore her out. I lost sight of her in the trees and just focused on my own technique, racing through obstacle after obstacle. Eventually, shouting penetrated the haze of my concentration.

To my right, some guy in uniform was yelling and

waving his arms around. I caught a flash of Jennifer ahead of me. I ignored him, picking up the pace. I had only about a quarter of a mile to catch her before the end of the course, and the way we'd dictated the rules, every second was going to cost me dearly in points. Maybe weighing this part so heavily wasn't such a bright idea after all.

I saw Jennifer scrambling up the second rope obstacle—this one was supposed to be a simple swing across a mud pit, but like an idiot, I'd agreed to Jennifer's modifications.

She'd gotten halfway up when she, too, heard the shouting. I saw her look at the man as I cleared the one obstacle between us. She climbed back down, then swung herself across the mud to the grass on the far side. I leapt up, grabbed the rope, and started climbing. She said, "Pike, there's someone shouting at us."

I reached the top and said, "So?"

I got on top of the beam just as the man reached Jennifer, screaming about what the hell we were doing here. He pointed up at me and said, "Get down from there."

I said, "Okay," and tightrope-walked to the far side, arms out for balance. I hung from the beam, then dropped. I saw him with his hands on his hips, glaring at me, Jennifer looking like a toddler in trouble next to him.

And I knew I was going to win. Jennifer had an innate moral streak that would prevent her from not following the man's instructions. She would try to calm him and explain that we had permission to be here—which we did.

I, on the other hand, would finish the course. I saw both of their mouths drop open when I took off at a sprint toward the final obstacles, then heard Jennifer shout, "Pike! Get your ass back here!"

If I were smart, I really would have. But I had a bet to win.

By the time I'd finished the course and circled back through the woods, she was in a fine fury, glowering at me as I walked up with a *what did I do?* look on my face.

The man said, "She says you have permission from the Marine Corps to use this."

The Marine Corps ROTC department at the Citadel managed the O course. They'd actually built it, using their funds, but it was on Citadel property, so there was always a little push and shove over who actually had the right to grant permission to use it.

I said, "Yeah, Gunny told me it wouldn't be an issue, with it being Sunday morning and all."

"Well, he didn't clear it with the grounds department. There are releases, legal issues, a whole host of things—especially with the way you were doing the obstacles. We have an SOP for this thing, and you were way outside of it. I'm within my rights to call the police on you for trespassing."

I raised my hands and said, "Okay, okay, we're done anyway. Won't happen again. Sorry for the trouble."

Indignant, he pointed his finger in my face, saying, "And I'm going to talk to the Gunny about this."

I was surprised he wanted to push it, given whom he was talking to. At six feet two, I was carrying more than two hundred pounds—and it wasn't from a beer belly like he was sporting. With a day's stubble highlighting a scar that ran down my cheek, I looked like a pirate, something Jennifer hated. She was always pestering me to shave because she said it made me look less than savory. Actually, she said scary. I decided to test that theory.

I slapped his finger away and leaned into his personal space, saying, "Fine. Can we go now?"

He took an involuntary step back, his eyes widening. He nodded without saying a word, and I began to walk to the start, supremely satisfied, Jennifer right behind me. When we were out of earshot, she punched my back and hissed, "I thought you said you had permission for this."

"I did."

"No, you didn't. I've never been so embarrassed. And you kept going, leaving me there to try to explain. I don't even know what a 'gunny' is."

I laughed and said, "So, is this about being embarrassed by that groundskeeper, or losing the bet?"

That really set her off. "Losing? Losing! If I hadn't stopped, he would have called the police. We'd be in the back of a squad car right now."

We reached the parking lot, where I'd prestaged a vehicle, and in a pious tone I said, "Always remember the mission. Mission comes first. I finished the O course ahead of you, which means I won every event. Which means I'm the winner."

She became apoplectic, her mouth opening and closing without a sound coming out.

I said, "And I'm holding you to the double or nothing. I think you can pay the first installment when we get home."

Livid, she spat out, "I'll do *no such thing*. You are *disqualified* for cheating."

I laughed and said, "Calm down, little Jedi. You're going to blow a blood vessel in your head."

She took off her armor and got into the car without another word, slamming the door. I did the same, getting behind the wheel. Having had my fun and wanting to smooth things over, I said, "We'll call this one a draw due to outside interference."

She muttered, "Because you knew I was going to beat your ass."

Before I could get out a smart-aleck reply, my phone rang with a special tone. The one telling me it was a secure call. Meaning we might have some business.

I looked at Jennifer and saw the same little thrill I was feeling, the earlier fight lost to history. No matter what I thought about the physical abilities of the fairer sex, there was no denying that mentally—at least for those like Jennifer—females were solid in a gunfight. I'd seen that numerous times firsthand. She wouldn't admit it, but she lived for the missions just like I did.

I put the car in drive and tossed her my phone, saying, "You can do the honors."

Driving back to our row house on East Bay, I got only her side of the conversation, but from what I heard, we were headed out pretty quickly. She hung up and laid the phone down. I said, "Well?"

"Well, it looks like that Panama Papers scare has surfaced again. Kurt wants us in DC today. He's got us tickets on a flight in a couple of hours."

"I thought they'd scrubbed that data and we were in the clear."

"Yeah, they did, but apparently there's an 'Agent Zero' out there who's got another load he's going to release."

4

Dexter Worthington glanced at the time once again, then went back to his computer screen, searching a news story, willing it to have additional information. He'd been doing the same series of motions every thirty seconds for the past ten minutes.

Where the hell is he?

He scanned the story for the hundredth time, and it didn't get any less explosive. The International Consortium of Investigative Journalists—a collection of networked reporters who spanned the globe—was preparing to release a second data dump of the so-called Panama Papers.

The first leak had occurred in the spring of last year, and it was the largest illegal data dump in history, encompassing terabytes of information, so much so that one could stack WikiLeaks, Snowden, and every other leak together, and the Panama Papers would far eclipse them.

The target was a Panamanian law firm called Mossack Fonseca that specialized in offshore shell companies. Completely legal on the surface, its main focus was hiding wealth from authorities, as the intricacies and subterfuge of the shell companies were almost impossible to decipher—unless some insider calling himself Agent Zero decided to leak the information.

None of this would have mattered a whit to Dexter, except Mossack Fonseca was the same company that he'd used with the Saudis more than a decade before. When the first leak had occurred, he had lived in terror for a month, consumed with the fear that his association with Tariq and his father would be outed—along with Dexter's long-held suspicions that they'd had a hand in 9/11.

It had not. Even given the enormous scope of the leak, Dexter's shell company had remained ensconced inside Mossack Fonseca's digital fortress, protecting him from discovery. But now there was supposedly another leak on the way, and Dexter had much, much more to lose than he'd had fifteen years ago.

Although he'd never spoken to Tariq again—afraid of confirming his darkest fear and convinced that any communication would be monitored by federal authorities—he had taken the contract in Saudi Arabia, and it had proven lucrative.

He learned that having a contract begat more contracts, and he began to expand his business, branching out from simple aviation services to full-spectrum military industrialist titan. He had defense contracts encompassing everything from providing interpreters to SOCOM in Uganda to electronic perimeter security at a US consulate in Mali.

In short, he was now a player, and with that power came a duty to prevent this new leak from bringing everything down. He'd worked too long and hard, developing influence both in the halls of Congress and in the halls of the Pentagon, and in the ensuing years he'd learned to play hardball better than most. It was why he was successful.

He leaned forward and punched an intercom button, saying, "Janice, has Johan called you about being late?"

Before she could answer, he caught a movement at the door, then recognized his head of security, Johan van Rensburg.

Dexter said, "Where the hell have you been?"

Speaking with a light Afrikaans accent, Johan said, "I just got in. I was delayed at JFK and had to spend the night."

"I thought you were coming in two days ago."

"Couldn't get out of Jordan. You told me to make sure the work was done before I came home."

Dexter's latest venture was a contract from Jordan's King Abdullah II Special Operations Training Center, providing armorer support to the various courses run there, with an eye toward increasing beyond that into the security realm itself.

Created jointly between the United States and Jordan in 2009, KASOTC was the only Special Operations training facility of its kind in the Middle East, with ranges and mock-ups that rivaled anything in Europe or the United States, and it was used by multiple countries on an invitation basis. Run solely by ex-operators from various countries, one could just as easily run across a Brit formerly in the SAS as an American from US Army Special Forces. It was where Dexter had initially met Johan, and had convinced him to leave his current contract as a CQB instructor with KASOTC and come work for Icarus Solutions as the head of Dexter's fledgling security division.

A former member of South Africa's famed Reconnaissance Commandos—the Recces—Johan had left the military after the turmoil in his country in the early nineties. He'd bounced around from job to job, most on the African continent at various hot spots. He'd fought with Executive Outcomes in Sierra Leone, Sandline International in Liberia, and, most recently, at the behest of the Nigerian government against Boko Haram. He'd eventually tired of getting shot at and decided to go the route of training instead of operations, landing the job at KASOTC.

Unlike the Hollywood portrayal of SOF supermen, Johan wasn't a bulked-up Arnold Schwarzenegger, but more wiry, with ropes of muscle clinging closely to his frame and what looked like a permanent tan baked into his skin. Dexter didn't know all he'd done, but he'd heard enough from rumors, and he knew the scars on Johan's body hadn't come from playing rugby.

Johan said, "What's the fire? Why'd you call me back?"

Dexter pointed to a seat and said, "I've got an issue. Something that could cause significant problems with Icarus."

Johan sat down and said, "Okay."

Dexter toyed with a paperweight biplane, realizing he would need to measure his words carefully. Dexter worked in the "defense industry" as a manager of aviation assets, but all of his employees were support. He had no real "security" experience at the sharp end of the spear. Johan was the only man he knew who could prevent the leak, but in so doing, Dexter would be placing significant trust in him. Giving him knowledge that could be used against Dexter in the future.

There was also the problem of Johan's willingness to execute. He was a hard man, no doubt, but he'd shown a perverse sense of honor. Johan was a cynical killer on the surface, but underneath, he believed. He would not do anything against his personal code of conduct. And that code was written in stone.

While thinking of how to present the problem, Dexter had had a stroke of genius. He remembered a conversation he'd had with the South African when he'd initially hired him: The man hated traitors and considered organizations like WikiLeaks to be enablers of the theft of national secrets. On top of that, he absolutely despised the press for perceived transgressions against South Africa, and that had continued on into his mercenary days.

One night, after a few beers and a single question from Dexter, Johan had become apoplectic, ranting like a madman. To the point that Dexter had felt fear. The Panama Papers bore none of those taints, but it was similar in technique. All he had to do was spin it the right way.

Johan said, "Well?"

Dexter formulated his words but couldn't look him in the eyes. Johan had a way of peeling back the soul, as if he were mentally flaying you, and it was unsettling. Dexter was sure he'd falter if he locked eyes with the man.

He continued playing with the paperweight airplane, saying, "Do you remember the Panama Papers last year?"

5

Johan said, "Yeah. Some fuck stole a bunch of proprietary information and gave it to journalists. What about it?"

"I told you about how this company was founded. About the first contract in KSA. You remember that?"

"Yes."

"Well, it was predicated—and I'm not proud of this—on a bribe to a certain Saudi contact. I did it, and now I'm where I am. *You* are where you are. No more running and gunning. A nice job with a hefty salary."

"What was the bribe for?"

Dexter shifted the conversation, saying, "I used a shell company from that law firm in Panama. The first leak—before I hired you—was huge, but I wasn't in it."

Dexter pointed at the computer screen and said, "There's a second leak coming, and there's a good chance I'll be in it. If that happens, at best, I'll be crushed for the relationship by the prima donna politicians all looking for a score, and worst, arrested for illegal contract negotiations and insider trading."

He paused, wanting to see if Johan was on board, risking a glance across the desk. He couldn't tell one way or the other. The man's face was stoic, his shaggy blond hair partially covering his eyes. Dexter sagged back in his chair and said, "If that leak goes, I'm out of a company. And you're out of a job."

Johan leaned forward, brushing his hair aside and giving Dexter his full, uncomfortable attention. He said, "What do you want me to do?"

Dexter said, "Well . . . I know who the reporter is that's going to meet the leaker, a sorry sack of shit like Snowden and Manning. I was hoping you'd meet the leaker instead. Convince him it wasn't in his best interests."

Johan picked an M&M's candy from a bowl on the desk, popped it into his mouth, and said, "I could do that, I suppose. One less waste of flesh walking the earth, but it's not without risk."

"I understand. I'm prepared to pay you a great deal. This bribe I did can't see the light of day. Ever. It was nothing on the grand scheme of things, but it's everything to us."

Johan popped another M&M and said, "You keep saying that, but I've worked this side of the fence for a while. Bribes happen all the time, and you have leverage with the American establishment. Maybe it's better to let it out and fight it on the publicity front. My way is dirty."

"No. That won't work."

Johan straightened and said, "Why? You have the ear of sitting senators and half the generals in the Pentagon. Unless there's something more. What was the bribe for? Who got it?"

"It's not the bribe. It's the fact that it's Saudi Arabia. Ten years ago, that would be nothing. Now, with the Islamophobia rampant in the United States, I'll be crucified. I can't count on support from the Pentagon or Congress. Especially after the administration released those classified pages from the congressional inquiry into 9/11. The ones dealing with Saudi complicity in the attacks."

"Okay. Once again, what do you want me to do?"

"Interdict this 'Agent Zero.' Get his data and destroy it."

Johan considered the mission, then said, "You want him dead. Is that it?"

Dexter hadn't thought about that, the question startling him.

Johan said, "Let's face it, if I meet him as the journalist and I get his information, and it doesn't get exposed, he's just going to try again."

Dexter said, "Yes. I see your point. I suppose you couldn't just convince him?"

Johan barked a sharp laugh and said, "I could for the five minutes we were together, but once he's gone—and safe—he'll reconsider. He understands the risks. He's made powerful enemies with his release, which means he has courage."

Dexter nodded, realizing what Johan had said was true. The Panama Papers had exposed corruption from the highest levels of foreign governments to the biggest bosses of organized crime. Whoever Agent Zero was, there were plenty of people who wanted him dead. Which made the decision easier. With that many enemies, nobody would connect a lone defense contractor to the action.

Dexter said, "I don't want the information out. Period. You do what you think is best. You'll be well rewarded."

He withdrew an envelope and laid it on the desk, saying, "This is the information on the reporter who's going to meet him. Don't ask me how I got it. Just understand that it cost a significant amount of influence and money. You talk to him, find the meeting site, then assume his place."

Johan took the envelope and opened it. He glanced at the first page and said, "International Consortium of Investigative Journalists. Washington, DC."

"Yes. I'll pay for the airfare and hotels, of course. And a handsome bonus when it's done. I'd like you to leave tomorrow."

"What about the journalist?"

"What do you mean?"

"Well, I can't just ask him for the source and expect him to gladly give it to me. And once I leave, he'll contact this Agent Asshole and tell him to flee."

Dexter instinctively knew where the question was headed, but he didn't want to face the decision. Johan saved him from the problem.

He stood and said, "Don't worry about it. I fucking hate reporters. All a bunch of lying shitheads with rainbows and noble causes. They destroyed my country, then destroyed my employment in Africa, first with Executive Outcomes, then every other company I worked for. Now they're trying to destroy me again."

He pocketed the envelope and said, "I'll do him for free."

6

The sign read, BLAISDELL CONSULTING PARKING ONLY. FOR INQUIRIES, ENTER THROUGH MAIN ENTRANCE ON 10TH STREET. I pulled the rental car in front of the gate to the underground parking deck and pressed the button on the intercom because I didn't have a badge to wave in front of the card reader.

It buzzed, and a female voice said, "Can I help you?"

"Grolier Recovery Services here to see Kurt Hale."

I heard her shuffling around for a minute, checking clipboards and probably calling offices, and understood why. Nobody from the outside firms of the Taskforce ever came to the headquarters—but then again, none of the other outside assets were run by Operators.

Truthfully, I very rarely came to the headquarters in Washington, DC, precisely because we wanted to maintain a separation between the cover organization of Blaisdell Consulting and my own firm, Grolier Recovery Services. Just like criminals at a CSI crime scene, every time we touched, we left a little clue behind. Something someone could potentially use to unravel exactly what it was we did. It was the reason I'd conducted a surveillance detection route just to get here. Precautions, precautions, precautions.

Once a year or so, Kurt decided to have me up to headquarters just to get a feel for what had changed. Keep me in the loop with all the other shooters who were running operations. Only a few short years ago I'd still been on active duty, sheep-dipped from an Army Special Mission Unit into the Taskforce. Grolier was the only civilian company that actually conducted missions, an honor not afforded anyone else. Well, I called it an honor, but the truth of the matter was, I got results. Period. As such, I was a little bit of an outlier. All the other civilian companies—aircraft leases, boating companies, trucking firms, whatever we needed for operations—were strictly support.

Without another word from the speaker, the gate rose, and I entered. Jennifer saw all the spaces were numbered and asked where the visitors' parking was. I chuckled. Unlike me, she'd never been in the military or intelligence community and, as a result, had spent precious little time inside headquarters and truly was a civilian.

I said, "No visitors' parking in here. The Taskforce never gets visitors. Each space is reserved."

"So what are we going to do?"

Right next to the glass doors providing entry to the building was a free spot, marked KURT HALE, CEO. I said, "I'm taking the boss's spot."

She shook her head and dialed her phone. I parked and heard her say, "We're here."

Then: "Okay. Standing by."

She said, "I didn't tell him where you parked."

"He'll figure it out."

Thirty seconds later, the glass door opened and a man dressed like he was going to a *We Are the Eighties* reunion came out. He held it open, waving us in.

I exited the car, saying, "Retro, Kurt's got you running errands for him now?"

He smiled and said, "Knuckles ain't around, so I guess it's me."

Jennifer said, "Kurt's not going to mind where we parked, is he?"

"Beats me. I don't have a parking spot, so power to the people."

I said, "Where's Knuckles? You guys are on training cycle."

We went through the door to an elevator, him waving his card and punching in more numbers, saying, "Yeah, he's been tasked as a sponsor for a new hire. Leading him around, getting him settled."

Which was surprising. Knuckles was my second-in-command, so I should have been consulted on any new hires to the team. As the team leader, I wasn't about to say anything to Retro and decided to just act like I knew what was going on, waiting to see Kurt Hale.

We exited the elevator and walked down a broad hall-way, past offices full of people left and right who would glance at us, then turn back to work.

Retro knocked on an oak door, then opened it. Just inside was George Wolffe—the deputy commander of the Taskforce and an old-school CIA paramilitary officer.

He ignored me and said to Jennifer, "Well, well. Koko made the trip too."

She surprised him with a stone face, saying, "Yes, I did. I am, after all, half owner of GRS. Why wouldn't I come?"

With his use of her callsign, Jennifer immediately thought he was patronizing her. She was always self-conscious whenever we did anything with people out-side of our team, because she knew her position as a fe-male team member was precarious and, in some circles, hated. Jennifer had been inside the headquarters only a couple of times in her entire life, but George certainly knew all about her. First female operator was a hard one to miss, and, unbeknownst to her, he had been the deciding vote to let her try. He meant no harm, actually thinking he was giving her a compliment. He looked at me for support.

I said, "Welcome to my world. She hates that damn callsign. I'm thinking of changing it to Fluffy Rabbit or something."

He stuck out his hand, giving as good as he got, saying, "Well, *Koko*, I'm sorry your callsign is a talking gorilla. Mine is the Wolf. I didn't get it for my name."

She quickly realized her mistake, breaking into a grin and taking his hand. She said, "I didn't get mine because I look like a gorilla. Knuckles gave it to me."

He swung the door wide and stepped aside, saying, "I know, I know. We all suffer for our sins."

We entered a simple office that could've been found anywhere in DC, with the exception of the wall adornments. All of them were the last vestiges of some sorry asshole who had tried to kill Americans. A piece of metal from a Hellfire strike, a pressed kaffiyeh tinged with red, three pages of a manifesto describing the end of civilization as we know it, now hanging as a wall plaque in the office of the man who'd prevented just such a thing.

On the phone, Kurt Hale saw us enter and waved us to a couple of seats. He said a few words and then hung up. The air was silent for a moment, until I said, "Well, sir?"

He rubbed a hand through his hair, staring at the phone, lost in thought, then turned to us, switching from whatever was said on the landline to me. He said, "Hey, my favorite team leader. Glad you could come on such short notice. We have a problem."

I decided to get my issues out first. "What's up with the new team member? The one Knuckles is in-processing? If I'm the 'favorite,' why didn't I get a say?"

He looked confused, then said, "What are you talking about? She's not a new member of your team. She's just new to the Taskforce. That's not why I asked you to come up."

And it all became clear. I said, "Knuckles is a sponsor for a female support person?"

He said, "Yeah, but that's not why you are here."

Before he could say anything else, Jennifer said, "A CIA case officer?"

He looked wary and said, "Yeah?"

I said, "Named Carly Ramirez?"

Then he got aggravated. "Yes. Carly Ramirez. The same one you read on in Athens. How did you know that?"

I said, "Just a hunch."

He went from me to Jennifer, then said, "What's the big deal?"

Jennifer grinned and said, "You know they're dating, right?"

He said, "Of course I did." But the reaction on his face betrayed him. He said, "That's not why I brought her on board . . . She's the one who helped your fiasco in Greece. She's a good hire."

I realized he had no idea what Knuckles had in mind. I said, "Why is an Operator doing the legwork for support staff?"

"Because he knew her, damn it. She was a friend of Decoy, and a friend of his. It made sense. It's not a fraternization issue. She's support and he's an Operator. What's your point?"

"I'm saying he wants her in on the team. As an *Operator*. Did he say she could do more than case officer work?"

Carly was an operations officer in the CIA who had

crossed paths with us more than once, including having a heated relationship with a Taskforce Operator who had been killed in action. Since then, Knuckles—my 2IC— had taken a shine to her. She probably had no idea what Knuckles had in mind, but then again, neither had Jennifer. It wasn't that hard to figure out, unless you were Kurt Hale.

Kurt said, "Well, he did say something like that, but we don't work for the Department of Defense. This isn't a social experiment." He glanced at Jennifer and then said, "Understand, I'm not against it, but I'm not doing it just because some female wants to prove her bones."

Jennifer grinned and said, "Yeah, screw all of that 'proving yourself' crap, since she's handicapped as a female and all. On the other hand, maybe she'll be worth it on skill alone. Hard to tell."

Kurt nodded solemnly, completely missing the sarcasm. He said, "I had enough trouble getting you inside."

I stepped in, saying, "But *that* was worth it."

He finally laughed and said, "Yes, it was worth it. If only to keep your ass in line."

I said, "Can you at least give Knuckles some grief? Make him pay for the subterfuge?"

Jennifer poked me in the ribs and I said, "Okay, okay. Let him live. Why are we here? What's the forest fire?"

Kurt exhaled, relieved to be off the hot seat.

He said, "I have a mission that—believe it or not—I can't do with Taskforce assets. I need a cutout, and you're it."

7

Cutout? What the hell is he talking about? The entire Taskforce organization was a cutout. We were so illegal, how could the fact that I was a civilian company matter?

He said, "You heard about the Panama Papers, right?"

"Yeah, of course. It had everyone in a tizzy a few months ago, but we came up clean."

The Taskforce had no taint of official government on it, and so, in order to operate, we did much like the Mafia did—we created shell companies that were stitched together like a giant Frankenstein monster, making it impossible for anyone to figure out that the tail end was with Uncle Sam. All those various firms were covered under a shell company for the purposes of payment and leasing, and unfortunately, the Taskforce had chosen the law firm of Mossack Fonseca to create a lot of them.

Aircraft leases, transnational shipping vessels, in extremis medical care, intelligence/reconnaissance assets, and a host of other companies were buried in a blizzard of paper to prevent anyone from determining their true purpose. When the first leak had occurred, everyone had soiled their pants, but at the end of the day, we'd come up clean.

Honestly, I had some mixed emotions about the damn leak. While I hated the press just on general principle—because all they ever did was make things worse in my world—the ICIJ was a group comprised of *journalists*, unlike that saggy, self-important windbag site known as WikiLeaks. I hated reporters digging into my world, but I grudgingly respected them.

I did, after all, live in the United States, and somewhere underneath my constant fighting to get the mission done, I realized why I was doing it. Yeah, the ICIJ was reporting on things that might hurt us, but they were *reporting*. Unlike that foppish asshat hiding in the Ecuadorian embassy in Britain, who simply leaked classified information wholesale without any attempt at reflection or perspective.

Kurt said, "Yeah, we did come up clean last time, but we've got indicators saying there's another leak on the way, and we need to know what's in it."

"You mean you want me to interdict it?"

Grudging respect went only so far. If he wanted me to affect the outcome, I was more than willing.

"No. Just get visibility on the data. The Oversight Council won't approve of actually stopping a journalist from getting the documents. They only agreed to let us intercept what's in it so we can start with damage control. Closing down accounts, building new firewalls, that sort of thing."

The Oversight Council was the Taskforce's board of directors, so to speak. Thirteen men and women isolated from all three branches of government who had a vote on everything we did. We were way, way outside of any legal constructs—such as the Constitution—but when we were created, Kurt had made sure there were some checks and balances to prevent people like me from going hog wild.

I usually agreed with their orders, having the ability to see the second- and third-order effects, but in this case, it was ridiculous. I got along okay with the Council, having had a personal stake in saving the lives of some of their family members in the past, but this sort of myopic order was downright stupid. Either you were wading in the mud or you weren't. It's like they thought they could fight this kind of war and still maintain their dignity in their cloistered, oak-paneled room. They might as well order me to give Miranda rights to the next terrorist I saw.

On second thought, I'd be better off keeping that thought to myself, because they would probably agree.

I said, "So all you want me to do is obtain the data? Isn't that self-defeating? If I can get it, I can destroy it."

He said, "Yeah, yeah, I hear you. The problem is the source himself. You destroy this data, and he'll still have access. Nobody knows who he is, and he's not going to quit. Bottom line, the Council is not going to allow you lethal authority to prevent his disclosures. And I would, in no way, even ask for that."

I nodded, the statement making sense. I wasn't going to kill some whistleblower simply to protect my own ass. I guess, like the Council, I had some lines I wouldn't cross.

Jennifer said, "So what's the mission? Why is the cut-out with us important?"

Kurt put his hands behind his head and leaned back, saying, "Well, the Council isn't completely pure here. Even directing someone to interdict the press has them hot and bothered. They refused Omega authority for anyone on active duty under the employ of the United States government, be that CIA or DoD. They do, however, have a soft spot for you."

Omega authority meant unilateral Taskforce action and was really hard to come by. You had to prove beyond a reasonable doubt that the target was out to harm the

United States. In this case, it didn't meet the smell test, because this guy was only threatening Taskforce exposure—and not in a violent way.

I said, "You're kidding me. Is this going where I think it's going? I finally get the IMF mission?"

He grinned and said, "Yep. If you're compromised, they'll disavow any knowledge of you. Your company is a well-established entity—unlike some of the slipshod covers we use here—so the only way it'll be penetrated is if you roll over. They want you to do the mission but don't want the liability. In their minds, it's not real if no US government employees are used. I know it sucks, but that's just where they are right now."

"You mean because of the election coming up?"

"Well, yeah. That's a big part of it. President Hannister can't be caught in a scandal two months before the nation votes."

President Philip Hannister had assumed the office of the presidency six months ago, when Russian thugs in Ukraine had inadvertently assassinated his predecessor by blowing Air Force One out of the sky. He had done well in that disaster, preventing World War III when all considered it a foregone conclusion—and my team had been the linchpin behind that success. I genuinely liked him, and if he'd asked for this, I'd do it.

I said, "Did Hannister get a vote? Was he there?"

The Council met every quarter for updates on ongoing operations, but that didn't necessarily mean that the president was at the meeting. He was, after all, running a campaign.

Kurt said, "Yes, he was. In fact, he's the one who brokered the compromise. He personally asked for you."

Well, I liked him even more.

Kurt continued, "There's one more thing: We have

reason to believe that the release will hit the Rock Star bird. Which will lead to all sorts of questions about Grolier Recovery Services."

The Rock Star bird was a Gulfstream G650 that was ostensibly leased to our company for mundane travel as we flitted about the world looking at archeological sites. In reality, it was a flying weapons platform, with an arsenal hidden inside it to allow us to execute operations without worrying about host nation immigrations and customs finding the lethal tools. And it was really, really cool to fly around on.

I said, "That lease is Mossack Fonseca?"

"Yep. Hasn't come out yet, but it might now."

"Can I take it to do the mission?"

"Of course. It's your aircraft. As far as anyone knows. But if you fail, it might be the last time it's used. We'll have to burn it to the ground if the company leaks."

I said, "What do I have to go on?"

"We intercepted the email traffic between this Agent Zero and a journalist. Agent Zero is the one with the data. He's due to meet the reporter from the ICIJ this weekend."

I said, "How do you have that? If he's talking to journalists?"

We weren't allowed to eavesdrop on the American press, which made me skittish about the source of the information. If it was a "he said that she said that someone would meet," then I might balk.

Kurt said, "The initial journalist he contacted is from Spain, and he's also been communicating with known members of ISIS. Not in a bad way—he was simply doing research—but it was enough for us to be able to make an argument for investigation before we knew he was a journalist. We caught this on the ISIS investigation and had no idea that it would lead where it did. An American journalist is meeting him, passed off from the Spaniard. We don't know Agent Zero's name; we don't know the journalist's name; we only know when and where. You guys will have to figure the rest out."

I said, "Well, what's the when and where?"

Kurt said, "I saved the best part for last. It's at the Atlantis resort in the Bahamas. Apparently, that country is the host to a ton of Mossack Fonseca shell companies. Including ours."

I glanced at Jennifer, seeing concurrence to go ahead with the deliberations. I said, "Okay, who do I get from the team?"

"Nobody. You're it. The rest are active duty."

"You're shitting me. Just the two of us? How do you expect that to happen?"

"The usual way. Make a little Pike luck."

"Sir, that's asking a lot. Even of me. At least give me a network guy. I mean, I'm going in for computer crap."

Kurt said, "Maybe. They're on contract like you, so maybe."

"Seriously? Do you even want this to succeed?"

George said, "Pike, I get it's a stretch, but we're on a full-court press against 9/11 anniversary threats. Yeah, Knuckles is leading around a new hire, but he's also here, at the flagpole. As is Retro. As is Veep. As is the rest of your team. We might need them to react on short notice. Sorry for the news, but it is what it is."

I let the sarcasm leak out, "Well, hell, if I'm not good enough to stop the next 9/11 from happening, I guess this is the next best thing."

Kurt said, "Don't take it that way. Look, the Council needs your civilian company, but the president and I would have picked you anyway. Because of *you*. I need a surgical touch here. Just get the data and come home. No drama."

I glanced at Jennifer, not wanting to make a decision without her agreement. She was half owner of our business, and this was a little bit of a risk, but I knew what I'd see. Bahamas? Paid by the US government? For nothing more than a digital theft?

She winked at me.

I said, "Okay, sir. What happens if it goes wrong? Will we be hung out to dry?"

Kurt grinned and said, "You've never asked for backup before."

"Backup was always explicit with the Taskforce. You're saying it's not now."

I hated to do the negotiation, the very thought disgusting me, but I couldn't put Jennifer in harm's way for the US government only to have her roasted if things went bad. And they could most definitely go bad. Since it was a deniable mission, we could refuse and be good.

Kurt saw the reticence and said, "Hey, you know I won't do that. You get compromised, and you'll have the best legal team that money can buy. It's not really like *Mission: Impossible*."

Jennifer said, "A legal team that's also a shell company? Created yesterday?"

"Well, yeah. Of course. But they'll be good."

I leaned back and looked at Jennifer. George caught the eye contact and said, "Who's in charge here? You guys need a room to talk?"

I looked him in the eye and said, "We'll do it. But if you miss an attack because you're so worried about covering Taskforce ass, I'll be back in this office. And it won't be because I needed to consult with my partner."

8

Wearing chemical goggles and a protective mask, Anwar Suleiman looked at the crystals in the water, the largest batch he'd created yet. White, looking a little like rock salt, they floated about on the bottom of a Pyrex jar, giving no hint of their destructive capability.

Anwar picked up a set of tweezers with eight-inch legs and fished inside the jar until he held one of the bits of crystal. He withdrew the tweezers until the crystal was just below the surface, then leaned back as far as he could, turning his head to the side.

He pulled the crystal free from the water, and it burst into flame like a mini-star, burning at a temperature hot enough to melt the metal that held it.

Anwar tossed the tweezers into an old metal sink full of rusty water, starving the crystal of oxygen until it ceased burning.

He was supremely satisfied with his work. This batch, like the ones before it, had been clearly successful, and now he had enough white phosphorous to execute his mission.

Nicknamed "Willy Pete" by the military, white phosphorus was a chemical that burned extremely hot the minute it was exposed to the atmosphere. It had been used as an incendiary weapon as far back as the nineteenth century and still caused massive controversy when utilized on the modern-day battlefield, for both psychological and practical reasons.

Practical in the sense that the burning chemical created some of the densest smoke on earth, perfect for marking targets or hiding movement, and all one had to do to create the screen was expose the chemical to the air.

Psychological because when used against humans, the embers tended to burn right through the body, like hot coals dropped into a vat of soft butter. It was an excruciating way to die. Once it was on fire, the only way to stop it was to completely deprive the chemical of oxygen. Something that was hard to do with a man screaming and thrashing around as his insides were devoured in flame.

Even given this, the chemical had one aspect above all that Anwar desired: It wasn't that hard to make in his improvised lab, especially for someone as smart as he was.

He poured the latest batch in with the others he'd created, taking extreme care to ensure the crystals remained below the surface of the water. It had taken him close to a month to get enough, but now he had a pint-size mason jar filled to the brim with water and half filled with crystal. Enough to do the damage he envisioned.

He tucked the jar underneath the sink, washed his hands, and looked at the time. His mother would be home soon, and he wanted to be there when she came. She was growing suspicious of his activities, and he didn't want any more questions about what he was doing or where he'd been.

He exited the "lab," the ninety-degree heat actually feeling refreshing after the punishing temperatures within. At least out here there was a breeze. He clicked a padlock on the door of the abandoned Airstream trailer, then trudged through the broken asphalt and weeds toward his home, a derelict double-wide that sat at the end of a sorry row.

He reached the first occupied trailer and saw a mother and child listlessly staring at him, the child in a small plastic pool, projecting an air not so much of having fun but of simply trying to cool off, the mother nearby in a torn aluminum lawn chair.

He waved, but they didn't wave back. One more bit of proof that his online friends were right. One more reason to hate.

A first-generation American from a Somali heritage, he missed his friends in Minneapolis. Missed his father, but he knew that was wasted effort. His father had fled long ago, back to Mogadishu, and Anwar had heard he had been killed acting as a leader in Al Shabaab. Something that Anwar aspired to be. But that, apparently, wasn't his path.

He was more valuable here, in the United States. More useful because of his American passport. He'd made plans to leave—to flee his pathetic desert life in Nevada to a homeland he'd never known—but then he'd made a contact on the Internet. A very powerful and rich contact who had groomed him for something special.

He heard the roar of a jet engine and glanced skyward, seeing the small reflection of two F-16s circling in the sky. Something that happened daily, as Indian Springs, Nevada, was the practice range of the Air Force Thunderbirds' demonstration team. Stationed at nearby Nellis Air Force Base outside of Las Vegas, they routinely overflew Indian Springs, using the Creech Air Force Base ranges for their practice.

While the Thunderbird rehearsals were routine, Creech was also used for something else. Something that interested Anwar much, much more than any aerial demonstration.

He saw his mother's beat-up Toyota Corolla pull through the fence of their "gated community" and took off running, trying to get to the trailer before she turned down their lane. He didn't make it.

She parked next to the aluminum skirting of the trailer, exited, and stood waiting on him, a smile on her face. He saw she hadn't changed out of her slutty, shaming "uniform." Pants that clung to her buttocks and a halter top barely covering her breasts.

He hated what she wore and hated her job. The employment wasn't exactly new, but the hatred was. She'd worked as a waitress in his home of Minneapolis, back when he was younger. Back when he had friends.

Now he had no friends save the ones in virtual space. Here, in this desolate, weed-strewn patch of America, he was treated like a bug in a jar at his new school. In Minneapolis there had been a huge Somali diaspora. Here, none of these rednecks could even find the country on a map.

When he got close enough, she said, "Why are you sweating so much? Playing soccer?"

He knew she continually hoped that he'd make friends and take to playing like he used to, but that was impossible in Indian Springs. The town was a bleak outpost built mostly of cinder block and gravel, barely rating a post office. The sole employer had been a casino adjacent to Creech Air Force Base, and that had been bought out by the US government for security concerns. The action had left his mother looking for work, and she'd found it wearing that despicable outfit in a casino on the strip.

Thinking fast, Anwar said, "No, it's just really hot. I was out rock collecting on the other side of town."

The excuse was lame, but there was no way he could tell her about his makeshift lab. She'd already begun to question his use of the Internet and had even broached banning some of the websites he visited, stating that they were evil and destructive, just like his father.

But how could that be? Both his father and the websites were followers of the purest form of Islam. And they both had taught him that the only thing evil and destructive was the very land he was living in. Just look at how far his mother had fallen, from wearing traditional attire at a Somali restaurant in Minneapolis to dressing like a whore in a casino in Las Vegas.

Anwar bit his lip, wondering if his mother would ask him where the supposed rocks were that he'd collected.

She didn't, instead saying, "I got a big tip today. Want to go out to dinner?"

He wanted to snap out that spending money earned from an infidel ogling her breasts was the same as becoming an infidel, but he didn't. His friends had told him to be circumspect. To hide his true beliefs. And so he said, "That would be great. Downtown? In Las Vegas?"

She smiled and said, "Of course." She started to ask where he wanted to go when she noticed a UPS van pull into the trailer park and stop right outside their lane. Puzzled, she held a hand to her eyes as the driver pulled a box out of the back.

She said, "Did you order something?"

He had, but he'd had no idea it would come so quickly. Either way, he already had an excuse for the arrival, as he knew he could never hide the purchase from his mother.

"It's from my science teacher. For the science fair."

Confused, she turned to him and said, "He bought you something?"

"No, the school did. It's a drone, but I don't get to keep it. I only get to experiment with it for a week."

His mother slowly nodded and the man dropped the package at her feet. Anwar peeled back the tape and opened the corrugated box, exposing a cellophane-wrapped container proclaiming PHANTOM 3 PROFESSIONAL, with a picture of a quadcopter drone.

He tore into the box as his mother said, "The school bought you this? For no charge?"

He pulled the drone out, saying, "Yes. Well, I think so. Maybe Mr. Rickter bought it himself. Either way, I get to use it; then I have to give it to him."

His mother didn't look convinced, but she didn't press him further. She said, "Do you want to test it now, or go to dinner?"

He gazed at the legs protruding underneath, mentally measuring the gap between them and the camera. It would work. He would have to bend the legs inward, but the jar would fit.

His mother repeated the question, and in his overwhelming desire to test the drone he said, "Yes, I'd like to fly it right now."

Then he remembered that part of the flight controls required a smartphone. He had one, purchased through the same bank account that had bought the drone, but his mother didn't know about that—the phone was his little secret. He knew his mother would want to watch, but he couldn't test the drone without it, and there was no way he could claim Mr. Rickter bought him a phone as well.

His mother, misunderstanding his apprehension, and wanting his approval, said, "It's okay. We can get dinner later. Let's see that beast fly."

He stared at the box for a moment, then said, "It's got to charge first. That'll be a few hours anyway."

Twenty minutes later they left the gravel of Indian Springs, his mother entering the flow of traffic headed south on Highway 95, the sprawling Creech Air Force Base in front of them. They drove by the empty space where the old casino once stood—the one demolished because of "security concerns." The one that had forced his mother to start dressing like a harlot against the proscriptions of their religion.

Anwar felt the anger rise, and then they were passing the east gate of Creech, a steady stream of vehicles attempting to exit at the close of the business day. He saw the cars and smiled, the anger growing into anticipation.

His mother caught the look and said, "What so funny?"

"Nothing. Just thinking about the science experiment I get to do with the drone."

9

Jalal al-Khattabi took a seat at the rear of the main cabin, avoiding anyone else who had boarded the ferry, preferring to keep to himself. The less he had to interact, the less could be learned should someone be questioned later. He knew he was being paranoid, but he'd been taught specifically that such things had caused catastrophic failure in the past. The enemy was everywhere. After the operation, it would be very hard for anyone to connect the dots to this trip, but he certainly didn't want to give the authorities any extra help.

It had been thirteen long years since he'd left his homeland of Morocco, and in that time plenty of changes had occurred—most that the average person visiting would never blink an eye at. But for those like him, it was a danger.

The ship under way, he saw the people line up for the immigration officer, each dutifully handing a passport over and answering the usual questions.

He despised the fact that the Europeans were treated perfunctorily, while anyone of Moroccan descent was questioned more harshly. An indicator of what he fought for.

Directly in front of him were two Eurotrash couples, the males disheveled, with tattoos and backpacks, the females with disgusting dreadlocks that looked like cotton rope that had been dipped in wax. He knew exactly why they were making the trip, having worked the supply side of the Moroccan drug trade for most of his life, and he was sure the immigration officer knew as well.

And yet nothing but cursory questions on their intentions.

Jalal was a Berber from the Rif Mountains of Morocco, a land where the people fought for survival every single day, and through their trials, they'd found a method of success. The Rif had grown into one of the highest marijuana-producing regions of the world. When it came to Europe, forget about Mexico. If you wanted dope on the Continent, it originated in the Rif, and the trade was handed down from father to son in the hardscrabble life carved out of the rocks of the mountains.

The two couples in front of him were on a hashish tour, Jalal was sure. He was, after all, a primary conduit feeding the trade. At least he had been, before he'd found the true cause of his life. He still dabbled, but not nearly as much as he had in the past.

He listened to the questions and was disgusted at the lack of attention. The man simply rubber-stamped their passports and let them through. It was further proof of why his action was needed. Nobody could fight the West when one hand was in the pocket of those same people. The fight had to be pure, which is what he had become.

He presented his passport and, unsurprisingly, was subject to much more scrutiny. He answered the questions, hiding his anger, and had his passport stamped, then returned to his seat in the back, fuming.

The ride from the Iberian Peninsula was relatively short, no more than a couple of hours even with the berthing and unloading time, and soon Jalal could see the new Mediterranean port of Tangier slowly growing outside of his window.

It was located about thirty kilometers from Tangier itself, and built in the time Jalal had been gone. He had never seen it before, but he'd been told it was a better place to use for infiltration. The port was four times the size of the aging one inside Tangier and, as such, strained the authorities' ability to maintain security. With so much going on, there would be little chance that Jalal would be stopped and interrogated a second time.

The boat began docking procedures, and he climbed out to the deck with everyone else, watching the trucks and cargo vans parked underneath the passenger area preparing to disembark. The heat of the deck, greasy and steaming, began to settle, and he wondered if they would be forced to wait until the vehicles had left. He would not.

He saw a signal from the woman manning the gangplank, and the passengers began shuffling forward, most with roll-aboards, but some with gigantic garbage bags full of whatever they'd found on the Continent. One lady, clearly cresting eighty years old, was struggling with an oversize suitcase as the others passed her by, rushing to get off.

Underneath her hijab, he could clearly see her pain as she tried to muscle her baggage onto the cleated stairs. She was knocked aside by other passengers too impatient to wait. He stepped forward and, speaking Arabic, said, "May I help you?"

She looked at him gratefully and nodded. He hoisted the bag and turned to the narrow iron stairwell, and was promptly bumped aside by someone else. He dropped the bag and hammered the man who'd done it, throwing him into the steel wall of the ship. The man looked at him in surprise, not saying a word. They stared at each other for a split second, and the man retreated down the stairs. The line following him stopped. Jalal looked at them and said, "Will nobody help her? Is this what we've become?"

Everyone glanced away. He carried her bag down, then returned to help her navigate the stairs, no other passenger daring to venture forward. She reached the bottom and said, "Thank you, I've been blessed. Thank you."

He nodded and shouldered his small backpack, following the flow of people off the ferry and toward a bus. He showed his passport one more time, the man checking only to make sure he had his stamps, and, after a ten-minute ride to the new terminal, was hailing a taxi to the city.

After forty minutes of bouncing on the winding blacktop of the coast road, the windows rolled down to offset the stifling heat, they reached the outskirts of the sprawling port city of Tangier. Jalal marveled at how much it had changed. He had read how the city was rivaling Casablanca as a commercial hub, but he hadn't translated that in his mind.

He asked how much longer and was told about ten minutes. They wound past the old port—much smaller than the monstrosity built on the coast thirty kilometers away—and finally turned inland to the teeming city. The cabby went through a traffic circle, then left the main road, entering a zigzag of streets, the walls closing in on a lane barely wide enough for two cars. Eventually, he stopped and pointed at an American flag, saying, "American Legation."

Jalal nodded and asked how much. The man told him, and Jalal asked if he would take euros. The driver agreed and gave a new amount. Jalal paid, spending the final bit of euros he had and knowing he was being wildly overcharged. He didn't care; it wasn't his money.

He took his small backpack and walked up the white

stairs, passing through an arch with the United States' Great Seal. He ignored it, and the museum it represented—the first American delegation to Morocco, formed here even before the nomenclature of "embassy" had been created. He passed by the door, disregarding the guard out front, and wondered if the Sheik had found a safe house at this location because he thought it was the most secure, or because he thought it humorous.

He wound down a brightly colored pedestrian lane, the walls close enough to touch with outstretched arms, passing an attractive woman headed the other way. One who was wearing Western clothing, with no hint of her Moroccan heritage. Clearly, some other things had changed here as well. Some things he intended to reverse.

After three turns in the alleys he stopped in front of an apartment labeled with the number twenty-four. He withdrew a key and was mildly surprised that it worked.

He entered, seeing a small flat with a kitchenette and a separate bedroom/bathroom combination. On a table next to the stove was an envelope.

He opened it, finding instructions for his meeting today, along with a set of car keys and a bundle of Moroccan dirham currency, the bill on top having writing on it in Arabic.

Not even bothering to explore the apartment, he left, retracing his steps until he was back on the street, the Great Seal behind him. He read the instructions and walked south down rue de la Plage. He made a right turn and saw his landmark—a century-old Spanish theater called Cervantes, crumbling and decrepit, with boards over the windows and an iron gate outside. He was surprised at the state of the building. When he'd last visited Tangier, it had been operational, a symbol of the multiculturalism of Morocco. But that had been years ago, and truthfully, his family couldn't have afforded the price of admission even then.

Lining the street in front were cars parked in parallel and a man wearing a reflective vest studiously helping someone park. Jalal waited until the man was through, then handed him the hundred-dirham note with the Arabic instructions. Initially surprised at the amount of money, the man read the bill and nodded, leading the way to a Toyota Land Cruiser wedged between two other cars. Jalal thanked him, handing him another bill as he entered the car. The man guided him out, and in short order, Jalal himself was battling the traffic in Tangier.

He headed north, forgoing the main arteries out of the city. He threaded through the winding streets until he hit a single ribbon of highway going southwest, now out of the city. Once again he paralleled the coast, only this time on the Atlantic instead of the Mediterranean.

He passed through a forest maintained by the monarchy, the trees interrupted every so often with gigantic homes—palaces, really. One would think, given his bitter upbringing, that they would cause Jalal some umbrage, but they gave him no concern, as he knew who owned them: the same people who had taught him the true meaning of Islam. The Wahhabis of Saudi Arabia.

Over the last two centuries, Morocco had seen colonization by the Spaniards, the French, and finally the Arabs, and through it all the Berbers had been the bastard children, discriminated against no matter who was in power. Eking out a living in the Rif Mountains, Jalal's heritage was one of sorrow, with the Berbers' language erased, their society and tribes marginalized. Moroccan law even forbade their families from anointing their children with traditional Berber names.

Jalal knew none of this when he and his cousins set out for Spain to make their fortune so many years ago. Barely able to read and write, he had no knowledge of anything religious—most certainly not the rabid brand he now professed. That all changed in the immigrant neighborhood of Lavapiés in Madrid, Spain. Struggling to survive, Jalal and his cousins had been befriended by an imam from Saudi Arabia—one of the many the kingdom sent out to proselytize to the Arab diaspora. There, in a living room mosque, hidden from view of the authorities, they learned the true reason for their hardships and began to embrace Islam as it was meant to be. Pure, without the equivocation of the Takfiri or the outright apostasy of the unbeliever.

It was there, in that small makeshift mosque, that Jalal had met the holy warriors who would strike a terrific blow in 2004. Moroccans like himself, they blew up the main Madrid train station, killing nearly two hundred infidels. While others lamented the attack, Jalal and his cousins, led by the imam, silently cheered.

The mosque held another milestone in Jalal's life. It was there, six years ago, that he was first introduced to a Saudi Arabian called the Sheik.

10

Driving toward the Atlantic coast on route des Grottes d'Hercule, stuck behind one Moroccan tour bus or tractor after another, Tariq decided he wouldn't have time to meet his father. The thirty-minute commute had become close to an hour, cutting out the time he had allotted for that chore.

He passed by a sweeping mansion situated on the cliffs of the Atlantic, glimpsing the blue of a pool fronting a pillared veranda, and a pair of armed security out front clinging to the shade of the outer wall. Adjacent to it was the hotel Le Mirage, looking just as ostentatious, the scattered buildings on the campus impossibly white, with luxurious fountains sprinkled across the grounds, as if it were competing with the mansion next door.

He knew this wasn't the case. The mansion was one of many properties in Morocco owned by the royal family of Saudi Arabia, and the hotel was built and owned by his father, just one of the varied businesses controlled by the Saudi billionaire.

Tariq passed by the resort's immaculately sculpted landscape, the barren desert on the right side of the road providing a stark contrast to the lushness of the grounds on the left. He reached another traffic circle and wound around it, entering a drive proclaiming the Caves of Hercules. His meeting site with Jalal.

He parked and dialed his father, immediately hearing consternation.

"Where are you? The meeting's in ten minutes."

"I'm here, at the meeting site. I got stuck behind a line of traffic, following a police car. I didn't want to risk passing."

"Do you have the phones?"

"Yes, sir. I have everything I need." He paused, not wanting to ask the next question. "Unless your package arrived."

"No. It won't be here for a few more days. It arrived in Algeria by air, but it's coming overland to here."

Tariq felt the tension leave his body. Yousef bin Abdul-Aziz was a doting father, but he was prone to spasms of anger when his instructions weren't followed to the letter. If the package had arrived, it would only have given him ammunition against Tariq for his lack of time management.

Yousef asked, "How do we stand with Ring of Fire?"

The comment made Tariq grin. His father had a flair for the dramatic, and while he had applauded the glorious attacks of 2001, he had always despised that it had been called simply the "Planes Operation."

Tariq said, "I have nothing more than I told you before. I'll know more after the meeting. Jalal said he had a plan for Norfolk, and I need to discuss it with him."

"I told you I have no ships going to the ports in Norfolk. We should be looking at Charleston or Seattle."

"Let me hear what he has in mind. Norfolk is ripe with targets, with both the US Navy and commercial shipping. I'll come to you when I'm done."

"Okay, but remember, we are in charge. We are the captains; they are the soldiers. We have spent four years developing this operation, and I don't intend to turn it over to a tribe of Berbers you recruited."

"Yes, Father."

Tariq hung up, watching the tourists traveling down to the caves hollowed out by the ocean—or by Hercules, depending on which belief system one followed. He checked the time, retrieved a small knapsack from the passenger seat, then entered the flow himself, passing by a courtyard souvenir shop before descending roughhewn steps cut into the rock.

To his left was a smaller cave with a man accepting money to enter; to his front was the primary cave, free of charge. He tossed a couple of coins in the bowl just to be polite and continued on to the larger cave.

He entered and immediately felt the breeze coming from the Atlantic forty meters to his right, the ocean crashing against the rocks beneath a huge craggy opening, a large gaggle of tourists standing behind a knee-high fence taking pictures.

To his left the cavern wound back into the darkness, small lights set into the floor providing feeble illumination. He went left, and the tourists grew sparser. He entered another huge cavern, a couple on the far side using a selfie stick, the woman fully covered in black Gulf attire, including a niqab, as if two different centuries were colliding. He ignored them and continued deeper, until he reached a smaller cave with an entrance hole that stopped at waist level. He stooped underneath the rock and saw Jalal sitting on an outcropping in a space about the size of a small kitchen.

He was a thick man of medium height, but his head didn't seem to go with his body. The face was long and narrow, with prominent brows and a sharp chin, as if it were meant for an Ichabod Crane–type frame instead of the slightly pudgy one Jalal owned. He was clean-shaven, but his black hair was matted on his scalp, long overdue for a cut.

Scooting under the limestone entrance, Tariq found he could stand upright. He held out his hand and said, "Salaam alaikum."

Jalal took it, replying, "Alaikum salaam." Jalal withdrew his hand and touched the palm to his heart.

Tariq said, "I trust your trip was uneventful?"

"Yes. No problems."

"And you have your team in place? At each one?"

"Yes. Your father's supertanker is docking in Gibraltar for repairs the day after tomorrow. Karim is on the shift schedule as the master mechanic. He'll have access to the engine room and hull; all he needs is the explosives and the timers."

"They're coming, but he knows how to use them? It does no good to simply cause the ship to stop running."

"Of course. He didn't get that job based on nepotism. He got it from skill. He was taught the weakest parts of the ship as risk mitigation."

Tariq ignored the implied insult, saying, "And the port in Algeciras? You have someone who can insert a package in a container on a ship?"

"Yes. Badis is working as a stevedore. He's got all necessary security clearances. He just needs the ship to put it on, and, of course, the package."

"The ship is coming into port in two days. It's headed to Los Angeles, California, and you'll have the package before then. I expect to receive it tomorrow. We'll meet again, and I'll give it to you. Badis can rig it with explosives?"

"Yes, but Los Angeles won't let it leave the ship. You wouldn't believe the security there. They'll find the explosives long before it's allowed to board a truck."

"That is a risk, but a small one. As much as the United States screams about scanning every container before it's left the ship, they're still only doing four percent in the port. The trucks all pass through a detector on the way out of the port, but we don't care about that. The bomb will go off before then."

Jalal nodded, saying, "Okay, if you're confident. That leaves the eastern port. Why can't we simply repeat the same attack?"

"That is what we wanted, but my father cannot get the material. He has enough for one, which brings me to your idea. What is it?"

"There are a multitude of ports in Norfolk, and it's also a hub of tourism. Plenty of places to hide, and plenty of waterborne traffic. We attack there, and we drive home the other attacks."

"Yes, but I told you earlier, my father has no ships going to that area. How can we do this? You yourself just told me that United States port security has exponentially increased. It's one thing when we own the boats or already have people working within the system. It's quite another to attempt an attack on foreign soil without any infrastructure in place. Especially in America."

Jalal told him. When he was finished, Tariq nodded. The plan wasn't without risk, but it seemed valid. With one huge hole.

"You have men who would be willing to do this?"

"Yes. Three of my cousins left Madrid a couple of years ago, returning home. You don't remember them, but they met you in the mosque. They are brothers, and they were going to be a part of our original cell but left due to an illness in the family. They're now working in Fez, in the medina tannery. It's a nightmare existence that has only fueled their desire. They are willing."

Tariq bent down to the knapsack at his feet and said, "Let me speak to my father. If he agrees, I'm assuming you'll need lots of money."

Jalal said, "Yes. I can make it on my own, but that will take time."

Tariq snapped back up, saying, "You're not still smuggling hashish, are you?"

"No. Not really, but I can if I need to. I still have that conduit, and it's easy money."

"What do you mean, 'not really'?"

"I mean I do enough to survive. You don't pay me a salary, and unlike the others, I don't have a job to fall back on."

Tariq handed the knapsack to Jalal and said, "Do you still have the account in Madrid? The one tied to the offshore account?"

"Yes."

"Well, quit with the smuggling. I'll put enough money offshore to cover the expenses of your plan, and a little extra for you to live on. The last thing I need is for you to be arrested smuggling drugs."

Jalal nodded and held up the bag, saying, "What's this?"

"Smartphones. They all have an application called Wickr. It is end-to-end encrypted, and you can set a time for your messages to be wiped from the memory of the phone. It is how we'll communicate. I have five phones in there. Use them as you see fit; just send me a message when you hand one out, so I know who has what."

Jalal peeked inside the bag, then looked at Tariq, a bit of wonder on his face. Up until this point, it had all been discussion. Grand plans, but little action. He said, "We're really going to do this?"

"Yes. The time for talk is past."

"You were right about Syria. I'm glad I didn't take my brothers with me there."

Tariq smiled and said, "I told you then that was the wrong decision, and I was correct. The Islamic State is hunted all over the world. We are unknown, and because of it, we're going to light a ring of fire around the West. Cripple them."

11

Sucking on a twelve-dollar virgin daiquiri, I studiously ignored the skinny man who'd taken a barstool four feet from me. He'd sat at a table at first, then had fidgeted back and forth, as if he didn't like the choice. I kept an eye on him from the corner of the bar. After a few seconds, he'd left the table and hesitantly sidled up to the stool. Right next to me. Which I was sure would earn me no small amount of grief from Jennifer. After all, the first rule of surveillance was to remain invisible to the person being followed.

He was older than I would have imagined, maybe fifty-five or sixty, and was dressed like he didn't belong on a Caribbean vacation. Pale legs, pasty arms, a white T-shirt with stained pits, showing that it had clearly been worn as it should be—under a suit—and to cap it off, white socks jammed into a pair of brand-new Teva sandals. He looked exactly the opposite of someone I would have expected to be siphoning off secrets from a myriad of offshore accounts in the largest data dump in history.

Truthfully, his sitting down near me wasn't that big a deal. All I needed to do was keep an eye on him while Jennifer did the heavy lifting. My job was to provide early warning in case the target attempted to go back to his room, something I was more than capable of doing even if he sat in my lap, although the "virgin" of the daiquiri was a little annoying. If Jennifer would hurry up, I could order us both a real one.

We'd been in the Bahamas a total of two days, and it had taken a little effort to find our target. Kurt wouldn't let me take anyone from my team, but he did give me my choice of computer nerds to help locate the source. I'd picked Bartholomew Creedwater, a guy Jennifer and I had worked with in the past. He had a secret crush on Jennifer, which was annoying but not enough to overshadow his computer skills. He was almost supernatural on the keyboard, and I'd need that skill to locate the leaker.

Coming down here, we'd known two things: the location of the meeting—the Atlantis resort in the Bahamas—and the MAC address of the laptop computer that had been used to send the only email we'd intercepted.

We'd gotten a couple of rooms in the so-called Royal Towers; then Jennifer and I had gone down to the pool and left Creed to his work. We needed to conduct a reconnaissance of the grounds for contingencies. At least that was what I told Jennifer. After I told her to wear a swimsuit to blend in.

At the mention of the location for the meeting, I'd just assumed the source was bleeding the reporter's expense account dry, but after seeing it, I began to believe he actually had a method to his madness. The resort was huge, including everything from a water park to a dolphin pool, and it was swarming both with people staying in the hotels and with passengers disgorged from cruise ships just to play on the grounds. It was a perfect place to disappear, having a transient population that rotated out daily.

And it had some really cool swimming pools.

After I'd convinced Jennifer to check out the lazy river

tube ride—you know, just in case we needed to escape on an inner tube—she'd finally demanded that we act like we were actually on a secret mission. She was always a Debbie Downer about such things while we were on official business. I told her I'd agree to go check on Creed if she'd agree to ride the shark tube—a water slide that actually went under a lagoon full of sharks. She'd given me her disapproving-teacher glare, and I'd given up.

Getting back to our small tactical operations center, I'd found out my little bit of fun was over and it was time to go to work. Tunneling through the hotel Wi-Fi, Creed had found the MAC address—a specific numerical identification tied to a specific computer the source had used in the past—and once he had that, like a dog with a bone, he'd necked down the room that housed the computer on the network of the resort complex. It turned out, it wasn't in our tower. It was in a separate tower called the Cove, down a stretch of land with its own private pool and beach.

He'd handed us the information, saying he was going to get his swimsuit on as a jab at my earlier indiscretion, and we'd gone to work, first renting a room on a lower floor from the target's in the Cove tower, then building a pattern of life for a break-in.

We'd placed a wireless button camera across from his door, and then Jennifer had practiced her technique with an under-the-door penetration device—really just a flexible metal rod with a wire attached that would allow her to pull the door handle from the inside. Since all hotel doors were made to be opened on the inside for fire escape—no matter the lock position—it would facilitate penetration and we wouldn't have to worry about duplicating key cards or having our electronic-lock log-ins captured by the system.

After she was comfortable with getting in, we'd watched our little camera feed, the fish-eye lens making it look like we were viewing the world through a door peephole, waiting on him to leave. Thirty minutes later, he had done so, and our first attempt was under way. I'd immediately gone to the elevator of our floor, getting down to the ground level before him, leaving Jennifer the task of breaking into the room.

I'd decided to let her crack the room because if anything went sideways, she'd be less of a threat and able to talk her way out, acting as management or guest, depending on who initiated contact in the room.

She'd smiled at that and had said, "Talk my way out, or climb?"

Creed had gotten all bright-eyed at the statement, having seen her at work once before, now fantasizing that he was Tom Cruise in a *Mission: Impossible* movie. I'd scowled at him before saying to her, "Climbing won't be necessary, but hey, if it comes to it, that skill doesn't hurt."

For security reasons, the mission was a two-step process: First she'd just ensure she could get in, find the computer, and employ a thumb drive to identify encryption protocols so Creed could develop a bypass after the fact. She would spend no more than a few minutes in the room. The actual penetration of his laptop would occur later, after we had the lay of the land and Creed had developed a way around whatever security he'd put on the computer.

While Jennifer was doing her work, I'd keep an eye on Johnny White Socks.

Staged in the lobby, I saw him exit the elevator, then turn toward the beach access. I gave Jennifer the go to penetrate. He'd made it only halfway down before

Jennifer had called, pulling me off of him. She'd gotten in but couldn't find the computer.

I'd returned, meeting her in the TOC. We reviewed Creed's logs, seeing the target had logged off the Internet two minutes before he'd left the room, meaning the computer was inside somewhere, because he wasn't carrying anything when I'd seen him, which most likely meant it was in a hotel safe. Good for us, bad for him.

Every hotel safe looks secure, but is, in fact, quite a sham when it comes to protection. Because it had to be repeatable for guests over and over, it had to have a fail-safe for the occasional idiot who forgot the code. This was usually a hidden key access or a universal code. All we had to do was figure out which one.

We'd returned to our room, opening the closet that housed our own safe. One look and I knew which one it was: a hidden key access behind a metal plate with the safe's manufacturer advertised on it. I broke out a Leatherman tool, unscrewed the label, and saw a pathetic lock that could literally be picked with a screwdriver and a paperclip.

I gave Jennifer the Leatherman, and she rummaged around in her suitcase for a lockpick kit, then went at the lock. With a little practice, she was able to get it open in under thirty seconds. Plenty of time.

Jennifer had wanted to have a go at it right then, but I didn't want to risk breaking in without eyes on the target, so we sat around most of the day waiting on him to return. He finally did, but then stayed in for the night, which was no big deal. Intelligence work was always a game of patience.

The next morning we were up bright and early, staring at our fisheye camera feed. Eventually he left the room, around ten in the morning, and once again, I beat him to the ground floor. I saw him, gave Jennifer the go, then picked up the follow. He headed to the adults-only pool, with me trailing behind. I went to the bar while he did his table dance, and then the jackass sat down on a barstool four feet away, checking his watch every few minutes.

Even at ten in the morning, the place was starting to pick up, with a DJ setting up equipment and more and more hotel guests swarming around ordering piña coladas, some already showing they were on the inebriated side. A guy in board shorts and a man bun asked me if the stool between us was open, and I said yes; then my earbud crackled.

"Pike, Pike, this is Koko. I've got an issue. He's placed some sort of lock over the hotel safe."

I raised my phone to my ear as if I was getting a call, sliding off the stool and moving toward the back of the pool area, getting some privacy behind a bunch of lounge chairs.

I said, "Koko, Pike. Say again?"

"There's a band on the front, like the Club steering-wheel lock. It might be alarmed."

I said, "Creed, this is Pike, you copy?"

"Roger all. Koko, is there a brand name or anything?"

He sounded breathless, I'm sure probably feeling an erection at actually getting to talk on the radio. Okay, that was harsh.

Jennifer came back, "Yeah, it reads, 'Bloxsafe'"; then she spelled the name.

I heard nothing for a moment, then: "Stand by. I'm looking."

I glanced at the target and saw he had something on the bar in front of him. A plastic box of some sort. I circled around the bar, the phone still up to my ear, my sunglasses hiding the fact that I was doing anything but retrieving my drink.

It was a portable hard drive.

Holy shit. He's doing the meeting this morning. That's why he keeps checking his watch.

12
★★
★

The Nevada sun began to heat up the rock-strewn field, rapidly burning off the coolness of the morning and causing the first beads of sweat to form on Anwar Suleiman's forehead, sprouting in his scalp for a split second before being sucked away by the avarice of the desert air. As he struggled to mount his small mason jar of death to the legs of the Phantom 3 drone, the heat was the least of his concerns.

He'd spent a day practicing with the drone, testing its flight characteristics first with just the drone, then with a weight attached. He knew he could pilot it, but he'd never really concerned himself with physically attaching the white phosphorus jar to the legs of the UAV.

It was always the little things that screwed up the experiment, something he'd learned in spades during his high school chemistry and physics classes, and a fact he wished he'd paid attention to here.

The Phantom drone had two small skids jutting out underneath it, made to protect the camera slung below. Anwar had planned on simply bending the legs together, then lightly gluing the mason jar into the cradle he'd made, but the legs were much too brittle, threatening to break apart. And that certainly wouldn't work, because besides the jar, he needed them to hold the four carbide glass-breaker heads, one affixed to each corner of the skids.

He'd thought about it last night and decided to glue the jar's lid to the right skid, high enough that it wouldn't interfere with the glass breakers, then screw the jar on, leaving the payload hanging on the outside of the skids.

The glue had held up, and he'd carefully attached his jar of white phosphorous to the lid, but he now worried about the flight characteristics. He hadn't practiced anything like this, with the load not centered on the main thrust vectors of the drone, and he wasn't sure how the thing would fly. If he screwed up here, with everything committed, he'd end up spending another four months in his makeshift chemistry lab making more white phosphorous, and he certainly wouldn't have the conditions he was blessed with today.

A demonstration at the base was planned, and protestors would be diverting all traffic to the east gate, causing jams and stoppages and preventing anyone from traveling more than fifteen miles an hour. In other words, unwittingly facilitating his attack plan.

He affixed his iPhone 6 to the mount on the remote control, gained link, tested the camera, then took a deep breath. He fired up the quadcopter, and it rose in the air for a brief moment, then began skipping to the right, favoring the extra weight. It picked up steam, the gimbals applying power in an effort to hover, fighting the weight with a software program that had no ability to compensate.

The device began flying straight at Anwar's makeshift lab, furiously trying to stabilize itself. Anwar cranked the controls, twisting his arms and waist as if the body language would help, sure he was about to witness disaster. The drone went vertical, then began sliding much more slowly back toward him. He let out his pent-up breath and brought the drone overhead.

When it was directly over him, the four daggers of the carbide window breakers just above his head, he checked the video feed on the attached iPhone. It was perfect.

With only twenty minutes of flight time—and probably much less carrying his load—he had no time to spare for practicing. He launched the drone toward Highway 95, still fighting the weight of his payload.

He cleared what few trees were fronting the road and saw a mass of people around the east gate of Creech Air Force Base, some dressed as a vision of Death, complete with a scythe, others holding signs and placards. He zoomed in on one and saw NO MORE ILLEGAL DRONE KILLING.

It made him chuckle, given what he was about to do.

While known as the practice range of the Thunderbirds, Creech held another, poorly kept secret: It was the largest control location of unmanned aerial vehicles in the United States. Fully two operations groups comprising ten squadrons of Predators and Reapers were flown from this base, conducting ISR missions and strike operations worldwide, from Afghanistan to Yemen. And Somalia, where his father had been killed by one. One minute he had been training his men outside of Mogadishu, the next minute incinerated by a Hellfire missile. And now it was time to return the favor.

He did a slow turn with the drone's camera, until he could see the caravan of vehicles fighting to get onto the base through the protestors. He went over the top of the line, maybe thirty feet above them, going from car to car. He saw a protester point toward the drone, then others begin to notice, a ripple going through the crowd.

He centered over each vehicle, peering inside. Some drivers he couldn't make out because of the reflection of the windshield. Others held enlisted men or officers in

Air Force camouflage, going to work at some part of the base, but not his target. He was looking for a particular rank and uniform. A pilot's uniform.

Four cars down he reached a Ford Ranger pickup, the windshield clear. Inside was a man in a flight suit. Anwar clearly made out the rank of captain and the embroidered wings on his left breast, the camera strong enough to reveal the idiotic callsign "Bionic" beneath the wings.

Anwar felt his heartbeat increase. He saw the man looking upward out the windshield, trying to see what the protesters were pointing at.

He raised the drone higher, generating depth for the free fall that gravity would provide. For the first time in his life, he put his Advanced Placement physics classes to use in the real world.

Thirty-two feet per second squared.

13

I kept my eye on the target, hearing Creed come back, "Koko, it's just a secondary lock. It clamps on the outside of the safe, over the door. It's made to prevent maids or other hotel personnel from accessing the safe."

"You mean like me?"

"Uhhh . . . yes, I guess, but it's not alarmed."

"Pike, this is Koko, what's the call? You want me to abort or try to get through it?"

"Creed, what's the lockset?"

"Well . . . it actually has a lockset that's tamper resistant. Something called Mul-T-Lock. Resistant to picking and bump keys."

Shit.

Jennifer came on. "Pike, I recommend abort. Let me get out of here and familiarize myself in our room first, then reattack."

My target stood to leave. I said, "Can't do it. I think today's the meeting day, and after it we won't get a second chance. He might check out as soon as he's back."

Jennifer said, "Pike, I don't know if I can get through this lock. It could take some time."

"The lock is bad news, but the good news is he'll be busy for a while. Just do your best. Put out the do-not-disturb sign and get to work."

I could almost feel the steam coming off her head. She

didn't like improvising—even though she was pretty damn good at it. I saw the back of my target leaving the bar area, circling around the drunks at the pool.

I said, "I have to go. Just work it as long as you can. I'll let you know if the guy's headed back. The room is yours."

In a completely flat voice, I heard, "Roger that." I knew she wanted to give me some choice words, but she wouldn't do that with Creed on the net. Thank goodness I'd had the special insight to bring him along.

I quickly left the pool area, blending in with a small crowd behind the source. He continued away from the Cove tower, headed to the side entrance of the Royal Towers. He went into the giant hallway that spanned the base of the building, moving with a purpose, and I followed behind. He passed through the stores and somewhat cheesy art displays, reaching the main entrance, a sunken dining room next to a gigantic aquarium to his left. He descended the stairs, entering a hallway with a label calling it THE DIG.

I followed him down, briefly reading a placard at the entrance. It was some sort of fake archeological tunnel describing the lost city of Atlantis.

I gave him a five-second start, then went in after him, entering a tunnel with aquarium glass on the left that gave underground view into the lagoon that bordered the property. On the right were fake artifacts from the fabled city of Atlantis, with both sides full of families taking in the sights. My target ignored it all, forging ahead.

I keyed my radio. "Creed, Creed, target has entered something called the Dig. I need some intel. What's down here?"

"Stand by."

"Roger. Koko, how's it going?"

"I'm working it. I can't tell if the pins are seating or not. It's not a traditional lock."

"Keep at it. It's like the final test for Jedi. You crack that, and I'll give you a prize."

I heard, "Yeah, yeah. Promises, promises."

Creed came back and said, "It's just an exhibit that lets you see their marine life. It's supposed to be the archeological find of Atlantis."

Jennifer said, "Atlantis? I knew there was a reason Grolier Recovery Services was given this mission. Can't wait to see it."

Jennifer's comment was a thinly veiled joke directed at me and our cover. Ostensibly, GRS was hired by individuals, companies, or governments to facilitate the excavation or maintenance of archeological sites around the world. In reality, we used it for counterterrorism, leveraging the cover to get into nonpermissive environments and put a head on a spike. As an anthropologist and someone who really liked looking at old shit, she religiously attempted to force us to see the sites for "cover reasons," and she was poking me in the eye with her comment, because we rarely did.

I ignored her, saying, "Where does it go?"

"It winds pretty much linearly, paralleling the hotel itself. Looks like it exits near the casino."

Casino. Maybe that's it.

I immediately discarded the idea. If he did anything in there, he'd be on twenty different cameras. No, the meeting was going to occur down here. If he were headed to the casino, he would have just used the hotel hallways.

I kept behind him, and he made no attempt to look at anything other than his watch, even though we were walking right next to sharks, stingrays, and other marine life. We made a couple of turns and eventually reached an anteroom with floor-to-ceiling glass, the lagoon beyond full of "ancient" artifacts and underwater creatures. In the center of the right wall was the entrance to another exhibit.

He disappeared from view, going into it. The hallway extended past the entrance, and next to the Atlantis "runes" painted on the wall was an illuminated exit sign, so the room wasn't the way out. Afraid that it was just a small exhibit, I continued past, glancing inside.

The exhibit turned out to be a small circular room about thirty feet across, the wall ringed with mannequins in pseudo–*20,000 Leagues Under the Sea* scuba gear and a pit in the center breathing fog. Suspended over the pit was some sort of hanging ball—presumably something from the lost city. Behind it was the entrance to a gift shop.

My target was intently studying one of the mannequins, the first thing he'd wanted to look at since entering the Dig. The only other person in the room was a man in a white sun shirt, a baseball cap pulled low to his brow.

The linkup.

I went past the entrance, stopping on the far side near the exit sign leading to another hallway. I took a seat on a stone bench carved with make-believe runes, pretending to read a brochure. As much as I dearly would have liked to watch the meeting, my mission here was simply to protect Jennifer, and entering that small room would burn me for sure.

Four minutes later, the man with the ball cap came out, walking at a brisk pace. He went by me, following the exit sign, and I gave a warning order to Jennifer.

"Koko, this is Pike, meeting's done. You're running out of time."

"Roger. I think I've figured this thing out. Need maybe ten minutes to get through it, then the actual safe lock, then download from his computer."

"Roger all. I'll let you know when he leaves and what his intentions are. If we reach the lobby of the Cove and you're not done, put it all back like you found it and exfil. I'll delay him if I have to."

"Will do."

I waited another minute, wondering what the guy was doing in the exhibit. Maybe shopping in the gift store? Thirty more seconds and I got antsy. I stood to take a peek inside, afraid I'd missed an exit he could have used. I took two steps forward; then an awful shriek split the air. I took off sprinting, rounding the corner to the exhibit. I saw a young Bahaman woman wearing an Atlantis uniform and freaking out. She was screaming incoherently and pointing into the pit below the ball.

Through the fog bubbling up from some machine below, I could see my target. His legs were still outside of the hole, lying on the rock, but his body was on an iron grate that spanned the pit, the imitation fog making it look like he was being cooked on a barbecue grill.

His face was peaceful, like he was sleeping, but his throat had a ragged tear, the blood running freely through the grate.

14

Captain Steve Austin saw the line of cars outside the gate entrance and cursed. He was still out on Highway 95, and the line snaked from the road leading to the entrance gate and spilled back onto the four-lane blacktop. Right where the gate road met the highway he could see a crowd of people, maybe a hundred in all, dressed as if it were Halloween and carrying signs.

Then he remembered: The protest was today. He should have left his house an hour earlier to get to work on time, and now he'd have hell to pay from his commander.

Not that this job wasn't hell already.

A former F-16 pilot who'd flown combat missions in Afghanistan, he had a new job piloting an MQ-1 Predator for the 17th Reconnaissance Squadron. He'd joined the Air Force to fly—really fly—but with the explosion of requests for unmanned aerial vehicle support, the Air Force had quit relying on volunteers and had begun forcing pilots to run a tour with the UAVs. There was just too much demand and not enough pilots.

Some of his peers had volunteered and seemed to enjoy the shift work without the need to deploy, but he certainly didn't. He despised being a drone pilot.

The missions weren't the issue, per se. In truth, the 17th was a little bit special, in that its mission set was dictated by the National Command Authority. They didn't get any drudgery like a route reconnaissance tasking from a deployed battalion. They received target packages for terrorists out to harm the United States, and he preferred it that way. If he had to fly a drone, he'd much rather work with armed UAVs over straight intelligence collection. At least with the 17th, he was making a contribution. He'd dropped plenty of munitions in support of national interests while deployed in a fighter squadron, and the strike missions with the 17th didn't bother him at all.

It just wasn't flying, and he couldn't wait to get back into a real cockpit. Especially when he had to deal with idiots like the ones in front of the gate today. Ignorant of the massive intelligence picture he had, they were completely unaware that there were literally thousands of bad men out in the wild, all actively pursuing a goal of taking the naïve protesters' lives.

He inched forward on the highway and finally turned onto the gate road, the protesters held at bay by the base security, content to chant their slogans at him as he passed. He flipped them the bird and continued on, ignoring when two of them raised their hands attempting to return the favor. He saw a third raise her hand and realized they weren't making an obscene gesture. They were pointing.

He leaned forward into his windshield and looked up, seeing a speck about forty feet above him and rising. The car in front of him moved, and he followed another ten feet, then leaned forward again. The speck hovered right above his windshield about seventy feet in the air. Then it began to fall.

It took the rest of Steve Austin's life to realize that the object was growing in size. By the time he recognized it as an out-of-control commercial drone, it had smashed into his windshield, spikes on the skids shattering the glass and the weight of the drone punching a jagged hole.

He felt liquid splash all over his upper body and snapped his head back in confusion. Then the confusion turned to infinite pain as his face and neck burst into white-hot flame. He threw open the door, giving the protestors an event that finally stopped their chanting. Screaming in agony, he ran right at them, his hair now alight and his face melting as the white phosphorus burrowed into his flesh as if it were alive.

As he staggered through the protestors, looking like a grisly rendition of Johnny Blaze, the chemical cauterized his esophagus, burning to his spine. The protestors fell away in horror, the ghastly smell of burning flesh following Austin in a putrid wake. Mercifully, a second later, his arms dropped, and he collapsed on the side of the road, dead.

The white phosphorus continued to burn, tendrils of thick smoke rising from his melted face like steam from miniature volcanoes.

15

Jennifer felt the pin slip back into place and muttered under her breath. The lock was becoming an absolute demon, a test of wills for her to conquer. Unlike a traditional key, with ridges and valleys, the key that worked this lock had the ridges built into the side, with the key itself flat on both top and bottom. It made the entire pick a learning process, something she would really rather not have to do on a live mission.

She kept tension on the barrel and gently went at the pin again, knowing she was running out of time. Any minute now, she would get the call that the target was headed back to his room. And she absolutely despised failure.

When the call came, it was not what she expected.

"Creed, Koko, this is Pike. Target is down. I say again, target is down."

What on earth?

"Say again?"

"Too much to explain over the radio. Someone took out the target. Killed him inside the Dig. I'm still here, just outside the crime scene. Security is all over this place."

She felt the pin seat and gave herself a mental cheer. She said, "So what's that mean for me?"

"Not to be callous, but I think it means you've got all the time you need. Creed, I want you to break out the scanner. See if you can find the hotel security net. There's a guy right in front of me talking into a radio. I'm sending you a picture of the model of his radio."

"Roger that."

"Koko, how's it going?"

"I have one more pin, and I'm through the bar outside the safe. What happened to the target?"

"I don't know. Well, I know someone slit his throat, but I don't know if the whole 'meet the journalist thing' was a setup, or if someone beat him to the meeting. Either way, he's dead."

Jennifer felt the last pin slip home. *Yes.* She said, "Creed, Creed, this is Koko. I got the lock. How do I remove the bar?"

"Pull out on the handle and it will release the legs, extending them out."

She did, and miraculously, it worked. She tossed the bar onto the carpet and withdrew a screwdriver for the plate hiding the universal access key. Creed shattered her concentration, breathless. "Koko, Koko, I have the security net. They know who the dead guy is. They're sending security up your way to inspect the room."

She started unscrewing the label, asking, "How much time?"

"I don't know. They just called on the radio, telling someone to check the room. If they're in the building already, maybe seconds. If it's going to some command post, minutes."

She popped the label and said, "Okay. I'm chancing it."

She heard Pike say, "Your call, but plan an exit."

She glanced toward the bathroom, seeing it was just like the bathroom in their room one floor below—meaning the only hiding place would be behind the shower curtain. Not optimal. She surveyed behind her, and Creed burst through her earbud, sounding as if he were face-to-face with the devil, panicked. "*Koko, Koko, they're coming down the hall.* I see them on the fish-eye. They're at your door!"

She grabbed the Bloxsafe secondary lock and leapt up, jumping over the bed to the sunken television room next to the balcony. In one fluid move, she threw open the sliding glass door, whirled around it, and slammed it closed again. She looked below, seeing a fall of eight dizzying stories ending in manicured landscaping. She tossed the Bloxsafe bar out into space and threw herself over the railing, grabbing the lower bars and hanging, leaving her hands as the only thing left visible to the room.

She heard Pike come on in his bored, pizza-delivery voice, meaning he was worried. "Koko, Koko, this is Pike, status?"

She whispered, "I'm on the balcony. Creed, what do you see?"

"Two men entered. Door is now closed. Don't know what they're doing, but they're in your room."

Pike said, "Koko, can't they see you on the balcony?"

"I'm hanging below it."

She heard nothing for what seemed like a minute, Pike racing to exit the Dig, then: "Jesus Christ, Jennifer, I see you, I see you. *Anybody* can see you."

A little miffed, she hissed, "Anybody except the security in the room. What did you want me to do? Jump?"

Creed said, "They've left the room. One went back down the hall. One is standing guard outside."

Jennifer pulled herself up, flipping over the railing and taking a breath. She surveyed the exterior of the hotel and said, "I might be able to climb to our room."

Pike said, "No. Too risky. I don't mean the climb; I mean because someone will definitely see that."

"Pike, you're one floor below me. I can get there in about a minute. Two tops."

"No. You get seen playing spider monkey, and we're in a world of shit. And before you say it, I'm not letting you sit on that balcony until the sun goes down."

"What do you propose?"

"Creed and I will get you out. We'll distract the guard, and you slip out. Just tell us when you have the computer."

Computer?

"Say again?"

"You got the secondary lock off, right? Which means you can get in that safe in about thirty seconds. You no longer need twenty minutes to download anything. Just take the whole damn computer. He's not going to miss it."

She shook her head, realizing why he was against the climb. She said, "It'd be nice if you thought about my welfare instead of the mission."

"I *am* thinking about your welfare. That damn climb is dangerous, even if you don't think so. And I told you I'd give you a prize, but you have to accomplish the mission."

She grinned, carefully sliding the door open. She whispered, "That prize was for picking the lock. I did that. I'm a Jedi now."

"Okay, the Jedi prize was just some ice cream. The mission prize is much better."

Kneeling at the safe, careful to remain absolutely silent, she clicked her earbud twice, letting him know she understood, then went to work on the universal access lock. In fifteen seconds, she had it unlocked, swinging the door open and hearing Pike say, "Creed, meet me on his floor. We're going to walk down the hallway arguing with each other. When we get just past his door, with the guard's back to it, we're going to get into a fight. As security, he'll have to react. You copy?"

She saw a wad of bills and a Dell thirteen-inch laptop. She heard Creed meekly say, "Uhh . . . Roger that."

She closed the door, relocked it with the universal key, and began screwing the label cover back over it. She heard Pike say, "Okay, listen, do you want me to hit you, or do you want to hit me?"

Before Creed could answer, she heard, "Never mind. I'm on the way up. I'll talk to you then. Koko, give me one click for still working, two clicks for ready to go."

She clicked twice, then slid up to the door, seeing the guard through the peephole. She waited.

A minute later, Pike came on, saying, "Koko, Koko, we're thirty seconds out."

She clicked twice again and put her eye to the peephole. She faintly heard loud voices that grew stronger. Pike and Creed entered the vision of the peephole, Pike towering over Creed, waving his arms and shouting. They both ignored the man in front of the door. They got past him, the man turning to watch them go, and Creed drew back and walloped Pike on the side of the head with a clumsy hammer fist, hitting him so hard Pike's skull bounced against the wall.

Ouch.

She heard Pike shout, "Have you lost your fucking mind?" and wondered if that was an act or if he was actually pissed at the force of the blow. Pike dove into Creed, slamming him into the ground, and the security man leapt at them, grabbing both by the collar and attempting to break them apart.

Creed looked like he was about to soil his pants in panic and fear, screaming and kicking his legs like a child. Jennifer waited, knowing Pike would do more to protect her exit.

Lying on top of Creed, preventing him from moving, Pike slapped one arm around the security man's neck, bringing him close and pinning the man's face to his chest.

She opened the door and slipped out, preventing the door from slamming behind her. She began trotting toward the elevator, hearing Pike say, "Whoa, whoa, I didn't know you were security. I'm sorry. I thought you were attacking me . . ."

His voice faded into the background as she entered the stairwell next to the elevator. In seconds, she was back in their makeshift TOC, breathing heavily, the adrenaline still coursing through her.

Ten minutes later, she heard the door open, and Creed entered, by himself, smiling as if he'd just accomplished the impossible.

Jennifer said, "Where's Pike?"

"Did you see me out there? Did you see what I did?" He mimicked throwing a fist, his eyes glistening.

She said, "I did. That was a pretty good cover play," then repeated, "Where's Pike?"

"Oh, he's with security. We might be getting kicked out of here."

Jennifer rolled her eyes, and Creed said, "How about that mission? I did pretty good, didn't I?"

Jennifer smiled at him and said, "You did, Creed. You really did."

He flushed at the attention, and the door opened a second time. Pike entered, the first words out of his mouth being, "What the fuck is your problem? I said slap me. *Slap* me. Not punch the shit out of my head."

Pike stalked over to him, and Creed cowered, his early bravado gone. Jennifer stood and said, "Pike, don't you dare."

Pike stopped his advance, putting his hands on his hips and shaking his head, saying, "Tell me you got the computer."

She pointed at the desk where it sat and said, "Tell me you didn't get us kicked out."

He grinned and said, "Nope. Not tonight anyway. They agreed we could stay one more night, since all the flights have left for the day, but tomorrow we're persona non grata."

She nodded and said, "Okay, now tell Creed he did a good job."

Creed said, "You said to make it believable."

Pike laughed and said, "Okay, okay, Creed, maybe I wasn't specific enough. You did all right under pressure. Makings of a Jedi."

Creed beamed and said, "So I get a prize too, right? Like you promised Jennifer?"

Pike said, "I think you'd better call it a win with the ice cream. I seriously doubt you want the prize Jennifer's earned."

Creed looked confused.

Jennifer stood with her mouth open, not quite believing that Pike had just said what he had.

Pike said, "What? You know I'm right on this."

16
★★★

The insidious bleating of the fifty-inch high-definition television overshadowed the panoramic view of the Moroccan coastline, as both father and son were once again glued to another story about the single death in Nevada. The Sky News reporter, standing in front of Ramstein Air Base, an American Air Force base near Landstuhl, Germany, breathlessly repeated the exact same facts that had been cycled endlessly for a day and a half. The only twist was his attempt to interview a screaming mob of German protestors, all waving signs decrying the use of the air base as a staging ground for US Air Force drones.

Tariq said, "Who would have thought one small strike would cause so much interest. Perhaps we are working too hard."

Yousef grunted, spat an olive pit into a bowl, then said, "Sensationalism doesn't serve our purposes. I don't care about drone strikes. I don't care about Afghanistan. Or Yemen, Iraq, or Syria. I *care* about Saudi Arabia. We are being corrupted by the West, and the only way to stop the rot is to cripple those same people."

Tariq said, "But you have to admit, that attack was pretty ingenious. I told you my man was smart."

"Smart, yes. For that single attack. But dumb that you let him do it. He's the one who is supposed to be our sleeper cell. Our inside man, and now he's hunted worse than Osama bin Laden when he was alive. I cannot believe how much attention this attack generated."

Tariq said, "It was the price of doing business. He was on his way to Somalia, more than willing to become cannon fodder in some tribal fight. I recruited him by playing on his desires."

"By paying for the drone and giving him information on the air base?"

"Yes, Father. I had no idea his little attack would generate so much interest. I thought it would be a minor blip on the news, with him crashing the drone into a fence, but I was prepared nonetheless. He has a complete set of new identification, a new bank account, and a string of safe houses. And like I said, he's smart."

"Where is he now?"

"In Houston. Waiting on the arrival of your tanker. He knows not to do anything else. He'll just keep his head down."

"You're sure?"

"Yes, of course. I talked to him yesterday on the phone I gave him."

"Does he still have access to the original bank account?"

"No. Anything from his life in Nevada has been severed. We have multiple different accounts to use. Why?"

"Because I don't want to confuse missions. His is done, for what little good it did. Ours is now beginning. The real mission. Where do we stand with Ring of Fire?"

Tariq inwardly sighed but was afraid to show any reticence at the questions. His father had done none of the work, other than provide the money, and yet he expected instant results. He still had no understanding of how much effort the Planes Operation had taken, and this one was no different.

"Nothing has changed from two days ago. The tanker left Gibraltar, and the explosives are in place. It was clean, so no problems there. The container ship is in port in Algeciras, but it's leaving soon, and I can do nothing with it until I can deliver the package to Jalal. He's still here, waiting."

Offhand, Yousef said, "So we miss September eleventh."

Confused at the turn of the conversation, Tariq said, "Yes. We talked about this. We can't do a synchronized attack because each attack has to be different. We do one, and they'll defend against the method. So we do a different one. Then a different one again. That was the plan all along."

Yousef said, "I like the symmetry of another spectacular attack on the same day as the one before."

Before Tariq could answer, the doorbell to the suite rang. Yousef said, "That would be the package you need."

Tariq opened the door, finding a bellman for the hotel holding a canvas satchel. He took it, tipped the man, and closed the door. He held up the satchel and said, "So, do I finally get to hear what the mystery is all about?"

Yousef smiled, saying, "You remember my new venture in food sterilization in Riyadh? The new plant we invested in?"

"Yes? The one designed to prevent diseases in produce and meat? What's that got to do with this satchel?"

"The method is irradiation. It's done with an isotope called cobalt 60, the same thing used for radiation treatment in cancer patients."

Tariq opened the satchel and withdrew a slender cylinder, capped at both ends. He said, "And this is the isotope?"

"Yes. The plant is going into production next week. It was some work, getting the isotope out of the official controls for such things, but I managed to do it."

"And if I include this on the container ship from Algeciras, what does that get us?"

"When I decided to invest in the plant, the only thing everyone could talk about was how deadly the isotope was and how it would contaminate city blocks if the plant exploded. Getting the approvals was like convincing everyone I wasn't introducing Ebola into the kingdom. Blow up that tube, and you'll contaminate the entire port for a minimum of forty years. You'll turn it into another Chernobyl."

"Is it safe? I mean, do I need to tell Jalal anything specific?"

"It's safe in the container. Once it's out, no. It's deadly."

Tariq smiled and said, "So at least two of the events will succeed."

Yousef popped another olive and said, "The final one concerns me. We don't control the ship. We don't even control the men."

"Father, trust me as you did in 2001. We didn't control those martyrs then any more than we do now, but it worked."

Yousef slapped his hand onto the table, causing the bowl of olives to jump. "No, it *didn't*. One plane ended up in a field. The one that was to strike the capital. The greatest target. It was missed. I don't want to repeat that."

He stabbed a finger at the screen and said, "I don't want another symbolic attack. I want *destruction*. I want them to bleed."

Tariq said nothing, knowing his father, once on a

familiar tirade, would continue until he ran out of energy. It was a speech he'd heard many times before. Although not a member of the royal family, Yousef was a powerful entity of the ruling elite of Saudi Arabia, equal with the Bin Laden construction group and just as staunch as them about preserving the Islamic traditions within the holy lands of the kingdom. Traditions that he believed were being assaulted on a daily basis by the West. Women's rights, religious freedom for those who didn't practice Islam—even discussions about the blasphemy of homosexuality—were now tolerated by the royal family, and it was all because of the influence of the West, led by the United States.

His father's fever had been quenched somewhat after the attacks on the United States in 2001, but then, in 2015, a new king of Saudi Arabia had taken the throne, and with the accession had come a royal shakeup. The new king's son, Mohammed bin Salman, had been named deputy crown prince and had been given the portfolio of both defense and oil, overtaking the power of even the crown prince himself.

To make matters worse, the deputy crown prince began to take his position seriously—and his father, the king, seemed to let him. Mohammed bin Salman had come up with something he called Saudi Vision 2030—a plan to wean the country from the stranglehold of oil, divesting the future of the country from the very asset that defined it, instead focusing on such things as the hospitality and tourism industries. Something that would only increase the calls for reform away from Wahhabi traditions that, in Yousef's mind, defined the very existence of the kingdom.

All of this, he was sure, was being done insidiously by the West. Even the developer of Saudi Vision 2030 was a global consulting firm founded in the United States. Yousef was convinced the young prince had been seduced and bamboozled by hucksters in suits from Savile Row, in essence forsaking his very heritage in some deviant quest to become more Westernized.

Yousef's voice began to rise, the thunder of his words bouncing off the walls of the suite. "Killing a single drone pilot generates press and propaganda. It creates terror, but that is *all*. We must strike a blow that will actually hurt—just as our martyrs did in 2001. Billions and billions of dollars were lost, the attack forcing them to turn inward, bleeding money on security. We must repeat that. Leave the spectacle of beheadings and fear attacks to those without a vision. If that final plane had struck, we would have won."

"Father, we can't account for outside events. The aircraft was brought down by the very passengers on it. This is different. There will be no passengers to interfere."

Yousef looked out the bay windows, watching the surf crash onto the Moroccan coast. He said, "Yes, all it took were the passengers to stop that attack. Civilians. Since then, because we failed, there are much worse monsters out in the world, some working with our own royal family, others hunting in this very country. Coordinating with every government in the world to stop us."

Tariq stood and placed a hand on his father's arm and said, "I have the martyrs, and there is nobody who can interfere like before. Bin Laden was a known enemy in 2001. Al Qaida was hunted. ISIS is the same now, but nobody's looking for us."

17

I watched a man waiting in line at the ATM, wondering if he was the one. He fidgeted back and forth, from one foot to the other, wearing bedraggled jeans and canvas shoes. He *could* be the target. He was standing behind a couple who were clearly tourists. Dressed in ratty clothes, and at an age that we would call a MAM— military-aged male—he fit the profile of our target set.

The couple took their money and left. The MAM inserted his card, and I waited on the call from Creed. The man punched a few buttons, withdrew his cash, and left. I received no call.

I shook my head and Jennifer said, "He'll come back, soon enough."

I said, "Maybe. Maybe not."

"Well, Creed's got a handle on the account, so if he does something anywhere, we'll know."

Surveillance work was always boring, but I couldn't really complain this time. I was sitting at an outdoor café called La Vinoteca at the Plaza Santa Ana in Madrid, Spain, drinking a blackberry mojito that looked like it had taken an hour to make.

In essence, this detour was nothing more than a date with Jennifer, and the US government was paying the tab. Well, they wouldn't pay for the mojito unless I camouflaged it as lunch, but Jennifer wouldn't allow me to do that.

The last forty-eight hours had been a whirlwind, to say the least. Not that I'm whining. Living in the whirlwind sure beat binge watching *House of Cards* on Netflix—which is what I would have been doing after the Bahamas.

We'd reported back to the Taskforce, and, as expected, the first thing the Oversight Council had done was go apeshit over the fact that I had murdered a "whistleblower" in the course of my duties. I should have been pissed at the accusations, but given my past transgressions, I'd earned the right for them to be suspicious. Jennifer was another story. They'd questioned us both, spending most of their time on me, but ran out of steam on her within ten minutes, because there was just no way she would ever do such a thing.

The grilling took about an hour, and by the time we'd left the grounds of the White House and returned to Taskforce headquarters in Clarendon, the computer data had been analyzed, and it looked like the Taskforce was in the clear for whatever leak had been planned: There were no bank accounts associated with any of our cover organizations. Not that it mattered now anyway, as the intrepid leaker had met his fate head-on.

Nobody in the Taskforce was too keen on looking into the death, as his previous leaks had upset just about every organized crime outfit on earth. It would be a waste of effort to determine who'd killed him, as there was undoubtedly a long line, and it had nothing to do with our charter of counterterrorism. Then, unexpectedly, some of the data we'd brought back *did* have a connection.

Three days earlier—when we were operational in the Bahamas—some asshole had flown a commercial drone into the car windshield of a US Air Force UAV pilot in

Nevada and had killed the driver with a homemade white phosphorus grenade. The fiery death had ignited cable news and social media, so much so that it had been non-stop coverage since it had occurred and was just now winding down.

The authorities, of course, jumped all over the crime scene like a hobo on a ham sandwich but found very little. FBI, ATF, local police, sheriffs' departments, DHS, you name it, they all took a turn behind the microphone to say one thing: We have no leads. They tried to dance through it politely, but the brutal truth was they had nothing at all to go on.

The drone had self-immolated in the attack to the point where the only thing they could ascertain was the model, but that was about it, and there was no further evidence at the scene. There were plenty of witnesses of the event, but none for the drone pilot himself. Unlike today's usual crimes, for this one there was no cell phone camera or surveillance footage, no reports of someone fleeing the scene, and no suicidal jihadi spraying bullets after the fact. Nothing. The killer had vanished.

Strangely enough, there had also been no claim of responsibility. The attack had been meticulously planned, involving reconnaissance and some expertise with both chemicals and electronics, and had been executed perfectly, implying it wasn't some individual nutcase who just decided to kill after he woke up one morning, and yet no group was crowing about the death. Strange all the way around.

The authorities had been running on fumes, with an increasingly angry press hammering them at every update, when they got a break: A Somali immigrant had contacted Las Vegas police. She suspected her son was responsible.

He'd been gone two days, and she'd feared the worst, finally summoning the courage to contact the authorities, telling them she'd seen him looking at jihadist videos online. She'd let them into her shabby trailer, and they'd turned the place upside down, finding enough evidence to establish that he was the killer, but nothing as to where he'd gone or who had helped him. Well, nothing that they knew about, anyway.

It turned out that one of the many strange numbers they'd found in their search through his digital life matched an offshore account included in the planned leak that we'd brought back—tied to a US bank account his mother didn't know existed.

The US bank account had been cleaned out, and the link to the offshore account appeared to be dead—to him at least—but it was tied to another bank account in, of all places, Madrid, Spain. And *that* bank account was still active.

The US authorities had no idea about the offshore account—how could they, given how we'd gleaned the information—and it was determined that, while we'd pass along any information that would help find the killer in the United States, the Taskforce would investigate the Madrid lead. Which meant my team. I'd found the lead and would have screamed holy hell if it had been given to someone else.

We'd saddled up the Rock Star bird and flown straight to Madrid, and by the time we'd landed, Creed had hacked into the bank account in question and had a historical footprint of every interaction. The most prevalent had been at an ATM in Plaza Santa Ana, leaving my team to simply keep eyes on it, waiting on the target to trigger.

When he—or she, I suppose—did so, it would alert the hacking cell in real time, and we'd simply follow whoever was using the ATM. So far, it had been pretty boring. But I did get to have a single mojito with Jennifer. Small miracles.

Jennifer said, "You think they'll give us Omega to do anything, or is this just going to be a setup for Spanish authorities?"

We'd been given Alpha authority to investigate the bank account—meaning we could sneak around trying to build a case against whatever we found—but the Council had balked at giving us Omega, the authority to execute a capture.

I said, "Probably not, unless we can follow this guy to a safe house full of ISIS terrorists trying to purchase a biological weapon."

She smiled and said, "Shift's almost over. Want me to call Knuckles and Retro?"

"Yeah, but send them to the other café across the square. I'm not ready to leave yet."

The ATM withdrawals had all happened in the daytime, and we'd already decided that we weren't going to keep eyes on it 24/7. It was closing in on five o'clock, and the last three-hour shift belonged to Knuckles.

She made the call, then took a sip of her mojito, looking at me askance, like she was about to ask something uncomfortable. Which raised the hair on my neck.

She said, "You think Knuckles will get Carly a shot at selection? You think Kurt will allow that?"

The question was a minefield. I didn't know if she was asking for my opinion after our earlier arguments about females in combat arms and our little triathlon, or if she was demanding I help.

Cautiously, I said, "I'd wait and see if Carly even wants to do it first. It may be a moot point."

And just like that, I stepped on the mine.

Jennifer cocked her head and said, "That's a cop-out. She wants to do it. You know that. Will you support her or be like everybody else and stand in her way?"

Oh boy.

"Of course I won't stand in her way, any more than Knuckles stood in yours."

I saw yet another skeevy-looking guy walk up to the ATM. He was definitely local, with a swarthy complexion and a threadbare knapsack over one shoulder. He looked like a Spanish pickpocket, not a terrorist.

Jennifer said, "That's not what I meant. I know you wouldn't spew that he-man women-hater crap that all the other guys do, but will you *support* her? Knuckles holds some sway with Kurt, but *nobody* has your power. You say the word, and she's in."

What she said was true; Kurt knew I would never throw my weight behind someone who wasn't capable, but that was also the primary reason I hesitated: I *didn't know* Carly's capabilities. She was a CIA case officer with a penchant for getting into a gunfight—something she'd proved in the past with Knuckles—but from what he'd told me, she was impetuous. Maybe even a little bit of a loose cannon. That could have been just bar talk, with him bragging about her courage, or it could be real, which was a trait that wouldn't work well in the Taskforce. She'd have to give me something more before I made that leap. I wouldn't vouch for a male just because he was a friend of Knuckles's, and the fact that Carly was female alone wasn't enough for me to support her, but that was exactly why Jennifer was asking.

It was a no-win situation.

I considered my answer, Jennifer boring into me with her eyes, and then my earpiece blessedly crackled from a call half a world away. "Pike, Koko, this is Creed.

Account has been triggered. I say again, account has been triggered."

I saw Jennifer's eyebrows shoot up, and I pointed at the phone, telling her without speaking to get Knuckles, Retro, and Veep ready. I clicked my earpiece and said, "Templated location? At the ATM in Plaza Santa Ana?"

"Yes. Withdrew the max amount. Account still active."

I glanced at the ATM and saw the swarthy guy still there, messing around with the keypad.

Creed said, "He's checking the balance."

Then, "He's off."

Jennifer put her phone down, threw some money on the table, and stood. She grinned at me, the adrenaline of the mission pouring through the both of us.

She said, "Saved by the bell, Nephilim."

I said, "Boy, was I ever."

I keyed my encrypted earbud and said, "Break, break, Knuckles, you up on comms?"

"Roger that. Got Veep and Retro. What's up?"

"It's showtime."

18

Speaking into a smartphone, Jalal said, "I'm sorry, man. That's the way it has to be. I'm out of the business for at least the next month."

The man on the other end said, "I don't have the contacts you do in the Rif. How am I supposed to make this work?"

"Snyder is in Chefchaouen. He has the contacts still."

"That idiot American? That's who you left in charge on the Moroccan side?"

"Yes, and he's not an idiot."

"He smokes more of the product than he ships."

Jalal laughed and said, "Yes, you're probably right, but he has a business mind, and his brother will keep him from wasting too much product on himself."

"His brother isn't even in Morocco. He's in Granada, running around with a pack of street musicians."

That was news. "Granada? What's he doing there?"

"I sent him. I'm trying to grow our network, and that place is ripe for expansion. Plenty of European expats loafing around that city, which is why your timing is horrible."

Jalal heard a knock on his door, causing a moment of silence. He went to it and saw the Sheik through the peephole, impeccably dressed in an expensive suit and holding a canvas satchel. He said, "Look, this is just temporary. I'll be back. You got the money I promised, yes?"

"Yeah, I just withdrew some from the ATM. The card worked."

"And you still have the product from the last shipment, correct?"

"Yes."

"Well, that should tide you over until I can return."

Jalal opened the door, waving the Saudi into the little apartment. He started to speak, and Jalal held up a finger, pointing at the phone.

The man on the other end said, "Tiding me over depends on how long you'll be gone."

Jalal said, "Look, I can't talk right now. I have a visitor at the door. I'll call you later."

Before the caller could respond, Jalal hung up the phone. His unexpected guest, looking suspicious, said, "Who was that?"

"None of your concern. Why are you here in Tangier? We were never supposed to meet at this apartment."

The Sheik wouldn't let it go. Waving the question away with a hand, he said, "Why were you speaking English on the phone I gave you? Who were you talking to? Tell me it wasn't your drug-addict friends."

Jalal quietly set the phone on the table and said, "I could not simply walk away. I have partners who trust me. Business that was not yet complete. I told you I would no longer be involved personally, and I've kept my word to you. I must also keep my word to others."

He turned and placed his hands on the table, getting level with the Saudi's face. "Do not presume because we are allies that you control me."

The Sheik said nothing for a moment, Jalal reading the hesitation on his face. He continued, "Now, tell me why you have put our operation in jeopardy by coming to this safe house. If you are being followed in any way, you have now linked me with your actions. It's the very reason I made you come up with the off-site meeting place two days ago."

His visitor blustered and said, "Nobody is following me. I'm a Saudi. If anything, you would be the one under suspicion."

Jalal nodded and said, "True, and that suspicion will only grow when a lowly Berber waif is seen meeting with such an *important* Saudi man."

The condescension was not lost on his guest. He sought a different line of attack. "You talked to them on the clean phone I gave you? You accuse me of poor operational planning, and you taint the very means of success. I have done such operations before, and trust me, the digital world is much more dangerous than the real one."

Jalal stood up, moving to the sink and pouring a glass of water. He decided to end the fight. "I'm sorry. I had no other means of communicating. I won't use it again for such things. Let's stop bickering. Why are you here?"

"My father agreed to your plan for the third attack. I'll be putting significant money in your account to buy what you need. You're sure you can deliver?"

"Yes. If you give me the identification I requested. All I need is money, and a tourist visa for the four of us to get into the United States. I don't even need your inside man like you have for the other attacks."

"I'm arranging for passports from Saudi Arabia. I'll have those ready when you come back here."

Jalal said, "Come back here? What do you mean?"

He tossed the satchel on the table. "The delivery arrived, and time is of the essence."

"What is it?"

He explained the satchel and its contents, then said,

"This needs to get on the ship in Algeciras before it leaves tomorrow."

"Tomorrow? That's not enough time. I have to take the ferry from here, meet him, get the package built, and get it onboard in one day?"

"That's exactly why I didn't want to waste time on setting up a meeting. There's a ferry leaving to Algeciras this afternoon."

"I haven't talked to my men in Fez yet."

"You can do that when you come back, after I have the passports. You said the explosives were built, right?"

"Yes, but the containers are already in the holding area. Badis has access to the area, but he can't introduce a package in broad daylight—especially if they're loading the ship from that container zone."

"Then you'll have to accomplish it tonight. The port works twenty-four seven, right?"

Jalal said nothing, thinking of the timeline.

"Can you do it?"

"I don't know. I'll have to ask Badis. He's the one who will make the call. What if we can't?"

"The attack will be delayed, if not permanently stopped. When our other strike goes off, there will be an investigation. When they see it was sabotage, make no mistake, the security will be increased at ports all over the world. People will be screened. Areas will be locked down. We need this ship to be moving toward its target before then. And we need you to be moving with your men for the third attack."

Jalal nodded and said, "Insh'Allah, if it can be done, it will be."

The Sheik pointed at the phone on the table and said, "Use the Wickr app to let me know, and be sure to send the cell number of the triggering phone. I'll need to pass that to our man."

"This seems rushed. We took two years to get the men in place, and now we're racing around like chickens."

"I know, but it's why you were chosen. Remember our talks in Madrid. This is the way. When all targets are attacked, it will cripple their shipping industry, and in so doing, cripple America. When the path grows hard, *remember* where it leads."

19

★★
★

Held up by the traffic on Paseo del Prado, right next to a fountain that looked like it was supposed to be the god Neptune, I lost sight of our target. I called Knuckles, saying, "He got across before me. You have eyes on?"

Knuckles came back, "Got him. Crossing next to the national museum, and continuing west."

I'd sent the team a couple of pictures of the target, along with his direction of travel, as soon as I'd triggered the operation. He'd headed generally west out of the plaza, looking like he had a destination in mind. Jennifer and I had followed loosely behind until he came to a major four-lane road. Called Paseo del Prado, it was split by parks, with two lanes on the near side and two on the far. The target, like everyone else, was stuck waiting at the light. I didn't want to stand right next to him, so Jennifer and I hung back. When the light changed, we let him cross, then followed at the last second, making it across the first two-lane road but missing the light for the second, leaving us stranded in the park between the lanes.

I said, "What's up there? Where's he going?"

Knuckles was working with Retro as a team, and on the hunt directly behind the target. Veep, operating as a singleton and staged on the target's projected line of march, came on. "Pike, I'm up at the top of the hill.

There's a big-ass church here, and a national park. It's big as well. Wide-open. Looks like something you'd see in France."

Veep was at least ten years behind me in age, meaning he was someone well versed in the use of Google.

Our light went green and I said, "Veep, I'm walking across now. Do you want me to use my phone as I go, or would you like to do that research while you twiddle your thumbs next to the 'big-ass church'?"

Jennifer scowled at me, and I heard a contrite, "Roger. Looking now."

I was fairly sure he was kicking himself, which is exactly what I wanted.

Jennifer said, "Do you really think it's in our best interest to insult the son of the president of the United States?"

Which is how he had come by his callsign. He'd earned it the hard way, on an operation when his father was still the vice president. Heritage meant nothing in the Taskforce. Either you could operate or you couldn't— and in Veep's case, he most definitely could. He just needed some instruction.

I smiled and said, "You're just sweet on him."

She gave me her disappointed-teacher look and said, "No. I just think you're a jerk to anyone new."

We'd crossed the second two-lane road and started walking up the hill past the national museum before Veep came back on. "Pike, the park is 350 acres, called Buen Retiro. It's been around since the monarchy of Isabella in the sixteenth century. It's got trees from Japan, architecture from Europe, and lakes and fountains. It's been through several different—"

I cut him off. "Okay, okay, I don't need a history lesson. What's up there that the target would want?"

I heard nothing from him. Knuckles came on. "He's entered the park. We're still behind him, but getting hot. Veep, where are you?"

Veep whispered, "I see him. I got him. I'm on him. I'm behind him now."

To Jennifer, off the net, I said, "I think Veep's got eyes on."

She pinched my side, saying, "Stop it. You made your point."

We entered the park, and Veep came back on the net, saying, "Pike, he's not just cutting through here. This place is wide-open, with plenty of tourists, but he's off the concrete and into the trees. I think he's going to a meeting."

Which was the first bit of analysis that mattered. I said, "How do you know? What do you see?"

"He's walking down a dirt path, and he's taking it slow. This place is crisscrossed with them, for joggers or people looking to find a patch of grass to sit on. He's not doing either. There are police on the paved paths, and he's avoiding any stretch that has people on it. He's got a reason to be in here, and he doesn't want to be remembered. He's not just cutting through this park . . . Well, maybe he is . . ."

I grinned at the last statement, because Veep was losing confidence in his call. I said, "Veep, you got the eye, and I trust it. Keep on him, and click on the beacon in your phone. We'll leapfrog ahead and pick him up."

Jennifer smiled and said, "That wasn't so hard, now, was it?"

I said, "Find him on your phone, then plan a route to intercept his likely destination."

On the radio, I said, "Knuckles, Retro, you monitor last?"

"Roger all."

I turned on the beacon to my smartphone—basically just a software feature that allowed the team to track one another's movements—and said, "Koko and I are going to intercept. I want you two to run anchor, keeping us clean from anyone else in here."

Meaning, I wanted some countersurveillance in case our target was moving slowly precisely to see if he was being followed. We kept walking, reaching a large fountain, a man-made lake to the left with rowers sculling in circles around it. I said, "You got anything?"

Jennifer said, "Veep's in the trees to our right, moving south. If we go down this road, and he continues, he'll pop out right about here. If we hurry, we can set up beforehand."

She was pointing down a stretch of asphalt that paralleled the wood line the target was in. At the base was another road, running perpendicular and basically boxing in that section of the park. I said, "Mark it and send it to the team." On the radio, I said, "Knuckles, got a destination headed your way. Veep, tell us if he deviates from that intended location."

We took a right and began moving with a purpose, Jennifer staring at her phone from time to time. We'd gone only about a hundred meters when Jennifer said, "Veep's stopped. We just passed his position."

I started to call him, but he beat me to the punch. "Pike, target is now moving east. I'm off. If I go that way, he'll know for sure I'm following."

"How far ahead of you?"

"Fifty meters."

I looked at Jennifer's phone, did the math, and saw the guy was going to pop out right in front of us. Before I could say anything, he did, about forty meters away.

"All elements, all elements, this is Pike. We have the eye."

He crossed in front of us and immediately went into the wooded area on the eastern side of our path. I didn't want to run up and cross where he had, but I needed to keep eyes on or risk losing him in the trees. I glanced to the east and saw a well-worn path that looked like something tourists routinely used to meander through the trees. I tugged Jennifer's hand and said, "That way."

We entered the tree line, and I saw it was much more open than it looked, with wide gravel paths and various gardens, picnic tables, and benches scattered about. I caught a glimpse of our target still moving east. We followed, walking parallel and keeping our distance. Eventually we came upon some giant two-story greenhouse-looking things fronting another lake and swarming with tourists. Appropriately enough, a sign next to it proclaimed it the CRYSTAL PALACE.

I stopped at a bench and took a seat, both Jennifer and me scanning for the target. She whispered, "There he is. Eleven o'clock. Walking toward that policeman."

I casually swiveled my head and found him. He walked right by the cop, and I saw him pass something. The cop immediately stuffed it into his jacket.

It happened so quickly that an untrained eye would have missed the action. I wasn't even sure if I wasn't tricking myself.

Jennifer said, "Did you catch that? The brush pass?"

So it wasn't my imagination.

"Yep. Let's stay here."

The target took a seat across the lake from us, on a bench snuggled into a small copse of trees, leaving us with an angled view of his back.

Eventually, two young local men approached. He talked

to them for a moment, then surreptitiously dug into his knapsack on the bench. The men left. This happened two more times before I realized what was happening.

I said, "He's a damn drug dealer. And that cop is his protection."

Jennifer nodded and said, "Yeah, I think you're right, but how is he connected to a bank account tied in to a terrorist in America? It makes no sense."

"No idea, but we'll stay on him. Maybe something will pop up. Maybe he's fronting for someone. Half of AQ is funded by the drug trade."

Jennifer said, "You know when we report this back in our SITREP tonight, that'll be the end of it. We'll have to turn over everything and the Taskforce will punt this to DEA or CIA or someone else."

"Yeah, I know."

Knuckles came on. "I got eyes on you, but not the target. What's happening? Did you do something to spike?"

I told him, watching the target answer his cell phone, then asked, "Why the spike question?"

"I got two Hyenas who are very interested in your bench. One's on the phone now."

Hyena meant someone who wasn't positively good or bad, but potentially could compromise the operation either way because of his actions. Someone who caught our attention because they were acting funny, like a hyena pacing a lion's kill.

The target swiveled around, looking in our direction. I diligently studied the lake, taking Jennifer's hand in mine. I said, "Must be his internal protection."

"Just hold in place. Give me a direction and distance, and when the target leaves, Retro and I will pick him up."

The target got up, walking back to the cop. They

exchanged words, and the cop shook his head. Apparently not trusting the cop's ability to know if other police were after him, the target decided to leave.

And I had a great idea that would guarantee our ability to operate.

I said, "Target's moving. Coming right by us."

Knuckles said, "I'll get him. Stay put."

"No, Jennifer and I will get him. Keep eyes on the Hyenas. They'll probably move to interdict us. When they do, let it happen."

Jennifer whipped her head to me, and I heard, "What? Say again?"

The target passed us and I rose, bringing Jennifer with me. I said, "We're done after our report tonight, unless something drastic happens. This'll go into the intelligence slush pile, and we won't get Omega. But we always have the right to self-defense."

Knuckles said, "So? What are you saying?"

"I'm saying I want those two thugs you're watching to interdict us. They'll take us somewhere and you can then come in for the rescue."

We started following the target again, and Knuckles said, "That is the most harebrained thing I've ever heard. Pike, Hyenas are now on you, fifty meters back."

I said, "It's pure genius. A Trojan horse. Once I'm on the inside, we'll have all the authority we need to interrogate and exploit whatever we find."

"What if they just kill you?"

"Then you'll have failed."

I heard nothing for a second, then, "This is a really bad idea."

20

Sitting at his desk, trying to appear nonchalant, Dexter said, "So, I saw that the journalist met an unforeseen fate at a dangerous stretch of road. They should mark that highway better."

Johan said nothing, not even hello. He set a laptop computer on the desk and booted it up. Dexter continued, "The source in the Bahamas, not so much. That made a little bit of a splash."

Johan said, "Shut up. What I got out of that hit is the splash."

Dexter clamped his mouth closed. Johan clicked on an application, then began flipping through one document after another, saying, "Your account was, in fact, in that leak, and it's got some seriously strange activity."

Dexter said, "What do you mean?"

"I mean, if you used it only once, someone else has been using it ever since, and your name is all over each transaction."

Dexter leaned forward toward the screen; then his jaw dropped. "What the hell? I've never done anything with that account since then!"

Johan flipped through the documents, getting to a fuzzy scan of an original. "Is that your signature?"

"Yes. That's the founding document. I placed two million dollars in it, and it was withdrawn a day later.

After that, the account was closed. I was given the closing documents."

Johan flipped to the next document, saying, "Does this look like it was closed? Cash transfer to Yemen, 2002." He flipped again. "Cash transfer to Nigeria, 2004." And again. "Cash transfer to Libya. *Libya*, 2012."

Dexter's mouth went dry. "I . . . I didn't do any of that."

Johan zoomed in to the signature. "Is that you? Because it sure looks like it."

The signature was, in fact, Dexter's. He said, "What the fuck is going on with this thing? Who are these people?"

"That's my question to you. What have you been involved in? You just had me kill two people. Why? For Icarus? Or for you?"

Dexter licked his lips and said, "Johan, I had nothing to do with this. Those assholes are using the account from my original bribe, using *my* name. We have to stop this."

Johan kept flipping the documents, which recorded transactions up until the present day. He said, "The last transfer you made was to a company in Gibraltar called Mint Tea Maintenance. What was that for?"

"Johan, I have no fucking idea. I didn't do it."

"I looked, and it's a company that doesn't even have a webpage. It's got an address, but that's about it. Looks to be some singleton repair shop on the naval shipyards there. I can't find anything else on them."

"Johan, you have to believe me, I haven't done anything with that account. Ever." He turned and started tearing through a filing cabinet, saying, "I have the closing papers right here."

He turned around, holding a folder and finding Johan's blue eyes on him, the color of a mountain lake, hiding what was below. Johan brushed his hair aside and took the folder, saying, "What, exactly, did you do in 2001?"

"It's irrelevant now. I gave a bribe. Nothing more. Or, apparently, much more than I wanted." He put his head into his hands and pulled at his hair, saying, "This is a fucking disaster."

Johan tapped him on the head to interrupt the whining. Dexter looked up, waiting. Johan said, "If you're lying to me . . . if you asked me to take the lives of people to protect some bullshit operations for your business . . . I'll fucking cut your throat."

Dexter said, "It's not like that. It's *not*." Now in a panic, he said, "Jesus Christ, those fucks had no right to keep using that account."

Johan said, "What 'fucks'? Who did you give the money to?"

"I . . . just . . . it was a man who . . . a nobody."

"A nobody? Well, this 'nobody' has accounts that span the globe."

Dexter sat upright and said, "Johan, I had nothing to do with these accounts. I did nothing wrong. For Christ's sake, all I did was bribe someone. Why are you so angry?"

Johan sat on the desk, leaning into Dexter's face. "I believe you, for now. But your bribe is going to get out, and when it does, it's going to be tied to some very bad things."

"What do you mean? What bad things? All you have is that those sons of bitches used my name. What are you saying?"

"Take a look at the accounts. Every transfer happens

to go to some bad-guy land. You, by your name, have probably funded terrorist attacks."

"Wait a fucking minute. You can't make that claim. Yeah, the Saudis gave money using my name. So what? I *did not* have anything to do with terrorist attacks. All I did was make a business. One that employs you now. One that gets you out of the line of fire."

Johan stood up, his face hardening. "You think I work for you because I'm afraid of the guns?" He leaned in close enough for Dexter to smell his breath. "Is that what you think?"

Dexter's secretary entered, saw the confrontation, and scurried back out of the room. The door closed, and Johan continued, his voice scraping along like a rake over asphalt. "Let's be clear, you and I, just to be sure we understand each other: I have fought terrorists my entire life. I started in South Africa, where I found women raped for no other reason than they were a different color of skin. I've seen things that would cause you to tremble just in the telling. I have fought against evil for my existence, and I will not be a participant in the same."

Dexter said, "Johan, I promise, I had no idea about any of this, and I want it stopped." He tried to read him, but he wasn't sure what Johan thought.

Johan said, "So, what now?"

"I . . . I don't know. I mean, I don't want to have anything to do with this. You stopped the leak. I guess, let it go. Let's get back to business."

"That guy in Gibraltar is working on something. He's not going to quit. And your name is tied to it."

Hearing the words, Dexter realized how deep he'd become embroiled in the state-supported system of Tariq's family from Saudi Arabia. But he couldn't tell

Johan that. All he could do was mitigate. Mitigate, mitigate, mitigate.

He said, "What do you recommend?"

"Let me go there and interrogate him. Find out what that last transfer was funding. Find out who's actually behind all of these accounts. Find out how they're using your name."

Dexter already knew the answer to that, but he was more than willing to plead ignorance. He knew why they were using his name. Knew that his entire corporation was built on the death of others. He had never wanted to face that reality, but now it had come home. He decided to destroy the facts instead of embracing the calamity he had engendered. He took one more step into the abyss.

"Yes. I think that would be best. Figure out what that guy is doing, and how he has an account tied to my name. Figure out who is to blame."

Johan relaxed, the violence in his demeanor escaping like air from a balloon.

He said, "I'm on it. I will."

Dexter smiled, missing the menace behind the words.

21

I jerked Jennifer along by the hand, with her cursing my every step. "Pike, this is *really* stupid. Don't do it. You remember the criteria for assault?"

I said, "Yeah, of course. I'm the one who wrote them."

"Then you *know* you can't engender the reasons for Omega. You *cannot* design an operation where you are forced to react. It's in the damn charter."

"We always have the right to self-defense. I'm not asking for anyone to interdict, but I can't plan for that."

"You *just did*."

I looked shocked, saying, "I'm just following a target. How could you say that?"

She gritted her teeth and said, "I should call this off right now. Run back to Knuckles."

"And miss the opportunity to show the value of the weaker sex?"

Her eyes flashed at that, and I knew I'd overstepped. She said, "So if I don't do this, it's because I'm a woman? Are you really trying to manipulate me like that?"

I backed off immediately, because it was a pretty shitty thing to say. "Hey, come on." I squeezed her hand. "I wouldn't do this if I didn't think you'd save my ass."

The scowl remained, and I said, "Okay, okay. If you want to quit, I will. But you have to admit we'll never get a second shot. These guys are tied into a pretty sophisticated terrorist attack on US soil, and the Taskforce won't want to investigate the thread. They'll get arrested as drug runners, and that'll be the end. Nothing will come out of that bank account."

She exhaled, blowing the air out of her cheeks. I said, "Someone else is going to die. Maybe not because this guy is selling dope, but because of what he's attached to. You know it, and I know it. It's always the nothing threads that lead to success. A parking ticket that catches a serial killer. Or an innocuous email leads to a terrorist in Bosnia. Isn't this the right thing to do?"

That was a reference to a bad guy we'd ended up chasing after I'd first met her. There, I was the one who wanted to quit, and she'd given me the same "right thing to do" speech. I saw a small grin slip out. She said, "You had better make sure we can get out of this."

I said, "Me? That's Knuckles's problem."

The target reached the man-made lake and made a beeline for the exit of the park, spilling out of the same gate he'd used to enter. He walked about the length of a football field down Calle de Alfonso, getting away from the park entrance and into a networked neighborhood of expensive apartments. We, of course, followed.

I called Knuckles. "Status on Hyenas?"

"They're still on you. This could go on for miles."

I said, "No, it won't. He's going to make a left or right to confirm we're following, and then they'll make their move."

"What do you want me to do? Attack them? We didn't bring any weapons, and I'll bet they have some."

"No, no. Let it go. Both my phone and Jennifer's are active. They'll take them to prevent us from calling for help, but they probably won't take our Bluetooth. They have no idea that we're connected via real-time radio.

And the beacon will remain with us, even if I can't manipulate the radio. Let it play out."

The target took a right on a side road, and we followed. Knuckles said, "Pike, I think this is seriously dangerous. We'll have to go back to the hotel to get weapons, then design an assault plan, then come in. You might be dead. I recommend abort. Just start walking away from him."

I saw a black van, no side windows, pull up next to the target. He leaned into the driver's window and started talking. We either held up, which would look stupid, or we kept walking past him. I said, "Too late. This is it. Head back to the hotel ricky-tick. I'm going to need you soon."

Next to me, but on the net, Jennifer said, "*We*. We're going to need you soon."

Knuckles said, "Don't blame me for your choice of partner. You brought this on yourself."

We pulled abreast of the van, and I said, "You want Carly to go to selection, you'd better not let me die."

I heard, "What the fuck does that mean? Who said anything about Carly?"

Then the door slid open and two men with pistols came out, jabbing them into our guts. The two Hyenas behind us closed the distance, shoving us into the van. We reacted exactly like we should have: in abject fear, cowering and showing no threat whatsoever. As the van rolled, we were forced onto our stomachs and searched, with both cell phones taken, but they didn't do anything to our Bluetooth earpieces—which were still slaved to the phones.

Our original target leaned in and said something in Spanish, a language I couldn't understand. When I didn't answer, he cuffed me in the head. I glared at him and said, "I don't speak Spanish. Why are you doing this? If you're terrorists, we have no money. We can't pay."

He leaned back, reassessing. He said, "I know you aren't police. So who do you work for? Why are you following me? We've never intruded on Marco's terrain. Do you work for him?"

I had no idea what he was talking about and told him that. He punched me in the head, causing me to grit my teeth to keep from slaughtering everyone in the van. Forcing myself to remember the end state.

He said, "I'll figure out who you are, make no mistake. It would be easier if you just told me now."

I reiterated our innocence and got another cuff to the head. I took it. The van eventually stopped, and we were hoisted out. I had one quick look and saw we were in a depressed area, with graffiti everywhere. We were hustled into the foyer of an apartment complex and slammed against a wall. The men around us scurried about, unlocking a door; then we were jerked forward. We entered a small apartment and were thrown to the floor. Under my breath, I checked my radio, "Knuckles, Knuckles, we're home. Acknowledge."

I heard, "I got you, I got you. At the hotel now. We're probably twenty minutes out. Can you hold?"

"Yeah. I think so. Don't waste any time."

The target jerked me upright and sat me in a chair. Another man did the same with Jennifer. The target said, "Okay, enough of the bullshit. Why are you following me? Who do you work for?"

Acting like I was terrified, I trembled and said, "I have no idea what you want. We're American tourists. I have some money, if you want it."

He squinted his eyes, then slapped me, hard. "Tell me what you are doing."

A man moved next to me and used a pistol to poke me in the cheek, in his mind telling me he was a threat, not realizing he would be my first target.

I moaned, "Nothing. I swear, nothing."

The leader glanced at the men surrounding Jennifer and said, "I can hurt you, but I don't think that would be the quickest way to our answers."

"What do you mean? I swear, we were just walking in the park."

He said, "We'll see." He walked over to Jennifer, raising the level of the interrogation. Pushing me toward the breaking point.

He said, "You like her?"

I felt the first tremors of real fear. The assholes were supposed to focus on me. I could take the slaps until Knuckles showed up. This was not part of the plan.

I said, "Yes. She's my wife."

Jennifer looked at me with a touch of amazement, then shrank back as the two men next to her closed in. The target said, "Well then, maybe you'll tell me what you were doing before we destroy her."

He flicked his head, and his minions jerked her out of the chair, forcing her onto her hands and knees. Jennifer screamed, "Pike!"

I said, "Don't do this. Please. Don't do this." I triggered my earpiece and said, "Where the fuck are you?"

The men heard the words and looked at me in suspicion. I heard, "Five minutes. Loaded for bear."

I said, "Things are going bad swiftly." The target smacked me in the head, not realizing I was actually talking to another human being.

Two men held Jennifer's arms, and she screamed again, "Pike! Pike!"

Jesus Christ. This was a bad idea.

I knew why she was screaming, and it wasn't because she wanted me to save her. She wanted me to let her loose. But if I did, we would lose our ability to interrogate anyone, because she'd slaughter them like lambs.

I made one more attempt, shouting, "Stop, stop. I'll tell you what you want. I work for the United States Drug Enforcement Administration. The DEA. That's all. We're looking at marijuana infiltration from Morocco. Please, this isn't necessary. You aren't even the main target."

The men in the room had worked themselves into a frenzy, like a school of sharks in bloody water, circling my partner. Circling the one thing I held dear. I saw their faces and knew it was too late. They were going to do what they were going to do. And because of it, I was going to end their lives.

The target said, "Well, it looks like you're about to learn what happens on my terrain." He walked away from me, getting behind Jennifer. And then he flipped her sundress over her back.

Jennifer, on her hands and knees, with her ass hanging in the air, looked at me and said once again, in a much quieter voice, "Pike?"

I squeezed my eyes shut for a split second, resigned to the outcome. I opened them and locked onto her. She was trembling, but it wasn't from fear. She was a finely tuned machine with the engine revving, waiting on the light to go green. I flicked the switch. "Take them out."

I sprang out of my chair, grabbing the weapon of the guy to my right, maintaining control and aiming it toward the ceiling. I drove my knee into his crotch, lifting him off the ground and causing his eyes to fly open comically. His arm turned into a noodle as he snapped forward in pain, raw saliva coming out of his mouth, his body now devoid of resistance. I torqued his arm back, snapping the elbow, then slammed his face into my knee, shattering the nose. He dropped, leaving me with the pistol.

Our original target was stunned at the action, simply standing with his mouth open at the speed of events. Jennifer flattened herself on the ground, breaking the hold on her arms, then rotated around on her back. Surprised, the men attempted to contain her, but it was like trying to catch a dog on the loose.

She lashed out with her foot, shattering one guy's jaw, his teeth puncturing through his cheek as her foot demolished his face. She rotated her legs and wrapped them around the neck of a man bent over trying to trap her, jerking him to the ground from her back and snapping it by slamming his head into the concrete floor.

She leapt up, and the target finally understood the threat. He raised a pistol, pointing it at her. I sprang at him, and the door behind us exploded inward. Veep came in, eyeballs behind an assault rifle, his face a vision of rage. The rifle spat two suppressed rounds, and the target's head snapped back. He dropped like a cold bag of ground meat.

The world went quiet for a moment, the only noise coming from the rest of the team entering. As they cleared the apartment, I checked on Jennifer. She collapsed into me for a split second, breathing hard, then remembered why the whole thing had happened. She smacked me in the gut, saying, "I *told* you this was stupid."

I surveyed the damage, seeing two men on the floor, one definitely dead, the other bleeding out from the split in his jaw. Behind me was another unconscious man, his arm irrevocably destroyed and his balls somewhere near his throat. The target himself had a third eye and wouldn't be talking anytime soon.

Knuckles came back into the room and said, "Well . . . this went pretty much like I thought it would."

I said, "Start SSE. Find me something."

22

Jalal leaned back in his chair, exhausted from his trip and not wanting to hear the words his friend was saying. "What do you mean, you can't get this into the shipment? You're on the inside. You're the man who has access to the containers. It's just a tube."

Badis said, "You don't understand how hard it is. The ship is being loaded tonight, which means all of the containers that will be boarded are in a secure holding area."

"Can't you get into it?"

"I could, but it wouldn't matter. Each container has a cable seal with a bar code."

"You don't have additional seals?"

"I do, but the United States requires the manifest for anything headed to their country to be sent twenty-four hours in advance of the ship even being loaded. They have all the seal numbers. Even if we made it in, broke into that container, and then replaced the seal, it wouldn't be allowed to board because the new seal number wouldn't match the manifest. It would only draw attention to that container. They'd break it down and search every article. They'd find the explosives."

"And the explosives are already inside the container?"

"Yes. I had to load it when I had the chance. Before the seals went on. Jalal, forget about the tube. Just let the explosives go off. It will be the same thing."

"No, it won't. How much of a charge did you place inside?"

"It'll blow half the container open. If the container ends up in the middle or bottom of the stack, it'll cause the entire stack to fall into the sea. Spectacular."

"So we get a visible display, but it won't do anything to the port."

"It will once they realize that a bomb was smuggled in. Right now, they search a fraction of the containers. With this attack, and the tanker one before it, they'll be forced to search every container. It will destroy their shipping industry. They can't possibly do it without disrupting the shipping chain globally."

"I agree, which means they *won't* do it. They'll scream and yell, and show flash and pomp, but they won't let the trade stop. Only we can do that, by damaging the port."

Badis rubbed his hands together, like an old woman afraid of confrontation. He said, "You don't understand, there is no way to get that tube into my container. Just no way. We can't penetrate a secure area, find the right CONEX, then open the doors, breaking the seal, and dig around to find my explosive package. It looks like every other package in the CONEX, and the place is under constant surveillance. This isn't like Tangier, where we planned the attack. They don't care what comes into port. America does."

Jalal squeezed his eyes shut for a moment, then said, "Can you get me in?"

"Yes. I have a temporary badge. The one they issue while the real one is being made."

He held out his own badge, a thick piece of plastic with Badis's face emblazoned on it. "This is what you would end up with, and it's embedded with biometric information. In this case, a retinal scan. I wave this at the reader, then lean in to look into a machine that reads my eyes. It takes a while to get them made, so in the interim, new hires are given a temporary badge. But you have to be with me to enter. Or with someone who owns a real badge."

"When are they loading the ship?"

"Tonight, starting at ten P.M. They'll run until one A.M., and we'll have a shift change, which is when I work. We'll continue for six hours straight, loading forty containers an hour, until it's done. The ship is due to leave tomorrow at eight in the morning."

"Besides the seal mix-up, what would prevent a container from being loaded?"

"What do you mean?"

"What would cause the contents of one of those metal containers to be transloaded to another container?"

"Nothing. They're already packed."

"Nothing?"

"Well, if the container was shown at the final inspection to have some structural flaw, maybe. If the dockmaster thought that the container posed a threat to the stability of the stack. I mean, they stack those things up like buildings. If something like that happened, they might halt the loading."

Jalal stared at the wall, lost in thought. Badis said, "What are you thinking?"

Jalal said, "You load the containers, correct?"

"Well, yes, in a way. I take the containers out of the holding area using a top-pick and transport them to a shuttle carrier, which then takes them to the cranes for loading on the boat."

"So this top-pick is like a forklift?"

"Yes. A giant one, but it lifts from the top. It can transport an entire forty-foot steel CONEX."

Jalal lapsed into silence again. Badis said, "What?"

"Could you get me in during the loading?"

"Yes, with my visitor badge, but what would you do? You don't know anything about being a stevedore. Someone will ask what you're doing there."

"You'll take care of that."

"How?"

"You're going to lose your job."

Six hours later, Badis drove his small pickup truck through the gate of the port of Algeciras, the sixth-busiest port in Europe. At the tip of the Iberian Peninsula in the Strait of Gibraltar, it was the closest operating port to the Maghreb, a mere ten miles to the African coast, and as such, a major transit point from Africa into Europe. Moroccans of all stripes made the daily one-hour ferry commute from Tangier to Algeciras to work in Spain, and this was one of the reasons Jalal had chosen it for infiltration. It had taken two years of work to embed Badis deep within the trust of the port authority, and yet Jalal had never been inside.

Badis slowed at the primary entrance, but the woman inside the gatehouse barely looked at him. He continued on, driving past the ferry terminal, and Jalal said, "That wasn't much security."

"That's just to enter the public side. Everyone taking a ferry travels through that gate, so it's really nothing more than show. The real security is deeper."

They hit a traffic circle, and Jalal saw the cranes in the distance, giant booms hanging out over the water. Badis took a road leading to a chain-link fence and another gate, this one with a drop bar, but unmanned. Beyond the fencing were rows of cars. Badis ran his badge over a card reader, and the bar lifted. He pulled in and parked, saying, "This is as close as they let private vehicles get."

"How do we get in?"

"We walk. Make sure that tube doesn't slip down your pants."

Jalal ran his hand down his calf, testing the tape holding it in place. "I'm good."

He followed Badis across the lot, hitting another gate, this one only wide enough for pedestrians, manned with a guy in uniform holding a radio.

Badis nodded at him, waved his badge in front of another card reader, then placed his eyes into what looked like an outsize set of binoculars attached to the wall. A light buzzed green, and the pedestrian gate opened.

Badis said, "Show him your temporary badge." Jalal did, and the guard wrote down the number on a clipboard. Badis said, "Orientation night for him."

The guard smiled and said, "Good luck with that. Going to be a rough one."

Jalal said, "So I've heard," and they were through the gate, into a holding area towering with row after row of twenty-foot and forty-foot SeaLand containers.

Badis said, "The security here is a separate company from the loaders, so they won't question your being inside. I'm a top-pick driver, so let me deal with the foreman. I'll tell him you're just going to right-seat ride for the night."

"Okay."

Badis pointed to a small office in the ocean of steel and said, "I need to clock in. Obviously, you can't do that. Stay out here."

Thirty minutes later, Jalal was in a vortex of what looked to him like controlled chaos, top-picks driving back and forth hauling CONEX boxes to shuttle mules, which then took them to the gantry cranes, the cranes never ceasing movement loading the ship.

Jalal said, "There are four top-pick drivers. How will you guarantee we get the right container?"

"The way we divided up the lot. Trust me, it looks confusing, but it'll be our top-pick. You just be ready to help with the reload."

Three routes back and forth later, and Badis lifted the steel harness of the top-pick to the rack of containers, pulled one out, then leaned toward the windshield. He said, "This is the one."

Jalal rubbed his leg, feeling the tube. He said, "Do it."

Badis manipulated the controls, lowering the twenty-foot container until it almost blocked his vision. He began driving toward the shuttle carriers, building up speed, then jerked the vehicle to the left, causing the left side of the container he was carrying to clip the stack in a rending of metal. He immediately backed up, as if shocked, then lowered the container.

Before the dust had even settled, the dock foreman was outside, screaming his head off. Jalal and Badis exited, seeing the container had a small split along the seams of the corner, the rivets popping out. The foreman began berating Badis, demanding to know if he'd allowed Jalal to work the lift as an apprentice. Badis said no, it was completely his fault.

The precision timetable of the container loading ground to a halt, and it was a schedule that had to be maintained. The cranes could mount forty containers an hour—and needed to do so to keep the port in operation. Now they had a problem, because it wasn't a misstep of paperwork on the part of the freight forwarders or an error of the company that contracted the port for shipping—it was the port operation itself, and they would pay a hefty penalty for this load not making the ship.

Something Badis knew all about.

In short order, an empty container was brought out, and as the ship was being loaded with all the other containers, men simultaneously manhandled the freight from the damaged container to a new one. Including Badis and Jalal.

Passing across boxes of linens and crates of plastic donkeys from China, Badis finally hit the crate he wanted: one that looked like all the others but was decidedly different in composition. He said, "Jalal, help me with this one."

Jalal felt the sweat break out on his neck, looking at the four guards watching the transfer. He nodded, picking up one side of a wooden-crated box four feet square. They walked past the guards and entered the container, moving to the rear. They sat it on top of a similar crate, and Jalal hissed, "Block their view."

Badis turned around, the harsh lights of the port leaving him in stark silhouette. On his knees, Jalal stuck his hand under the leg of his jeans and ripped the tube free, stifling a scream as it took his hair with it. In between the wood slats, he jabbed a hole in the paper wrapping and shoved the tube through.

He had no idea if it was close enough to the explosives to do the damage he wanted, and he feared it would simply be launched intact into space. But it was all he could do.

He stood up and nodded at Badis, and they continued loading. Forty minutes later, they watched the security team seal the new container, a cable band placed on the locking mechanism and the number recorded.

Twenty minutes after that, it was transferred to the

ship. One container out of millions that traversed the high seas, the last one loaded on a ship crossing the ocean toward the port at Los Angeles. The event would be logged, as were all anomalies, but the ship would sail. After all, there were schedules to keep.

When the loading was complete, the dock foreman said, "Badis, you've been a hard worker, but I can't protect you from this. Too much potential monetary loss. The container you were lifting was destroyed and we almost missed the departure of the ship."

Badis said, "I understand, and I don't blame you. It was my mistake."

The foreman said, "I'll vouch for you. I don't want to lose you." He jerked a thumb to Jalal and said, "This guy, on the other hand, can head on back to where he came from. He knows shit about port operations. We hire him, and it will be a disaster every night."

Jalal said, "Not every night, I promise."

23

I could hear the rest of the team behind me, all nervously fidgeting in their seats as the screen cleared on our VPN. The first person I saw was Creed, who said, "Hey, Pike. Kurt will be here in a minute. He got held up somewhere."

Creed's statement was promising. I'd sent a detailed situation report last night and then had gone to bed. When I'd awoken this morning, all I had in my inbox was a curt message saying that I was to connect for a video teleconference via an encrypted virtual private network. No mention as to why.

The consensus from the team was that I was going to get flayed alive by Kurt, but Creed would have known that and would have said something to that effect as soon as he saw me.

I said, "Did Kurt get a chance to read the SITREP I sent?"

"Yeah. He did. I guess I should warn you, that might be an issue for continued operations. You've already upset the applecart in Spain, so he might have to pull you instead of following through on your request."

That's it? He's just worried about operational security?

Being proactive in my defense, I said, "We already know the lay of the land; swapping me out with another team isn't the way to go. There's no footprint of our involvement."

Before Creed could answer, I saw a shadow behind him, then heard him say, "Hey, sir. Pike's up."

Kurt Hale sat down in front of the camera. *Here we go . . .*

He turned away from the camera and said, "Everyone but George leave the room."

Ordering everyone out but the deputy commander could be good or bad, like getting an ace on the first card of blackjack. After the door closed, he returned to the screen and said, "Who's in the room with you?"

"Everyone. Jennifer, Knuckles, Veep, and Retro. They're just too chickenshit to get on camera."

"Good. So I don't have to worry about you twisting up my words when you brief them, like you did with this SITREP."

I said, "Sir?"

He shook his head, saying, "Really, Pike? You were following the target and got captured? Without any intervention of the team? Just you and Jennifer?"

"Well . . ."

He held up a palm and said, "I'm not even going to ask you flat out what happened."

"Sir, it seriously did go bad. I mean, I didn't expect it to, I thought I could control the outcome, but I was wrong, so, yes, that was a mistake, but they brought it on themselves. It wasn't like I jumped in their van and started spitting on them. *They* did what they did. I really didn't mean for the damage to come about."

He tapped his fingers on the desktop and said, "Two civilians dead, two civilians crippled. It doesn't look surgical from my optic."

Which, reading between the lines, was a key phrase. *My optic.* I said, "But it doesn't bother the Oversight Council?"

He grinned and said, "You had better relish your brief moment in the glowing embrace. President Hannister doesn't care, and because he doesn't care, neither does the Oversight Council."

Taken aback, I said, "Really?"

"Yeah, really. You've managed what I haven't been able to do in eight years. The president of the United States is willing to take your SITREP at face value. A drug ring destroyed after attempting to kill Taskforce personnel? No, he doesn't care. All he cared about was whether you were compromised, and I take it you weren't."

Will wonders never cease . . .

"No, sir, of course we weren't. It was all detailed in the SITREP."

While I would fudge—and had fudged in the past—the circumstances that led up to an operation, I would never, ever falsify the detail of the action itself. It was a bedrock principle of the Taskforce, and Kurt knew it. If we'd been compromised, or if the hit had gone horribly wrong, I would have outlined that in painful detail—even if it caused my firing.

I reiterated, "Sir, we're as clean as the driven snow. Nothing at all to connect us to that action. I'm assuming you turned over my intel to the host nation, correct?"

Kurt said, "We did. We laundered it through DOJ staff in the embassy, using the real DEA liaison, and sure as shit, they found a ton of stuff in that apartment, but it's all drug related. Just like your SITREP. I'm having a hard time even wanting to convince the Oversight Council to let you continue. We aren't the DEA."

"Except for that bank account. It has nothing to do with drugs."

Kurt leaned back for a moment, then said, "Pike, I'm

torn here. I could go ask for further exploration, but if I do, I'm leaning toward a new team. Someone fresh. I know you say you're clean, but you're leaving a trail just by existing, digital and otherwise. You have a footprint in Madrid, and moving on to Granada will just add to the number of threads they can piece together. Especially if you find something and need to action that intelligence."

At that point, I knew I'd won. I'd started this VPN session worried that I'd be jerked back to the US forthwith, and now all I had was Kurt worried about my footprint. If Kurt wasn't barbecuing me for my actions in Madrid, he would collapse under the weight of my incredibly intelligent argument. All I needed to do was present it in the most compelling way possible, detailing how I was the only person on the earth who could solve the problem.

I said, "That's bullshit, sir, and you know it."

I saw his face contort in anger and prepared myself for the debate, one I'd had many times in the past with this very same man. I started to continue with my inevitable mass assault on his argument, knowing I would wear him down, and heard Jennifer hiss at me. I flipped my head to her, and she said, "Don't say another word. You'll bury us."

I waved my hands like I was washing a window and hissed back, "What are you talking about?"

On the computer, Kurt said, "What was that?"

I flipped back to the screen, then heard another bark from the peanut gallery. I turned back to the team and Kurt said, "What the hell is going on?"

Knuckles said, "Don't go where you're about to. I've seen this show a hundred times. You aren't going to win by bludgeoning him. You need to win on the merits. On logic. Not on how much you can bark."

I put my hand over the microphone of the computer and said, "What the hell are you guys doing? We're *about* to win."

Knuckles said, "No, we're not. We're about to be ordered home because you're stubborn. Back away from the computer. Let Jennifer give it a go."

"Why?"

Jennifer locked eyes with me and said, "Because you'll make this personal. All about you and your intuition. We all believe, but you'll piss off Kurt, and we'll be taking the Rock Star bird home. Come on, honey, let me do this."

My eyes snapped open at the "honey" comment, and Jennifer realized her mistake.

Knuckles saw my reaction and said, "Don't go there. Ordinarily, I'd take you to task for her statement, but I happen to believe you're actually on to something here. Don't turn this into a fight to prove who's in charge. Let her get on camera. Now."

24

Johan idly watched a small boy kick around a rubber ball, the mother keeping a close eye on the youth, especially when the ball rolled to Johan's bench. Johan tossed it back to the kid and smiled at the mother. She gave him a small wave in return, but not in a friendly way. Johan worried about the exchange. Not because it was significant, but because he might be remembered, and his next actions could make that problematic.

He was sitting on an iron bench inside an expanse of green called the Commonwealth Park, watching a door that housed his target, so close to the ocean he could smell the salt in the air. He'd been there a good two hours, and it certainly didn't escape him that he might look like a pedophile by spending his time surrounded by children in the largest park on the Rock of Gibraltar. But, given the trade-offs, he couldn't believe how lucky he had been, as the park was adjacent to the single-door entrance to the office of Mint Tea Maintenance. A happy coincidence, given his lack of detailed planning.

He'd flown into Madrid last night from JFK airport in New York, eschewing landing in Gibraltar itself, preferring not to have his information on any manifests that connected him to the territory. Madrid was only a couple of hours to the north, but an entire country away as far as immigration records were concerned. He'd rented a car, driving straight south to the fabled Rock of Gibraltar, holding a small nagging doubt throughout the trip that he might need a special visa to visit. He'd Googled that and believed he was good, but the truth would be at the point of entry.

The one sore point of Johan's international work was the fact that not many first-world countries allowed a South African citizen to enter without preapproval, a byproduct of the country's tumultuous past. Unlike an American citizen, who could travel pretty much freely to any state in Europe, a South African had to have a reason.

Johan's passport was littered with visas: an H-1B worker's permit from the United States, a Schengen visa for the twenty-six member nations in Europe, and a United Kingdom ancestry visa, obtained as a part of his Commonwealth heritage, as he was lucky enough to have a grandfather on his mother's side born in Great Britain. While the Schengen visa allowed him entry into Spain, he hoped the ancestry visa worked for Gibraltar.

Located at the foot of the Iberian Peninsula, "the Rock" was one of the world's anomalies: an outcropping of earth attached to one state that was the sovereign territory of another, in this case, the United Kingdom. Taken from Spain by an Anglo-Dutch force in 1704, it had remained a British territory ever since, even as Spain repeatedly laid claim to the small piece of land.

Driving south, he'd hit the coast road on the Mediterranean Sea and instantly saw why Gibraltar had the nickname it did. A mountain of white rock topped by clouds, it towered over the Spanish coast as if God had plopped it there when he was shaping the earth, intending to use it elsewhere.

Johan had driven into the queue for immigration and happily discovered that his earlier fears were unfounded.

The gate was manned by British immigration officers, and after a perfunctory check of his passport and some simple questions, they'd waved him through.

He'd crossed the flight line of the British airbase and international airport on Winston Churchill Avenue—the entry road literally crossing the runway, a peculiar situation necessitated by the fact that it was the only flat piece of terrain large enough to allow landing an aircraft on Gibraltar territory—and had parked at the first garage he could find on his GPS, a shopping mall called the International Commercial Centre.

As the entire landmass of Gibraltar was little more than two and a half square miles—with most of that taken up by the sheer cliffs of the mountain itself—he'd already decided to walk to his target, using his GPS to locate the address of the suspected business.

He'd followed the arrow on his GPS to the target, which had required some back-and-forth, with him walking up and down Line Wall Road, passing the door to Mint Tea Maintenance three times before realizing that the GPS was off by about a hundred meters. Eventually, he'd found it.

Set into the stone of the ancient casement of the King's Bastion, once the foremost defense of the city, it was a narrow office next to a modern entertainment center grafted onto the same historical defenses. The dilapidated office door existed in stark contrast to the modern-day entrances for the bowling alley and cinema next to it, and Johan wondered how on earth his target had managed to lease it.

With one small window in the door, Johan could glean little from the outside—but there was no way on earth he was going to enter this early in his mission. He decided to establish a surveillance post and simply watch.

He'd surveyed the surroundings, seeing few options for long-term observation. Line Wall Road was a narrow strip of asphalt, jammed with parked cars and mopeds, with nothing more than a sidewalk snaking alongside it. He'd retraced his steps and found the park right across the street, hidden behind a concrete wall. After a little bit of jockeying, he'd located a bench that had a view through the portico entrance to the office door.

He'd taken a seat and waited, ostensibly watching the children play in the park. Three hours into it, with the sun starting to set, the mother of the child with the rubber ball finally started giving him pointed stares. As if she was thinking about reporting him. She took the hand of her child and exited the park, using a different portico, but not before glancing back at him with a mama-bear look.

Not good.

But then again, he'd done nothing wrong. Yet.

25
★★
★

Knuckles stood up and crossed the room, putting his hand over the camera lens and glaring at me, his expression telling me I was wrong, even as he knew he was asking me to swallow my pride.

He said again, "Let Jennifer handle this. Yeah, the Council loves you, but they aren't Kurt Hale. After the last hit, he'll wonder if you're playing him."

I heard Kurt say, "Move your damn hand. What the hell is going on there?"

I started to reply, because I was always right, and Knuckles held my eyes. I pulled my hand away from the microphone and said, "Nothing, sir. Just some team stuff."

Knuckles smiled, saying, "Good job."

I backed away from the computer, knowing it was just my ego talking, but it *still* hurt. I said, "Jennifer's got something to say. Apparently, I'll just stick a fork in your eye."

Kurt laughed and said, "So old dogs can in fact learn new tricks. Putting in the A team now. Jennifer, what's up?"

She sat down and said, "Hey, Kurt. You know I wouldn't do this if I didn't think it worthy, but we went through the phones and computers inside the house, and they're tangentially connected to a bunch of tethers inside Morocco. We haven't found a direct thread to terrorism, but we have a lead with an American citizen in that country. From the email trail, it appears he's in Granada, just south of here, trying to develop a new market for his marijuana. We have his face, and we have his target location. It'll take a little work to locate him, but he's real."

Standing over Jennifer's shoulder, I could see her argument didn't cut a lot of weight. Kurt said, "So you want to bust up a nascent drug ring in Granada now? I don't see a lot of payoff here. Only downside."

"Except for the bank account. The guy we hit had no established use of that thing until two days ago. Someone gave him the access. And that someone is whom we're hunting. I can't tell you that we know the connection right now, but you let us through, and we'll find it."

Kurt said nothing, doing the tap routine with his fingers. Behind him, George said something too faint to hear. I didn't know if it was good or bad.

Kurt talked to him for a few seconds, then returned to the screen. "You think this new guy is going to give you a thread? Beyond just another drug bust?"

Jennifer said, "Yes, I do. And you know where I stand." She glanced at me and said, "I'm not saying that because I just want some high adventure."

Which was a little insulting.

She went back to the screen and said, "It's convoluted right now, I know, but there's no way a bank account for a terrorist in the United States is innocently tied into a bank account for a drug dealer in Spain. Let us pick the thread. We won't do any harm. Unless you let us, that is."

I saw a rueful smile leak out of Kurt's face. He said, "Is Pike still there?"

"Here, sir."

"Is Knuckles there?"

"Here, sir."

"Whose idea was it to put her on-screen? You or Pike?"

Knuckles said, "It was nobody's idea. She just felt strongly about it."

Kurt laughed and said, "Bullshit."

Jennifer became incensed, saying, "What the hell does that mean? We're trying to stop a terrorist attack. Why on earth does me on the computer matter—"

Kurt cut her off. "Calm down, Koko. You win. I know Pike inside and out, and I was prepared for his inevitable request, because I know what's in his heart. I also know what's in yours. And I'm giving you the go-ahead. Alpha only. Track the guy in Granada and report back."

We all sat in silence for a second, amazed it had been that easy. Kurt said, "You guys still there?"

Belatedly, I said, "Yes, sir. Thank you."

"Yeah, yeah. Just get me something that doesn't involve you getting kidnapped. I can only sell that so many times. Show me some finesse."

I said, "Sir, I promise this isn't a fishing trip. Something bad is being planned, and I'm going to find out what it is."

Kurt glanced at George behind him, then said, "I believe you. Give me some Pike magic."

I said, "I will."

He said, "But do it with a little Koko restraint, if you don't mind."

Jennifer beamed, then broke open the applecart. "So does that mean Carly gets a shot at selection? Giving a little female restraint to the Taskforce overall?"

Kurt's eyes flew open, Knuckles practically did a rain dance, and I just sagged back. Nobody said anything for a couple of seconds, then Veep, the millennial of the group, said, "I don't see why this is such a big deal. I've seen Jennifer in action."

Knuckles whipped to him and snapped, "Shut the fuck up."

Knuckles flicked his eyes back and forth between Jennifer and me, caught between the conventions of the Taskforce and his experience working with her. It was the same place I'd been in when I'd first met Jennifer. But back then, I'd been kicked out of the Taskforce and had no constraints on me, unlike Knuckles.

He was still on active duty, and I knew the pressure he was under. We still lived in a he-man women-hating club, and he was worried about his reputation, even as he was silently plugging for Carly. He didn't understand what I had learned: His reputation would stand for itself. Just like mine had. And if Carly was worthy of the attempt—which I wasn't convinced of just yet—nothing he did would alter that one way or the other.

From the VPN Kurt said, "Just get to Granada. Carly will take care of herself. If it even matters."

He disconnected.

Knuckles lightly smacked the back of Jennifer's head, causing her to say, "What did I do?"

He started to retort, and I cut in, defusing the situation. Becoming the team leader again. "Let's get packed and check out. I want to be in the air in less than sixty minutes."

26

★★
★

Thirty minutes after the mother left the park, a police officer entered, searching the area with his eyes, clearly looking for something. Johan had no illusions about what that might be. The woman had reported him as suspicious.

He stood up and began sauntering toward the portico he'd used to enter the park, studiously avoiding eye contact with the police officer and running through alternatives for continued surveillance of the office. He needn't have worried.

He reached the wall and saw his target door open. A wiry man of about thirty-five exited, wearing a Berber jacket that was coarse and homespun, the cloth rough, with small wooden dowels instead of buttons or a zipper, the hood lying flat on his back. To Johan, it looked like a coat worn by someone from Tatooine in *Star Wars*, which wouldn't matter, except the hood sat high enough to prevent Johan from getting a good look at the target's face. The man locked the door as if he were in a production of *Scrooge*, pulling out a ring and using a key much too large for the modern day.

Johan glanced behind him and saw the policeman still searching. He exited the park, now forced with a choice: follow the target, or penetrate the office. He watched the man walk away, growing smaller with every step, and decided on the latter, with a little bit of a wait.

He crossed Line Wall Road and entered the pedestrian area of the main downtown tourist section. Walking down Main Street, he contemplated his next move, but he already knew what that would be. He'd seen the target lock the door. Seen the ridiculously old key. He could defeat the lock on that door in about fifteen seconds using a paper clip and a flathead screwdriver. All he needed was some time.

Walking three blocks and looking for someplace to park for a spell, he passed yet another liquor store, the sign out front blaring the great deals within. Just like the last one had. *What on earth?* He was no stranger to drinking in his hardscrabble life, and never one to run from a beer, but this was a little ridiculous. Unlike in Madrid, where one had to search for a place to buy something besides wine, here there seemed to be a liquor store on every corner.

How could they all stay in business?

He assumed it was the tourists. Or that everyone here was a drunk. Given the number of pubs in the area, it could be either. Not that he minded. He saw a sign for a pub down a narrow alley and followed it to the source. He took a seat at the outdoor patio, ordered a Guinness, and waited for the sun to go down.

Two hours later, he paid the bill and retraced his steps, walking back down Line Wall Road. He reached the office of Mint Tea and glanced around, the night giving him shadow. Cars passed, but no pedestrians were on the sidewalk. He went to work on the lock, getting it open in under a minute.

He glanced around again, seeing no threat, and cracked the door. He hesitated a moment, listening. He heard nothing from inside.

He entered swiftly, closing the door behind him. He ran

his hand along the wall, looking for a switch, and found it, the light blazing into his eyes. He saw a narrow space, less than eight feet across, a shelf running down the wall. On it was a computer and a printer, then a collection of schematic drawings. In the back was a wider room, without a door.

He advanced slowly, not sure if there was a hallway connected to it or some other entrance to the narrow office space. He reached the small alcove and waited a beat, hearing nothing. He felt along the wall again and found the lights. Inside was nothing but trash. Iron rods, bits of wooden dowels, cans of paint, and drop cloths, all haphazardly scattered about. Nothing of interest. He went back to the office, finding a filing cabinet underneath the shelf, with a sheaf of papers on top of it.

He picked up the paperwork, seeing a work order made out to Mint Tea from a company called Gibdock, apparently for work on an oil tanker named *Dar Salwa*. The first page held a laundry list of various maintenance procedures that had to be accomplished. Underneath it were the schematics for the double-hulled crude carrier, with certain sections highlighted in red. From the date in the top left corner, it looked like the order had been completed two days ago. It meant nothing to Johan. He turned to the computer and swiveled the mouse, causing the screen to illuminate.

He saw a password block and then heard a knocking on the entrance door, freezing him in place. Holding his breath, he waited. It happened again, this time turning into pounding, the door reverberating with the blows. He heard, "Karim? You still in there?"

Johan said nothing, breathing through an open mouth to lessen his presence. The voice said, "You got the light on, so I know you're in there. Quit hiding from me. You owe me. Open the door."

Johan slid to the back area, walking ever so softly, leaving no trace of his crossing. He checked for an exit but found none. He was cornered. Hiding behind the small entrance wall of the alcove, he turned out the light and withdrew a pocket blade, flicking it open. Waiting.

He heard nothing more. He remained still for another twenty minutes, then advanced to the front of the office. He slid to the right of the door and peeked out of the small window, seeing the street empty.

He glanced at the computer, wanting to return to it but knowing he shouldn't. Not tonight, anyway. Too much risk. He turned out the lights and exited, locking the door behind him. Tomorrow was another day.

27

Knuckles wasn't too concerned about the company to his left and right, but he did mind the smell. And the filth. He watched the clique of human waste around him lay about and wondered just what it was that led someone to this. At what stage of life did you decide to congregate on a street corner and do nothing but stare at one another? They looked for all the world like a pack of dogs trying to escape the heat. Some passed a joint back and forth; others simply leaned against a wall, coveting the shade. Most were barefoot, with a crust of filth coating the soles of their feet.

The majority were under twenty-five and would probably escape the pack once they'd experienced whatever lesson they were searching for. Others would remain forever. One fifty-something began juggling balls in the air like he'd found the reason for his existence, making Knuckles feel like he was in a zoo experiment. Into his earpiece, he said, "Pike, you are going to pay for this."

He heard, "Pay for what? You're the only one who looks like a hippie. You blend right in."

Knuckles glanced at Veep, sitting cross-legged two feet away, seeing a smile. Off the radio, he said, "You've got a bill coming due as well for thinking of this idea."

"Not if it pays off. Which it will."

The team had few threads to begin the search, but they weren't starting from scratch. While they had no name, address, or electronic tether, they did have a dark selfie of the target and a batch of emails detailing a couple of locations where he intended to generate more drug revenues, all signed with the letter *F*. They'd flown to Granada right after getting the sanction from Kurt Hale, and then spent a day and a half conducting reconnaissance, eventually locating this congregation of Woodstock wannabes.

The email threads indicated that the target intended to use groups like this to make inroads into the marijuana market, so while the rest of the team conducted reconnaissance of other locations, Knuckles and Veep were stuck playing vagabond hipster.

On the surface, Granada looked like any other cosmopolitan city in Spain, but it was unique in two respects: One, it had the largest university in the country, spread out over five campuses in the city; and two, it had been the capital for the Muslim Moorish kingdom called the Emirate of Granada—the name *Granada* actually coming from the Arab rulers rather than the Spaniards—and a last vestige of that kingdom still existed.

At the base of the Sierra Nevada, on the banks of the Darro River, stood the castle of Alhambra, a giant walled citadel that had once been the royal palace of the Moorish sultans, and then the emperors of Spain after the Moors were pushed off the Iberian Peninsula in the fifteenth century.

Those two unique anomalies—the university and the citadel—led to Granada being a logical choice for expansion of the marijuana trade, as the city was bustling with a transitory population of students and tourists. While Knuckles was positive none in his little pack of loafers was a tourist, some of them might be students.

Just across the Darro River, in the shadow of the

Alhambra, Knuckles watched the juggler continue with his tennis balls, a small hat in front of him for passersby to toss him coins. Knuckles wondered if he was truly delusional.

Veep finally leaned over and said, "I don't think they sit here all night. Take a look at what most of them have with them. Bongos, guitars, and other props."

Knuckles saw he was right. "You think this is just a gathering spot before breaking out to various street corners?"

"Yeah. With a few groupies thrown in."

"Well, that's good news. I don't want to spend any more time here than necessary."

Initially, Knuckles had fought the insertion, saying he was on the university thread and someone else could pretend to be a new-age hippie. Nobody had listened, with Jennifer putting in the final, crushing blow.

"If I had to grind on you in the Cayman Islands to get inside, the least you can do is dress a little ragged."

Knuckles said, "That was about the mission. This is not." But nobody was listening. Veep said, "I think it'll be a little cool," and everyone had laughed. Everyone but Knuckles, that is.

Knuckles had been picked because he had a bohemian vibe already. While he was a tall man with a CrossFit-looking body, he had a mane of black hair that he refused to cut, in defiance of the military. Pike made fun of it relentlessly, saying it bordered on Fabio territory, and now that small fact had been the deciding point of who would infiltrate.

Veep was the second choice simply because he could blend in to the crowd of students. Young enough, his face would lead the way, the team hoping the hipsters would ignore the fact that he, too, was a little burlier than the average skinny drug addict. Knuckles and Veep had found a secondhand store and had dressed the part, getting input from the peanut gallery the whole way, with Veep scrupulously selecting what he thought they'd need to blend in, and Jennifer forcing Knuckles to tie his long hair into a man bun.

Knuckles was disgusted, but when they'd eventually wandered into the group of shiftless malcontents, they'd been accepted without question. While they appeared a little more scrubbed than the average person in the group, nobody looked askance at them, and a couple had actually come over to talk, one with a guitar. Initially, the fact that they were Americans generated some interest, but eventually that wore off and they'd been left alone, sitting by themselves on the outskirts of the pack.

Veep said, "Maybe I should just flat out ask someone if they have any weed for sale."

Knuckles said, "No. Not on first cycle. We'll let this break up, and if we have to come back, maybe tomorrow night." He quit talking as two females came across from the other side, leaving behind the guitar player who had spoken to them earlier. Both were clothed in flowing skirts that went to their ankles. One was wearing cheap rubber flip-flops, with a nose ring; the other was barefoot, her hair tucked under a loose knit cap.

Veep turned around, following Knuckles's gaze. Nose ring asked, "You are American?"

"Yep. I am."

She pointed at Knuckles and said, "You too?"

"Yes. I'm going out on a limb—by your accent: You're French?"

She smiled in a vacant way and said, "Yes. We're here for a week. Do you know Frank McDermott? He's American."

Veep hid a grin, and Knuckles wondered if she'd fried her brain cells forever. He said, "Well, no. Not offhand. Should I?"

She looked disappointed in the answer. She said, "Do you have any hashish you want to sell?"

Veep took the opening. "Actually, we were looking for some ourselves, but we just got here."

"So you don't know Frank." She said it as a statement, as though Knuckles's answer had finally settled in the fog of her brain. She glanced at Veep and said, "He's the one with the hashish. Do you know if he's coming tonight?"

Veep glanced at Knuckles, letting a smile leak out. They knew their target was American and that he had the initial *F*. Knuckles made the same connection. He said, "I'm not sure, but I'd like to meet him. How often does he come?"

"Usually every night, but he hasn't been by for a couple of days. It's aggravating. I mean, don't sell yourself as some great conduit, bragging about what you can do, and then leave me high and dry. Especially after I've fucked you."

Veep was a little stunned at the openness. Knuckles said, "Maybe we could help. Where does he live? Maybe we could talk to him."

The girl said, "I have no idea. He said he'd keep coming by here. It's why we're all waiting."

Veep started to reply when the barefoot woman glanced behind him and breathlessly said, "There he is!"

Knuckles turned around and saw their target striding into the plaza with a backpack, the two girls running to him. He made a quick call. "Pike, Pike, this is Knuckles. Jackpot. I say again, jackpot. Peel off what you're doing."

Jennifer came back, saying, "You sure? We're staking out the university site, and the folks here say he's going to show up."

"Well, he might be showing up there later, but I've got him here right now."

Pike came on, saying, "You got the Dragontooth?"

"Of course. Veep's ready. Get Retro working."

"Roger all. Let me know when it's emplaced."

Unlike everyone else in the confab, Frank McDermott was dressed in a pair of simple jeans, Converse sneakers, and a short-sleeve button-up shirt. His hair was cropped close, and his ears were not adorned with gauges or other piercings. With the exception of a full-sleeve tattoo on his left arm, he looked like a tourist.

Knuckles let him enter the ring of people, content to simply watch, not wanting to be remembered. The women immediately fell on him, and Knuckles heard, "Yeah, yeah, I got some stuff, calm down."

The ring-nose woman whispered a thing or two and, surprisingly, pointed at Knuckles.

McDermott walked over and said, "She tells me you're an American."

Shit.

Knuckles took on a deadpan expression and said, "Yeah, I am. What of it?"

"What part?"

"Here and there. Why the questions?"

McDermott nodded, sizing Knuckles up. "Not very friendly, are you?"

Knuckles said, "You got anything I can buy? Like right now?"

"Maybe. Depends on what it's worth to you. I might want something more than money."

Knuckles locked eyes with Veep, then returned to Frank. He said, "What's that mean?"

Veep sidled up to the target's left side, then brushed the outside pocket of the knapsack on his back. Frank turned, pushing Veep back, saying, "Get the fuck away from me."

Knuckles grabbed McDermott's arm, saying, "He's with me. He's okay."

McDermott jerked his arm away, looked between them, then said, "I don't have time for this. Either you two jerk-offs want my product, or you don't." He flicked his head at the girls and said, "I know they do."

The Dragontooth beacon emplaced, Knuckles decided to get the drug dealer on the move, a little aggravated that he had been singled out. "You mean you want me to let you fuck me? Because that's apparently the price these girls paid."

He stood up, towering over the drug dealer. McDermott staggered back, having never encountered hostility in the ranks of the hipsters. He said, "You just lost whatever I have to sell."

Knuckles said, "Fine by me. You're about to lose a lot more."

McDermott took one look at the venom in Knuckles's face and retreated, running back the way he'd come. The two women began berating Knuckles, demanding to know why he'd attacked Frank. He nudged one back, saying, "He started it."

The juggler saw the exchange and stood up, saying, "Hey, man, we don't need this shit here."

Knuckles said, "Sorry. We're leaving."

Veep tensed, sensing the shift in mood, and the guitar player backed up the juggler, saying, "You fucking Americans always screw up everything."

The nose-ring woman tried to slap Knuckles, but he grabbed her hand before it landed. She jerked it away, incensed, shouting, "You don't understand what we're about. Get out of here."

Knuckles saw the juggler looking at him with satisfaction. The man slid forward, crowded him, backed up by four other greasers. Dropping his tennis balls, as if that was a threat, he said, "You don't belong here."

Knuckles said, "You got that right," and punched him straight in the face. The juggler dropped to the pavement, mewling and holding his nose. The men around him were shocked, amazed that someone would actually use violence, even as they insinuated it. In their world, the violence never really happened.

Knuckles glared at them, but they made no move. Knuckles flicked his head to the square, and Veep started walking. Knuckles waited a beat, then followed him. When they were safely out of fighting range, the crowd began hurling invectives, but nobody made any attempt to give chase.

Moving fast across the plaza, Veep said, "I can't believe you just did that. We're supposed to remain covert." But he looked at Knuckles with a little bit of admiration.

Knuckles glanced at the crowd behind them and said, "Yeah, that was probably wrong, but sometimes wrong is better than right. Bunch of assholes."

Veep said, "What are we going to tell Pike? He'll kill us for this."

Knuckles laughed and said, "You have a thing or two to learn yet."

Veep didn't look convinced.

Knuckles said, "Pike would have punched that jerk a hell of a lot sooner than me. Don't worry about it. You're still on the payroll."

Knuckles clicked his radio and said, "Pike, Pike, Dragontooth is placed and he's on the move. Track him."

28

Johan resumed his place on the park bench very early in the morning, wanting to start building a pattern of life on his target. He couldn't very well break into the office during the day, so he'd decided to follow the man, hoping to learn his residence, then return to the office after nightfall.

At eight A.M. he saw the target enter the office, and he settled in to wait. His greatest fear at this point was that the same woman would return to the park, only to find him sitting in the same spot—especially if he were forced to sit here all day waiting on the target to leave.

At eight forty-five he decided to scout other possible locations, just in case he was forced to move. He entered the King's Bastion entertainment center, finding the bottom floor was consumed by a bowling alley. He went up to the second floor, going around the perimeter, finding a movie theater, an arcade, and, finally, a restaurant/pub that wrapped around the exterior of the old fort. He went to the deli counter and ordered a Coke, then picked a table next to the east wall overlooking Line Wall Road. No sooner had he sat down than he saw his target locking up the office, a bulky backpack over his shoulders.

What the hell?

Johan looked at his watch, seeing it was only a little after nine in the morning. Too early for lunch. Maybe he was headed to the wharf for a work order. If so, it would mean that Johan *could* break in during daylight.

Johan waited to see which direction the man took. Sure enough, he began heading south—toward the dry docks and shipyards.

Johan grabbed his Coke and speed walked to the first floor, taking the steps three at a time. He exited back into the park and made a beeline for the portico entrance. He glanced down the street and saw the target. He reentered the park and jogged south, paralleling Line Wall Road. When he reached the end, he exited, now with the target behind him. He continued walking, finally stopping at an outdoor ATM. He messed with the machine, checking his balance, withdrawing money, and generally killing time until the target passed him.

He knew Line Wall would begin to go farther east, away from the docks, so eventually the target would drop a block to Queensway Road, the logical thoroughfare for reaching the shipyards. Only he didn't.

Line Wall made a sharp left turn, and the target stayed on it. Johan let him get about a hundred meters ahead, then picked up the follow again. The target passed through an ancient stone gate, now widened for the passage of vehicles, and Johan let him continue by himself for a moment, not wanting to be silhouetted against the stone should the target turn around.

Johan checked his GPS, seeing nothing on this line of march that would be useful, as he was walking away from the docks. Unless he was headed home.

After counting to ten, he walked through the stone gate, seeing a gaggle of tourists but no target. He jogged forward, circling a sunken garden of some sort. He saw nothing on the street. He retraced his steps, searching more closely, and then saw his target, sitting on a bench inside a cemetery, carefully looking at the stairwell that led down to the garden.

He whipped his head away and passed by the stairwell, feeling lucky that he'd waited earlier, before going through the stone gate. If he hadn't, he probably would have followed the target straight into the cemetery. He reached the stone gate again and read a placard proclaiming the TRAFALGAR CEMETERY, which held the remains of Lord Nelson and other British sailors. Johan ignored the history of the place, focusing on why the man was in it.

The target was looking for someone following him.

The stop wasn't random, and the location was chosen for a reason. It was sunken into the ground, forcing visitors to descend stairs to enter, and full of paths that canalized surveillance.

Two things stood out for Johan: One, the target was up to something shifty, and, two, more important, he'd been trained.

Johan really wanted to get a look into his backpack, sure there was something in it that would prove his theory about the bank account. He sat on the bench next to the stone gate, waiting on the target to leave and wondering if his boss, Dexter Worthington, knew what was occurring. Wondering if he shouldn't start looking left and right himself.

He knew how such things worked, and if Dexter wanted him killed, Johan had no doubt that he'd use his money to accomplish it.

That is paranoid. He didn't believe Dexter had the balls for such an act. Maybe the man in the cemetery was simply evil, and Dexter wanted the same thing he did: to find out what he was doing.

Seven minutes later, the target exited the cemetery, now walking with a purpose. Johan took one glance around him, then followed. The target went around a traffic circle, and the tourist cable cars that traversed to the top of the Rock appeared. Inexplicably, the target entered the ticket building for the cable car system.

Johan hovered outside, hesitating. Surely he wasn't actually taking a cable car to the top of the mountain, was he?

He went back to the parking lot servicing the tourist attraction and waited. The cable car left the enclosed dock, and he saw a middle-aged couple standing inside, and his target on the bench.

What the hell?

There was only one reason that man was visiting the top of the Rock of Gibraltar: Something was happening at that location. His earlier countersurveillance attempts made sense now: He was about to do something suspicious and needed to ensure he was clean.

Johan walked up the stairs to the ticket queue and found it empty. He ignored the winding ribbon of nylon fencing and walked straight to the ticket counter. The lady behind the glass asked which ticket he wanted, a simple trip to the top or complete access to the park.

He had no idea. He decided to throw caution to the wind.

"There was an Arab man here a minute ago, with a backpack. What did he buy?"

She looked at him curiously, and he said, "He's a friend of a friend of mine. I was supposed to meet him here, because he doesn't know his way around. I'm supposed to be his tour guide, but there was some miscommunication. I came here and saw him already on the way up."

She smiled and said, "He just bought a cable car ticket. You'll find him at the top. He can't enter the park itself, so you should be able to find him."

Johan nodded, and to drive his cover story home, he said, "Can we buy new tickets once we're up there? If we want to explore?"

"No. Sorry. You'll both have to come back down and buy new tickets."

He nodded, then walked upstairs for the car itself. He waited, seeing the cable car descend toward him, asking the man working it, "How often do these run?"

"Every ten minutes."

Ten minutes. The target would be loose for ten minutes.

Johan impatiently watched the car descend from the top, the cable rotating around the giant spindle at a snail's pace. Eventually, the car nestled into the pocket of the terminal, empty. The attendant punched a button, and the door opened. Johan entered, all alone. Before the attendant could close the door, he asked, "Where are all the tourists?"

The Brit said, "Picks up later in the day. Watch yourself." And closed the door.

Johan rode up, the view spectacular, seeing the ports and shipyards from the perch of an eagle. The car passed an intermediary stop but kept going, the platform providing a brief moment of parallel terrain, and then the car broke free again to fly high above the rocks. He reached the top, sliding into a building housing a restaurant and tourist shop. He remained in the car a moment, like an aircraft waiting on the jet bridge, and then was allowed to exit.

A man slid open the door and welcomed him, and

Johan asked, "What was that other stop? The one we passed earlier?"

"We don't use that now. Off-season."

Johan nodded and said, "Where can I go from here?"

He took a look at Johan's ticket and said, "Just a couple hundred meters up that path." He pointed at an asphalt walkway snaking up into the foliage away from the cable station and said, "But the view is as good as you'll get with any ticket, and there are some old World War Two buildings that are pretty cool."

Johan nodded and exited, getting the view the man promised, the city splayed out before him as if he were looking out an aircraft window. He ignored it, working to find his target, a stiff breeze from the altitude rippling his hair.

He walked up the path, away from the terminal, seeing a multitude of concrete structures built into the hillside, all crumbling. There were a few tourists about, wandering the terrain and taking selfies, but no sign of his target. He continued deeper, ignoring the history.

He was considering his options, developing a plan, when he saw a man and woman toying with a monkey. He thought his eyes were playing tricks on him, but no, there was a monkey sitting on the path. What the hell was that doing up here? He watched for a moment, then noticed two more, finally realizing that the damn things were everywhere. Monkeys with babies on their backs, monkeys picking themselves, monkeys climbing trees, and tourists taking selfies with them.

What in the world?

The monkey snatched the sunglasses off the tourist's face and scampered into the tree line, the man shocked at the sudden turn of events. Johan laughed and returned to his mission, continuing on the path, the only direction his target could have gone.

It wound higher and higher, entering a literal cloud, the buildings and trees becoming cloaked in mist, giving the surroundings an otherworldly feel. He rounded the corner of a dilapidated brick building, an ancient radio antenna rusting on the roof, and saw a form come out of the mists. The figure drew abreast, and Johan recognized his target. Without the backpack.

29

Johan ducked his head and paid the man no mind, continuing forward. The target was alone, so whomever he had given the backpack to was ahead. Johan sped up, going another seventy meters before he came to a dead end, the path stopping at a modern concrete wall about four feet tall, connected to a building bristling with some type of weather monitors or cell towers. He leapt up onto the brick wall and swiveled his head around. He saw nobody.

What the hell?

The transfer of the backpack had to have happened before the target reached the wall, and there was only a single path going back down the hill. He leapt off the wall and started to retrace his steps, glancing at every cut and game trail off the path, sure he'd missed something. He passed a gaggle of the small rock apes bouncing back and forth over a decrepit brick cistern, agitated about something. He was passing it by, trying to come up with a plan, when a monkey ran by him carrying a bit of nylon.

He watched the monkeys, the pack starting to fight over some prize at the bottom of the cistern. Intrigued, he left the path and shooed them away. He squatted over the cistern, peering inside. He saw nothing but sticks and trash, but the branches on top were new, with green leaves.

He reached in and pulled the detritus aside, surprised to see the backpack. He glanced left and right but found himself alone. He hoisted the backpack up and split the zipper. Inside were seven or eight small metal cylinders the size of cigarettes and bricks of white clay. He recognized them immediately. Blasting caps and plastic explosives. But why put them here?

Because he's already used what he needed. Johan was sure he was getting rid of the evidence, dislocating himself from the explosives, if they were found, but leaving the ability to retrieve them at a later date.

Which meant whatever he'd planned was already set. Whatever it was, it was something local. Blowing up a tourist pub, destroying a monument, or, hell, cutting the cables on the cars that went up and down the mountain. Whatever it was, it was in the works, and the only way to solve that problem was to interrogate the man himself.

He slung the bag over his shoulder and went back up the path, debating his next steps. Call the police? Or do the work first? If he went the police route, he'd have to explain how he'd come upon the threat, which would negate the very reason he had come here. He'd have to expose Icarus Solutions' bribes.

He passed a tourist couple, and the man tagged him on the shoulder, asking if he would take a picture of them overlooking the Med. He shook his head no and continued forward, leaving them behind, fuming.

He reached the depot for the cable cars and slowed, checking the deck. No car was there, and his target was gone. He went forward, seeing the next car approaching. It slid into the stall, and he entered, taking a seat on the bench at the rear. He glanced out of the back window and was shocked to see his target approaching the door, licking an ice cream cone.

Jesus Christ.

He waited for other tourists to gather around the entrance to the car, but none did, still content to explore.

The man entered, took a step away to the other side of the car, and stared at him. Johan sat still, trying to appear nonchalant, covering the rucksack with his body.

The car broke free in a sickening split second of free fall, then began its downward trek, high above the earth. They traveled for about five seconds before the target said, "What do you want of me?"

Startled, Johan said, "Excuse me?"

He saw that his accent confused the target. The man said, "I saw you on the street. Outside of the cemetery. What do you want? Why are you following me?"

Johan said, "I'm sorry. I don't know what you're talking about. You followed *me* into this car."

The man said nothing, appearing to relax at the words. Then he caught a glimpse of the rucksack Johan was trying to hide, and his face hardened. He slid his hand into his waistband and withdrew a five-inch fillet knife, saying, "Even if I die, you won't stop me. What I've done is already in motion."

Johan saw the blade and threw his hands up, saying, "Whoa, whoa, what are you doing?"

The target said nothing, advancing on him. Johan, trying one last time, said, "Don't! Don't!"

The target jabbed forward, attempting to spear his heart. Johan exploded, springing off of the seat and snapping to the right, dodging the blow and trapping the knife hand at full extension. He locked up the wrist joint and rotated the blade away, twisting the arm upward and bringing the target to his knees, the knife falling to the floor. He heard the man wail, but he kept the pressure on.

Holding the joint lock, Johan exhaled, then said, "Now that we know each other, I have a few questions."

The target screamed and then did something completely unexpected. He sprang upward against the joint lock, snapping his own wrist and rendering Johan's hold useless. The broken appendage flopping, he slammed his head into Johan's face, throwing him back into the window of the car, the force of the movement causing the car to rock on the cable.

The target punched him in the face with a flailing blow, then scrambled on the floor for the knife, getting it into his good hand. Dazed from the head blow, Johan sprang up in a fighting stance. The target stabbed forward again, and Johan dodged the strike, slapping the knife hand away and punching his attacker in the face. The man fell to a knee, slashing with the blade and forcing Johan to spring back.

The target stood, breathing heavily, at the far side of the car. They looked at each other for a moment; then the target came in again, slashing the blade left and right.

Johan dodged one, then took another on his forearm, the blade slicing through his clothing into the skin. He lashed out, smacking the man with a back fist, connecting hard, then wrapped his arms around the knife hand.

Fighting for control, they sank to the floor, the car continuing its inexorable slide back to the earth. Lying on top of him, both men panting for control of the knife and struggling like demons, Johan pushed his elbow into the man's neck. He saw the man's eyes spring open and felt the struggle beneath him, the legs violently trying to alter the outcome but meeting empty air. He kept control of the knife and jammed his forearm deeper, feeling the ringed tissue of the esophagus begin to succumb.

His target began to flail, now no longer fighting for dominance but struggling for survival. The broken hand slapped him in the side of the head like a drunken man waving a party favor. Johan slammed his forearm hard, using the blade of his bone, and felt the break. He held it for a moment, the man underneath him twitching uncontrollably, weakly combating his fate. Then the body sagged, releasing its bowels. The ungodly stench filled the cabin, and Johan knew he'd won. It wasn't the first time he'd smelled such a thing.

Johan sat up, immediately assessing his situation. He was on a cable car that would end up at the bottom with two things: a bag of explosives and a dead man. Which meant he had to get out.

He searched the body, finding a bunch of useless pocket litter, but also an address book, a passport, and a phone. He stood up, breathing heavily from the exertion. He glanced out the window, seeing the midpoint stop approaching, and came up with a solution to both his escape and his inability to alert the authorities.

Leave the man here, with the explosives. Let them figure it out.

He dug into the bag and pulled out two bricks of Semtex and four blasting caps, scattering them around the floor. He then whipped around the car, looking for a way to open the door. He saw an emergency pull tab just as the car slid into the midpoint stop. He hit it, and the door lock released. He slammed down the handle for the door, and it slid open. He grabbed the rucksack with the remaining explosives and rolled out onto the ground as the car continued on.

He watched it for a few seconds, knowing he'd be on half a dozen cameras as having entered with the dead man at the top. He scrambled off the shelf of the midpoint, onto the winding road walked by tourists who were too cheap to pay for the cable ride.

He started jogging down the mountain, convinced he'd done what he could to prevent whatever the man had planned. Now all he had to do was get out of Gibraltar.

30

Sitting on a cinder block next to Knuckles, I took a swig from a water bottle and watched Jennifer down the road, pattering on about something with Veep. I saw him laugh and her put a hand over her mouth, looking all the world like a couple on a date. Out of nowhere, I wondered if they were talking about me. *Jennifer's probably bastardizing the story of our triathlon earlier, getting on the millennial's good side.*

Knuckles said, "He's got her number. Maybe you should've put Retro in that position."

I glared at him, and he smirked, saying, "Touchy. With so little confidence I'm surprised she's stayed with you."

I laughed and said, "I'll see how that works with Carly." He started to retort, and I said, "Retro has to coordinate with Creed for Veep's ridiculous plan. You'd better hope he's not burned."

"He's not. Not with normal clothes on. I'm the only one who's no good for surveillance against this guy. He never got a look at Veep's face. He was focused on me the whole time."

Jennifer and Veep were sitting at an outdoor table next to a narrow hotel entrance—one we'd conveniently rented the night before. We were up the street behind a temporary wall of a construction site, the ground littered with scaffolding, two-by-fours, and paint cans. Retro was about fifty meters behind us in a minivan, working his Wi-Fi magic with Creed on one of the few roads big enough for cars. Our ambush was set. It only remained to be seen if Veep's idea was worth a shit.

Personally, I thought it was nuts, but he had been adamant, and I was willing to give it a go, if only to develop him as a leader. It was the first time he'd taken charge, and I wanted to encourage that—and the plan did show some out-of-the-box thinking.

Yesterday, we'd tracked the Dragontooth around the ancient Moorish neighborhood of Albaicín, right up the hill from the Darro River and the plaza with the hipsters, seemingly wandering the narrow footpaths aimlessly, to the point that I wondered if the equipment was malfunctioning.

The Dragontooth was a crowd-sourced beacon that utilized the cell network to leverage unwitting cell users on that same net. It worked on Bluetooth and sent data to anyone within range who had a smartphone—which was just about everyone nowadays, outside the odd grandparent still using a flip phone. Basically, it was malware that infected the local population's phones as if they'd asked for the app, and when our beacon registered with the phone, it sent us an alert with a time and location. Once the beacon was activated, it would talk to any cell phone in range, and that cell phone would talk to us, whether it wanted to or not, letting us know where the beacon was.

It wasn't perfect, because the beacon could travel along a lonely highway at seventy miles an hour, passing cars going the opposite way at the same speed, or the beacon could wander for hours outside of any other cell phones, giving us imprecise or latent data, but if someone was on foot in a crowded area, it was pretty damn precise.

In this case, the beacon seemed to be wandering aimlessly through the neighborhood. It would stop for about half a minute, then wander on, winding through the twisting roads and alleys. We watched it, with everyone on the team having an opinion, but nobody could determine exactly what the guy was doing. He didn't stop long enough to do any drug deal, and he was going up blind alleys and roads that made no sense. Eventually, I'd gotten sick of the beacon-only tracking, not trusting the results, and had sent Retro and Jennifer into action, on foot.

They had picked him up right at the Darro River, on the main road that paralleled the water about a hundred meters from where the hipsters had been, and then had followed him right up into the Alhambra itself. On the way, he stopped every couple of hundred meters and messed with his phone, standing still like he was taking a picture of something, only nothing was there. And instead of pressing the photo button, he flicked his touch screen up and down repeatedly.

I'd gotten a third call from Jennifer giving me the same report, which was, "He's looking at a patch of grass and flicking his phone."

I replied, "Come on. Something's there."

"No. Pike, I'm telling you, I think he's on drugs."

I said, "Keep on him. Keep on him."

She said, "He's walking up the road to Alhambra. He can't get in without a ticket, and they sell out early. If he has a ticket, we won't be able to follow."

I said, "Just stick with him. Figure out what he's doing. If you have to peel off, don't worry about it. At least we know the beacon's working."

They reached the summit, discovering there were some areas free of charge inside the Alhambra, including a couple of hotels, squashed right in the center. The target passed through the taxi stands cloistered outside the gate, looking at his phone and walking forward, as if it were telling him where to go.

Throughout the surveillance, Veep had been working the computer for research and reported that there were two hotels on-site: one a five-star and one a dump. I gave the information to the team, directing them to the less savory hotel, figuring that was where the target was headed.

The citadel was huge, with most of the historical constructs available to ticket holders only—gardens, waterworks, castles, and art museums—but there was a large part that anyone could enter, centered around the hotels. Most of it was apparently a tease to get you to buy a ticket.

They followed the target past the first hotel, and he stopped again, doing his incomprehensible cell phone dance, this time in the parking lot just outside the entrance. Honestly, the repeated action was driving me nuts. Nobody does anything that strange unless he is up to no good. We just needed to figure out what it was.

Jennifer gave me another stale report, and I said, "Come on, you guys call yourselves commandos? I'd expect this out of the Air Force. What the hell is he doing?"

Inside our hotel, Veep—an Air Force Special Operations member—gave me a look but backed down when I'd glared back. Knuckles said, "Veep, you really don't have to take that shit. You can tell him he's an asshole."

I clicked back on the radio and said, "Correction. You're acting like a bunch of SEALs."

Retro said, "Pike, I have no idea what he's doing. I've analyzed every stop. There's nothing of interest at any of them. Nothing."

Off the radio, Veep said, "Get me video. Get me a clip."

I looked at him and he said, "Sorry. Can I ask that?"

I said, "Of course you can. Jesus. Why, though?"

"I don't want to say. I got a feeling."

I nodded and said, "A feeling . . ."

Knuckles had laughed and said, "It's worked for you."

I went back to the radio and said, "Give me a video. From two angles. Veep thinks he's got something."

Veep looked a little startled at my call, like he was surprised I gave the order.

Jennifer came on, saying, "Pike, we can use this place for cover reasons. It's a UNESCO Heritage site. We need to get on this if we're going to do any work here. Get the cover of Grolier Recovery Services engaged."

Which was her way of saying, *I really want to go look at a bunch of old shit.*

But it did make sense. I glanced at Knuckles and he went to the computer, sending a message to the Taskforce. I said, "Okay, okay, Koko. We'll go look at Alhambra if we have time. Knuckles is working it now."

The target made a stop right outside of a kiosk selling beer and popsicles to the line of people waiting to enter Nazaríes Palace—a place that required an additional ticket to enter. He repeated his weird actions, and the team caught it on video and sent it to us.

We watched the video, and I swear it was exactly what they'd described. A guy with a cell phone pointing it into the dirt and then flicking the screen over and over again.

I said, "He's obviously marking territory. He's building a kill box, or a target set, or something."

Veep studied the video a second time and said, "No, he's not." He turned to me and said, "We have a way to get him."

Knuckles and I both looked at him like he had a third head. Now animated, Veep said, "We need to get Creed on the line. Get some hacking capability. We can build a trap for this guy."

Knuckles glanced my way with an expression that said Veep was a loon, then went back to him. "What the hell are you talking about?"

Veep grinned and said, "He's playing Pokémon Go, and he's addicted."

31

I said, "Pokémon Go? That stupid video game?"

Veep smiled triumphantly and said, "Yep. That's what he's doing, and he's playing it all over. All we need to do is create a gym that he'll want to come to. We can build it wherever we want, and he'll walk right into it."

Knuckles said, "What are you guys talking about? What the hell is Pokémon Go?"

Veep looked startled and said, "The game? Come on, surely you've heard of it."

Deadpan, Knuckles said, "No. I haven't."

Veep looked at me for help, but the extent of my knowledge was a couple of news stories I'd seen. I shook my head and said, "I'm just as clueless as Knuckles."

Veep exhaled, then glanced at us as if he were trying to explain airplanes to a pair of cavemen. He said, "Okay, Pokémon Go is a cell phone game that transposes virtual digital creatures into the real world. When you boot up the application, it uses the GPS to determine your location; then you walk around using the application's mapping function. When you get to a Pokémon, the camera function of the app is enabled, and you're looking at the actual scene in front of you, but also a digital Pokémon. You then flick a ball at the Pokémon, capturing him."

Knuckles said, "What the hell for?"

"What do you mean?"

"Why do you do it? Do you win something?"

"Uhh . . . no. Well, you win the Pokémon."

"The fake, virtual thing?"

"Yes. I guess that's one way of looking at it, but it's extremely popular."

Knuckles laughed and said, "Mighty big endorsement for your generation."

I said, "How does that help us?"

"Well, besides finding virtual Pokémon, there are PokéStops and—"

Knuckles interrupted, "PokéStops?"

"Yeah, those are where you get the balls to throw at the Pokémon."

Knuckles held up his hand. "Please . . . I'm losing faith in humanity."

Veep glanced at me, and I said, "Keep going. What were you going to say?"

"Besides PokéStops, there are 'gyms,' where one team owns a piece of terrain, and other teams can try to knock them off of that terrain and claim it."

Knuckles said, "There are teams? You can make teams?"

"Well, yes and no. There are three teams set by the game maker—with names like Mystic, or Instinct—and you have to pick when you reach level five."

Knuckles rubbed his face and said, "Do you guys ever think about just reading a book? *Harry Potter* or something?"

"What, now you want to quiz me on Hogwarts? Have *you* read them?"

Knuckles just rolled his finger, telling Veep to continue.

Veep said, "Annyywaayy," drawing out the word, "if Creed can get into the system, we can build our own gym, and I'm sure he'll come to it. Spain is a relatively new release country, so it'll be novel to him. He'll want to come fight."

I said, "Why go to all of that trouble? We're still on him. We can just track him to his house."

"Yeah, but we don't know where his house is, or if he has roommates or dogs or alarms or anything. We don't control his bed-down location, but we would control the gym. With this idea, we control the environment. All we have to do is locate where we'd most like to take him down, then build a gym there."

Which actually made a hell of a lot of sense. Maybe we could use this on every terrorist we encountered. I said, "How do you know so much about it?"

He leaned back, silent for a second, then said, "I've played it a few times." Knuckles started to laugh and he said, "Just to test it out. I mean, I'm on Team Valor, but that's about it."

"So you're a level five?"

"Well, yeah. You have to be to join a team."

"Few times my ass."

I said, "This all sounds good, but who's going to believe a Pokémon gym at the end of a dark alley? Won't that be a trigger for an alarm?"

"Not really. The company is throwing those things out worldwide based on nothing more than a Google map. They aren't doing any demographic work before building the virtual background. There's already been Pokémon activity in the Holocaust Museum in DC, which naturally caused a little snit, and people are getting mugged playing the game in various cities. Hell, the troops are playing the game on the outskirts of Mosul, finding Pokémon in what was previously an ISIS safe house. No, it's safe to say that the company isn't looking at anything specific."

I glanced at Knuckles and said, "What do you think?"

"It's actually pretty ingenious. We aren't on a timeline, so it's worth checking out. We can always fall back to the bed-down location if we have to. The two biggest obstacles right now are that we don't have Omega from the Oversight Council, and we don't know if Creed can penetrate the system. Even if he does, we don't know if he's smart enough to create one of these gyms."

Veep said, "There's one more thing about Pokémon Go. When it first came out, it had a huge zero-day vulnerability. You signed in with Gmail, and when you did, the Pokémon site had access to everything. I mean everything. They could read your emails, send emails, see your web history, see your photos stored in Google Photos, and check wherever you've been if you used Google Maps for navigation."

I said, "You're shitting me."

"Nope. It was pointed out fairly quickly, and Pokémon built a patch immediately after the outcry, but the user still had to opt out. Most people didn't care. And I'll bet our drug dealer didn't bother."

I took that in, impressed with his imagination. I said, "Maybe we should start calling ourselves Team Valor."

He looked at me in defiance, and I laughed at his expression, saying, "You did all right, young Jedi." I slapped him on the knee and said, "Bring the team back."

He grinned and got on the radio, calling Jennifer and Retro. To Knuckles I said, "I guess it's time to get to work. I'll talk to Kurt; you talk to Creed. See what's in the art of the possible."

We both attacked our directed paths. One was productive. After a brief pen test, Creed said he thought he could get in, but it would take him the night to build the code.

The other was a dead end. Kurt told me that without any evidence of terrorist activity—without our target doing anything besides selling drugs—he wasn't going to bring it up to the Oversight Council for Omega. We could continue with Alpha authority to explore such a connection, but no Omega until we had one. I tried to tell him that the connection was in the guy's head, but it did no good.

We tracked the beacon to his bed-down site, and I sent out a reconnaissance just as a formality, but I didn't think it would matter. Turned out he was living large, in a unique cave apartment in the neighborhood of Sacromonte. Just east of the old Muslim neighborhood of Albaicín, it was higher in the hills and known for apartments that literally were dug right into the rock.

I told Creed to work on the code necessary for the Pokémon Go game, and he balked, telling me he had enough to do with other Omega operations that were actually going to happen. I played to his ego, saying that the Pokémon Go work had the potential to pay dividends across the Taskforce, and he'd get credit for thinking it up.

He finally agreed, and I sent everyone to bed. Later, lying on the bed next to me, watching some mindless movie, Jennifer had said, "Well, as long as we've wasted the tax dollars, we should at least enhance our cover company by visiting the Alhambra. You know, get some credit cards on file, get some tickets to show. That sort of thing. I'm thinking of a group tour tomorrow."

I said, "I don't really find that funny."

She rolled over and laid her head on my shoulder, her arm across my belly. "I know, I know. I'm sorry Kurt didn't bite."

I said, "I honestly can't blame him. We had nothing."

She snuggled in and kissed me slowly, and I said, "You're really working it."

She grinned and said, "Selling my body for a trip to the Alhambra."

I laughed out loud and said, "That won't be necessary." I kissed her on the forehead and turned out the light, saying, "You win. You set it up, and we'll go there tomorrow."

Which turned out not to be true.

32

As he had for the last three days, Anwar Suleiman trundled out of his decrepit safe house carrying binoculars and a backpack. A three-room clapboard structure in a historically black area of Houston called Sunnyside, it was a step up from the trailer he'd left in Nevada, but the neighborhood was still less than stellar. He didn't realize until after he'd moved in that it was one of the most crime-ridden areas in the United States. He wondered if his paymasters had known that and ignored it on purpose or had simply been cheap. It seemed every three days there was a phalanx of police cars in the area, yellow crime ribbon strewn about, and a body on the ground. The constant sirens made him jumpy. As would be expected given his past actions.

And his future one.

He loaded up into a '75 Ford F-150 pickup and threaded through the neighborhood, heading out to his overlook as he had the last three days. Today would be different, though.

He passed by the sad houses, interspersed in the gaps between overgrown shrubs. They were all in some state of disrepair, with the driveways crumbling and the roofs sagging. It was a neighborhood that one would say had seen better days, but Anwar was pretty sure that wasn't true. The people living in these houses had never seen a single good day, but they would. Once the caliphate came.

He drove by the Sunnyside community center, nothing more than a couple of ballparks and a defunct pool surrounded by acres of forest. The dense woods were littered with needles, beer cans, and other trash, revealing that it was used more than the ball field, but not for playing games.

He reached Interstate 610 and headed east, toward the Houston Ship Channel, one of the largest port facilities in the world. Stabbing inward from the Gulf of Mexico, it stretched like an out-of-control weed that grew to the outskirts of Houston itself. Close to fifty miles long, the narrow body of water had been dredged and widened multiple times as the ships had become bigger and bigger.

Once the channel left the blue waters of the Gulf of Mexico, it became a greasy, turd-colored, oil-coated mess that passed by the largest collection of chemical and petroleum facilities in the United States. The ExxonMobil refinery on the east shore was one of the biggest in the world, with the Shell Deer Park facility across the bay a close second. Those two only scratched the surface of the other chemical, liquid natural gas, and crude oil facilities that littered the shores of the waterway.

A veritable mecca of targets.

He left the 610 and got onto the Pasadena Freeway, entering the wasteland of refineries, huge tank farms, and chemical plants that paralleled the ship channel. He drove the speed limit, feeling the anticipation build. Wondering if his ship had finally made it into port.

He exited onto the Sam Houston Tollway, heading north, reaching a bridge that crossed the channel. He'd realized on his first day that there was no way to tell from ground level if his ship had arrived, because he'd have to drive through the refinery to see the port, and that simply wasn't going to happen. The bridge, however, had given him a vantage point.

When he reached the top, he slowed, putting on his hazard lights. He pulled over to the side of the road, blocking the right-hand lane and ignoring the bleating horns. Cars and trucks flew by him, none stopping to see what was wrong. He put the binoculars to his eyes and focused on four ships getting drained of their cargo on the north side of the channel.

He dismissed the nearest one as too small. He'd spent the days waiting for the arrival by doing research—a quirk of his inquisitive mind—and had learned that the ship known as the *Dar Salwa* was called a VLCC, or very large crude carrier. This class of ship had a lot of nick-names, such as Panamax or Suezmax—meaning it was the maximum dimension that either of those canals could handle—and its size was staggering, falling just short of the Empire State Building in length, with the capability to carry upward of 400,000 tons of crude oil. Today, it would be a floating weapon.

Anwar had no insider knowledge about the attack, as his contact hadn't told him a thing. All he'd done was give Anwar a cell number and a date, with instructions to start looking three days before. But Anwar did have the Internet.

He'd researched the vessel, gaining insight into the evo-lution of the shipping of crude oil in the modern day, start-ing with the *Exxon Valdez* disaster. That ship was basically a floating bathtub full of crude, and it had run aground off the coast of Alaska in 1989, sparking one of the largest eco-logical disasters in history, the hull splitting apart and leak-ing out its enormous load of crude. Because of it, all crude containers coming into US ports were mandated to have a double hull—the container holding the crude effectively shielded from the hull slicing through the water. Anwar had seen instinctively that this was useful for natural disasters involving a wreck but played into the hands of anyone looking to split a ship apart by other means.

It would be near impossible to hide a bomb on a single hull, because you'd be trying to either attach it on the inside, underneath the surface of the crude oil, or attach it on the outside, where it could be seen. The double hull was different. Because it was built precisely to prevent a leak, and the sea was unforgiving with respect to corrosion, the gap between the two had to be large enough to allow for inspections. In essence, large enough for someone to place an explosive charge designed to breach both the hull toward the water and the tank inward.

He didn't know any of this for sure, of course, but he assumed it to be so. It's what he would have done.

He kept scanning with the binoculars, searching for his ship. He found it, three over from the others. An enormous, hulking thing with tentacles snaking to it, draining the crude. It was positioned perfectly. Blowing it there would shut down the entire ship channel, preventing entry of everything from grain carriers to container ships.

He dropped the binoculars and brought out his cell phone. He pulled up his contacts list and typed OIL. A number came up. He stared at it for a second, thinking he should say something profound. Instead, he just hit the talk button.

He dropped the phone onto the seat, still ringing, and started his truck. He turned off his flashers and began to pull away, but paused when nothing happened. He slammed the vehicle back into park, watching. Another car honked, and he put the hazards back on.

33

Alejo Santos descended into the bowels of the ship, mildly cursing his luck at having to conduct inspections while his friends were all allowed off for shore leave. He supposed he should take it as a sign of respect, as the chief engineer had asked for him by name, something none of his Filipino brethren could claim.

The ship was fairly new, and as such, it had plenty of remote sensing equipment to warn the crew of any trouble, be it with the navigation, propulsion, or integrity of the tanks holding the crude. It was this last piece that he had been instructed to visually check.

The double hull of the ship was placed under enormous stress just by plying the ocean, with the steel flexing and rippling through the swells in the North Atlantic. Normally, this would simply be business as usual, but before the ship had left the Mediterranean, there had been work done on the starboard side midship wing tank. Alejo's job was simple: inspect the new welds and make sure they were holding, with no cracks, dents, or other signs that the ocean crossing had damaged them.

Reaching the bottom of the giant hull, the stench almost overpowering and the noise of the pumps evacuating the crude bouncing off the steel, he turned on his flashlight and began working his way toward the tank.

He had gone about fifty meters when his feeble light

bounced over something blocking his way. A shape he didn't recognize.

He approached it, finding a tarp covering something the size of an office desk, in between the hull and an inboard tank.

What in the world?

Using a handheld radio, he called the chief engineer, but the man couldn't understand him over the noise of the pumps. He gave up, holstering his radio and pulling out a knife. He slit the canvas, peeling it back. He saw wiring and a bunch of what looked like bricks wrapped in wax paper. Confused, he pulled the tarp further and saw a cell phone hooked to a motorcycle battery. And he knew instantly what he was looking at.

He dropped the tarp and began shouting again into the radio. The chief engineer repeated back to him that he couldn't understand, demanding to know what the trouble was.

Then the phone screen came to life, a call coming through.

He dropped the radio and ran as fast as he could, his flashlight bobbing over steel ribs and bulkheads, all threatening to cause him to trip to his death. He saw the ladder in front of him, tantalizingly close, and he prayed he would reach it.

His prayer was answered, as an enormous shockwave picked him up and hurled him twenty meters straight into it, ripping his body in half.

He was the lucky one.

34

Anwar picked up his phone and saw that it was connected. He was wondering if he should disconnect and redial, when he saw a brilliant flash of light; then the side of the ship nearest the dock split open, spraying flaming crude out in a fan and turning the majority of the shipping channel into a lake of fire.

He immediately put the truck into drive and began racing across the bridge, narrowly missing colliding with another car. Before he reached the far side of the channel, he saw the nearest tank on the land beyond the ship explode, the lid flying off like a bottle rocket.

He didn't wait to see further results, but he could hear the secondary explosions as he raced back to his safe house.

Thirty minutes later, he exited Interstate 610 onto the surface streets of Sunnyside, traveling south through the depressed area. Finally entering the run-down section he lived in, he passed a police car on the shoulder of the road, the sight making him nervous. He took a left, one block up from his safe house, and ran smack into a line of cars waiting to move forward. He leaned toward the windshield, holding his hand to his eyes to block the sun, and felt a shock of adrenaline.

There were two police cars on the road, and they were searching each vehicle before it was allowed to continue. *It can't be because of the port. No way.* Clearly, some other crime had occurred and they were looking for a suspect—but if he went through, they very well might handcuff him instead. He knew he was a wanted man for what he'd done in Nevada, having seen his traitorous mother on the news.

With only two cars ahead of him, he backed up, causing the vehicle behind him to honk. He wheeled into the other lane, hearing someone shout at him. He glanced behind him and saw policemen running toward his truck. He goosed the gas pedal, racing the other way.

He turned the corner and saw the original police car pulling into the road to block him. He torqued the wheel to the left and rocketed by, scraping the cage on the front of the squad car's bumper.

He glanced in the rearview and saw the police car pull out directly behind him, lights and sirens going. He skidded around another corner, the truck vibrating in protest. He immediately took a left, trying to lose the police by reaching the major thoroughfare that ran next to Sunnyside Park. Moving too fast, the truck's tires broke contact with the pavement, sending him into a wild spin. He bounced through a ditch and across a sidewalk and slammed broadside into the trees at the edge of the park.

Shaken, he cleared his head, hearing the siren growing. He leapt out of the truck just as the police car slid to a halt. He ran straight into the thick woods of the park, the branches of the underbrush whipping and scratching his arms and face as he barreled through.

He heard the policeman shouting at him to halt, but he kept going. He hit a tangle of undergrowth and sprawled face-first onto the ground. He lay panting but heard nobody following.

The thicket, he knew, was only a couple of acres, and

they were going to surround it. Then they'd bring in the dogs. He needed to get out before he was trapped.

He jumped up and began running again, straight west, toward the South Freeway, which bordered the woods. If he could get across that—put it between him and the park—he would stand a chance. He heard sirens on both his left and his right, realizing they were setting up observation points on the surface roads, but that would be harder to do on the expressway.

He heard the noise of cars on the freeway first, then saw a break in the trees ahead. He kept running until he reached the edge of the wood line, then squatted down, cautiously peeking out. No police.

He'd started to step out when he saw a police car to his right, at the corner where the freeway met the northern surface road. He pulled back into the wood line and ran south a hundred meters. He tentatively tried again. The south road to his left was still clear of police vehicles, but the freeway was a problem. It was two two-lane roads separated by a fifty-foot swath of grass. From his position, the woods on the other side of the freeway were about a football field away. A long distance to run in the open. The only good news was there wasn't a lot of traffic.

He broke free, running flat out toward the freeway, waiting to hear someone shout. He heard nothing. He made it across the northbound lanes, then was forced to stop in the grass median, frustrated by traffic. He glanced behind him at the police car to the north but saw no reaction.

A break appeared in the southbound lanes, and he raced to the far wood line. His lungs on fire, his legs wobbly from the exertion, he finally reached the first shrubs and stunted pine trees. He pulled himself into the woods, now staggering forward. He went far enough inside to be hidden, and collapsed.

Gasping for air in the humid Texas heat, he thought about his options, which were few. He couldn't go back to the safe house, so anything in there was lost. He had plenty of money but no transportation. Maybe he could steal a bicycle, but that wouldn't get him to Los Angeles, and he was supposed to be there in four days.

He decided he would call his contact. Let him solve the problem. In the meantime, he would put as much distance between himself and Sunnyside as he could. He thought about which way to go and logically decided to continue west, toward Los Angeles.

The next target.

35

The following morning, I'd been awakened by my phone buzzing with an alert, annoying the hell out of me. I looked at my watch, seeing it was only six A.M. I snatched up the phone and saw it was the Taskforce telling me to call in secure, immediately. I did the quick math and realized it was midnight in the United States. Which was foreboding.

Jennifer propped up on an elbow, her hair all over the place like she'd rubbed a balloon to get the static electricity to make it stand on end. She wiped the sleep out of her eyes and said, "What's going on?"

I said, "I think our trip to Alhambra is going to be put on hold. Kurt wants to talk."

She perked up at that but couldn't resist a jab. "But I already paid for the tickets."

I got on the computer and said, "You did not. You never did anything with the laptop after I turned out the light."

Behind me she said, "Yes, I did." And then I got the joke. I dialed up on the VPN, saying, "So it was all work for you, huh?"

She started to reply, and the screen cleared. I held a finger to my lips as Kurt appeared. Without preamble, he said, "You've got Omega for your target."

I glanced at Jennifer and said, "Why? What's changed?"

Kurt said, "You guys seen the TV news lately?"

We both said, "No. What happened?"

He told us about a strike on a ship in Houston, something that had caused enormous damage tactically, with millions of dollars in destruction and a body count climbing north of 150, but even more strategically. Now one of the largest ports in the United States was shut down. I flicked on the television while he was talking and saw a repeating newsfeed showing a burning lake of fire next to a gigantic tanker ship.

I said, "Okay, got it. What does that have to do with our target?"

"Everything. Right after this happened, but completely unrelated, some uniformed Houston police were looking for a gangbanger and ended up chasing a guy avoiding their checkpoint. He crashed his vehicle but managed to escape. The fingerprints in the vehicle were from the terrorist in Nevada."

"So . . . you think there's a connection between the two?"

He gave me a weary smile and said, "Really? A wanted terrorist with a penchant for complex attacks ends up in the city that has a complex attack? Yeah, I do. More importantly, so does the Oversight Council—and you have the only lead in existence, as tenuous as it is. If I'm right, he's no longer a lone wolf. No way would he have been able to execute this mission by himself, which means there's a complex plan in play."

"You don't think this was a one-off? It's pretty spectacular. You think more hits are coming?"

"I honestly don't know, but Tower One was pretty spectacular as well. Before Tower Two and the Pentagon."

"Who are we looking at? Al Qaida? It can't be ISIS. Those yokels don't have the brainpower to manage something like this. All they can do is spray and pray."

"You have hit the conundrum of the day. We have no idea. It's not al Qaida—or if it is, they've managed to avoid about a thousand different intel feeds, which just isn't possible given the scope of the attack. It's not anyone on our radar."

That was scary. A terrorist group that announced itself with an attack like this was unheard of. Even al Qaida had done multiple lesser attacks before the big one, including the botched World Trade Center bombing in 1993 and the attack on the USS *Cole* in 2000.

Kurt said, "You mentioned earlier you had a plan to roll this guy up. Can you execute?"

I said, "That'll all depend on Creed." I told him about Veep's millennial trap, and that we were still waiting on the code to be built. He said, "I'll get more manpower on it. If he can get it done, how soon can you execute?"

"We still have to find an ambush location, but that won't take too long. This evening?"

He said, "Get it done, because I don't think this asshole is finished yet, and we need whatever is in that drug dealer's head."

Twelve hours later, Veep and Jennifer were whispering sweet nothings to each other at an outdoor table, while I was forced to listen to verbal abuse from Knuckles, sitting on a cinder block at a construction site.

We'd been stationary for close to an hour before we got our first nibble, like a fish causing the bobber to bounce. Retro came on, saying, "Dragontooth is in the neighborhood, down on the river, and it's doing the usual." Meaning he was playing the game.

Now we only needed to see if we could sink the hook.

36

A muted television on in the background, Johan van Rensburg tried another four-digit combination on the iPhone 6s, and, as expected, came up blank. He'd hoped the man he'd killed in the cable car had been stupid enough to use 1234, 1010, or 1111, but he hadn't. Giving up on the keypad, he tried several outdated hacks involving Siri, the voice activation application, on the off chance the owner hadn't updated the iOS software. He asked the phone for the weather, the clock app, and email, hoping to get a backdoor around the passcode. Each time he was stymied.

Damn it. Why do they publicize that shit?

While deciding on his next move, he idly placed his thumb on the Touch ID fingerprint reader, and, of course, that didn't work either. But it did give him an idea.

He went to the explosives he'd brought with him, laying the two blocks on the bed and looking closely at the wax paper wrapping. He found a multitude of fingerprints on the wax—some probably his own—but he continued searching anyway. He located four on the glossy paper that he determined were thumbprints. Using his pocketknife, he carefully sliced around each one, then picked up the individual slips of wax paper with the edge of a napkin, placing them in separate pint-size Ziploc bags.

It was something he could work on later.

He turned his attention to the passport, the face of the man he'd killed bringing the death home, but not in a bad way. He had no regrets about what he'd done, and he now had a name—Karim al-Khattabi, from Morocco.

Johan ignored the eyes staring at him from the passport photo, instead searching for something that could help. Outside of work visas for Gibraltar and Spain, there was nothing of interest. Karim had entered Spain more than ten years ago and had been in Gibraltar for at least two years, but he'd returned home only twice—presumably to update his visa.

He picked up the small address book, flipping through it. He saw scribbles, all in Arabic, which was no help. He was about to toss it aside when he found a list of names, all ending in *al-Khattabi,* with an address in Fez, Morocco. *Family?* Johan didn't know. In truth, he didn't know why he was even looking.

He'd managed to escape Gibraltar without incident— simply by walking back to his car and driving out. He'd continued straight to Madrid, finding a cheap hotel near the Royal Palace. He'd turned on the television, hoping to see some news about the discovery of the dead man, but the only English-speaking channels in Madrid were international ones: the BBC, CNN, and Sky News. None of them had picked up on a small-time murder in Gibraltar.

He knew Karim had been up to no good, and he hoped the police would discover the plot before some tourist was blown apart, but beyond that, he wasn't sure what his next move should be. The target using the bank account was dead, so he'd cauterized whatever fallout might be coming to Icarus Solutions.

He wished he'd left the address book, passport, and cell phone with the dead man. The authorities could certainly use them more than he could. They needed them to stop whatever was about to happen, and he felt no small amount of angst about taking them.

He caught a news flash on the television, bringing him out of his self-pity. He focused on the report, seeing an oil tanker surrounded by fire, the ticker below the screen saying it was from Houston, Texas. He turned up the volume, listening to the description of the attack as the camera zoomed in on the wreckage. He saw the name on the hull and realized life as he knew it was over.

It was the same ship whose name he'd seen in Karim's office. The one with the work order.

Christ. He blew up an oil tanker.

He watched the screen, mesmerized at the carnage and feeling the revulsion build at his running away from the crime scene instead of attempting to stop whatever the man had planned. Feeling sickened that he was connected.

But he was, inescapably. In his heart, he knew there was nothing he could have done, as the attack had already been in motion even as he was tracking his target, but the images on the screen caused his stomach to roil. It was the same feeling he'd had in Africa, entering a small hamlet and seeing the destruction. The raped women and dead children. Something he could have prevented, had the government let him.

He slept with that knowledge every single night.

He watched the carnage, seeing the body count, feeling the rage grow. Dexter's name was on that bank account. Somehow, whether he knew why or not, Dexter was at the root of the attack. And now, so was he.

He checked his watch, seeing it was one in the afternoon in Florida, and dialed the phone. Dexter answered on the fourth ring, saying, "Johan, I've been waiting on your call. Did you find anything out?"

"Yeah, I did. You see that attack in Houston?"

"Of course. Everyone here is going apeshit over it. The body count is still rising, and they're having a hard time putting out the fire in the bay. It's a catastrophe. Why?"

"Your bank account financed it."

"What? What the hell are you talking about?"

Johan told him what he'd found, detailing the evidence and the unmistakable connections. Dexter said, "How do you know all of this? Did you talk to the man? Maybe he's lying."

Johan stared at the ceiling, wondering if his boss was just acting stupid or was truly that dumb.

He said, "I fucking killed him. He didn't hand me his phone and passport. I took them from him after I found the explosives. He attacked me with a knife, and he paid for it."

The first words out of Dexter's mouth were, "You actually murdered him?"

Johan's voice turned cold. "Don't ever use the word *murder* with me. I don't murder anyone. He attacked me, and now I want to know what the fuck is going on. Your bank account is tied into all of this. *You* are the thread."

Johan thought he heard crying on the phone. He said, "Are you still there?"

"Yes, yes. I just . . . I mean . . . I don't know what to say. They killed over two hundred people in Houston. The port's shut down. It's costing millions of dollars a day."

"Who did you pay that original bribe to?"

"What?"

"Dexter, when I ask a question, and you answer 'what,' all that tells me is you're trying to think up an answer. You want to fuck with me, you'd better go to interrogation training. If you want me to give you the fucking instruction, I'll be home in a day. Now, I'll ask again: Who. Did. You. Pay. The. Bribe. To?"

"It . . . it was a guy who had inroads into the Saudi kingdom. Nothing more. He was a guy that could get me a contract."

"What's his name?"

"I . . . I don't remember. Tariq something. I could find out."

"Are you recording this conversation?"

Flustered, Dexter said, "No, why would I be?"

"Okay, listen to me, and listen closely. I do not work for anyone who helps terrorists. Unlike you, I have lost friends and family, and I have fought them my entire life. If I find out that you've helped this man in any way—if I find out you're lying to me—I'm going to kill you."

Dexter managed to come up with a little bit of bravado, but Johan could feel it was forced. "Hey, wait a minute. I lost my best friend on 9/11. Don't give me that. I would never help terrorists."

"And yet here we sit, you prevaricating on who you bribed, and a bank account from fifteen years ago used in a terrorist attack."

Dexter said, "I'll find out the details. It was so long ago."

"You'll do more than that. You'll go to the authorities with my information. Tell them what you know. Connect the dots from Gibraltar. Get them hunting the rest of them."

"The rest of them? What are you talking about? The

attack's over. Why should we throw ourselves to the wolves?"

"Because it may not be over. Those bank accounts that had your name on them are complex, and they're worldwide. I don't care how you do it, but get that information into the system. Do it anonymously, do it on the nightly news, do it with your friends in the Pentagon, I really don't give a shit, but get that intelligence out into the wild."

Johan heard nothing for a second, prompting him to say, "You still there?"

"Yes, yes. I'm just thinking. This could destroy us."

"It has *already* destroyed us. People are dead."

"But they'll ask about the first bribe."

"So what? You can smooth that one over. It was a charitable contribution, right?"

"You don't understand . . ."

"What do I not understand?"

"Nothing. I'll do it. I'll use my contacts."

"Good. You will do four things for me, in the order I'm telling you."

"Wait, what? Do what?"

"Shut the fuck up and listen. One, I need a visa for Morocco from Madrid. I have an H-1B visa from the United States, so I can leverage that for an expedited visa, but I need your connections into the country. Two, I also need plane tickets and a hotel to use on the application. You will buy those. Three, you will wire me a bundle of money here in Madrid. Four, you will use your contacts to get me a weapon inside Morocco once I'm there. A Sig Sauer P228, along with fifty rounds of ammunition."

"Whoa, whoa, wait a minute. Why are you going to Morocco?"

Johan wanted to strangle the phone in his hand. He hissed, "To clean up your fucking mess."

Dexter backed down at the tone. "How on earth can I get you a gun there? I mean, I'm not an arms dealer."

"You have the contract at Ouarzazate, correct?"

The shift in conversation caused Dexter to do nothing but breathe into the phone. Johan said, "The one providing armorer support to the movie studio?"

"How do you know about that?"

"I know because I don't do business with someone unless I check them out, which I'm now regretting. Do you have a contract for that film about Iraq, or not?"

"I do, but that's just a bunch of props. It's where everyone in the United States goes to film a movie if they need a desert. It's not an arms bazaar."

"They filmed *Black Hawk Down* there, right?"

"Yes . . . I think so."

"Well, they had real guns, then. You're filming a movie about the Iraq War, aren't you?"

"I'm not filming *anything*."

"Okay, someone is filming a movie about the fight in Iraq against ISIS, and you're providing them armorer support. Is that fucking right or wrong?"

After a pause, Johan heard, "That's correct, but all of those weapons are not allowed to fire. From what they tell me, they're basically props."

"Yeah, they're props on the set, but they work. All they did was remove the guts for the movie. They aren't fake guns. Get me one of those weapons."

Johan waited a beat, then heard, "Okay, okay. I think I can make that happen. But why are you going to Morocco in the first place?"

"I have an address from the guy I killed. I'm going to check it out."

"Wait, wait, you can't intervene somewhere else. Let the authorities handle it."

"I will, if you get them moving, but I'm not waiting. Get me the visa. If it isn't necessary, it isn't necessary."

Dexter relented, saying, "Okay . . . Okay. I can do that. What's the money for? Why do you need more than I've given you?"

Johan looked at the iPhone on the bed, tantalizing him with its information. He said, "I have a cell phone I need to hack, and it's going to require some specific kit."

37

Dexter hung up the phone, feeling the air conditioner for the first time, the cold breeze finally sweeping through the sweat on his body, a clammy, uncomfortable sensation.

His secretary knocked on the door, then stuck her head in, saying his next appointment was still waiting. A group that was willing to invest in his expansion into the bloodbath of Yemen.

She took one look at him and said, "Sir, are you all right?"

He said, "Yes, yes. Of course . . . Actually, no, I'm not. I think I've caught a fever. Can you tell them I'm indisposed? But make it look like it wasn't from me?"

She smiled and said, "Of course. Done it many times."

She closed the door, and Dexter sagged back in his chair, staring at the ridiculous icon he'd created for Icarus Solutions, realizing his life was about to be in ruins.

What on earth am I going to do?

The problem set was getting out of control. There was no way he could take what Johan had found and give it to the authorities. Forget "leaking" it to someone inside. Forget telling anyone outright. He had nothing to do with the attack in Houston, and yet he knew his name would be tied to it. Telling anyone would destroy him.

The fact that his original account was being used for further terrorist attacks was proof. Damning proof.

Now, in his heart, he knew he was responsible for 9/11.

He put his head into his hands, willing the world to be different. He thought about Chip. Thought about the other thousands who had died.

It *wasn't* his fault. Even Chip wanted what he was striving for. Even Chip wanted . . .

He stopped, knowing that Chip didn't want to die in an inferno.

So what now?

The answer was obvious. Give Johan the information on the Saudis. Get him the visa and the gun. Let him do what he would do, like turning a rabid dog loose, but there was no way he was going to tell the United States government what Johan found.

38

After a little bit of a wait, with all of us holding our breath, I said, "Okay, Retro, what's the deal? Is he coming or what?"

Retro said, "Sorry. He's in the neighborhood, but he's not biting. He's sort of wandering around."

"What's that mean?"

"He's doing what he does, finding his little Pokémon, but he's headed your way. Give it some time."

I said, "Shit. Really? I'm going to sit on a paint can all evening while this guy chases nonexistent creatures?"

Jennifer cut in, saying, "Pike, take a breath. If it works out, you'll get a prize."

Knuckles looked at me with a quizzical expression. I smiled and, on the radio, said, "That's what I was waiting for."

Off the radio, Knuckles said, "What was that all about?"

Before I could answer, Retro came on, saying, "Creed wants to know if it's ice cream or something else."

Knuckles raised his brows, and I said, "Ice cream for everyone. Except Jennifer."

The radio went silent, and Knuckles said, "What the hell are you talking about? This relationship stuff is getting out of control. Can we just kick the shit out of someone? For once?"

I smiled and said, "It's a hell of a lot more fun this way. Jennifer hates it, and I get to poke her in the eye."

"It's not what we used to do."

I said, "Yes, it is. I've ribbed you more times than I can count, and you've returned the favor . . . Wait a minute. Are you getting jealous?"

Flustered, Knuckles said, "No, of course not. That's stupid. I just think we should—"

The radio cut him off, Veep saying, "We have two unknowns moving your way."

I peeked over the wall and saw a twenty-something couple take a left turn away from the hotel and into our alley kill zone.

What the hell. I clicked on and said, "What's the beacon doing?"

"He's on the north-south alley two blocks over."

Which didn't mean a whole lot as far as timing went. The old Moorish neighborhood was built straight up a steep hillside and was positively claustrophobic, the brick buildings jammed together in a seamless mass. Constructed centuries ago, the few roads capable of automobile traffic ran along the ridgeline, with the majority of the neighborhood reachable only by foot using narrow steps and alleys that looked like they came out of a medieval fantasy novel, winding and twisting around without apparent rhyme or reason. The only indication that you hadn't traveled back in time was the boutique hotels and coffee shops interspersed throughout the maze.

I watched the couple, hoping they'd move on. They didn't. Instead, they both pulled out their phones and began playing with them. On the net, I said, "Veep, what's going to happen if someone else comes to the gym?"

I waited on a response, and Knuckles said, "You think they're playing the game?"

"Hell yeah, look at them."

Veep came back, "If they win, they now own the gym. It's no big deal, because the gym will still stand. He'll still come."

Retro came on, "Uh . . . Pike, Creed says the gym's not real. He only had a day to work on it, and it doesn't actually work. It just shows up as a phantom."

"What's that mean?"

"It'll register on the app as existing, but nobody can actually play there. It's a dummy gym."

Jennifer came on, "Pike, this is Koko, I have eyes on the target. He's on the way."

Off the net, I said to Knuckles, "This is going to go bad."

He chuckled and said, "I would expect nothing less."

The couple fidgeted around for a little bit, messing with their phones, then turned and retraced their steps. They rounded the corner of the hotel and disappeared from view.

I said, "Whew. That was close. Get your kit ready."

Knuckles opened a small satchel, using a syringe to mix two powerful sedatives together. He held the tube up and pushed the plunger, expelling the air in the needle.

Jennifer said, "Pike, we have an issue. The couple met the target on the way down. They're talking."

Shit.

"What's your read?"

"They saw him playing, and they're telling him the gym is a bust."

"Are you burned? Has he seen you with Veep?"

"No. He hasn't reached us yet."

"Okay. Keep eyes on him, if he looks like he's going to abort—"

"They're done. Moving in different directions."

"Is he headed your way?"

"No."

I looked at Knuckles, and he said, "Get Jennifer on his ass, now."

I nodded and, into the radio, said, "Veep, go into the hotel and wait. Koko, interdict him. Get him into the kill zone."

"How?"

Looking at me with a half smile on his face, Knuckles clicked into the net. "Show him some cleavage and ask him about the game. Work it. Tell him you want to see how the game is played."

I saw Veep stand, then heard Jennifer say, "Are you serious?"

I came on. "Yep. Just go the 'are you an American' route, then start talking about the game. He'll want to show you, and the only thing nearby is the gym."

She glanced up our way and said, "This is not my skill set."

Knuckles said, "Do it, and I'll give you a prize."

I scowled at the comment, and, he mouthed, *What?* But he damn well knew what the *prize* meant. I saw a little grin leak out and knew he was playing me. I said, "Execute the mission."

I watched her walk away, out of view, and said, "You'd better hope Carly doesn't come into the team, because payback is a motherfucker."

He laughed, checking his equipment and saying, "I think you're jealous."

And just like that we were clicking again. I grinned at him, saying, "Touché."

I waited a moment, then poked my head over the wall, seeing Jennifer walking up the alley with our target, her hand on his arm. Knuckles said, "She must like guys with tattoos."

I said, "That's what drew her to me in the first place."

He said, "You don't have any tattoos."

They made the turn, going to the fake gym deep into our blind alley, and I said, "None that you know about."

He poked his head over the wall and said, "None that exist."

The target looked our way, and Knuckles hunched down behind the wall. I said, "Maybe I got one after I left the Taskforce."

He chuckled and said, "No way. After the hell you gave me for my tattoos? You're too particular."

He had me there. I called Veep and said, "Lock down the exit. Keep us clean."

He said, "Roger. They've passed by me. They're on the way into the kill zone."

I said, "Roger all," and stuck my head above the wall, seeing Jennifer leading him in with a hand on his upper arm. They stopped, and she leaned into his phone, clicking into the net and saying, "How does this work? What do you do?"

I heard him start talking, explaining the game, and said, "Veep, it's on. Retro, stage the vehicle. We're coming back with a body."

Knuckles slipped over the wall and I followed. We slunk down the alley, closing in on them, watching the target valiantly attempt to vanquish the virtual character in the gym so he could get into Jennifer's pants.

I heard, "This damn thing isn't working. It's like what those other people said. It's a glitch."

He caught movement behind him and turned around. He saw Knuckles and said, "You!" Jennifer grabbed his arm and he slammed his leg into her crotch in a spasm of rage. I saw her eyes explode in pain, and she sagged forward. I started running toward him, and he went into a crouch, snarling. Then Jennifer got back in the fight.

Her face contorted in anger, she snapped low, whipping in a circle with one leg out, hitting him just above the ankles, flinging his legs up and sending him flat on his back. I heard him yelp, and we reached him just as his head bounced on the pavement. I grabbed his legs, letting Knuckles use the syringe.

He did not. Instead he leaned into the target's face, held up the syringe, and said, "This would have been an easy ride, but you chose to hurt someone I hold dear."

The target began thrashing about, me holding his legs still. He blurted out, "What the fuck is going on? What did I do to *you*? What does that mean?"

Knuckles leaned in and said, "It means you meet my callsign," and then hammered him in the temple.

Jennifer released his arm, letting it hit the ground. She sagged into the wall, taking deep breaths. She said, "Knuckles . . . that wasn't necessary."

He stood up and said, "Yeah, it was. There's a reason these guys exist and it's because they don't feel any consequences."

I flipped the inert body onto his stomach, peeled his pants down, then motioned to Knuckles. He used the syringe in the buttocks. I locked eyes with him while he administered the dose, and he said, "What?"

I said, "Nothing. Just wondering if you'd have done the same if it had been me on the receiving end."

He grinned and said, "No fucking way."

I laughed and started coordinating exfil.

39

Inside the Old Executive Office Building next to the White House, Kurt Hale and George Wolffe were forced, like everyone else in the room, to wait on the arrival of President Hannister.

Kurt glanced around the table, taking in who was missing from the members of the Oversight Council, trying to ascertain a clue as to why Hannister was late. Most were glued to the latest reports out of Houston—which was the reason they'd all been called together—but some were clustered in small groups, talking. Kurt couldn't find Nancy Rankin, the newly minted secretary of state, Kerry Bostwick, the director of the CIA, or Mark Oglethorpe, the secretary of defense.

He mentioned their absence to George, who said, "Palmer's missing as well." Alexander Palmer was the president's national security advisor, and the four being absent meant there was a separate meeting going on somewhere.

Kurt started to respond when the door opened and President Hannister entered the room, followed by the four missing administration officials. The assembled Council members found their seats, and Kurt stood up. President Hannister said, "Colonel Hale, before you brief, I'd like Director Bostwick to give an update. We just came out of a VTC with his counterpart in the United Kingdom, and we've made some headway."

Kurt sat back down, interested in the British connection, and Kerry Bostwick moved to the head of the table. He said, "We know that the ship was a Kuwaiti-flagged vessel, owned by a Saudi Arabian company. We've tracked its course since loading up with crude in Kuwait. It came through the Strait of Hormuz, around the Cape of Good Hope, and headed up to its first port of call, which was in the United Kingdom. This is where it gets interesting."

He clicked on a PowerPoint showing a picture of a dry-dock shipyard. "The vessel claimed some internal problems—we're still working with the shipping company to determine just what the issue was—and detoured into the Med, going to the British port at Gibraltar. They were delayed for five days. During that time, a company called Mint Tea Maintenance was one of six that worked on the vessel but was the only one that did anything near where the vessel was breached."

He clicked the screen, bringing up a picture of a badge from the shipyard with the face of a thirty-something Arabic man. He said, "This is Karim al-Khattabi. He's the sole proprietor of Mint Tea. He worked on the vessel for a total of five days."

He flipped the screen again, showing the same man lying on a steel floor, his eyes half-open and his mouth agape, the tongue rolled back. "This is Karim now. He was found dead on a cable car descending from the top of Gibraltar. Next to him were two bricks of Semtex and some blasting caps."

He turned back to the room and said, "MI6 feels—as do I—that this man is responsible for the attack. What we don't know is why he was killed, but we believe it was a cleanup."

Richard Melbourne, one of the few civilians on the

Oversight Council, said, "Where's he from? He's clearly not British."

"He's from the Rif Mountains of Morocco, which is one of the reasons we believe he's the terrorist." Bostwick grinned sardonically and said, "I mean, outside of the fact that he was found dead with a bunch of explosives after being the last man to service the ship."

Richard said, "Why is that an indicator? The Rif Mountains?"

"The Rif has been a hotbed of revolt for over a hundred years, filled with Berbers who are staunchly independent. The *Rif* name itself is Arabic for 'the edge of cultivated lands,' and it has a rich history of rebellion. The people there have fought against the ruling party of Morocco for eons. It's most famous for kicking Spaniard ass in the 1920s, but the region has a peculiar tie to terrorism in the last few years. People from the Rif did the train bombings in Madrid in 2004. The Paris attacks in 2015, culminating in the Bataclan Theatre massacre, were committed by Moroccans with a heritage in the Rif. Same for the Belgium airport attack in 2016. Moroccans with one foot in the Rif. It's an area that breeds violence, and the fact that this guy was from there is a definite indicator."

Nobody said anything, taking the history lesson in, until Mark Oglethorpe, the secretary of defense, said, "Tell them what you think about further attacks."

Kerry nodded and said, "It's our belief, given the extensive nature of planning and coordination for this attack, that it's not the only one. This man worked at the shipyard for more than two years, patiently waiting before he was triggered, and he had help from a sophisticated network. In today's world, we don't see that anymore. We see lone wolves with rifles or bombs strapped to them, randomly shooting strangers or mowing them down with a truck. This is different and, honestly, scary. Someone placed him there, years ago, for this specific attack, and if that is true, then someone's been placed somewhere else. The timing of this attack is no coincidence. It wasn't exact, but September eleventh is now a rallying cry. They're using ships, not planes, but this hit, in my mind, was the North Tower, and more are coming. And it's very, very effective. Whoever is doing this isn't looking for death or propaganda, like ISIS. They're looking for an economic disaster."

Richard said, "What's that mean?"

"They know we can't shut down our ports without catastrophic effects, and they're attempting to make us do it. And it will be catastrophic. Our trade through shipping is hard to even calculate in monetary dollars, to be honest. Our ports account for fully eight percent of global trade. Billions of dollars would not do it justice, and that's per day. Right now, because of the attack, we're on so-called high alert at our ports, but that means little in the real world. We inspect, at best, four out of a hundred containers that pass through. If we try to do one hundred percent, trade will be destroyed. We simply cannot stop the ships coming in without a devastating impact."

He rubbed his eyes and said, "To answer your question more pointedly, unless we stop them, they win. Big-time."

George Wolffe said, "I thought Congress had mandated a hundred percent inspection rate a while ago. That's a law, right?"

"Yeah, it is, since 2006, but they might as well mandate changing the color of the sky. It's an impossible task. We actually do manage to achieve it in some ports, mainly when the trucks leave, *after* the ship is unloaded, but it's too hard to do at our major ports. Business trumps terrorism, so the law has been slow-rolled. Anyway, none of those provisions would have prevented the attack in Houston."

Wolffe said, "Who do we think this is? You mentioned a sophisticated apparatus, and I know that al Qaida is resilient and still alive. Is that what we're seeing here? A resurgent al Qaida?"

Kerry pursed his lips and said, "That's the million-dollar question. Karim has no known ties to any terrorist or extremist group. He's like a ghost that awakened with the capability to destroy an oil tanker. On top of that, no group has claimed credit. It's one of the most devastating attacks in the history of terrorism, and nobody's crowing about it."

Richard said, "We have no clue? What about a state? Maybe it's Iran, or even Russia."

Kerry said, "We're looking into that, but at this juncture, we don't think a state would do such a thing. It's too great a risk. They can hurt us, but we can destroy them. On top of that, harming our trade harms *their* trade too."

He turned off the monitor. "Having said that, whoever it is has the resources of a state. There's just no way something this sophisticated could occur without a huge bankroll."

40

Tariq turned from the television news report and said, "Excellent. Exactly what we wanted. Ring of Fire is working."

Not nearly as sanguine as his son, Yousef said, "Yes, it was spectacular, but they've tied the tanker strike to the drone attack. They've identified Anwar. It is only a matter of time before he is caught. We should have never allowed him to do that first strike."

"Father, I told you that was the price I had to pay. Anwar is intelligent. Inquisitive. He wasn't like the usual recruit, simply running from something. I had to negotiate."

"I know, I know, but it doesn't alter what has happened. We didn't need a bright, inquisitive person. We only needed someone to recognize a ship and dial a phone. Even your 'intelligent, inquisitive' man was almost arrested. Where is he now?"

"He's in Los Angeles, waiting on the ship *Al Salam II*. He should be able to remain undetected until it arrives, and then we are through with him."

"Can he remain hidden for an additional week?"

"Why? The ship arrives in three days."

"I've been informed that it's delayed because of the Panama Canal. The ship is too big to use the original locks, but planned on going through the new one that recently opened. Apparently, there have been multiple accidents with the new lock, with vessels getting damaged trying to navigate it. They haven't refined their operational tugboats, and the ship's captain has determined the management of the canal is unsafe. He's stopping and offloading the cargo on the Atlantic side, and it will be rail loaded to the Pacific side, then reloaded to a different vessel."

Tariq said, "Rail loaded? Can't you order him to use the canal?"

"That would be a little unusual. The owner of the shipping firm overriding the decision of an individual ship's captain for cargo he shouldn't care about? No, that's not going to happen. Why does it matter? Can your man remain undetected or not?"

"Yes, he should be fine. I've loaded a different bank account with money, completely severing any ties with Houston, and he has a safe house to live in, but every day is a risk. More importantly, he's looking for the name of a ship. If the cargo is transloaded, how will we know which vessel it's on?"

Yousef pursed his lips, then tapped his fingers on the table, thinking. He said, "I hadn't considered that."

"Can you track the containers? Through the freight forwarder?"

Yousef toyed with a pen, then said, "It would be strange, but I can get the feeds for the containers. It'll probably be two separate ships, but I can tell you when they arrive."

Tariq nodded, not wanting to antagonize his father, but needing to impress on him how critical the information was. "If the boats don't arrive at the same time, he could dial the phone and do nothing more than cause an explosion in the middle of the ocean. I need to know *exactly* when the boat holding that container arrives."

His father stood up, his corpulent waist bumping the table, aggravated at the news. He stabbed a finger into the air and said, "Then I *need* to know what container holds the explosives. I need to know which shipment holds the method of destruction. I tell you over and over that planning is the heart of our success, and now I hear that you don't even have a plan for a simple shift in shipping. After I've run a shipping company for your *entire life*."

Tariq said, "I don't know that information. I didn't think I had to. I left that up to Jalal, but I can contact him."

His father glared, and then Tariq saw his face soften. He said, "I'm sorry. I shouldn't speak such a thing to my son. I understand the risks you take. I just want to make sure that this time, we do what we set out to do. As the prophet—peace be upon him—said, 'If thou comest on them in war, deal with them so as to strike fear in those who are left behind, that they may remember.' That is what we are doing. Our actions are just, and our will needs to be strong."

"Father, we have to be careful. The Americans are still researching the redacted pages about Saudi involvement of our attacks on 9/11. The ones released last year. Nobody has made the connections yet, but they might. The kingdom professes innocence, but make no mistake, the trail is there. We must be circumspect here."

Yousef clenched his fists and said, "We were right then, and we are right now. The king is selling out our entire country. Our culture. Maybe we should let it be known that we helped the attack back then. Let it be known that the Kingdom of Saudi Arabia is against the West. I'm sick of hiding it."

Aghast, Tariq said, "Father, please. You can't do that.

We can't do that. The king is *the king*. He supports what we're doing by his actions around the world."

Yousef sat back down and muttered, "The king is a traitor. The entire house of al-Saud is traitorous, and has been for decades. Osama bin Laden was right, and so are we. You *will* execute our mission. I don't want to hear excuses like I heard fifteen years ago."

Tariq said nothing, not having the courage to agree out loud to what his father had said. Yousef turned away, regaining his composure. He picked up a glass of water and took a sip, as if the words had never been spoken. He said, "What of your Berber friends? Are they still on track?"

Glad for the change of conversation, Tariq said, "Yes, sir, they are. Jalal is now in Fez, preparing the men for their trip to America. He is strong."

Yousef smiled and said, "Good, because I've been thinking of our attacks. Thinking of another one."

Confused, Tariq said, "What does that mean? Everything is in place."

"Yes, it is, but we're missing the final piece. The same one we missed in 2001. We hit them financially and we hit them militarily, but we missed the greatest blow."

Hesitant, Tariq said, "What are you talking about? We're doing the Ring of Fire. We're attacking ports around the entire country."

Yousef said, "Yes, we are, but I want the one where we hit them at their heart. The one that crashed in Pennsylvania."

"Father, there are no ports near Washington, DC. What do you want to strike, the one in Baltimore?"

"No, that's not what I mean. You saw the attention that mini drone attack garnered."

"Yes, but you said that was just symbolic. You disparaged it."

Yousef said, "Make sure your drone man in Los Angeles can get out clean. I have something else in mind for him."

41

Inside the Oversight Council meeting, Richard Melbourne exhaled and said, "Well, that was a pretty good scare briefing. How does this information help us?"

Kerry Bostwick looked at him with disdain but gave him an honest appraisal. "Very little. We have quite a few threads to pull, but nothing is concrete."

Kurt had developed an instant dislike for Richard. He was one more blowhard who knew more than anyone else about how to defend the nation, but he did have a point. One that Kurt himself might be able to solve. He said, "The dead guy in Gibraltar is from Morocco?"

Sensing a lifeline, Kerry said, "Yes. He was."

"That's tracking with what Pike's finding."

President Hannister said, "He's got a lead from Granada?"

Kurt tapped his pen on the table, realizing he'd given too much hope. "Not exactly. He's found a lead that goes to an American drug facilitator in Chefchaouen, Morocco, in the heart of the Rif."

The secretary of defense said, "Another drug dealer? Seriously? That's what Pike's found?"

He said, "Yes and no. The person in control of the bank account that started this thread—the bank account that was also tied into the terrorist attack in Nevada—is a Moroccan from Chefchaouen. He's the leader of the drug ring, but apparently he's taking some time off. The man we captured in Granada doesn't know where he is, but his brother does. And he's in Chefchaouen."

Richard said, "So we're rolling up a drug ring and getting nothing but ghost leads? How long do you expect this to go on? It seems like every time we authorize an Omega operation, all we get is 'the *next* one' is the key."

Richard Melbourne was a hedge fund manager who had once been a naval officer and had spent the rest of his life dabbling in politics, advising one administration after another. He'd been brought onto the Oversight Council after the death of President Warren because President Hannister saw in him an ability to cut through the bullshit, but Kurt couldn't look past the fact that he'd also done an enormous amount of work on President Hannister's current election campaign. In Kurt's mind it wasn't disqualifying, but it was a little smelly.

Kurt said, "Sir, yes. That's what I'm telling you. This work isn't like a movie. You rarely get the smoking gun, or the guy handing you the bomb. You have to follow where the leads go, and in this case, the lead is solid. The man's name is—"

Richard cut him off, saying, "We don't have time for that shit. We need to resolve this problem soon, or the president's poll numbers are going to tank. We need to be able to hold someone's head in the air, talking about success. We had the huge bump last year with your work in Poland, but it's evaporating. Christ, just turn on the television. President Hannister is now being played as the 'weak on security' guy, even after the Baltic States stare-down. A position he held absolutely a week ago, and it's only going to get worse."

Kurt said nothing, looking at President Hannister. The president shifted in his chair, uncomfortable at the turn of the conversation. Kurt wondered if his faith had been misplaced; then Hannister spoke.

"Rich, this room is not a place for politics."

He waved his hand around the collected members and said, "This body is not designed to get me elected. It's designed for one thing: protecting American lives. Kurt does what he does, and he does it with a precision that I, personally, have seen. Please, never bring up my campaign again."

Flustered, Richard tried to protest, and Hannister showed Kurt why he deserved to be elected. "Rich, don't. I appreciate your dedication. Show me the same on a nonpartisan level, or you can wait outside."

In the heat of a presidential election, with Hannister being accused of being weak on national security, the entire room saw what was truly important to the man. Kurt was impressed, thinking, *You've come a long way.*

Hannister looked at Kurt and said, "So, you want Omega to go to Chefchaouen? Is that what I'm hearing?"

"Yes, sir. I think this next guy will give us the lead we want. I was interrupted before I could give you the best part." He looked pointedly at Richard but spoke to Kerry Bostwick. "What was the name of the guy found dead in Gibraltar?"

"Karim al-Khattabi, why?"

"The leader of the drug ring is named Jalal al-Khattabi, and he's from the Rif region." He bored his eyes into Richard's and said, "Strangely enough, they have the same tribal name. That enough smoke for you, Richard? There's a Moroccan at the end of this trail, and this guy in Chefchaouen will give him to us."

Richard broke eye contact, pretending to scribble notes on the pad to his front. At the head of the conference table, Kerry's mouth hung open at the news. Kurt winked at him, then turned to President Hannister. "Sir, I'd like Omega for Pike's team."

Hannister smiled and nodded, saying, "I'm inclined. Kerry, your thoughts?"

"Hell yeah. Get them on it, now."

Hannister said, "Let's put it to a vote."

But that was really just a formality. All thirteen Council members voted yes, including Richard. The meeting broke up, and Kurt stood to leave. President Hannister waved him forward. Kurt muttered, "Shit," to George, but went to him.

President Hannister said, "You caught that bullshit about the election, right?"

"Yes, sir. Hard to miss. Richard's a jackass."

Hannister laughed, then said, "But he's right. I won't use this organization for political purposes, but make no mistake, if these assholes keep killing, the Taskforce is done. It's ironic, but the death of the Taskforce will happen because of the very terrorists we designed it to hunt, because I won't be elected if they keep killing. You know that, right?"

Surprised at how quickly Hannister had changed from threadbare economist to cutthroat candidate, Kurt said, "Of course. Yes. But I can't make rainbows for you. I can only do what I do."

Hannister smiled and said, "Don't look at me that way. I'm still the same man. The one you helped stop World War Three. I just want that again."

Kurt stepped out on a limb and said, "Because you want to get elected?"

Hannister bristled at the implication, then said, "No. Because I want to prevent American deaths."

Kurt said nothing, the tension thick. Hannister broke it, putting his hand on Kurt's shoulder and saying, "Okay,

okay. Yes, I'm in a campaign, and it's hard to separate what's right for me and what's right for America, but this one is easy. Give me what you did in the past."

In a monotone, Kurt said, "Yes, sir."

Hannister said, "I don't want a yes-man. I get that from everyone around me."

Kurt pointed at Richard and said, "I can't give you what he wants. I can't make headlines saving the day. I can only do what I've been doing. Sometimes it works out, like Poland, and sometimes it fails, like 9/11."

"Kurt, I understand. Just do your best."

Kurt nodded, and Alexander Palmer caught the president's attention, starting to talk about something unrelated. Kurt turned away, and the president of the United States tugged his arm, shutting Palmer down. Kurt paused, and Hannister said, "I meant what I said."

In no mood to engage in more politics. Kurt said, "I know."

Hannister looked at him, not as the president of the most powerful nation on earth, but as the same man he'd been when Kurt had guided him through the rocky shoals of a near world war.

Hannister said, "I trust you. Give me some Pike magic."

Kurt smiled and said, "Don't blame me if the magic ends up being black. With Pike, it can go either way."

Hannister chuckled and said, "Black magic is still magic. Get it done."

42

We landed at an obscure airfield on the Mediterranean coast of Morocco called Sania Ramel, in the city of Tétouan. It was about an hour and a half north of Chefchaouen, but the closest strip of asphalt that could handle the Rock Star bird. The distance presented some issues, though. Ordinarily, I'd leave all of the killing tools on the bird, returning to it as necessary. With our target city so far away, I'd decided to send the aircraft with our prisoner to a rendition team in Ireland, and thus had to make an early call on what to bring with us. Instead of dictating, I threw it to a floor vote, after customs had cleared us.

I watched the immigration guys walk down the airstairs and said, "We're going to need more surveillance kit than lethal. But then again, we *might* need lethal more than surveillance. Knuckles, what do you think?"

Knuckles said, "Yeah. I'm with you. Take out the level-one package for surveillance. GPS trackers, Dragontooth, lipstick cameras for the cars. On the lethal stuff, I say we leave the long guns. Bring suppressed pistols. We aren't going to get into a firefight. The most we'll need is self-defense."

Veep said, "We thought that in Poland, and Retro ended up using the Punisher."

I nodded, then said, "Okay. No Punisher, but bring

two breakdown long guns. I'm not going to try to hide a sniper rifle with a twenty-two-inch barrel everywhere we go. The PWS rifles will have to do."

Retro said, "What about exploitation? I'm going to need some tools."

"How much? I don't want to drive out of here with fourteen Pelican cases."

"We need the exploit kit for cell phones and computers. I'd recommend two Gryphons, one for Android and one for iPhone, along with two Grapples, one for Windows and one for Mac. I don't think we should wait for the Taskforce to exploit. Let's get what we can on-site."

I nodded. All of that would fit in a backpack, and I could live with it.

Jennifer said, "What about nonlethal?"

I said, "That goes without saying. Tasers are loaded in the bug-out package. Anything else?"

Nobody spoke. I said, "Last chance. I don't want to hear shoulda woulda coulda in a day."

Met with further silence, I said, "Okay, let's roll. Jennifer and Knuckles, break out the kit. Veep and Retro, head to the terminal and get us some rental cars. Two SUVs."

They left, and Jennifer and Knuckles started removing the panels of the aircraft, breaking into the walls to bring out the specified kit hidden within. I went to the pilots, passing our prisoner near the bulkhead, handcuffed to an eyebolt in one of the leather seats, his left eye swollen and black from Knuckles's blow. He was snoring softly into a pillow against the window.

He'd ended up being perfectly compliant, telling us anything we wanted to know, to the point that we didn't even need to hack his Google accounts through the

Pokémon application. He'd simply unlocked the phone for us.

Our target was his brother, Snyder McDermott. Both were college dropouts from Chicago and had come to Spain for nothing more than the usual "see the world" wanderlust. They'd financed the trip by selling Oxycontin in their hometown and had ended up running out of money, so they began doing what they knew—this time selling marijuana in Madrid. Eventually, they'd moved from dealing on the street to actual distribution.

A Moroccan man named Jalal al-Khattabi had recruited them, and a job that was originally designed just to get them airfare home had become a career.

At twenty-seven, Snyder was a few years older than his brother Frank, but apparently he was the immature one of the two. Through Frank, we had plenty of photos of him, and almost all of them had him sampling the product, stoned out of his mind. One video, however, showed him doing flips off of walls, hurdling railings, and hanging from balconies. An ascetic-looking man with a pronounced nose, he was all skin and bones and didn't look athletic, but when asked about the video, Frank said Snyder was a fan of parkour—a sport of free running where the runner utilizes an urban environment as a giant obstacle course, leveraging anything in his path for efficiency in getting from point A to point B.

Invented by French Special Forces as a way to economically navigate an urban environment in a hurry, it had become a little bit of a cult, with people training in it all over the world. I found it strange that a dopehead would do such things, and Frank told me Snyder began practicing precisely to get away from the police on foot.

Should have guessed that.

The real target, of course, was Jalal. His last name

coincided with that of the suspected bomber of the tanker in Houston, and Frank had said he believed that if anyone had the bank account, it would be Jalal. Unfortunately, Jalal al-Khattabi had apparently taken a leave of absence from the trade, placing Snyder in charge. Frank had no idea where Jalal was, but he said Snyder would know.

So now we'd turned over one more rock in our quest to walk up the chain to the actual terrorists. Frank would be flying to Shannon, Ireland, and turned over to a Taskforce rendition team, who would fly him to America for a much more thorough interrogation.

After that, I had no idea what they'd do with him, and really didn't give a crap, but I suspected he'd probably get put into the general prison population as a drug dealer.

I conferred with the pilots, making sure that they'd be gone only as long as it took to drop off the human waste, then would return back here. Given the flight time from the United States—the long pole in the tent, as the flight time from Morocco to Ireland was only about three hours—I didn't expect to have them available for at least another cycle of darkness.

I double-checked the crew chief, making sure he was good with the drugs to keep Frank unconscious and had no qualms with the mission. He seemed squared away, reassuring me that he'd done such missions before.

Satisfied, I returned to Jennifer and Knuckles, seeing them boxing up the small amount of kit into specially configured suitcases, on the inside padded with foam but on the outside looking like ordinary Samsonites.

Forty-five minutes later we were bouncing down the N2 highway, on our way to the city of Chefchaouen, with Retro doing some research on our target's location.

We knew he was staying at a *riad* called Lina high up

the hill in the old town, but nothing about atmospherics of the operational area. Retro gave us our first bad news: Like the Moorish neighborhood in Granada, it was pedestrian-only.

I said, "Surely they drive around somehow?"

"Doesn't look that way. The road ends at the main plaza next to the original Kasbah that protected the city."

Jennifer said, "Well, that makes a little sense. The city was founded in the Middle Ages by the people fleeing the persecution of the Spanish Inquisition. They just built what they'd left."

Retro said, "Okay, Professor, tell us why it's blue."

I said, "Blue? What do you mean?"

He twisted his tablet around, showing a densely packed alley, with every building plastered in stucco and washed with blue paint. I mean every building. I said, "What's the point of that, Jennifer?"

She tucked a strand of hair behind her ear, and I thought Retro had finally stumped our team historian. I was wrong.

She said, "A bunch of different rumors, but nobody knows for sure. Some say it was started for religious reasons; others say it's to ward off mosquitos. Either way, the entirety of the old town is repainted blue every year, with individual owners collectively doing it. It's more for the tourism aspect now."

I squinted my eyes, and she said, "I'm not making it up. I'm not you."

The group chuckled, and I said, "Well, that doesn't hurt or help. Show me the location of the *riad* he's using."

A *riad* was an establishment that equated to a North African bed and breakfast. In Arabic, the term meant a house with a courtyard, but in modern times it signified a house that someone had revamped to allow travelers to stay in it—just like one in, say, Alabama, only without the grits.

Retro pulled up Google Maps, showed me where the Kasbah was located, then the *riad*. It looked to be about a five-minute walk straight uphill, but the way the maze was built, it would probably be longer. There wouldn't be a cross street that ran right up to it.

I said, "Okay, on the plus side, if we can't get cars up there, *he* can't get cars up there, so the surveillance problem of him going foxtrot to vehicle while in old town doesn't exist. But we can't capture this guy without vehicle support, so we need to follow him until he leaves the old town into the new section of the city. Make sense?"

Knuckles said, "Yeah, but we need to confirm him first. Retro, any ideas about boxing that *riad*?"

"Stand by. Let me check the area."

After another ten minutes, he said, "There's another hotel with a balcony in view of the rooftops, and a café at the base of the stairs leading up to the front door, but that's about it."

I nodded and said, "So the Starsky and Hutch stakeout it is."

43

Two hours later, I was on the small iron balcony of our new hotel room, looking out across a sea of roofs onto the outdoor deck of the Lina Ryad. Built onto the roof of the *riad,* it stood four stories above the ground—five if you counted the narrow stairs that led to the alleys below—and was eye level with my balcony, about seventy meters away.

From up here, the entire city looked like a congested, tangled mess, with haphazard roofing material ranging from red tile to corrugated tin, each building jammed next to the one beside it, some roofs higher, some lower, with random alleys providing the only break and every roof seemingly having a clothesline on it. Apparently, the blue whitewash was only for ground level, as it was a multicolored mess up here.

Jennifer was on the first floor at the hotel's small café, with eyes on the base of the stairs. She couldn't see the door, but that was my job from the balcony. Retro was at the main plaza, drinking mint tea with a host of locals and watching our cars. Knuckles was to the west of me, up the alley at the first intersection he found. Veep was to the east, doing the same thing.

We couldn't capture the guy in the old town, because getting him out on foot would be a little problematic, so we intended to follow him until he breached the old town and entered the newer section of the city—one we could drive on.

I would trigger him leaving the *riad;* then Jennifer would relay east or west. Either Knuckles or Veep would pick him up, and we'd all collapse around him, using the maze of alleys to keep him in sight. From there, we'd just develop the situation. It might take a day or two, but eventually, we'd have him.

Retro called from the plaza, saying, "Just a heads-up; two police cars pulled into the plaza."

I said, "From the checkpoint?"

During our drive down from the aircraft, we'd passed multiple checkpoints anytime we entered a town, manned by some guys in brown uniforms. They didn't stop us, or even slow us down, so I figured they were just for show. We'd passed one more as we'd entered the city.

Retro said, "No. These guys are in blue uniforms. I think they're the actual city police force, and those guys on the road are like state troopers or something. They just went by me, four of them, headed into the old town on foot."

I said, "Roger all. Bumper positions, you copy?"

I got an acknowledgment from them, and we continued to wait. I saw the door to the upper deck open, and I'll be damned if our target didn't appear, talking on a cell phone. I alerted the team, telling them I had eyes on—which was good, since we only had the word of his brother that he was staying there. He glanced down into the alley below, and I got a call from the east. "Pike, Pike, this is Veep. The policeman just passed me headed your way."

Uh-oh. I prayed they'd walk by the *riad* before our target decided to leave.

"Koko, let me know if they reach you."

The target went back inside in a rush, talking into his cell phone, and it clicked: He had someone staged like we did, only it was for early warning. I hoped that the police weren't coming for him, but my sixth sense said they were—or Snyder wouldn't have prepared a tripwire to alert him.

Jennifer said, "They just passed me, and they're headed to the stairs."

Damn it. We were going to lose our next lead because he was getting arrested. I began mentally exploring options for leveraging the Taskforce to get us into his cell, when the target burst out onto the balcony, wearing a backpack and looking over the side. The police spotted him and began racing up the stairs, banging into the lobby of the *riad*. I could hear faint shouting, and Snyder put away his phone. He backed up, then took a running leap, clearing the railing of his rooftop deck and soaring onto the next rooftop. He rolled, then stood up at a dead run. He planted his feet, then threw himself into the air, clearing the alley between us—floating through fifteen feet of open death—landing on the roof to my left.

Holy shit. I stood up, saying, "Target's on the run, target's on the run. He's on my side of the alley, on the roof."

I heard noise behind me, and Jennifer came out onto the balcony, saying, "Which way?"

I pointed to the roof attached to our hotel, two balconies over, and said, "He's running. Get on him."

She didn't hesitate. She leapt onto the railing, then jumped to the next balcony, scattering wineglasses and a bottle on a table. A man came out, shouting at her, and she ignored him, repeating the maneuver, leaping to the next balcony, then jumping to the adjacent roof. She said, "I got him, I got him, and, man, he's moving out."

Parkour . . .

I saw the police burst out onto the deck, looking around. One of them pointed across and they all began running back down, the leader shouting into a radio.

I got on the net and said, "This is going to be a foot-race. Veep, Knuckles, track from the ground. Follow Jennifer's phone. Sooner or later, he's leaving the roof."

I heard, "Roger."

"Retro, Retro, give me a route. Where's he going? He planned this beforehand, so he's got to be headed to a vehicle."

I was sure he was a junior El Chapo and had planned this escape long ago. Retro said, "I'm on it."

We had only about five minutes before he left the old town. I ran off the balcony, saying, "I'm moving to you."

Jennifer watched their target leap up onto a wall and barely touch the top before using his legs to springboard sideways to another roof. She was impressed.

There was one roof between him and her, and she leapt to it, scrambling upright.

She saw him run to the edge of his roof, abutting another alley. He glanced over, and she thought he might be boxed in. She crouched down below the parapet, waiting.

He backed up ten feet, swung his arms, and took off sprinting. He leapt up to the top of the wall and launched himself across like a long jumper, arms and legs forward, backpack straining against his shoulders. She couldn't believe it. He began running across the roofs as if it were flat terrain.

She leapt up and repeated his maneuver on the earlier roof, jumping forward to an adjacent wall, gaining height, then planting her feet and pressing off, rolling on the new roof. She heard Knuckles say, "Holy shit, he just came over my head. He cleared my alley."

She ran to the gap, seeing about a twenty-foot spread, and the target moving to the next roof. She glanced down and found Knuckles looking up at her, two women in hijabs closing up a spice store next to him. Into the radio, Knuckles said, "Can you do that?"

She said, "I don't know. That's a big gap."

"I can't get parallel to him on the street. He's going to get away."

Jennifer nodded at him and said, "Catch me if I fall?"

He said, "I'll do my best."

She took a deep breath and backed up. She heard movement behind her and whirled around. A child came out, saying something in Arabic. She smiled at him, then ran as fast as she could, knowing if her foot slipped, she was going down.

She leapt up, planting both feet on the wall, and launched herself through the air. She sailed forward and saw she wasn't going to reach it. She hit the next parapet at the waist, getting the wind knocked out of her. She scraped her feet on the wall, seeking purchase and hearing Knuckles say, "Koko, you going to make it?"

She pulled herself over the parapet and sat down, holding her ribs. She heard Knuckles say, "Pike, she's over. This is getting nuts."

"Find another way to parallel. Keep on him. Through satellite imagery he's got about three ways to go."

Veep said, "Cops are on the move. Knuckles, you should see them in ten seconds."

"I got 'em, I got 'em, but they have the same problem I do."

Jennifer kept running, her target now two roofs away. She heard, "They just ran into a spice store."

Veep said, "Follow them. They know this place a hell of a lot better than us. There's probably a cut-through."

Knuckles said, "Good idea."

She saw her target leap up to an iron bar and swing himself sideways, dropping to a roof forty feet lower on the hill. She leapt across to the next roof, saying, "He's coming down. He's no longer moving parallel to the ridgeline. He's traveling down the hill toward the plaza."

She ran forward to the edge and said, "I can see the plaza and the Kasbah. He's almost to you." She jumped, grabbing the same iron bar he'd used, and swung herself sideways, using the momentum to generate centrifugal force. She released, falling to the lower roof and hitting hard. She rolled upright, and the target was gone.

44

In the plaza, sitting next to Retro working a tablet, I heard, "I lost him. He's off the roof."

Knuckles said, "I have him, I say again, I have him. We punched into another alley, and he dropped right in front of me. He's in between me and the cops. They're running like a bat out of hell, but they don't know he's behind them."

I looked at the tablet, seeing the position of his phone no more than thirty seconds out, and said, "Okay, okay, everyone slow it down. He's going to try the nonchalant route. Knuckles, keep on him. When he gets to the plaza, it will be critical. I need a direction. Veep, where are you?"

"Still up high."

"Get your ass down here. Stage at the Kasbah. Jennifer, you get off and go west, near the entrance to the plaza. Retro and I will stage the vehicle."

I saw the police twenty meters away, busting out of an alley in between two cafés, running together and looking left and right at the locals and tourists in the paved area, the people gathered in the afternoon sun mildly surprised at the activity. I said, "I got eyes on the police. Let him escape."

I heard, "Pike, Koko, I'm in the square at your three o'clock."

She was maybe forty meters away, casually strolling to

the Kasbah, but looking like she'd just rolled down a hill, her hair all over the place and sweat running off her face.

I couldn't resist. "Holy shit, Koko, did that guy smoke you?"

She said, "Oh yeah. He did."

Veep said, "I'm here. At your ten o'clock."

I said, "Okay, get in the rear SUV. Start it up and wait. Knuckles, status?"

"He's hanging back. Letting them go."

"Roger that. Everyone take a breath and let it play out."

I watched the police, now separating and starting to search, questioning people on the square. They would realize soon that he hadn't come running through here and would know he was still trapped in the old town. Two more police cars arrived, spilling out men.

I said, "Knuckles, they're searching hard, and he's boxed in. He's going to get captured if he hangs around."

"What do you want me to do, go tell him?"

And then I had a stroke of genius. "Yeah. Yeah, I think so. Tell him you're from Frank and Jalal and that you've got a vehicle for him. Get him across the square and into my SUV."

"Will they see him crossing the plaza?"

"They might, but it's pretty crowded, and we can head straight out. By the time they get to their cars, we'll be gone."

"It's a single highway. Gone where?"

"Gone to the first intersection, the one going up the mountain next to the gate of the city. The road that goes into the national forest. Break, break, Veep and Jennifer, stage there. We'll transload the package and keep going."

"Then what?"

"You guys head back to the hotel, and we'll meet you there."

I saw Jennifer start moving across the square and heard, "What if you're arrested?"

"For what? Driving the same type of Toyota everyone else does?"

Knuckles said, "This is starting to sound like Madrid."

I saw Veep moving to the vehicle and said, "Yeah, and that worked out fine."

Jennifer said, "I'm going to ask you later for your definition of *fine*."

Knuckles said, "I'm moving to him now."

Off the net, Retro said, "What do you want me to do?"

"Nothing. Stand by here, monitoring the net. We'll all have our phone beacons on. Just keep track in case something goes wrong."

He laughed and said, "Like it's going to?"

I scowled at him and said, "Give me the keys."

He did, and Knuckles came back, "Okay, I've talked to him."

I broke across the square to our Land Cruiser, saying, "How'd that go?"

"He's eye-popping scared. We're coming. He's a believer. Get the car ready."

I saw Jennifer and Veep already on the road. I jumped in the seat and fired mine up.

Knuckles said, "We're out. Where are you?"

I saw them and said, "Look to your eleven o'clock."

"Got it. On the way."

Retro said, "Hold up, hold up, the cops are clustered together like they're quitting. Might not be necessary."

"Too late. We're in the open."

I said, "Get him across."

They made it halfway before Retro said, "They've spotted you."

I said, "Make his ass run."

Knuckles practically carried the skinny man to my vehicle, the target's eyes bulging out of his head in fear. I heard the cops start shouting and leaned over the seat, throwing the door open. Knuckles bodily shoved our target inside, then jumped in behind him, shouting, "Go, go!"

We took off out of the square, hitting the main highway out of the city. I called and said, "Retro, status?"

I heard the target say, "Who are you guys? How do you know Frank?"

Knuckles said, "Shut the fuck up."

Retro said, "They're loading up. They're coming."

"Time?"

"You got about a two-minute head start."

I went screaming around a corner, threading through the new city, and hit open highway, goosing the gas pedal. I said, "Snyder, we're going to pass you to another car and then keep going, pulling the cops with us."

He nodded, then said, "Who's paying for this? How did you know they'd find me?"

I said, "Jalal."

He didn't look convinced, and I said, "Come on. You didn't think you were the only American working for him, did you? We have to stick together."

He nodded, soaking it all in as he was rocked back and forth from the driving. We hit the outer gate and I reversed completely onto the switchback, jerking up the parking brake and causing the wheels to lock up into a slide, the tires smoking and the vehicle skipping into the turn. I saw our other vehicle and slammed on the brakes.

I said, "Get the fuck out."

He hesitated, and Knuckles kicked the door open, saying, "Get out, get out, get out." He rolled onto the gravel, and Veep jerked him upright. I withdrew my Glock, handing it to Knuckles. I said, "Give Veep our weapons."

He looked at me quizzically, and I said, "Just in case . . ."

He shook his head and passed our weapons out the window. I glanced at Jennifer behind the wheel of the other vehicle. She pursed her lips and shook her head, her face still grimy. I grinned and gunned the engine, swinging the vehicle around and blasting back onto the road.

We raced down it for about a quarter of a mile, then hit the checkpoint we'd seen on the way in, but this time, it was active, with two trucks blocking the road. We slowed to a stop, and I rolled down the window, waiting on one of the uniformed members to approach.

None of them did; instead they pointed FN FAL rifles at us from across the hood. I said, "This doesn't look good."

Knuckles jabbed a finger to the rear of the trucks, where a Mercedes was tucked, the door opening. A man exited, walking toward us. Knuckles said, "No, that definitely doesn't look good."

The man waved his hand, and the rifles lowered. A tall guy of about six feet, dressed in an impeccable suit, he approached me, and I saw a thin face and the ubiquitous Saddam Hussein mustache, then noticed a small discoloration on his forehead, like a bruise.

In flawless, unaccented English, he said, "Where is Snyder?"

I said, "I have no idea what you're talking about. We're just tourists."

He shook his head and said, "Okay, license and registration, please."

Shocked that he'd ask for something like I was on a

highway in California, I immediately complied. He saw me reaching for the glove box and said, "That was a joke."

Confused, I leaned back, saying, "What have we done?"

He said, "I don't know, but I'm going to find out."

An unmarked panel van pulled up. He rattled off some Arabic to the men around him. I glanced at Knuckles, saying, "Sir, we're just tourists."

He said, "Yes. Yes, of course. Get out of the truck. And for God's sake, whatever you do, keep your hands in view. I really want to talk to you, but not at the expense of my life."

45

Johan tossed his final package on the bed, next to the cell phone he'd taken off of the dead man in Gibraltar. It was at 2 percent, and about to die.

Fuck. He'd forgotten to purchase a charger when he'd bought the scanner, and now he might not have enough time to get there and back. Once it went dead, the phone would ask for the passcode after charging before allowing anything else to happen. The Touch ID would be worthless.

He grabbed his hotel key card, preparing to once again go to the Fnac electronics store off of Plaza Puerta del Sol, when he had an inspiration. He dialed housekeeping, asking for lost and found. When it connected, he said, "I'm afraid I've left my iPhone charger at my last hotel."

The dimwit on the other end said, "We wouldn't have it here at our lost and found, sir."

Johan rolled his eyes and said, "Yes, I realize that. I'm wondering if I could borrow one from your lost and found. One that's been there for a spell?"

The bellman hesitated a moment, then said, "Let me ask my manager." A minute later, he came on and said, "I'll send it up. Just return it before you check out."

Johan thanked him, then began unpacking the equipment he'd purchased, courtesy of a wire transfer from Dexter. First, a digital flatbed scanner/printer combination. Next, a laptop computer and digital imaging software. Finally, a collection of art supplies: latex glue, graphite powder, a roll of clear packing tape, squares of double-stick tape, and plastic, transparent overhead projection slides for the printer.

He heard a knock on the door and cracked it open, preventing the bellman from seeing inside the room. He was handed the charger and tipped the man ten euros in return, guaranteeing the charger would be forgotten.

He closed the door and plugged in the phone, seeing the charging icon appear. It would take at least an hour, but Johan didn't mind. He had plenty of work in front of him.

He placed four pieces of double-sided tape directly under the lamp on the glass table next to his bed, then slit open the first Ziploc bag containing a section of wax paper with a thumbprint. Using tweezers, he pulled it out and placed it on the first section of tape, then repeated the action with the other Ziploc bags until he had four sections stuck to the end table.

He then used the graphite powder and a brush to dust each of the thumbprints, the fat and sweat left behind causing the graphite to reveal the print. He gently blew away the stray graphite, then cut a five-inch strip of the packing tape. Ever so slowly, knowing this step was crucial, he lowered the tape over the graphite, picking up each print, one by one.

Once that was complete, he placed the sections of tape on the flatbed scanner, sticky side down, in essence gluing them in place.

He booted up the computer, connected to the scanner via Bluetooth, and scanned the image at 2,400 dpi, the highest resolution available. When it came through, he smiled. The image was clearer than the images he'd produced when he'd learned the technique in training. A result of the march of technology. Even so, he brought up the graphics suite and digitally enhanced each one, sharpening the ridges and whorls of the prints. Once he was satisfied, he reversed the prints, making them into negative images.

He returned to the printer, removing the tape and cleaning from the glass the residue of graphite and adhesive. He inserted a plastic transparency slide, then used the thickest toner setting available. When the slide came out, it looked like an overhead transparency from an FBI briefing. It had the fingerprints on it in reverse, but the slide wasn't actually flat. The toner had been applied on top of the plastic, creating a tiny mold, which was why he'd used the greatest resolution. More toner meant more realism for the mold.

He gingerly set the sheet next to the printer, then applied the latex glue over each print, building two layers. He left it to dry, checking the phone. Almost 70 percent. Good enough for government work.

Ten minutes later, he peeled the first piece of latex glue off of the transparency. He used an X-Acto knife to trim the edges, then stuck it on his thumb. He powered up the phone, getting the lock screen. He breathed on the mold to give it a little bit of "human" moisture for the sensor to work through, then applied it to the Touch ID. The lock screen jiggled left and right, telling him it wasn't a match. He adjusted and tried again, getting the same result. He gave up after five attempts, moving to the next latex mold.

Thirty minutes later, on the second-to-last print, the phone magically unlocked, surprising the hell out of him. In truth, he had started this as nothing more than a time killer while he waited on his visa application to be approved for Morocco. He'd given it about a 5 percent chance that he'd have the right print. There were just too many variables in play, but it looked as though 5 percent was all he needed.

He quickly went to the phone settings, bringing up the Touch ID interface, intending to add his fingerprint. The phone asked for his passcode. He cursed, knowing he was now stonewalled. He had the ability to turn off the autolock, but that was a catch-22. Without the screen locking, it would drain the power at an exponential rate, forcing him to plug the phone in three or four times a day to prevent it from dying and locking him out completely. His only other option was carrying around the dummy print everywhere he went.

He spent the next hour inspecting the phone, finding some loose information in text messaging, but most appeared to be for the target's actual work. He found an app called Wickr, something he'd never heard of. He Googled and discovered it was an end-to-end encrypted messaging platform, with a self-destruct feature for specified messages. The homepage caused him to chuckle because of a statement hailing the application as empowering democracy. He was fairly sure the man he'd killed wasn't using it for anything good.

He opened the app and hit a password. *Just perfect.* He attempted to open the mail app and ran aground again with a password screen. He was thinking about typing in something like JihadJohnny when his own cell phone buzzed. He picked it up, seeing it was Dexter. He answered pleasantly, remembering the threats from his last conversation. Since then, sitting around his hotel room, he'd seen the news about a sinister connection to Gibraltar, and he assumed that Dexter had done what he'd asked. Maybe he had been too hard on the guy.

"Hey, boss. What's up?"

"I see you got the wire transfer."

"Yep. Already used it, and it was money well spent. I got into the guy's cell phone. Hey, do you have any contacts with IT forensic guys? The hardest part about cracking an iPhone is actually getting past the lock screen. I've done that, but I have some programs that have passwords. You know anyone who can bypass them?"

"I'm not sure. What are you trying to do?"

"Read his email. Check a messaging app. Things like that."

"I don't know of anyone in the private sector, but I might be able to locate someone in the government."

Johan chuckled and said, "You really think I'd hand this phone over to the government? It would directly tie me to the dead guy. By the way, I see you got that information out. The news is talking about a—quote—possible connection to Gibraltar—unquote. I'm assuming that was you."

There was a pause; then Dexter said, "Yes, yes. I told you I'd get it done."

"Well, did they find anything out? Did they make any connections?"

"I . . . I don't know. I'm not read on to the investigation or anything. It's not like I'm at the Pentagon."

"So you don't know if they're exploring leads in Morocco?"

"I'm sure they are. There's no reason for you to continue. They're very good at this sort of thing."

Johan gave a mirthless laugh, saying, "Yeah. I've seen how that works. Where does my visa stand?"

"Well . . . that's why I called. It's available tomorrow. You just need to show your credentials with Icarus and your H-1B visa. I got it done, tying you to the armorer on the movie set, but there's really no reason to go now. You saw they've made the connection."

"I saw some reporter stating there *might* be a connection. What I *know* is that attacks like this aren't a one-off. There's a planner behind it, and he'll just keep on planning for the next one. If you don't wipe out the queen, the nest keeps working."

"How are you going to do that? You're just a single man."

"I have an address in Fez. I'll just go check it out. If it leads to something, it leads to something. If not, I'll come home. Where are my tickets?"

"I'll email them to you. They're vouchers you can redeem for any flight."

"Okay, thanks. And the weapon?"

"That's a little bit harder. I'm in contact with my guy, but he can't get it free. It's a controlled item."

Johan let the first bit of aggravation come through. "Dexter, we talked about this. Shit, you just told me I'm ostensibly going there to help him. How hard can this be?"

"I know, I know. He's got a shoot in Fez for something. Using the medina. I think I can do it then. I'll have to send you coordinating instructions."

"Perfect. I also want the bank account information as well. The one that led me to Gibraltar."

Johan heard nothing for a moment, the pause so long he said, "Dexter? You there?"

"Why do you want that information?"

"Because it might provide another thread. I can cross-check accounts, discover linkages, maybe find something in Fez that will help me."

"The file's too big to send over email. It's huge."

"So create a file-sharing account. Dropbox or something. I don't need the entire Panama collection. Just the ones that are tied into that account. The ones with your name on them. Come on, boss, why are you jerking me around?"

"Because you're putting my company in jeopardy! That's why!"

Johan heard something more. "Is that all you fucking care about? Have you seen the dead in Houston? Do you want to be responsible for the next attack?"

"Why are you saying that? Why do you keep *accusing* me? I have *nothing* to do with this."

As before, the vociferousness of the response raised Johan's fine-tuned antenna for bullshit. He'd lived in a world of duplicitous lies for so long, he could no longer determine whether Dexter was truly concerned about his business—or whether he was worried about something else.

Either way, Johan needed Dexter on board, if only for the funding. He said, "I wasn't implying you did. I'm saying you have the means to prevent it. It's why you sent me to Granada, isn't it? It wasn't only about the money, was it?"

Johan waited a moment, growing suspicious yet again. He repeated, "*Was* it?"

Dexter said, "Okay . . . Okay. I'll do it. Are you planning on flying tomorrow?"

"If I can get the visa in time to catch a flight. If not, I'll wait another day."

"Keep me informed of what you find."

"So you can feed the beast? Or protect your interests?"

"Both."

Johan hung up, once again wondering if his boss wasn't hiding something. For the first time, wondering if Dexter had said a word to anyone about Granada.

He toyed with the terrorist's phone a little bit longer, but his heart wasn't in it. He kept returning to the central question, which wasn't who was doing the attacks, but why he even gave a shit.

But he knew why. At the center of it was a village in Africa. And a lot of dead children.

46

Jalal hoped the cab driver knew where the Blue Gate to the medina Fez-el-Bali was located, because he sure didn't. He'd never been in Fez before, and, even as a Moroccan native, he felt out of place. He was used to the bustle and hum of the city, with the usual honking traffic and pedestrians who seemed to believe they were invincible, but it was new in other ways. Unlike his hometown of Chefchaouen, this city had modern steel and glass competing with buildings created eons ago.

And the tourists were everywhere. It seemed there were more foreigners than Moroccans here.

His driver seemed to want to talk, acting as a free tour guide, pointing out sights and explaining what they were. He droned on and on, but Jalal paid little attention. He was more worried about finding his cousins inside the medina. A walled city, it had been around since the ninth century and was the oldest living medieval habitat. More than 150,000 people called it home, and it was composed of 9,400 alleys, some barely two feet wide, others dead ends. It was a labyrinth that now stood as a mix of tourist attraction and a living, breathing piece of Moroccan life, and it confounded visitors because there were no detailed maps of the area. You either knew the terrain, or you had a guide who did. Wandering inside alone was asking to get lost.

Yes, there were some tourist prints, and Jalal had one,

but from what his cousins had said, they were all designed to focus the traveler on the specific shopping areas. Spices, copper, silver, leather goods, and the like. Which, given that the four men he was meeting were working in the tannery, should help.

At the very least, he could talk like a local. And because he looked the part, wearing a T-shirt, torn jeans, and running shoes, there was little chance he'd be given bad directions by someone looking to pull a prank on a European.

The taxi pulled into a cul-de-sac and was immediately stymied by a myriad of double-decker vans parked around a platform with elevated lights and cameras. The area in front of the platform was roped off, with a man in US camouflage, body armor, and an assault rifle arguing with a local woman about something. The driver pulled around the ropes, generating shouts from the men on the platform.

Jalal said, "What is this?"

The driver ignored the shouting, saying, "Movie. They're making a film about Iraq." He waved his hand and said, "This is supposed to be Baghdad," then began laughing.

Jalal said, "So, where do I go?"

The cabby pointed across the square to a stone gate, the opening shaped like a minaret and the outsides sprinkled with indigo tile. He said, "That's the Blue Gate. Entrance to the medina."

Jalal paid him, saying, "Wish me luck."

The cabby laughed and said, "You'll need it!" Jalal exited, hearing him bark back at a man on the platform before wheeling his cab away, leaving the plaza.

Jalal shouldered his rucksack and wove around the cameras and lighting. Within seconds, he'd escaped the chaos of the cul-de-sac only to hit the chaos of the medina.

He fought through the swirling mass of humanity—through donkeys carrying propane, gaggles of women in hijabs, and Europeans wearing sun hats and Teva sandals. It was a claustrophobic smorgasbord of activity that dwarfed his youth in Chefchaouen.

The lanes in the medina went from arm's width to large enough for a car, as if a child had built the place by squeezing out mud from his fingers, laying out the paths without thought.

He continued to the west, not really attempting to read the map, because the tannery was one of the most famous places inside. He passed a meat market, one stall having the newly severed head of a camel hanging to show the freshness of the product, then walked by a sign proclaiming Wi-Fi for an Internet café, the past and future fighting for supremacy, much like in Islam itself.

Eventually, after thirty minutes of weaving through the crowds, he inadvertently punched out of the medina, finding himself next to a canal, the walls made of fresh concrete. Somehow, he'd missed the tannery.

He reentered, and for the first time, asked for directions. In short order, he was walking down an alley with a distinct odor, like socks worn for days. Or dead things. From his conversations with his cousins, he knew he was close. He passed a sign proclaiming TANNERIE CHOUARA with verbiage in French and English. He took the next set of narrow stairs to his right.

He reached the top and saw hundreds of leather purses, vests, and jackets, all in various multicolored hues. A man approached, thinking he was a customer, and immediately began a hard sell in English.

In Arabic, Jalal said, "I'm not here to shop. Sorry. I'm

here to visit my cousins." He gave their names and the man said, "Yes, yes. They are working right now. Do they know you're coming?"

"Yes, but they didn't know the time. I was supposed to be here yesterday, meeting them at their house."

The man smiled and said, "Follow me." He walked up another set of narrow stairs, reaching a balcony. Before exiting, he pulled a sprig of mint off of a shelf and held it out. Jalal said, "What's that?"

"Put it under your nose for the odor. Those who come for the first time might want it."

Jalal shook his head, and they stepped out into the sun. Into what looked like a scene from Dante's *Inferno*. Looking over a balcony into a pit of hell, he saw raw hides stippled with fat draping over rails and tanks of caustic chemicals, each having a man knee-deep in the solution, stepping and sloshing about, washing or dying the leather. Other men were scraping the sheets of skin of impurities or stretching the hides out for drying. Overshadowing it all was a stench like the back side of death, a rotting animal odor cloaking the entire area, making Jalal's stomach flip. He smiled at the man next to him but wished he'd taken the mint.

Jalal looked about the facility, then spotted Wasim, waist-deep in filth and chemicals. He shouted his name, and Wasim looked up, breaking into a smile. He held up a finger, then left the tank, washing his legs and feet with a hose of dirty water.

He came running upstairs and hugged Jalal, saying, "What happened? You were supposed to be here last night."

Jalal said, "Nothing. Just had some problems getting on the road."

Wasim said, "I was worried. I thought you'd changed your mind. We are ready."

Jalal flicked his eyes to the salesman and said, "We can talk about this later. Not here."

Wasim caught the look and immediately backed off. He said, "Yes. Of course."

Jalal didn't question what Wasim meant by *We are ready.* Didn't plumb the depths of someone so willing to give his life in the pursuit of otherworldly goals. He understood it, of course, having been steeped in the value of jihad, but he himself would never take that step. He respected it, but a part of him wondered if he could hold the same commitment.

He would never tell Wasim this, but he took pleasure in sending them to their deaths. He was the architect. He was the controller of destruction, just like the prophet had been. Others would die—for *him*—and it was intoxicating.

47

Tapping his feet in the hallway of the West Wing lobby, Kurt Hale was growing impatient. George Wolffe said, "I know that look. Storming down the hall without a security badge isn't going to win you any friends. And you need some friends at this point."

Kurt said, "Yeah, okay, but if I find out that Alexander Palmer is making us cool our heels out here as some sort of power play, I'm going to throat punch him."

George heard someone coming down the hall; then Palmer turned the corner. "Speak of the devil."

Palmer handed them both badges with a bright red *V*, indicating visitor. He said, "Kurt, I hope this is important, because President Hannister has a busy calendar."

They started walking and Kurt said, "It is. I've had to make some decisions, and I need to let him know."

Palmer snapped his head to Kurt and said, "Don't tell me you've initiated some operation without sanction of the Oversight Council."

"Not exactly, but I had to move some personnel, and I need Kerry's assistance. He's here, right?"

Palmer opened the door to the Oval Office and said, "Yeah, he's here, but don't expect a lot of love. You jerked him out of something hot as well."

Kurt walked in first, followed by the other two. At the Resolute desk, Hannister heard the door and lowered his glasses. He said, "Kurt, I don't have a lot of time. What's up?"

Kurt shook hands with Kerry Bostwick, then the president. He said, "Sir, the operation in Chefchaouen was only partially successful. We captured the target, and he's talking. We have a lead on Jalal al-Khattabi in Fez through some relatives of his. They work at the tannery in the medina, and the target firmly believes that they'll know where Jalal is and what he's up to."

"So you want Omega authority to go after them? You know I can't do that unilaterally. Is this time sensitive? Are we looking at an imminent threat?"

"Yes, sir, I do think there is an imminent threat, but I'm not asking for unilateral Omega without Oversight Council approval. As I said, the operation was only partially successful."

He paused for a minute, not even wanting to say the words. But he did. "Pike and Knuckles were arrested."

He saw the collected group begin to wind up with questions, and he held up a hand, saying, "It's not that bad. The target was being chased by the police, presumably for his drug activities, and Pike managed to snatch him from right under their noses. In the process of securing the target he was arrested, but it's all circumstantial, based on nothing more than the fact that his vehicle looked like the one that had left the scene. The biggest piece of evidence—the target—is missing. They have nothing else, the Grolier Recovery Services cover is very solid in that region due to the historic nature of the area, and both Pike and Knuckles have plenty of training in SERE activities."

"So why the meeting?"

"Two reasons: One, because I need him back in play. I'm

sure there's another hit coming. Maybe more than one, and Pike's on the thread. The length of time it will take to resolve this on their own leaves the team pretty much non–mission capable, and putting in a new team will cause us to lose ground."

Palmer said, "Just order them to continue the mission without Pike and Knuckles."

"Yeah, I could do that, for the active-duty guys, but Jennifer won't. No way. It'll split what's left of the team."

"Tell me again why we put up with this civilian shit? Tell me why we don't just use active-duty folks?"

Kurt glared at him and said, "Because they get results. More than anyone else, and part of that is predicated on their loyalty to each other."

President Hannister waved his hand, interrupting the exchange. He said, "And point two of why you wanted this meeting?"

Kurt let his anger subside, focusing on what was important. He said, "Because Pike and Knuckles have been taken to Casablanca. We tracked the beacons embedded in their phones, and they're currently being held at the headquarters for DGST."

Palmer said, "DGST? What the hell is that?"

Kerry said, "Direction Générale de la Surveillance du Territoire. It's their version of the FBI, except it doesn't really care about human rights. It's more of a secret police."

President Hannister said, "So why are the Taskforce Operators being held by them? Are they responsible for drug interdiction?"

Kurt said, "No, which is why I'm here. They deal with terrorism and state security, and Pike getting pulled into them, for whatever reason, gives us an edge."

Hannister said, "How?"

Kurt pointed at Kerry and said, "Because the CIA deals with them on a daily basis. Shit, after the attacks in France and Belgium, *everyone* deals with them on a daily basis. They have the pulse of the Moroccan extremists."

A suspicious look on his face, Kerry said, "How's that help?"

"Remember Carly Ramirez?"

"Yeah. You stole her from me."

"I prefer to think she chose a different career path, but anyway, she's still on the CIA books. I want to use her as a CIA liaison. Get her into DGST headquarters and cause a little smoke about who they have, get them to release Pike and Knuckles as a gesture of mutual cooperation, but that'll depend on leveraging the station there. Technically, she's still a CIA asset."

"What are you talking about? I can't have her walk into the chief of station in Morocco and demand help. The first thing he'll ask is why he wasn't read on to a covert action on his soil. The next thing he'll ask is what section of the agency the two knuckleheads who were arrested work for. And I can't defend either one."

"Yeah, you can. Don't paint it as an operation. He doesn't need to know what caused the arrest. Paint it as a transit."

"Even a transit would be included in cable traffic. He'll be livid that someone entered his domain and he wasn't informed. It's why we have a chief. You don't understand the significance."

"Yes, I do, and no, he won't. He'll be pissed, but he'll understand he can't be read on to every single covert action around the globe, and if some crew had to transit Morocco on a mission, then it just happened, and now you're going to ask for his help."

"What, specifically, are you thinking?"

George Wolffe, a CIA paramilitary officer who'd done more than his fair share of operations just like this, stepped into the breach. "Simple, sir. Carly shows up at his doorstep and asks for his help with DGST, using your weight as the director. She tells him a bullshit story, then endures his wrath for a few minutes. He sends a cable back to the mission center for Africa or the Near East—whoever's controlling Morocco nowadays—bitching about being left outside the loop, they tell him to comply, and he gets in touch with his contacts in DGST. Then she gets them out as CIA assets."

Aggravated at an old CIA hand short-circuiting his excuses, Kerry said, "And then what? They're going to continue the mission in Fez, right? How can I do that without including the CIA?"

Kurt nodded and said, "Actually, I *want* to include them, at least on the face of it. I think the DGST will help us find these assholes. It's just a hunch, but I believe that they're involved here for the same reasons we are. They're on a thread of terrorism, even if they don't know what it is. There's no other reason for a simple drug bust to end up in their hands. Let Pike develop the situation. Let him figure it out, but get him out of their custody under CIA auspices."

"So you're saying we're going to read on the chief of station to the Taskforce?"

"No. Come on. Don't tell me you can't build a bodyguard of lies around Pike. Jesus, do you actually work for the CIA, or do you just pretend to? Give the chief of station a reason to feel important, then cut him free."

Kerry remained silent. President Hannister said, "Can you do that?"

Kerry nodded, then said, "I can do it, but I can't contain the fallout if it goes wrong. I can't drag in the CIA after the fact. All of you need to be aware of that. If you include the chief of station, you open the operation to investigation after the fact. If this blows up, I'm not going to have the chief of station interrogated on the Hill by the House and Senate intel committees on a covert action for which they never got a finding."

Kurt said, "Don't worry about that. Just get Pike out. Nobody's asking you to betray your men."

Alexander Palmer said, "How soon can you get Carly there?"

"She'll be there in about two hours. I put her on a flight as soon as I heard about Pike and Knuckles."

President Hannister said, "You did what?"

Kurt raised his hands in surrender, saying, "You wanted the black magic, sir. I'm just rubbing the bottle."

48

Jalal took another breath of the fetid tannery air, wondering if the stench was penetrating his skin. He said, "How can you stand working here?"

Wasim glanced at the salesman and said, "You get used to it."

Jalal nodded and said, "We'll talk tonight. Can I get a key to your apartment? I'll meet you there."

Wasim said, "Yes, of course. You know how to get there?"

Jalal laughed and said, "I barely made it here."

Wasim pulled out a key and said, "Tell a cab to take you to the old Jewish quarter, next to the royal palace. If they don't know that, tell them Fes Mellah. You'll get dropped off at the front of the palace."

Jalal took the key, saying, "And?"

Wasim explained how to get to the apartment, the instructions a convoluted mess of turns. Jalal had him write the directions on a piece of paper. When he was done, Jalal asked, "Is this going to be like finding you in the medina?"

Wasim laughed and said, "Yes, it might be, but the people there are friendly. The neighborhood is all like us. Families struggling to survive."

Wasim left him, and Jalal watched until he began to work again, wondering what on earth would make any man willingly do such labor. Jalal thanked the salesman, then retraced his path to the movie set. He flagged a cab and gave the cabby the Fes Mellah address. Fifteen minutes later, the cab stopped on a street called rue Bou Ksissat.

On his left was the royal palace of the monarch of Morocco. On his right was a decrepit maze of buildings long past their prime. Initially the quarter for the Jewish faith in Morocco, it had existed since the fifteenth century. The area was now held up to the tourists as the integration of the faiths in Morocco, omitting the fact that the reason the Jews lived there was because they were forced to, sometimes behind walls. Even so, it had once been the prosperous section of the city, where one went to buy gold, diamonds, silk, or other precious items, and had valiantly tried to hold on to that reputation through the years, but instead had witnessed a slow decline, right up until the state of Israel was created.

Once that happened, the majority of Jews in the country emigrated, with the Arabs of Morocco encouraging them in not so subtle terms to get the hell out.

Now the area was a rotting ghetto of decrepit wood and draining sewers, with the modern day grafted onto the past through electrical lines draped between windows and television dishes hanging off carved wooden balconies that should have been treated as precious museum pieces.

Jalal followed Wasim's directions, hitting a market selling everything from homemade pharmaceutical remedies to bridal fashions, the people shopping in their own cloistered world. He took a covered alley that reminded him of a tunnel, stooping not to hit his head and searching each door he passed. He went by a narrow slice cut into the alley and saw four boys sitting on the ground, playing video games in a pay-for-play cave, a cheap desk in front with a teenager willing to take money.

He kept going, searching each steel door, finding the

one that matched the key at the end of the alley, a bare lightbulb providing illumination. He unlocked it, feeling as if he were back in Tangier. Once again, the key worked. He entered, finding a squalid two-bedroom place, with mattresses on the floor, a small kitchen consisting of a table and a camping stove, and a closet with a hole in the floor for a toilet, a bucket of water next to it.

He set his bag down, satisfied.

He initiated the Wickr application on his cell phone, updating the Sheik.

In Fez. The men are ready. When will we receive the passports?

He waited for a minute, then saw a bubble.

Another day or two. They're coming in a diplomatic pouch to the king's palace next door to my father's hotel.

What about the plans in America?

Good. I have the safe house in Norfolk. Still waiting on the money transfer for the purchase.

I need them when I arrive. I can't do the mission without the assets.

The response wasn't something Jalal wanted to hear. **It's almost easier to get explosives than what you want. At least there we can hide what is in the boxes. We can't buy three of what you want from an offshore account and then have them delivered to a house in Norfolk that nobody's in. You can buy them when you get there.**

Aggravated, Jalal said, **Are you crazy?**

What? Buy them with the money I send.

HOW IS THAT GOING TO LOOK? FOUR STRANGE ARABS BUYING THINGS? DO YOU NOT REMEMBER THE PLANES OPERATION?

Jalal saw, **What do you suggest?**

Get them delivered to the safe house before we arrive.

Jalal waited, and nothing came back. He wondered if the Sheik was discussing the problem with someone else. Finally, a bubble appeared with a message on the way.

Okay. I can do that, but you will have to receive them. I have nobody there.

Fine, as long as they show up the day we arrive.

Won't be that quick. I can't initiate until you confirm you're in the house.

Jalal became aggravated again, wondering if the Saudis understood what was at stake. He banged out the next message, pounding each key harder than necessary. **We will only have a short span of time before someone starts questioning why four foreign males have moved in. America hates us now. We can't live in a safe house without someone eventually calling the police.**

What is your point?

We need to train. We've never done this before. We can't just get the vehicles and execute.

So get some rentals. Train with them.

Jalal considered the recommendation, wanting to push back, but it made sense, if only because it cut the time down. He typed, **That is the same risk. But less of one. Are you sure the explosives are in place?**

Yes. Are you sure you can wire them?

Of course.

Good. Know that everything is a risk, but Allah always finds a way. Just like the Planes Operation. Allah is with you.

Jalal closed the app without responding. He believed in the mission but had never trusted Tariq or his father. They never contributed anything but money, never sacrificed anything beyond a bank account.

And then he remembered Wasim, feeling the depth of his hypocrisy. He heard the call to prayer echo through the ghetto. Not wanting to risk attending a mosque, he found four rolled prayer rugs neatly tucked in a corner.

He faced east and began praying, searching for salvation.

49

The cell clanged open, and Knuckles was led into the room. They removed his handcuffs, then slammed the door closed. I said, "Well? How was the second one?"

I knew the cell was bugged with both cameras and microphones, because it was the only reason they would put us together in the same room—trying to get us to maybe spill some secrets when we thought we were safe. Knuckles knew it as well, so he wouldn't give anything up.

He said, "About the same. They keep asking what we're doing here. I tried to explain Grolier's mission, but they don't want to listen. They keep asking about that American named Snyder McDermott."

I said, "What the hell is this all about? Did you tell them we want to talk to our embassy?"

He hid a smirk, then said in an anxious tone, "Yes! They claimed that they have no responsibility to contact the embassy at all."

He put his head in his hands for effect and said, "I can't believe this is happening. It's like *Midnight Express* or something. They're going to kill us." He looked at me plaintively, as if he believed our life hung in the balance, and I said, "Hang in there. Grolier Recovery Services won't let us down. We've done nothing wrong."

In Chefchaouen, we'd been ripped out of our Land Cruiser, splayed on the ground, and searched. They'd found nothing suspicious to tie us to the mysterious Mr. McDermott, which didn't keep us from being loaded into the van. They'd found only our passports, the hotel key card for the room we'd rented to conduct surveillance—which was not the hotel that had our kit—and business cards for Grolier Recovery Services.

We'd bounced down the road for a good thirty minutes before the suit-wearing guy had turned from his tablet and said, "Grolier Recovery Services. So you men know something about history."

Because I was a hell of a lot smarter than some third-string Moroccan trying to tie me to a drug deal, instead of saying, *I want to contact my embassy immediately,* I said, "Yes. We're just here to look at the historical sites surrounding Chefchaouen."

I was taking a risk and running against what I'd been taught: Don't think you can outsmart the interrogator. If you have something to hide, just shut the hell up.

But I was pretty sure he didn't believe we were drug dealers, especially after looking at our business on the web.

I said, "You have a remarkable grasp of the English language. I could have used you yesterday."

He laughed and said, "My father was a diplomat. I spent my formative years first in Canada, then in Washington, DC. What about you?"

I said, "What do you mean?"

"Who are you? You aren't like Snyder." He waved a hand at Knuckles and said, "Neither one of you are like Snyder. It worries me."

I said, "Who is this Snyder you keep asking about?"

He rubbed his face and said, "Truly, to build trust, you must exhibit trust."

I said, "You've kidnapped us in the back of a van. What trust do you speak of?"

He was very smooth. Completely relaxed. He said, "Okay, I will play your game. We have a six-hour drive to Casablanca, so let's talk. Snyder is a major conduit of hashish out of this country. But he's American, which makes it easy for me to arrest him. I can't do the same with the hashish farmers here. They have to make a living, and interfering with them would incite the population. Your friend, on the other hand, gives me the ability to show I'm hunting drug runners while leaving the locals alone. Which, as you Americans say, means you're shit out of luck."

I said, "Look, we have no clue about any drugs. We came here for the historical sites."

He ignored my words and said, "We have a problem with drug running into Europe, and it's not because of the drugs. It's because of where the money from the drugs goes. Snyder can't possibly do what he does without Moroccan help. And that is where you come in. I want that man."

I said, "How in the hell would I know? I just told you why we're here."

"You helped Snyder escape."

"We did *no such thing*. You stopped us at a roadblock for no reason. You are going to be in big trouble with the United States after this."

He repeated his earlier question. "So Grolier Recovery Services facilitates work on archeological sites. Is that what you said?"

"Yes. That's what we do."

"So you know the history of this country?"

"A little."

"Do you know its history of terrorism?"

That one took me aback. I said, "I have no idea what you're talking about. Are you saying I'm a terrorist? Because I drove into your roadblock?"

He tapped his thigh, then looked up, saying, "Yes. That's what I'm saying. Do you know who has you right now? Who owns your life? It's not the local police force. My name is Ahmed al-Raffiki. I represent the Direction Générale de la Surveillance du Territoire. I'm responsible for keeping this country safe. And I think you're responsible for doing something bad."

I heard the words and knew we were in deep trouble. The DGST had some pretty horrible human rights abuses. A state-run secret police, it had gone hog wild after the Casablanca bombings in 1994 and had been supported by the monarch every step of the way. The only thing going for us was that we were Americans, and he apparently wasn't too sure of our guilt.

I said, "We have done nothing wrong, besides driving down a road."

Ahmed glanced out the window, then turned back to me. He said, "History. That's what you deal in, right?"

Now wary, I said, "Yes."

"Do you know the history of what you're doing right now? The deaths you are engendering through your drugs?"

"I keep telling you I don't know what you're talking about, but if it's terrorism, you're looking at the wrong class of people. It's you guys who strap on the vests and kill. *You* are responsible for the deaths. Don't give me that crap about 'Americans are the biggest terrorists.' Look in your own house."

He surprised me. He said, "Yes, I suppose you have a point." He chuckled and said, "We don't get a lot of Catholic suicide bombers over here."

Confused, I said nothing. He said, "I suppose it's all about Islam, isn't that right? Selling hashish isn't helping terrorism at all. You can't be responsible just because you're making a profit. It's the Islam thing."

I said, "I told you, we don't know Snyder. We don't sell hashish. We don't know anything about what you're saying."

His eyes bored into me. He said, "You understand Islam, though, correct?"

I said, "I understand the callus on your head."

The discoloration I'd seen earlier was from placing his forehead on the floor when he prayed. The only people who had it were devoutly religious, to the point that some intentionally created the physical mark to show their devotion. He was a true believer.

He smiled, apparently ahead of me, and said, "Yes. I am devout with my faith. And devout in stopping those who destroy my faith."

I remained quiet. He said, "But you Americans know all about it, don't you?"

I spat out, "Yes. I do. I've lived among Muslims. You want to charge me a *jizya* tax now? Can that get me out of this van?"

He raised an eyebrow and said, "No. That won't help. But I'm intrigued by the fact you even know the term. Where did you hear it? Where have you lived among the faithful?"

"My company has taken me many places. Iraq. Afghanistan. Beirut. Syria. A few other countries."

"So you have seen firsthand what I'm talking about. You understand the reason I have taken you in my van."

"What's that mean?"

"Islam isn't the Islamic State. It isn't the Taliban. It isn't Hamas. It isn't Iraq."

I leaned back and said, "I'm not going to argue about

religion with you. Let's just contact my embassy and sort this out."

He nodded, and said, "Okay. That would be fine. But because we have so much time, let's discuss why you're helping the very people you hate."

I said nothing.

He said, "So, now the cat's got your tongue?"

Truthfully, I was thinking furiously about where this conversation was going, and realized I should just shut the hell up. He was trying to trick me, and he held all the cards.

He said, "Do you know the history of this country? The actual history?"

I remained mute. He said, "Surely, as a company coming here to look at the past, you have done some studies."

He was twisting the knife of my cover, trying to find a seam. *Smart.* I said, "Yes, I understand the French and Spanish colonization. I know the Roman history. Is that what you mean?"

Thank God for Jennifer's history lessons.

He surprised me, saying, "No. I mean the history of modern day."

Now genuinely intrigued, I said, "Maybe? I'm not sure what you mean by 'modern day.'"

He toyed with a thread on his pant leg and said, "It's something you should study, if you want to sell hashish."

And that had been it, for the next four hours of our ride. He didn't say another word. We'd been locked up in DGST headquarters in Casablanca and left to rot. I was sure that Jennifer and Retro had contacted the Taskforce, and all we had to do was remain in our cover, doing one thing: deny, deny, deny.

I'd had one interrogation, which had been pretty light, with a guy in uniform. Then Knuckles had been taken out, and he'd had the same. I was thankful for being an American, because they couldn't make a mistake with us, and I was beginning to think they'd had second thoughts about arresting us. Especially after Knuckles's second interrogation.

When he hadn't come back lumped up, I was pretty sure we were good to go. And then the door to our cell had clanged open, a guard waving me forward.

It was my turn.

50

I was led down a narrow hallway, pristine in its cleanliness, making me wonder how much blood had been mopped up in the past. The guard pushed me against a wall and waved his finger, as if that meant anything to me. He unlocked one of the interrogation cells, then led me in. He handcuffed me to an eyebolt on a table, the door to my back, and left the room.

Same as before.

The door opened behind me, and a man came around the table. It was Ahmed, still dressed in his suit.

This was *not* like before. The first interrogation had been with some jerk in uniform who barely spoke English, and both of Knuckles's interviews had been the same way.

He took a seat in front of me and said, "I hope your stay hasn't been unpleasant."

I said, "No worries. You've been more accommodating than I expected. It's been fine. Except I'd still like to talk to my embassy."

He said, "I think I can make that happen. But first, let's talk about what you refuse to discuss."

I said, "I have nothing to do with hashish! My God. What evidence do you have?"

He said, "No. I want to talk about terrorism."

What?

"I asked you if you knew our history, and you became quiet. I'll ask again."

I said, "I have no fucking idea what you're talking about. What the hell does this have to do with anything?"

He leaned forward and said, "We fight the same thing, America and Morocco. We fight the bastardization of a religion, and it's fueled with money. Money from others."

Something different was happening, and I was off-balance, probably because he wanted me to be. The questions were way off base from what he should have been asking.

I said, "I get it, hashish is funding terrorism. But I have nothing to do with that."

He leaned back and said, "You Americans want our help when it suits you but disparage us when it doesn't. We're the 'good' Islamic country. Aren't we?"

Aggravated, I said, "Yes, I suppose as far as Islamic countries go, you're the 'good one,' but that's a pretty low bar to jump over, don't you think? I want to contact my embassy. Right fucking now."

He leaned back, a look of disgust on his face. He said, "So be it."

He pressed a buzzer, unlocking the door, and a woman walked into my cell. Short, about five three, with black hair that fell just past her shoulders. She turned around, and I was flabbergasted. Carly Ramirez. She was grinning, enjoying the shock.

She was wearing a pantsuit like she'd just come from an office cubicle, but she had a healthy tan that belied her being trapped indoors all day, with a sprinkle of freckles on her face and a little upturned nose that was cute for no damn reason whatsoever.

She said, "I see you're still making friends."

I remained speechless, unsure of what to say.

She said, "Ahmed, thank you for your courtesy. If there's any way to repay it, don't hesitate to ask."

Sticking to the cover, I said, "Are you from the embassy? Finally?"

Carly said, "Yes, it's the embassy, but it's a part of the embassy that Ahmed knows."

Meaning he thought I was CIA.

Ahmed said, "As we agreed, we work together. We stop this together."

She nodded. I said, "What's that about?"

Ahmed looked at me and said, "I'm your new partner, you bigoted asshole."

I looked at Carly, watching a smile leak out. I went back to him and said, "That's not really fair. You have a damn callus on your forehead."

Before he could get too upset, I stuck my hand out and said, "Sorry, it's just me."

He smiled and said, "It's just America."

I took his hand, squeezing a little harder than I had to, meaning I almost broke the bones.

Carly said, "Okay, dick measuring done? Because from what I hear, we have some intel that needs exploring. No rest for the wicked."

I said, "You know more than me. I've been stuck in a cell by this asshole for a couple of days."

Three hours later, I was having dinner at Rick's Café, a suitable location given that we were now planning skullduggery like we were in the movie *Casablanca*. The establishment wasn't from the movie, of course, but it still seemed to fit. There had been no Rick's Café when *Casablanca* was filmed, but a career foreign services officer had taken the idea and reproduced the movie set, right down to a Moroccan piano player named Issam. We were up-stairs, at a balcony/bar area that Carly had reserved for the night, meaning we had the entire room to ourselves. I had to admit, it was a pretty cool place—the best part was that they served actual steaks instead of kebobs made from camel meat. But then again, as Ahmed would gladly tell you, I was a bigot.

I, of course, was still a little pissed at the play that had been done to me. My last "interrogation" had been con-ducted by a man who knew I was innocent. Carly had been outside the door the whole time. It wasn't something I was willing to forgive, mostly because the asshole interrogator was in the restaurant with us.

Honestly, I didn't trust Ahmed. He was an Islamist with a burr on his forehead, and letting him stick his nose into our tent was crazy as far as I was concerned. Kurt had sanctioned it, and I understood working with a liaison, but for me, this was asking for trouble. He be-lieved we were true-blue CIA, so the Taskforce was cov-ered as far as his service was concerned, but he *still* had a seat at the table.

One that we were now sitting around trying to plan our next moves.

Jennifer said, "So, we know that Jalal al-Khattabi has cousins in Fez, and we know he contacted them—"

Knuckles interrupted, saying, "Let's not get ahead of ourselves. We know that Snyder *thinks* he contacted them. Sticking to the facts, all we really know is that Jalal said he had cousins here. And said that he *thought* they'd been in contact. It's not that strong of a thread."

There was a little bit of cross talk, with everyone giv-ing an opinion, and then Ahmed waved his hand, saying, "I can find them."

I said, "Find who?"

"The cousins. I can find them. We can bring them in. Get them to talk."

I glanced at Knuckles, and he shook his head. I said, "No, thanks. You're just an observer here. We really can't be involved with some draconian Gestapo shit, but we understand it's your country, so if you feel like kicking in some doors and using the rack, that's on you. Just understand that we won't be a part of it."

Ahmed slammed his hand on the table, livid. He said, "Do you really believe I'm a torturer because I'm Muslim? Is that where we're at? I'm trying to stop an attack. On *your* soil. Don't think I'm doing this because I give a damn about America. I care about Morocco."

I was startled. It was the first time he'd shown emotion. I said, "Calm down. Can you find out where the cousins live or work? Without using a cattle prod?"

He stared at me for a bit, then became the same calculating man he had been in the interrogation room, saying, "Yes, I can do that. But you have to include me on this. You don't know the culture or the area. *I do.*"

Carly gave me a small wave and a stare. I said, "Okay, okay. Sorry."

Mollified, he leaned back, muttering about Americans.

I said, "So, Ahmed will check his database, and we'll go from there. We'll fly out of here tomorrow at, say, noon? Will that give you enough time to do your research, now that you have a name?"

"Yes. That will work, but I don't have the money for a plane ticket. My government won't pay for that. I think we should drive."

I said, "Don't worry about it. My company has a lease on an aircraft. It's coming to Casablanca right now."

The food was served, and I said, "Okay, it's Miller time. Sorry, Ahmed. It's mint tea time."

He laughed and said, "What makes you think I don't drink alcohol?"

"The damn stamp on your head."

He paused and said, "You really don't like me, do you?"

"It's not a question of 'like.' It's a question of trust. I think you'll help us because you have to, but you'll make sure attacks like this occur in the future. Maybe not as a participant, but by excusing those who do the attacks, ignoring the connection to your faith."

He looked shocked. I said, "You want honesty or some politically correct shit? That's just the way I feel."

"Because I worship Islam?"

I paused, then said, "Yeah. I guess so. It's just one giant excuse after another. Poverty, lack of opportunity, being shunned, whatever, it's just an excuse for the real issue."

The chattering in the room subsided, the conversation raw. Jennifer looked at me and said, "Pike, now is not the time or place for this."

I said, "Why not? He's supposedly on our team."

He said, "You equate Islam with evil. A blanket statement, yet you have your own evil, do you not?"

"I have no idea what you're talking about."

"Let me help, then. You have the Westboro Baptist Church, right?"

I was surprised that he'd even heard of such a thing. I said, "Yeah?"

"And they profess a bastardization of your faith to the point where they protest at funerals of your military members."

"What's your point?"

"Nothing. Just having a discussion."

But he drew me in without even trying. I said, "Yeah,

well, I haven't seen a lot of beheadings by Baptists. Even at our worst, the low bar is someone holding a sign and chanting shit. At your worst, someone's getting raped before getting stoned to death. You want to preach to me, do it without a callus on your head."

He took the insults without emotion. He said, "Yes, that's true. But can you separate the difference? Can you see that Islam isn't evil, in and of itself?"

I stood up, saying, "Maybe. Maybe not."

Alarmed, Jennifer rose next to me, mistaking why I'd stood. She said, "Hey, what are you doing?"

I said, "Going to the bathroom before I rip his head off."

51

I went to the men's room, then to the downstairs bar, getting a beer and killing time listening to Issam bang away on the piano. Deep down, I didn't really think Islam was evil, but there was no denying a connection between the mass murderers and the faith, and it aggravated me when I confronted apologists. Even so, while I held my views, I knew we had a mission to accomplish, and acting like an asshole in Ahmed's world wasn't the best way to go about it. We *did* have some terrorists to find, and if Ahmed helped with that, it was fine with me. My personal opinions could not be allowed to interfere. I finished my beer and figured the heat had bled off from our conversation. I went back upstairs.

The first thing I saw was Knuckles and Carly, canoodling in the corner. Well, maybe not that bad, but they were definitely ignoring the rest of the table. I really wanted to break that up, but after my argument earlier, it would be a bridge too far. They got to live another day.

I saw Jennifer leaning over the table with Ahmed, deep in discussion, Veep and Retro listening in. I wandered over, getting close enough to hear but not close enough to shut down the conversation.

"But you can see what he's saying, can't you? It's not like there are a lot of Christians cutting off heads. I mean, he's right. Everyone talks about poverty or a lack of opportunity being the genesis of terrorism, but in the

Philippines, the poverty goes across religious lines, and the country is predominantly Catholic, yet all of the terrorist-related killings there are done by Muslims. In fact, that group just joined the Islamic State."

Ahmed said, "No, no, you're exactly right. But it isn't Islam, per se. It's the very ally America courts. It's Saudi Arabia."

"What do you mean? Islam is Islam."

"No, it's not. Islam is *not* Islam, any more than the various faiths of Christianity define that whole religion. Abu Bakr al-Baghdadi proclaims a caliphate, and everyone in the West paints all of Islam. How many Protestants listen to what the pope says? Yet they are all Christian."

Jennifer smiled and said, "That's true, but nobody in Christendom is running around lopping off heads."

"Look, there is a cancer here, and it has a name. It's Wahhabism, and it's coming from Saudi Arabia. We're fighting that cancer now, but we embraced it early on."

I started to intervene, then backed up, wanting to hear what he had to say, knowing that Jennifer would get more out of him than I could.

She said, "Everyone blames them, but it's not borne out by the evidence. We just had the redacted pages released from the 9/11 report, and there's no hard proof of their involvement. How can you say that Saudi Arabia is the root of a Moroccan terrorist in France?"

"It's not an excuse, but it *is* real. Involvement doesn't mean you carried a box cutter. The house of al-Saud made a deal with the devil. Way back when, they partnered with a bunch of extremists and said, 'If you back me as the supreme ruler, I'll support you in your view of Islam.' They did, and the Kingdom of Saudi Arabia was born, a state held hostage by the Wahhabis and their fundamentalist thinking. This would be nothing but one more agreement in a million of them in the sands of history, except Saudi Arabia found oil. Since then, to keep their kingdom intact, the royal family has funneled money into that extremist brand of Islam all over the world, precisely to keep the radicals in their own country happy. Without their support, the kingdom would fall, so they continue to do so, even as it causes attacks in their own country."

Jennifer said, "I don't see it. The strain of Islam you're talking about can't be bred by an infusion of cash. There's something more at play."

He took a sip from his glass and said, "What if the entire GDP of the United States funded the Westboro church or David Koresh's sect? Do you think that would make a difference? Especially if the government made that brand of religion the official state-sanctioned one? What would happen if the enormous force of the United States began pushing a certain church and sending out snake charmers all over the world? Trust me, it's possible, and we bought into it."

"How? What do you mean?"

"Saudi Arabia had the money. Haven't you seen the palaces here in Morocco? That country spends it like we drink water. And our previous king, when offered the money to build mosques, agreed to let it happen. He was looking to increase our respectability, but the mosques came with a catch—the imams came from Saudi Arabia. And because of it, their brand of Islam began to infect our society, like it has infected every Muslim country on earth."

Jennifer considered what he said but didn't back down. "But the Moroccans from Belgium and France had never been to Saudi Arabia."

He said, "And they've never been religious inside

Morocco. They were Berbers from the Rif who had no religious learning in our country. They were radicalized somewhere else, and that radicalization was done by a Wahhabi imam. I promise."

Now I was actually getting interested. Jennifer said, "So your brand of Islam is the open-arms one? Is that what you're saying?"

"You make a jest, but yes. It is. It's called Maliki, and it's inclusive. Sufism. We don't preach hate or intolerance. In fact, the new king has forbidden Wahhabis from our mosques and is exporting Maliki imams for that very reason, fighting fire with fire. Here, unlike Saudi Arabia, he is known as the commander of the faithful and is the ultimate arbitrator of the faith."

"So you allow Christianity to practice here?"

"Yes, of course."

"Then why is it against the law to have a Bible written in Arabic? What's the fear there?"

He stammered, saying, "That's . . . that's just a law. You in America have such things."

"Are you saying we made it illegal to have a Quran printed in English?"

"No, no. I mean you have such things as blue laws."

"Really? You're going to tell me that not being able to buy liquor on Sunday is the same thing as stifling an entire religion? And why is it that I, as a woman, can't worship in the company of men. Is that right?"

He said, "That is completely misunderstood. Men have needs, and having women bent over in front of them is not godly. That is all it is about. Temptation."

I saw her stutter, amazed, and I knew she was going to make the same mistake I had. She could chastise me all day long about being a Cro-Magnon, but when it came to women's rights, she was just as bad. Not that I didn't think she had a point, but we did have a mission to accomplish.

She said, "You don't think that's backward?"

I walked forward, getting their attention. I said, "We need to get some sleep. Long day tomorrow."

Ahmed looked at me in relief, clearly not liking where Jennifer was taking the conversation. He'd been so sure of himself right up until the last thirty seconds. She gave me the stink eye. I was pretty sure the discussion wasn't over.

I held out my hand for her and said, "I, for one, would never make you pray in the back. It would be depriving the world of a view they should see."

Which, naturally, went over like a lead balloon with both Ahmed and Jennifer. She jerked her hand away and stomped out. He looked at me like I was a lunatic.

I said, "Sorry, man. Just trying to help."

He shook his head and walked away. I watched him leave the balcony, and I, being me, ended up going for the trifecta. I started to follow them downstairs but saw Carly and Knuckles still in the corner, and I couldn't resist.

I went over to them, ending their conversation. They both looked at me expectantly. I said, "Carly, I appreciate the intervention today, but it won't matter at selection."

She looked at me quizzically, while Knuckles scowled like he wanted to stab me in the heart. She said, "What are you talking about?"

I said, "I'm going to bed. Ask your sponsor."

She turned to Knuckles and said, "What's he talking about?"

Knuckles spat out, "He's an asshole. I have no idea."

52

★★
★

Johan wound across the ridgeline in his small rental car, a tourist map of Fez on the seat next to him. He could see the large castle clearly on the slope, but trying to find the actual road that led to it, like everything else in Fez, was a trial. For all he knew, the bit of blacktop he was on would sail right by the fortress.

Called the Borj Nord, the castle had been built in the sixteenth century on the hills overlooking the original medina. It, along with its counterpart in the southern hills, was designed more to control the restless people of Fez than to protect from outside threats. Today, the Borj Nord was a military arms museum, but that wasn't why Johan was trying to find it. According to Dexter's contact, the Iraq war picture he was supporting was filming at that location.

He turned off avenue des Mérinides, pleasantly surprised to see a sign directing him to the fortress. He rounded a curve and saw the castle. With four triangular sally ports at each corner, and the top parapet notched all the way around, it looked more like something from King Arthur than from any King Abdullah.

Johan wound into the parking lot, seeing it crammed full of cranes, cameras, and vans. He slowed, looking for one van in particular. He found it at the back of the lot. He started to pull forward, and a Moroccan security guard blocked him. As instructed, he rolled down the window and, in an authoritative voice, said the name of the movie,

"*Home of the Brave, Home of the Brave.*" He knew the man spoke little English, if any at all. It worked. The guard stepped aside. He thanked the man and drove around to the back, ignoring the cast and crew.

He pulled up next to the driver's window, seeing it was down. Inside was a heavyset man with a full beard, wearing a T-shirt with a USMC globe and anchor, the clothing soaked through with sweat. Eyes closed, he appeared asleep except for the fact that his left hand was working a small travel fan back and forth across his face.

Johan said, "Terry Broadwell, I presume?"

The man started, then sat up. He looked left and right, then leaned out of the window. He said, "You Dexter's man?"

"Yes."

He glanced to the passenger seat, and for the first time, Johan noticed a Moroccan boy of about thirteen or fourteen. Terry said something to him and exited the van, going to the rear. He came around to the passenger side of Johan's car carrying a leather satchel.

He popped the door and slid into the seat. Johan said, "What's the film about?"

"Iraq." Terry laughed and said, "This is supposed to be one of Saddam's palaces. Doesn't look like any palace I stayed in."

"Then why do they use it?"

"Hollywood. Nothing has to be accurate. Just different."

Johan chuckled politely and said, "You have my request?"

"Yes and no." He patted the satchel and said, "Inside is a Beretta M9. It's all I could give you."

Johan rolled his eyes and said, "I hate that damn pistol. Come on, you don't have anything better?"

"Well, believe it or not, they have a military advisor on

set, and he provided the production company with the different types of weapons. This is standard US issue in the military."

"So they have to be accurate with that shit, but not with anything else?"

Terry nodded. "Pretty much." He reached into the bag and said, "This is one of four spares."

He passed it across, below the dash. Johan did a functions check and said, "Will someone know it's gone?"

"No. Only me. They aren't accounted for by serial number to anyone but our company, so nobody's going to miss it."

"Ammo?"

"Box of nine millimeter."

"Okay. Thanks."

Looking hesitant, Terry said, "Can I ask why I'm doing this?"

"No. But trust me, it's not for something evil. I'm on a contract for Dexter, and I might need the protection. That's all. I'm not looking to use it."

Terry smiled, the relief flitting across his face. "That's what Dexter said, but you never know. I've done a few contracts that were sketchy, to say the least. I like this gig and don't want to lose it."

"You'll be fine. I just have to go to some dicey areas down south. That's all. If something flames up, you won't be connected in any way."

"Be careful down there. It's truly a no-man's-land."

"I will." He pointed to the van and said, "Who's the boy?"

"Some kid who glommed on to me. He speaks pretty good English, and he's a wizard at knowing the area. I got him a pass for the set and pay him five bucks a day. He's a lifesaver."

Johan slowly nodded, thinking, then said, "Can I use him?"

Terry squinted his eyes, saying, "What do you mean?"

Johan laughed and said, "I have to find an address in this maze of a city, and I had a hard enough time trying to find a damn castle. Can I show him an address?"

Terry chuckled and said, "Sure. Sorry about that."

Johan hid the pistol, and Terry hollered out the window. The boy came scampering over, wearing sandals that were too large, a greasy T-shirt that could use a washing, and pants that didn't fit. Terry said, "This guy needs to find an address. Can you help?"

The boy nodded, glad to be of assistance. Johan said, "I don't have any idea where this is." He held out the address book he'd taken in Gibraltar, pointing at a page. The boy stared at it for a moment, then said, "Yes, that's in the mellah. Next to the palace. I know it. There's a video game place on that street that I've used."

Johan pulled out the tourist map and said, "Can you show me on this?"

The boy looked at the map, sliding his finger down roads, then pointed at an area. He said, "It's in there, but this map is not nearly good enough to show you. There are many, many alleys."

Shit.

Terry said, "Take him with you."

"What?"

Terry looked at the boy and said, "Want to triple your pay?"

The kid nodded eagerly. To Johan, Terry said, "Surely it's worth ten bucks, right?"

Johan said, "Oh, yeah. Easily."

Terry turned back to the kid and said, "You be back here tomorrow? Can you do that?"

"Yes, Mr. Terry. Of course."

"He's yours."

Terry said good-bye and exited the car, swapping places with the boy. Johan put the vehicle into drive and began retracing his steps from earlier, winding back down the mountain. He said, "What do I call you?"

"Fonzie."

"Fonzie? Come on."

"That's what Mr. Terry calls me."

"Why?"

"Because I learned English from watching American television." He began singing, "Sunday, Monday, happy days . . ."

Johan laughed and said, "You didn't learn in school?"

"I don't go to school."

Johan had no answer to that.

53

Our small group was dropped off at the so-called Blue Gate, right outside the Fez medina. I'd sent Retro and Veep to check in at our hotel, then contact the Taskforce for the latest dump we'd received from the capture of Snyder, hoping they'd find something more than just a name. I'd opted to bring Knuckles, Carly, Ahmed, and Jennifer into the medina with me.

By the time we'd linked up with Ahmed, he'd done whatever secret-police stuff he could and had found a group of al-Khattabis—Berbers from Chefchaouen—working in the tannery at Fez. That was the only lead we had. The flight up was only forty-five minutes, but it had been instructive in two ways: One, Ahmed had remarked that the aircraft we were on was just like the ones that had done rendition flights to Morocco in the early 2000s, meaning he didn't trust that it was just a plane we used, and two, Jennifer cornered him again.

I'll admit, Ahmed was certainly game, and fervently wanted to get Jennifer to understand that groups like ISIS or al Qaida were not Islamic. It seemed he was almost on a mission of his own, and this time he'd come prepared.

They spent the forty-five minutes in the air sparring back and forth, and I ignored most of it, only tuning in when I heard Ahmed say, "So because of some cultural restrictions in various countries, we're all terrorists? Is that what you're saying? Culture is different all over the world. Women in tribal regions in Africa run around without a top on. Do that in America, and everyone would demand clothing. It's just culture. It doesn't make it evil."

Jennifer said, "Women can't drive in Saudi Arabia. In some Islamic countries they can't leave the house without a male member of the family to take them. That's not cultural. That's religious. How on earth do you think that's fair? How is that inclusive?"

"Once again, you might not like it, but it doesn't mean we're all terrorists."

Jennifer said, "Well, you're certainly all a bunch of bigots."

He smiled and said, "Really? Who's America's greatest ally in the Middle East? In the land of all of us terrorists?"

Wary, knowing she was walking into a trap, she said, "Israel."

"Correct, but ultraorthodox Jews in Israel don't even want women on public buses that the males ride. They're forced to sit in the back."

Jennifer said, "That's not true—"

He cut her off, saying, "It *is* true. It's very true. They even have a name for the segregated bus lines. Israeli ultraorthodox Jews are just as bad as any example you can give for Islam. In Israel their own sons are excused from military service based on religion, while everyone else has to join. You won't find that here. You can't look at Morocco and wave such accusations, then turn around and say Israel is your friend. It's hypocritical. And, by the way, women drive in Morocco. Don't make me defend an entirely different country on the mantra of religion."

Ahmed had clearly come ready for the fight, his earlier retreats last night long gone. Jennifer, for a change, was now on the defensive. She trickled off by repeating what she'd said last night, "But you make women pray in the back or in a different room."

Ahmed said, "Check a synagogue in Israel."

"Two wrongs don't make a right."

He chuckled, then nodded. "Yes. That is a valid point, but not the one I want to make. Just because I practice Islam doesn't mean I'm a terrorist. I lived in the United States for a long time, and you had Baptists who forbade dancing and alcohol. It was their choice, based on a reading of the Bible. We choose our own direction based on the Quran."

He looked directly at me and said, "It doesn't make us terrorists."

I nodded. "I never said you were a terrorist."

"You implied I help them by excusing Islam. I'm trying to teach you that Islam isn't the threat. *Terrorists* are. And I will kill them wherever I find them."

His hatred was so strong, it actually turned me a little, but he still hadn't convinced me. His conviction didn't alter the facts. There was a reason that ISIS was killing people on a holocaust scale, and it wasn't because they were all afflicted with the same mental condition. Or maybe it was.

The pilot had come on, saying our short flight from Casablanca was almost over. I said, "Buckle up. Time to land."

Once on the ground, I'd sent Veep and Retro to the hotel. The rest of us would explore the medina with Ahmed. He would act as our "tour guide," and we would be two couples on a sightseeing event. Given Knuckles's obvious infatuation with Carly, we should be able to pull it off pretty well.

We passed through the gate, facing down donkeys

and a surging flow of people, all moving with a purpose, apparently knowing exactly where they were headed in the maze of the medina. I said, "What is it about Moroccans that you don't like anything allowing vehicles? Everywhere I go, it's pedestrian-only."

Ahmed said, "Maybe it's because our civilization is a thousand years older than yours."

He looked at me to see if he'd pissed me off, then said, "Believe it or not, this medina is the largest city on earth that has no vehicle traffic. We're proud of it."

Jennifer said, "It sure keeps you in shape. I don't see a lot of fat people."

He chuckled, and we began weaving through the medina, going deeper and deeper. It was a chaotic environment, with a constant flow of people trying to either buy or sell something, and had an otherworldly feel.

One thing was sure: If the cousins we were trying to question escaped into this maze, they would be long gone. There would be no interdiction by vehicle, or radioing someone to intersect, because every single alley had a branch that led somewhere else. It would take a battalion to lock down the area.

Ahmed said, "See that?" He was pointing at one of the ubiquitous pictures of the king, walking in front of a palace.

I said, "Yeah, what about it?"

"The woman behind him. See her?"

I leaned in, seeing an attractive middle-aged woman wearing a modest dress and sunglasses. I said, "What about her?"

"She is the queen."

"So?"

Exasperated, he said, "She's uncovered. She wears no hijab, and certainly no burqa."

I said, "What's your point? She gets the benefit of not being forced to dress in accordance with Islamic code because she's the queen?"

He clenched his fists and said, "No! She does that because the king is the commander of all faiths in Morocco. She refuses to wear the hijab because it would be disrespectful of other religions. She must represent the totality of Morocco, and she does."

Knuckles said, "Seriously?"

"Yes. We are serious about that. To the point that the queen made a choice, as a Muslim."

I nodded, grudgingly giving some ground. "Okay, Ahmed, I admit, that's pretty good."

He smiled, then said, "I'll convince you yet."

I said, "I doubt it, but keep trying."

He chuckled, and we continued walking. We took a left into yet another alley, and I said, "How do you know where we're going?"

"I've done a lot of operations inside here. I'm no expert, but it's not that hard to figure out after a few days. Some of these smaller alleys will get me lost, but I know the main ones."

Eventually, we reached a lane with a distinct odor. And by odor, I mean it smelled like someone had farted into a Ziploc bag holding a dead cat. Ahmed said, "Here we are."

He pointed at a sign describing the history of the tannery, then went up a narrow stairwell. We got to the first landing, and he said, "Let me do the talking. We need to corner the cousins inside. The tannery is enclosed, but if they flee into the medina itself, we will never find them."

I said, "Okay, but I want some backup. Where are the exits?"

He nodded and said, "That might be smart. There are

three, all on the same alley we came in on. One is the door at the base of the stairs, the other two are up and down the alley. They'll be the first doors you see. They won't have any signs selling anything. They'll just be wood doors in the stone."

I turned to Carly, Knuckles, and Jennifer. "Stage at the bottom. One of you go left, the other right. Jennifer, post on the door right below us."

They nodded and went back down. We continued up, getting accosted by some guy trying to sell me a leather suit. Ahmed flashed his badge, and the man immediately became obsequious. Ahmed spoke to him in Arabic, the man answered, then Ahmed turned to me.

"They do work here, but they didn't show up today. He has no idea why."

54

Jalal paced down the narrow tunnel as if he were entering a lion's den. He didn't like the positioning of the cloistered room the cousins had rented, but there was nothing he could do about it. He passed the gaming center, seeing the same teenager out front, playing with a phone and ignoring him. He was amazed at the poverty of the place, and yet this man still had money for a smartphone. It was all that was wrong with the world.

He reached the door to the apartment, and before he could even knock, it was opened by Wasim.

Startled, he said, "How did you know I was here?"

Wasim smiled and said, "Tanan has a camera set up at the entrance. He uses the Wi-Fi of the game center, and it transmits into here. We can see everything."

Jalal said, "Good, good. Smart thinking." He entered the hovel, seeing one of the men cooking tagine stew on the tabletop stove, the aroma of the food making his stomach rumble.

He said, "Are you men packed?"

"Yes. It's not like we have a lot of baggage."

He saw the other three sitting around the chipped kitchen table, waiting on him expectantly.

He set his bag on the floor and said, "This will be our last meal here. It's time. The passports have arrived."

They said nothing, and he saw fear on their faces. The fear of stepping into the unknown. He pulled up a chair and sat down, looking at each man in turn. He said, "Are you committed? When we leave here, it will be the end game. I don't want anyone who is questioning."

They nodded hesitantly. He said again, "Are you committed? Truly committed?"

They nodded again, now forcefully. The one known as Tanan said, "I have waited all of my life for this. Yes. Insh'Allah, yes."

Jalal smiled and said, "That is more in line with what I expect. Powerful people have helped our group. You will be the lions that accomplish what others could not."

In his mind, he had rehearsed a rousing speech, designed to ensure their dedication, but now he decided it wasn't necessary. They were Berbers from the Rif. They had struggled together since birth. He had not seen them for close to a decade, but he knew their commitment. They would not let him down.

He unzipped his backpack and pulled out a gallon-size Ziploc. Inside were the passports they would use. He said, "This is your ticket to paradise," and began calling out names.

Sitting on a broken metal chair underneath an umbrella that was listlessly sagging, Johan licked his popsicle next to Fonzie. The boy was enamored of the rare treat, slurping his tongue over it as if he'd never been allowed one before. So much so that Johan wondered if that were true.

He said, "You like that, huh?"

"Yes, yes, Mr. Johan. This is like what Americans do."

Johan said, "But they don't enjoy it like you do."

Fonzie smiled and said, "Because they get this all the time. One day, I'm going to be an American. You wait."

The boy licked his frozen treat, watching the people

walking by in the ghetto, feeling for the first time superior to those around him. *He* had a delight that they couldn't afford.

Johan felt the melancholy creep into him, memories of impoverished children in Africa only wanting a chance. And the fact that he'd let them down.

He said, "What do you want to be when you grow up?"

"I'm going to be a pilot. Flying airplanes."

Surprised, Johan said, "What makes you think that?"

Smugly, Fonzie said, "I have skills. I've been told so."

"By who?"

"I helped a pilot last month. I was his guide. He said I had the makings of a pilot. He's going to help me. I have his email address. He told me to wait until I was eighteen to send him a message, but he's going to help."

Fonzie was so sure of himself that Johan felt sick. Some asshole tourist had used a toss-off compliment and an email address to plant a time-delayed destruction of the boy. It reminded him of another boy. One who used to service their camp in Angola. He was a smiling, rambunctious kid who lived in the village down the road and had told Johan he wanted to be a soldier. He hadn't even made it to eighteen, his village destroyed by terrorists, all within spitting distance of the army camp.

Johan had found his dismembered body next to his mother's.

He shook his head, remembering why he was here. He said, "So, the address is right down that tunnel?"

"Yep." Fonzie looked comically sly and said, "Well, maybe not. It might take me a little more time to find it."

Johan laughed and said, "You mean, maybe another ice cream?"

Fonzie nodded forcefully and said, "Yes. Maybe one more and I can find it."

Johan saw a man with a backpack walking through the market. He was one of many strolling around, but this one looked furtive. The man glanced his way, then quickly looked away, as if he didn't want to be remembered. After a lifetime of hunting men and being hunted, Johan could almost smell the tension radiating from the traveler.

Fonzie caught the shift and said, "What's wrong, Mr. Johan?"

He faked a smile but kept his eyes on the man, saying, "Nothing, Fonzie. Nothing at all."

When the man turned into the tunnel, Johan felt a hardness settle in his soul.

55

Standing with the salesman, I said to Ahmed, "Can he tell us where they live?"

The man looked at me with annoyance and said, "I speak English."

Ahmed laughed, and I said, "Okay. So, can you tell us where they live?"

"No. I have no idea, but they have a friend. Someone who hangs out with them occasionally. He's here."

Ahmed said, "Point him out."

We went up to a balcony, and the stench became overbearing, like I had been thrown in front of a fan with the devil farting on the other side. I closed off my nose and pretended I didn't notice. The salesman leaned over the railing, and I saw row after row of cylinders like septic tanks, men stomping in each one, working raw leather. He shouted something in Arabic. Someone shouted back. Ahmed said something to the man, and I said, "What's going on?"

"He's trying to find the man. I told him not to mention DGST."

The guy shouted something again, and Ahmed punched him in the arm. The salesman looked shocked. I said, "What's going on?"

"He didn't mention DGST, but he said the authorities want to talk to him."

I looked down into the hellish pit and saw everyone

had stopped working and was looking back at us on the balcony, confused. Then I spotted a man slinking toward the exit. I said, "Who's that? The guy moving?"

Ahmed rattled off something in Arabic, and the salesman said something back. Ahmed shouted over the balcony in Arabic. The man took off running.

He said, "That's him!" and started leaping back down the stairs.

I followed him, slamming down the steps four at a time, calling on the net, "He's on the run, he's on the run, everyone get ready."

Jennifer came back, "How will we know who it is?"

"If someone comes by you at a sprint, take him down."

We flew out of the tannery back into the alley of the medina, then swiveled our heads left and right. I saw Jennifer, but she shook her head. I called, "Knuckles, what do you have?"

"Nothing."

I looked at Ahmed and said, "You sure he can only escape back into the medina? Can he get out the other way?"

He said, "I'm almost sure."

I said, "Shit, man! You've let him—"

My radio broke open with traffic. "I got him, I got him! He just ran by me."

It was Carly. I started sprinting in her direction, saying, "Where's he going?"

"Right! He just went right."

Given that we were running by one alley after another, it wasn't a lot of help. I said, "Carly, I need something more. Give me a lock-on."

I heard nothing. Knuckles caught up to us, and we kept going. I said, "Carly, Carly, we need a lock-on."

I heard a grunt on the radio, then, "Knuckles, get your ass here. I got him, but he's fucking strong."

We passed by alley after alley, pausing to look into them and seeing nothing. I heard, "Damn it, stop fighting!"

I said, "Carly, give me a damn lock-on."

We reached another alley, and I saw a crowd. Knuckles blasted past me and separated them, exposing a simple wooden door that was ajar. We went through it, entering an amazing, wide-open room with a marble floor and twenty-foot ceilings, golden chandeliers and intricately carved wooden wainscoting throughout.

It was a restaurant, and on the floor was Carly, riding some poor skinny shlep like a broncobuster, him facedown on the tile, arms swinging about wildly, and her doing whatever it took to keep him from standing up.

Knuckles stepped in, pushing Carly off the man's back and locking him up in a half nelson, causing him to squeal.

Some of the patrons in the restaurant began to try to intervene, and I pushed them back. Jennifer went to Carly, checking to ensure she was okay. I saw a bruise on her cheek and a split lip. I turned to Ahmed and said, "Time to get that badge out."

He did, talking to the hostess. Watching Knuckles control the man, I said, "Seriously, man, is that the level of instruction you gave Carly? She can't fight worth shit."

He grimaced and said, "We aren't there yet. Can you help me here? This guy is like an eel."

I bent down, getting control of his loose arm and tweaking his wrist, causing a yelp. He quit fighting. I looked over at Carly, breathing hard with a touch of blood on her face. I said, "Maybe you are worth the effort."

She said, "What does that mean?"

Knuckles, still on top of the man, said, "Don't you dare."

I smiled and looked up at Ahmed, saying, "Talk to him. Get us an address."

56

Johan continued his surveillance of the narrow alley, but the only activity had been the children coming and going from the makeshift game room. No other adults had arrived. He was in no rush, so he'd let Fonzie drive a hard bargain and purchased him a third ice cream, letting the little urchin slobber it down.

It had been a good thirty minutes since he'd seen the man with the backpack, and he was beginning to believe his suspect was in for the night. He stood up and stretched, saying, "I'll be right back." Fonzie nodded without even looking up, focused solely on his ice cream. Johan casually strolled up the street, glancing into the alley as he passed. He saw multiple doors on both sides of the narrow lane, the only gap in the wall the game room.

He came back to Fonzie and said, "When you're finished with that, I want you to find the correct door, then come back out here and describe it to me exactly, to include what's to the left or right of it."

Fonzie licked his treat and said, "No problem, Mr. Johan."

Wanting to get a feel for the atmospherics of the area as the workday came to a close, and needing a reason to remain in the area, Johan said, "You do well, and I'll rent some video game time for you."

Fonzie's eyes widened. He said, "You promise?"

"Yes. Now, go check it out."

Fonzie jammed the treat in his mouth, getting the last of it, then nodded, his cheeks comically full. He glanced back once, then entered the alley. Johan changed his vantage point so he could watch him walk all the way down.

Fonzie studied the first door, then the next, determining which way the numbers ran. He skipped the next two but stopped at the video game cave, staring at the screen and the children playing for a good five minutes. Johan was contemplating tossing a pebble into the alley to get his attention; then Fonzie continued on his own.

He walked deeper and deeper, so far in that Johan would occasionally lose sight of him in the murkiness between the hanging lightbulbs. Eventually, he stopped at the final door on the right side, directly underneath a bare bulb. He paused for a moment, then raised his hand to knock.

Watching Ahmed talk to the head of the district police, I could see his impatience beginning to show at the length of time it was taking to cordon off the area. Every minute counted, and we both knew we'd probably get only one shot at this.

Back in the medina the runner had not hesitated to answer any question—especially after Ahmed had shown his DGST credentials—starting off by protesting his innocence about anything and everything. Ahmed asked why he was running, and he said he wasn't sure. He'd just heard his name and panicked.

Later, Ahmed told me he was convinced the man was up to no good—drugs, counterfeiting, something—but it wasn't within the DGST purview. All we cared about was the cell of al-Khattabis, and the runner was more than forthcoming, giving us an address in the old Jewish quarter, now a run-down ghetto. Then he'd given us something a little more ominous: He said that the three men had met a cousin of theirs and were planning on leaving the country with him. Going to the United States.

After getting the translation, I had Ahmed ask where in the United States, specifically, and the man didn't know. I then had Ahmed ask how they would travel. Did he know if they had visas? Did they go through our consulate? He didn't know that either. All he knew was they were flying tonight out of Casablanca. As to the big question of why, he proclaimed ignorance.

Ahmed had calmed down the workers and patrons in the restaurant, and we'd taken our capture out of the medina. Along the way, Ahmed said, "We should coordinate this with the district police here. The Jewish mellah is much like the medina, and if they run, they may escape."

"But they could be loading up in cars right now to drive to Casablanca. If the flight is tonight, they've got to be leaving soon."

"I can coordinate while we travel. Like I said before, I've done many operations here and I have a point of contact."

I didn't say anything, and he said, "It's a ten-minute trip anyway. It can't hurt."

"Okay, okay."

Returning through the Blue Gate, Jennifer took the wheel of our SUV, Carly next to her providing directions to the ghetto. Jennifer said, "We have a list of names, right?"

On the phone, Ahmed nodded. She said, "The least we should do is get that into the system. Stop them from boarding a plane."

Carly snapped her fingers and said, "Give me the list. I know who to call."

Ahmed passed it to the front. Pretty soon everyone was doing something except Knuckles and me. I said, "What do you think? Should we stomp right in? Or wait on Barney Fife?"

"I'm leaning toward Barney Fife. It's their area, their culture, and we have three names, with a fourth unknown. Even if we could take them all down with just our force, we're still going to need police cover for the disturbance. I mean, we might actually cause a riot if these guys are upstanding disciples of the ghetto."

All good points. I said, "But the time is concerning me."

He said, "Can't have everything perfect."

Jennifer came abreast of the royal palace and Ahmed, still on the phone, waved his hand and pointed. She diverted into the parking lot, and he said, "My contact will meet us here. The address is less than a hundred meters away from here."

Carly said, "Talked to my guys. They'll get the names in the system."

At least that was something.

A man pulled up in a police car, and Ahmed went into a deep discussion, then began coordinating the lockdown of the area. Twenty minutes later—ten minutes too long, as far as I was concerned—and now even Ahmed was showing some impatience.

He said, "I apologize. My friend is not used to working on a strict timeline, but his men are good. Just a little slow."

Meaning they were on Moroccan time but weren't really lazy. They'd thump heads when push came to shove.

I said, "Don't worry about it. I understand. I would like to stage a little closer, though. Can we do that?"

He nodded and said, "Yeah, let's go." He turned to his contact and said something in Arabic, holding his phone in the air. The policeman nodded and pointed at his radio.

Ahmed said to me, "Same profile as before. I'm your guide, you guys are tourists."

I laughed and said, "Tourists in the ghetto. That's stretching it."

"No, it isn't. Believe it or not, the old Jewish mellah is a constant stop for tour guides. It has a lot of history, showing the inclusion of other faiths in Morocco."

We crossed the street and I said, "Meaning this is a government-mandated stop for that reason?"

He said, "No. It's some Islamic plot and I'm lying to you."

Jennifer rolled her eyes and said, "This is like a tourist trip from hell."

Ahmed laughed, then said, "Okay, right through that alley we'll be in the mellah proper. I recommend only going a few meters inside, because our address is less than fifty meters from here, and the police haven't positioned yet. There is a spice store around the corner. Jennifer, if you could do the honor of leading us to it, then ask me a question about it, I would appreciate it."

She said, "Of course," and started walking. Soon we were inside an area with different architecture than the Moorish examples we'd seen outside. Jennifer said, "Why do you call this 'mellah' instead of a ghetto?"

Ahmed said, "I don't know. I'm not really a tour guide. It's just always been called that." He flicked his eyes to the left and Jennifer caught the hint, saying, "Hey, what's that? That basket of stuff?"

Ahmed went into a speech about the spices, slowing our march to a standstill. We gathered around like it was fascinating, then Ahmed dialed his phone for an update on the district police.

A crack split the air.

Ahmed stopped talking, searching me with his eyes, asking a question without speaking. Another crack sounded, muted by distance, but I knew beyond a shadow of a doubt what it was: gunfire.

I nodded at him and said, "Time to go, police or no police." He hung up and we took off running toward the sound of the guns.

57

Jalal sampled the chicken tangine stew and found it delicious. He said, "Someone here has become quite the cook."

Wasim said, "It's what you learn when you have no women," and the table laughed. Jalal said, "Tanan, how did you set that video system up?"

Showing modesty, he said, "It was simple. You just buy a Wi-Fi camera, hook it and your computer to a Wi-Fi node, and you can start using it." He opened a cheap netbook computer and said, "I paid the teenager at the game stop ten dirham for the password. He didn't care, because it's not his Wi-Fi."

He raked a finger over the trackpad, bringing the screen to life. It showed a backward-looking view, as if someone was outside, at the gaming center, looking toward their door. Tanan said, "This way, we could see if anyone from the police were coming."

Jalal surveyed the feed, seeing a small boy at the gaming center. The boy began walking toward them, reading each door's address. Jalal recognized him, and an electric jolt of adrenaline raced through his body.

"Grab your stuff. Right now. Is there a way out of here that doesn't involve that alley? A back way?"

"No. There's a cut-through in the gaming center, halfway up the alley. That's our planned escape. That'll lead to the market on the other side. Why?"

"I passed that boy on the way in. He was sitting with a European eating ice cream. The European took an interest in me, and now that boy is checking door addresses."

"Jalal, it's coincidence."

"Nothing is a coincidence. I promise."

They watched the screen, and the boy came closer and closer, checking each door as he walked. Jalal said, "He's searching for our door. The man outside is against us. Do you have weapons?"

"Yes." Wasim flicked his head at Tanan, and he raced to the back bedroom, flipping over a mattress to expose a trapdoor. He pulled it up, revealing a shallow pit holding four folding-stock AK-47s and a Makarov pistol. He handed the AKs out, each man taking one and loading a round. He kept the Makarov for himself, looking at Jalal.

Jalal said, "Give me the pistol."

"What are you going to do?"

"If he comes to our door, he will have to die. We'll flee straight out. Get ready, because if I'm right, they'll be coming in. Who's leading through the game room?"

Tanan raised his hand and said, "I know the way. I can get us to the cars." Everyone except Jalal showed fear. The commitment was coming home much sooner than they'd expected.

Jalal returned to the computer. The boy kept coming, walking slowly and checking each door. He reached theirs, standing under the naked bulb, reading the address stuck in the tile next to the metal of the handle.

Jalal said, "That's it. Put on your backpacks. It's time to run."

The men began scrambling, and Jalal saw the child raise his hand, the first door he'd bothered to knock on after checking all of them. Jalal knew he was right.

He leapt across the room and ripped open the door. He saw the child's expression, shocked that someone had answered before he'd even knocked. The child said, "My mistake, sir."

Jalal raised the pistol, put it between the boy's eyes, and pulled the trigger.

On the street, Johan saw Fonzie raise his hand, then the door opened. The child was frozen in place, and Johan saw a pistol emerge. The man placed it right between Fonzie's eyes, and the world went into slow motion. Johan screamed, startling the people around him. He sprinted toward the tunnel. In the harsh glare of the naked bulb he saw the pistol cycle, the casing eject, the head explode backward. And the fall of the body.

He felt unbridled rage and lost control. He ran into the tunnel, seeing men spilling out of the far doorway armed with Kalashnikovs. They began filling the tunnel with fire. He dove to the ground, squeezing his own trigger to suppress their aim.

The rounds snapped the air around him, smacking into the walls and spackling him with spall. He scrambled back to the entrance, diving out and rolling up against the wall. He peeked around the corner and saw four men run toward the video game center, all wearing rucksacks. He screamed again in frustration, seeing the children from the gaming center begin fleeing toward him. They burst out of the entrance, running in all directions. The teenager who manned the center took one step out of the alley and was hit in the back with multiple rounds. He spilled forward, his eyes wide, and Johan knew he was dead.

He rolled into the entrance in the prone, seeing the

first of the men turn into the cave of the gaming room. Three made it into the cover, and Johan emptied a magazine at the fourth, seeing the bullets find their mark. The man dropped, and Johan changed magazines, running forward.

He cleared the small alcove of the gaming center, seeing it empty, then skipped over the downed man, kicking his AK to the side before rushing to Fonzie. He took one look at the shattered skull and felt another explosion of fury. He ran back to the man on the ground, seeing his body writhing in pain. He leaned forward, snarling, grabbing the man by his hair. The man said something in Arabic, and Johan put the gun to his forehead. The man's eyes finally focused, and he began begging.

Johan squeezed the trigger.

He turned to the gaming establishment, seeing a torn-open plywood wall. He started to follow when he heard the rushing of feet coming down the hall. He turned, ready to kill anyone who entered, innocent or not.

58

I drew my Glock as I ran, hearing what sounded like the Battle of Fallujah just ahead. People were fleeing the scene in all directions, a kaleidoscope of humanity all trying to escape whatever was happening. I heard multiple shots from an alley directly ahead of me and saw a Caucasian man on the ground, blond hair rippling in the afternoon breeze, firing crazily into the alley. I drew down on him, preparing to break the trigger, and he leapt up, sprinting down the alley, screaming like a maniac.

I ran to the right side of the alley, sliding into the wall. Knuckles took the left, Ahmed sliding in behind him. I heard two more shots, and Knuckles looked at me for a decision. I knew why. Hallways like this were notoriously hard to clear without the element of surprise, as there was no cover. A ready enemy could pick us off like the proverbial fish in a barrel. I wished we had flashbangs or some other diversion. Before I could assess the situation, Ahmed leapt up, rushing around Knuckles and into the tunnel. I saw Knuckles's eyes go wide, knowing we were now committed.

We both followed, racing into the funnel of death. The Caucasian saw us coming and got out two rounds. The first hit the wall, clanging away with a whine. The second hit Ahmed. I saw the round slap into his arm, and he screamed, dropping his own pistol. Knuckles raised his weapon, and I shouted, "Don't kill him!"

I closed the distance in the span of a single heartbeat, seeing him try to redirect to me. He was nowhere near quick enough.

I knocked his weapon wide and hammered him with a straight punch, splitting his nose open. He absorbed the blow and tucked in, and I knew he could fight. But nowhere near as well as me.

We tore into each other for a minute, and I gained dominance, trying for a rear choke. He hammered me in the gut with both elbows, causing an explosion of air. Knuckles reached him, with me holding his arms.

Knuckles snarled and grabbed his hair, then drove a punch into his face that would have knocked out a bull.

The man sagged, and I laid him on the ground, saying, "Check Ahmed."

I went into the cave of the game room, seeing the torn door and wondering what was going on. I came back out.

Knuckles had Ahmed up and moving, with a makeshift bandage on his arm. He said, "He'll live. What the fuck just happened?"

I said, "I have no idea. Ahmed, can you get us out of here? Help us avoid any police interrogation? The team—whoever they are—are on the run, and we need to find them."

Looking faint, his head rolling with sweat, he said, "I can. I can. But I can't get you into their apartment. Go. Go check it before the locals arrive."

I said, "You okay?"

He gave a wan grin and said, "Do I look okay?"

"No. You look like a terrorist."

He barked out a laugh and I clicked the radio, saying, "Koko, Koko, I need immediate exfil. I need Veep and Retro prepared to take out two bodies, one ambulatory and one unconscious. Knuckles will be bringing them both. Alert the Taskforce and get me some medical here in Fez."

Ahmed heard my call and said, "Where are you taking me?"

"To some first-class medical care. Don't worry."

The Taskforce, knowing that our work was dangerous, had planted medical doctors all over the world to treat injured members outside of the established medical system. I wasn't actually authorized to do the same for a nonmember of the Taskforce, but I would here, for two reasons. One, I wanted Ahmed to get the best care, but more importantly, I didn't want him entered into a system where I'd never get to talk to him again without an interrogation from the host nation.

He said, "I don't want to go to some rendition prison for medical care. Leave me."

I laughed and said, "You're going to our hotel. Just act like a drunk Muslim when you show up. Stagger up to the room. I'll talk to you then."

He smiled and said, "I'm sorry they escaped. We should have done what you wanted."

"That wasn't your fault." I kicked the Caucasian with my foot, saying, "He's the one who busted it open. And I intend to figure out why."

He leaned against the wall, his eyes still on me, and I said, "Give me two minutes in here. Can you do that? Keep me out of the police investigation?"

Ahmed pulled out his phone and nodded. Knuckles hoisted the Caucasian up into a fireman's carry and began walking toward the exit while he dialed.

I first went to the dead man in the alley, seeing his brain matter on the ground. I searched him and found a passport from Saudi Arabia but nothing else of interest.

I shouldered his rucksack for later inspection, then sprinted to the apartment, ignoring the child lying prone out front, his face shattered by a bullet. He was clearly dead, and had nothing of interest for me. A sad statement that more than likely symbolized his entire life. I raised my weapon high and kicked the door open. I cleared the area, seeing a meal on the table, then a mattress tossed aside and a hole in the ground.

The place was austere, without the usual flotsam and jetsam of life. No pictures, personal mementos, or even trash. Nothing. I started to leave and saw a cheap netbook computer on a shelf, the screen showing the hallway outside. I slapped the lid closed and jerked out the power cord, shoving the whole thing into the knapsack.

When I entered the hallway, I saw the beginnings of a police response, and Knuckles jogging up to me. He said, "We need to go."

I nodded, and we walked out of the tunnel, acting like we were petrified tourists, our hands in the air, leaving the mess behind us for the Moroccan police.

59

The Alitalia Boeing 737 closed its doors, and the flight attendant made the usual call to turn off any electronic components. Jalal relaxed for the first time. He leaned over to Tanan and said, "We're good. We're on the way."

Tanan nodded, still showing fear. Jalal said, "Relax. You will only raise suspicion with that face."

Tanan nodded again but didn't become any more sanguine.

The trip from Fez had been one trial after another, starting with the death of Tanan and Wasim's brother.

They'd broken out into the market on the far side of the alley, dumped their weapons, and raced out of the mellah to their vehicle, expecting to get arrested at any moment. Or die in a blazing shootout. None of that had happened.

Giddy with relief, Wasim had started the car, and for the first time, Tanan realized their brother was missing. He said, "Wait, where's Mustafa?"

Wasim had opened his car door to go back, but Jalal had stopped him. Jalal had said, "It's too late. I heard more firing as we were running. It wasn't us. It was someone else. He is martyred."

Jalal didn't know if he was captured or killed but knew he was a threat. He couldn't tell that to the cousins, though. Tanan demanded to go back. Jalal shut that down, saying the sacrifice was made and they needed to flee the country as soon as possible.

Wasim had fought him, saying that blood trumped any mission. Jalal had said, "Yes, blood is something real. Do you want to take his blood sacrifice and throw it away? Or use his sacrifice to continue?"

After a tense standoff, the cousins had relented, and they'd set out for Casablanca, four hours away. They'd parked their car in the airport lot and then settled into the Casablanca terminal for a three A.M. flight to Rome.

The cousins were antsy, clearly nervous. Jalal was morose. The mission shouldn't have started like this. He had no idea who the Caucasian man had been outside of their apartment, or even how he'd found it, but he was worried that their plot had been discovered. He wondered how the shipment to Los Angeles was going and whether it had been found out as well.

He used the Wickr app to text Tariq, letting him know they were on the way and asking about the container to Los Angeles. All he got back was that it was delayed but on track. He wanted to call. To talk to the man and get some answers, but he knew he couldn't. There were too many people listening to unencrypted cell phones.

They'd had two close scares when uniformed police had swept through the terminal, but both times, it was a false alarm.

Eventually, they'd boarded the plane, the three cousins looking exactly like a bunch of sweating terrorists out to take the aircraft down. He thanked God that they were flying out of Casablanca with a planeload of other Muslims. If they had been in Rome or New York, the entire crew would have been yanked off.

The plane began rolling to the taxiway and Jalal

leaned over, saying, "We'll be in Rome in a few hours. Then we'll regroup."

Tanan said, "I don't think I can do this. I can give my life, but I can't live under this pressure. They're going to know."

"It's okay. Quit worrying. You're going to make everyone on this aircraft nervous."

Tanan nodded, letting out a small smile. He said, "That was a pretty good escape, right? That camera and my escape route was good, wasn't it?"

Jalal patted him on the shoulder and said, "Yes. Yes, it was. Keep it up, because our next stop is Norfolk, Virginia."

60

I walked into the room, seeing Jennifer acting like a nurse in a World War II movie, tending to Ahmed as if he were her own child. I said, "Really? How long are you going to pull this helpless act?"

Ahmed smiled and said, "I didn't ask for the treatment. I think she feels guilty."

Jennifer tossed a rag at me and said to Ahmed, "Don't be fooled. He's been where you are now, and I didn't help him out of guilt."

Ahmed said, "I have no doubt of that." He turned to me, "What happened after we left? Did my calls work?"

"They did. Nobody on my team was arrested, but then again, none of the bad guys were either. They got away completely. It took the police time to build a coherent response."

I saw he took that as an insult. He started to say something, and I held up a hand, saying, "Not your fault. Not Morocco's fault. Your plan was good. We were short-circuited by a crazy man. I have no idea why he did what he did, but I will."

I could see the skepticism in his face. I said, "You did what you should have. I don't blame you."

Ahmed sagged back into his pillow. "So you don't believe I'm helping terrorists. That will be a first for you bigoted Americans."

I said, "We have a problem here. There are killers

headed to America. None of the names we gave were flagged, and we found a passport from Saudi Arabia on the dead guy. They're gone."

He said, "And?"

"And I could use your help. Because I trust you."

Jennifer snapped her head to me, surprised, and Ahmed squinted his eyes. He said, "I've been played before by the United States."

Jennifer said, "He doesn't have that in him. If he says it, he means it."

I said, "I do. I don't know who you worked with before, but I give my trust sparingly, and I would never use it to gain advantage."

He considered my words, then nodded, saying, "So, what's the help?"

"First, I have the man who shot you. He's in my control, but I need him. I can't turn him over to you."

Ahmed said, "You have lost your mind. He shot me. He is getting Moroccan justice. I don't care if he's American."

"He's not American. He's South African, and he has intelligence on the attacks that are *coming* to America. I'm sorry. If I thought he'd help out with your country, I'd toss his ass to you in a heartbeat, but that's not what's in his head. Please. I'm asking, not demanding."

He considered, then nodded, saying, "What else?"

"I need all of your databases, and I need it without a flag that we looked."

He said, "What information do you have to input?"

I smiled and stood up, saying, "I don't know yet, but I will." I held out a fist, and he looked at me quizzically.

I waited a beat, feeling embarrassed, and Jennifer said, "You're supposed to make a fist and bump him. It's a man thing."

He did so, with his left hand, and I said, "You sure you lived in America?"

He leaned back into his pillow, his bloody right arm held over his body, and said, "I'm getting tired of trying to measure up."

I patted him on the shoulder and said, "After the shootout today, there's no question about that. Regardless of religion."

He smiled, accepting the compliment, and I left him to Jennifer's ministrations, walking to the next room in our suite. Carly was outside the door. She said, "He's awake. You want me to get a recorder?"

I said, "No. I want to talk to him alone."

She said, "Let me come in with you."

I hesitated, and she said, "I'm a CIA case officer. I work with liars for a living. I won't say anything. I'll just assess him like I do with sources and assets."

I nodded, saying, "Okay, but no interrupting."

We were staying in a large suite at the Palais Faraj-Fes hotel, with three rooms each having a view of the medina and a great room in between them. It was bordering on celebrity status.

Two of the rooms were used as holding cells. One, for medical reasons, and another, as a true cell. Jennifer and I had the final room, with the rest of the team at reservations down the hall.

Carly and I entered the holding cell, seeing Johan van Rensburg handcuffed to a chair, each wrist locked down and his ankles taped to the legs. We'd found his passport and done a dive on his history, learning that he was a South African who'd recently been hired by some sleazy American company called Icarus Solutions. Now it was time to determine what he had in play. Why he was here, and what he was trying to protect. I'd met his sort many,

many times, and didn't have any illusions about his moral compass.

He tensed up when he saw us, waiting on the beatings to begin. Both of his eyes were black from the blows earlier, so he had some reason for the trepidation. I said, "We're not going to hurt you, unless you answer less than truthfully."

He nodded, then said, "And how will you know that?"

I looked him in the eye and said, "I'll know."

He said, "What do you want from me? I'm sure I can't explain anything that happened to your satisfaction. I was there, and I acted."

I said, "That's not going to cut it. You know it, and I know it. You're alive because I allowed it. There are children dead because of you."

My words sank in, but not like I expected. He became apoplectic, sitting upright and jerking against his chains, shrieking, "I didn't do that! They killed them. It wasn't me. I tried to prevent it. I tried. I tried . . ."

I took that in, letting him sag back into the chair, watching his chest rise and fall in anger. I went a different tack. "You're ex-military. Working for Icarus Solutions." It wasn't even a question. I was just throwing things out there.

He said, "Yes. It's how I came here."

I said, "Your passport is from South Africa."

"So?"

"You showed some skill with firearms today. Are you Recce?"

He looked at me in a new light. I chuckled and said, "Did you think an average civilian took you down?"

He said, "Yes. I was Recce. Still am. Always will be."

I said, "The fact that you're Special Forces will not

give you any leeway. I want to know where those guys were going. I want to know what they have in mind."

He looked shocked and said, "I'm not *with* them. I'm trying to *stop* them. It's why we had the firefight."

I said, "Sure. I believe you."

He became incensed again, saying, "They killed the boy. They killed a child. I sent that boy in. He was there because of me."

He jerked against the handcuffs hard enough to draw blood and shouted, "I *murdered* him."

I leaned back into the wall and looked at Carly. She imperceptibly nodded, letting me know the guy might be speaking the truth.

I said, "Why would you be chasing these men? If you're from South Africa? Why do you care?"

"I have my own reasons."

"Okay, let's cut the psychobabble and go straight to the evidence. How did you find them? I mean, if you're a true-blue terrorist killer, what led you to them?"

He scowled, then sank into the chair. "I have nothing to say."

That pissed me off. I leaned into him and said, "Really? Because I'll fucking bury you. I am judge, jury, and executioner. I am God as far as you're concerned. The only thing that will save your ass is you telling me what I want to know."

"Who *are* you?"

I said, "I'm the ghost. I'm the one who keeps America safe, and if carving you up is the price, I'm willing to pay it."

I went face-to-face with him, giving the full force of my potential for violence. I said, "If you want to test me, so be it."

I could see the emotion roll across his face. He tossed

his head a bit, pulled up on the handcuffs, then sagged back in the seat. He said, "I had a bank account number. That's what I followed. There was a man about to embarrass my company, and my boss asked me to check it out. What I found was . . . strange."

I said, "Bank account? You mean from the Panama Papers leak? Is that what you're talking about?"

He tried to hide it, but I saw a reaction. I said, "I'm following the same lead."

He rolled his head away, refusing to talk. I grabbed his hair, forcing him forward. I said, "Look at me. There is a terrorist attack on the way, and it's tied in to what you know."

He tried to jerk his head out of my hands but failed. He said, "Why should I trust you? You might just be another company looking for an edge. Why should I talk to you about what I've done? What protections do I have?"

I glanced at Carly, then went back to him and said, "What's that mean? I don't care what you've done. If I find out you're some low-life criminal, I won't do anything about it if you help us."

He looked me in the eye and said, "What about extrajudicial killings of terrorists? You won't hold that against me?"

That statement took me aback. I paced a bit, then said, "That depends. I'm not going to let you slide for some murder you did. That's not how this works."

I saw him study me, judging. He said, "You are Special Forces, too."

I said, "That's not pertinent."

He said, "Yes, it is."

I said, "Okay, I am. Now what?"

"Because you understand what the real world is like," he said. "I killed a man. Because of this."

I was now sure he was just a nutcase who was trying to use me to get out of some sociopathic bullshit. I said, "We're done here unless you give me what you know. Right. Fucking. Now."

He said, "I just did. The man in Gibraltar who caused the explosion in Houston, I'm the one who killed him. I followed him because of a bank account. I didn't know he was involved in a current attack."

And it all came home. I connected the dots and said, "You were in the Bahamas."

He looked shocked. "I was never in the Bahamas."

I said, "Oh, yes, you were. You killed the source, didn't you? And you are the man they're looking for in Gibraltar."

"I'm not saying anything else."

I said, "Yes, you will. One way or the other. There is another attack on the way, and I will stop it, either with your willing cooperation or . . . unwilling. Either way, you're going to cooperate."

Hesitantly, he said, "All I was trying to do was help. That's all."

"And here in Fez? What were you doing?"

"I honestly don't know. I was just following a lead."

I said, "Following a lead. Sure."

Carly said my name, and I went to her in the corner of the room. Splayed out on a table were the things we'd found on him, including his passport, a smartphone, and a strange Ziploc bag with a piece of rubber in it.

Carly whispered, "He's hiding something about the Bahamas, but I think he's credible."

"Why do you say that?"

"Watching his body language, for one, and this, for another." She held up the smartphone, using her frame to keep it concealed from Johan. She pulled out the rubber and put it on her index finger, saying, "He hacked this iPhone by making a fingerprint."

She put her index finger on the Touch ID, and magically, the screen cleared. She said, "The phone's not his."

I was impressed at what she'd put together. *Thank God we didn't throw away that piece of rubber as trash.*

She finished by saying, "Threaten him with the cell. If I'm right, you'll be surprised at the reaction."

I returned to Johan, holding the phone. I said, "You want us to start looking, and we can go deep. We'll dissect this handset down to the ones and zeros, retrieving a digital trail that you can't hide. When I find out you've lied to me, I'm going to cause you pain, and not gentle, like before."

He said, "I wish you *would* go deep. Rip it apart. I can't defeat all the password protections on it. I barely got past the lock screen."

I looked at Carly, then said, "It's not your phone?"

"No. It's the terrorist's phone. A member of a group we're both trying to stop."

61

Tariq lounged in his father's chair as if he had no concerns in the world. But he did. Ring of Fire was turning into a debacle, and as much as his father talked about heritage and history, he knew that their bottom line stopped right here in the present. Despite the barking about Islam and the selfless nature of the fight, at the end of the day only one thing mattered: Could anyone prove their company had a hand in something heinous?

And it was looking more and more like they could.

He saw the door swing open and his father enter the room. Tariq stood, sweat building under his armpits. He knew his father had heard about the fiasco in Fez. It had actually made international news. A sleeper cell that had escaped the authorities. There was a manhunt going on for the very men he was going to use, and the only thing that helped was that the names the authorities knew were not the identities the men were traveling under.

His father walked behind his desk and fell heavily into his chair, saying nothing. He rubbed his forehead, then looked up, asking, "Are we done?"

"Do you mean us, as in me and you, or the mission?"

His father leaned forward and said, "I mean Ring of Fire. Why on earth would I feel threatened?"

"Ring of Fire is progressing. Yes, they were found out in Fez—"

His father cut him off. "Why should I feel threatened? Is there a reason you parsed my question?"

"No, Father, I just misunderstood, but there is no reason to worry. We are completely dislocated from any actions involving the cell. Different countries, different heritage, different everything. Jalal is the only one who's ever even met me, and he doesn't know my real name. Only that I'm Saudi Arabian and rich. He certainly doesn't know you. Even if they catch him, he can't say anything that could harm us."

"Yet we thought the same thing about the cell. They were supposed to be invisible, with nobody looking for them, much less finding them. How did that happen?"

"I don't know, but the DGST is vicious, and they are everywhere. Maybe one of the cousins said something suspicious to an informant, and they were just going to be questioned. Maybe they panicked, leading to the shootout. Either way, they got out of the country."

"You don't fear them getting caught in Rome?"

"No. I think the entire event in Fez was a fluke. I truly do. As I said, the authorities are looking for Moroccan citizens with Moroccan names, and our men are traveling as Saudi Arabians, with preapproved tourist visas for the United States."

Yousef leaned back, staring at the ceiling. After a moment, he said, "Okay, okay, we'll continue. How soon before they attack?"

"A few days at least. They first have to get to the safe house I rented, then we need to ship them their vehicles, but it will work."

"You lost a man in Fez. Will two be enough to accomplish the mission?"

"Yes. Jalal says it will."

Yousef reached into a briefcase and pulled out a sheaf

of papers. He said, "The container from Algeciras is across the Panama isthmus." He slid the top paper across and said, "It'll be in the port of Los Angeles in two days. That's the new ship."

"Excellent. I'll inform Anwar."

"He's still in Los Angeles?"

"Yes. He's growing impatient because I told him to keep his movements low."

Yousef pushed another sheet of paper across the desk and said, "I want you to travel to the United States tonight. I've already purchased your tickets. Go to Norfolk and retrieve the explosives that were going to be used in the third vehicle, then give them to Anwar. Have him construct another one of his flying bombs."

Tariq studied the sheet, then looked up at his father in surprise. He said, "What is this?"

"The final target. The one we missed fifteen years ago."

62

Stuck in the midday traffic on the memorial bridge, Kurt could see the Washington Monument a short distance away, but it might as well have been on the moon. His phone chirped, and he answered, saying, "We're on the way. A little traffic. We should be there within twenty minutes."

He hung up. From behind the wheel, George Wolffe said, "If they wanted a meeting within five minutes, they should have called it at midnight."

Kurt said, "Apparently, the president has to get on the campaign trail, and they really want to know what we've found. He's going to be out of pocket for the next week."

"Well, you could have told him what we have in less time than that phone call."

George was using hyperbole, but not much. It had been a little over twenty-four hours since Pike had contacted him, asking for reach-back technological and intelligence support, and the Taskforce had worked furiously, developing a few thin leads. Kurt would have preferred to wait until they'd managed to at least flesh out a possible course of action instead of just finding data points, but apparently that was not to be.

George said, "Maybe we should ask the Oversight Council for approval of lights and sirens."

Kurt laughed and said, "I'm not sure they'd appreciate a clandestine force racing around DC with lights blazing."

"It worked for S.H.I.E.L.D."

After bumping along for another fifteen minutes, they eventually pulled into the security access point for the White House, and then to the portico of the West Wing. Alexander Palmer was waiting under the awning, waving them forward.

They pulled up and he said, "George, find a parking spot. Sorry, but Kurt needs to get inside now. The president is running late."

Without another word, Palmer turned and walked to the entrance. Kurt raised his eyebrows at George, then jumped out, trotting to catch up. Palmer handed him his access badge, and they entered the White House.

They reached the Oval Office and Kurt asked, "Is the entire Council in here?"

"No. Just the principals, but President Hannister wants an update."

Meaning it was the director of the CIA, the secretary of state, the secretary of defense, and the president. The four members who habitually hashed out Taskforce business before bringing it to the full Council.

He opened the door and ushered Kurt inside. Kurt saw the principals sitting on two couches facing each other, with President Hannister in a chair at the head.

Kurt nodded at the members, then said, "Sir, sorry. I understand you have a flight to catch."

Hannister smiled and said, "Unfortunately, yes. Apparently, part of the job description of president means I have to campaign so I can keep the job of president. I've received briefings from the other parts of the intelligence community, which amounted to a bunch of guessing about groups, motives, and possible follow-on targets. After your report from Pike, I was wondering if you had anything concrete."

Earlier, Kurt had given a detailed SITREP describing the trail that Pike had followed, ending with the action in Fez.

"Sir, yes and no. We have a bunch of data points right now but haven't analyzed them enough to weave a story. I will say, unfortunately, that I believe one or more attacks are in motion right now. It's undetermined how far along they are, but I can state with some certainty that it's coming."

Palmer muttered, "Shit."

President Hannister said, "Why?"

"The threads are too spread out. We had an attack originating in Gibraltar from a Moroccan, then a team of Moroccans engaged in a shootout in Fez, all of whom have disappeared, and now a link to someone else in Algeciras, Spain. All of that wasn't for the Houston attack. It's spread over three different countries, and it's for something greater than a single attack."

Kerry Bostwick, the D/CIA, said, "What did you find in Algeciras?"

"You read about the man from South Africa in my report, correct?"

"Yes, we saw that."

"He had a phone that he'd hacked on his own but couldn't get anything out of it because of further encryption and password protections. The Taskforce hooked up to it remotely, and we digitally drained it of everything we could find. In it is an application called Wickr. It's an end-to-end encrypted messaging service, and a Moroccan ship worker having that, in and of itself, is suspicious."

"So you were able to break the encryption and get the messages?"

"Unfortunately, no. The application has a built-in

design that allows the messages to self-destruct after a predetermined amount of time. There were no messages in it—but there was the contact information for someone else with a Wickr account. In effect, the owner can hide his messages, but not who he's talking to. They both have to have a Wickr account."

Palmer said, "And this other contact is in Algeciras?"

"Yes, and I think it's the root for a second attack."

"Why? Maybe it's just a friend of his."

Kerry said, "Algeciras is the location of one of the biggest ports in the Mediterranean." He looked at Kurt and said, "You think a second attack is coming from that port, like the first did from Gibraltar?"

"I do. I'd like a modified Alpha authority to go check it out. Modified in the sense that we don't have a lot of time here. I want to check out the contact and, if he's Moroccan, conduct an Omega rendition operation. If we're wrong, we're wrong, and we deal with it. I think that option's better than not interdicting, given the stakes."

Palmer said, "You want to capture a guy solely based on his nationality?" He turned to the president and said, "Sir, I really think we should bring this to the entire Oversight Council. That's a pretty big precedent to set."

Kurt said, "Sir, please don't spin it that way. I'm talking about capturing a Moroccan who's been using a highly sophisticated encrypted messaging service tied into another Moroccan who blew up the Houston Ship Channel. I think it's warranted."

President Hannister said, "And if you're wrong? What do we do with him? If he's innocent, we can't throw him in the Cloud to protect Taskforce involvement."

Referring to the Taskforce's unique detention capability where true terrorists were imprisoned without experiencing the US justice system, Hannister was asking a valid question. Kurt said, "Pike can mitigate that. Worst case, he'll get thrown back onto the street and we disappear. He won't even know where we're from. Hell, buy him a new car or something. I'm not talking about torturing the guy. Just questioning him."

President Hannister said, "Okay. Get the Council together and put it before them. You'll get your Alpha, I'm sure."

"Sir, we don't have time for that. It'll take another day, at least, to get a meeting established, and every minute is precious. The attack could be tomorrow for all I know."

"You feel this one connection is worth that risk."

"I think the risk of not doing it far outweighs the risks of bringing him in. For what it's worth, Pike is convinced he's bad."

President Hannister nodded, then addressed the assembled men. "Okay, we vote right here, right now."

In the end, even Palmer voted to allow Pike free rein. Kurt said, "Thank you. You won't regret it."

Kerry chuckled, saying, "If Pike can find a thread by chasing a drug dealer's bank account, I'm all about him continuing that streak of luck."

Kurt said, "That's the other data point we have. They aren't drug dealer bank accounts. The South African found the terrorist in Gibraltar by *also* following a bank account. Apparently, he works for a company that deals in offshore accounts and was worried about the Panama Papers leaks just like we were, but in this case it was because the owner's name was being forged on accounts he had nothing to do with. I sent Pike the Panama Papers data dump that we had, and the South African went through it, highlighting several accounts tied to his boss."

"Who is his boss, and why is he messing around with offshore accounts?"

"His name is Dexter Worthington. He owns a defense contracting company called Icarus Solutions. As to why, I don't know and don't really care. That's something for the FBI to look at. Anyway, we did our own analysis and a name triggered—Tariq bin Abdul-Aziz."

"Who is that?"

"Remember the redacted congressional committee report on 9/11?"

"Yes, of course. The conspiracy theories about that were deafening, but in the end, it was nothing."

"True. It *was* nothing, but now it might be something. Tariq is the son of a wealthy Saudi financier, and he was living in Sarasota, Florida, in September of 2001, the same place Mohamed Atta and others learned to fly. Tariq left the day before 9/11, and the FBI investigated the departure. It was very strange, with the house left fully furnished, to the point of leaving dirty dishes still in the sink and cars in the driveway. Apparently, he just woke up one day and took his whole family back to Saudi Arabia. The excuse was that he had to attend graduate school, but there was also some smoke about Mohamed Atta's car license plate being found in the gate guard's register as having come through Tariq's neighborhood at one point. Anyway, the FBI couldn't prove anything concrete one way or the other."

"So . . . what are you saying? Saudi Arabia is behind this?"

"No, no. Not at all. At least not at this point. What I'm saying is that it's beyond the realm of believable for a guy who turned up in the original 9/11 report to now be attached to bank accounts that have connections to another spectacular attack. In addition to that, the one dead terrorist in the Fez shootout had a Saudi passport, complete with a forged US visa."

The secretary of state said, "So how does that help us? You want State to lean on KSA for information on Tariq? See if they'll play ball?"

"No. For one, they refused to do anything about the FBI's information right after 9/11, even preventing making Tariq available for questioning. I don't think this will rise to a level that will change their minds, and I certainly don't want them to alert him that we're looking. For another, he's not in Saudi Arabia. What I want is to get his name into every single database and police station in the United States."

"What good will that do? Wait, are you saying . . ."

"Yes. I took the liberty of searching the ICE database this morning. Tariq bin Abdul-Aziz flew from Morocco last night and entered the United States in New York. His current whereabouts are unknown."

The secretary of defense said, "This is sounding more and more like all of the evidence prior to 9/11. We were running around like chickens, flailing in the dark, knowing a hit was coming but having no idea how."

"Well, it gets a little worse, but at least we have a focus this time. I'm convinced it's the ports. The ghetto apartment that the terrorists were using in Fez contained a laptop computer that they left behind in their haste to escape. It was a marginal netbook without a lot of power, and didn't have anything of special significance, but it did have a screenshot of Google Maps, and the location was of Norfolk, Virginia. By that, I mean the Norfolk shipyards, ports, and naval bases off the Chesapeake Bay."

The secretary of defense said, "Anything more specific than that? Norfolk is a mix of civilian and military assets.

I can definitely amp up the security on the military side, but short of stopping every single ship on the civilian side, there's not much we can do. This is different from 9/11. We can't stop the flow of trade like we did air travel."

President Hannister said, "Can we do it for a single port? Now that we have this information? Can we stop just this port from receiving ships?"

Palmer said, "Sir, we'd need to consult at least three cabinet positions on what that would entail. It would be a massive disruption of trade, and the very fact that we did it would signal a victory."

President Hannister turned to Kurt and said, "Are you sure it's Norfolk? If I make that call, can you tell me it's right?"

Kurt took a breath and then gave the bad news. "No, sir. I can't."

63

Third Mate Mitchell Redwing watched the cranes lifting the containers onto his ship, an endless chain of motion that reminded him of staring at an ant pile as a child. Docked in the port of Balboa on the Pacific side of the Panama Canal, his ship acted like a regional commuter airline, traveling back and forth between the West Coast of the United States and the Balboa terminal, taking container loads from the ships too large to use the canal.

They would offload their cargo at the Colón side on the Caribbean, and then the Panama railway would transport the containers across the isthmus to the Pacific side. Unlike the crew members of the enormous ships on the Caribbean side, he never had the pleasure of plying the high seas from one exotic port to another. He simply transported the goods straight up the coast, stopping like a bus at various ports. He didn't mind, though.

Graduating from the Merchant Marine Academy five years ago, he'd had visions of sailing all over the world, not being a back-and-forth truck driver, but it was a good living. A comfortable one. He certainly enjoyed his time in Panama. In Los Angeles, not so much.

He worried now because of the march of time. The railway line was old, and the new canal locks were open, allowing the enormous ships—much larger than his—to transit the isthmus. Currently, some companies were skittish because of a few collisions with the walls of the locks, but eventually, they'd work it out. And his employer of feeder ships would be left in the dustbin of history, like the taxicab was becoming with Uber.

He paced the deck of the ship, watching each container loading, checking his manifest and generally acting as if he knew what was being brought aboard. In truth, he did not. Nobody could. There were way more goods in the containers than any single human could track, and too many points of intersection for something not on the manifest to be introduced, from the initial port to the transload at Colón to the rail transport to the transload here in Balboa. He knew that smuggling using these points of failure was rampant, including drugs and even humans, but it was an overwhelming task, so like every other shipper, he relied on the paperwork. If it matched up, then it matched up.

After all, he wasn't responsible for what was loaded in the containers. That was the responsibility of the people across the ocean. When loading the containers, they had to adhere to the United States' Maritime Transportation Security Act—a law created after the terrorist attacks on 9/11. If they certified that the cargo met the requirements, all he had to do was certify that the manifest and seals were correct.

He did so, tracking one container after another. Two hours after the loading had begun, he checked off a specific container, watching as it was lowered to the deck and placed at the bottom of the stack.

Its cable seal was correct, so he signaled for the loading to continue. He did nothing more than ensure it was seaworthy, without any structural deficiencies. It sank to the steel of the deck, and the crew hands rushed to secure it in place, building a foundation for the multiple containers that would be stacked above it. It was one container of thousands Mitchell had loaded in his five years on the sea. One more container full of stuffed animals, auto parts, or interior lighting that he didn't give a second glance.

But he should have. This one would hold much more importance in his life than the modernization of the canal.

64

Carly leaned over Knuckles to get a view outside the jet's window and said, "What now? I thought we were cleared for Algeciras."

Knuckles saw Pike talking into a phone on the tarmac and said, "I have no idea. Just relax. You can't worry about every little thing. When he comes back on, he'll let us know."

"Doesn't that drive you batshit? I mean, with this guy, every day is a new adventure."

Knuckles said, "It's not him. It's the life. The one you signed on for."

Carly leaned back into her chair and said, "That's ridiculous. Even in the CIA we have plans. We don't fly by the seat of our pants every waking moment."

Knuckles said, "Neither do we. It might look like we do, but it's really the opposite. We react to changing conditions better than anyone on the planet, and we capitalize on those changes. Most would execute a plan that no longer had any meaning. We do not." A little miffed at the exchange, he said, "Maybe you should have just stayed in the CIA. It would have been easier."

Surprised, she said, "Hey, wait, what's that supposed to mean?"

He glanced to the rear, where Jennifer was sitting next to the man named Johan, and said, "I've seen what she's been through. Pike supported her every step of the way, but even that almost wasn't enough. She's succeeded because she has the drive. If you don't have the commitment, it's not going to work out here."

Carly said, "What are you talking about? Is this about us?"

Knuckles's eyebrows flew up. He hissed, "Don't say that out loud. We can't date and be on the same team."

Carly sagged back into her seat, chuckling.

He said, "What the hell is so funny?"

"Knuckles, everyone on this plane knows we're dating. *Everyone*, and it's not a big deal. I'm a case officer; you're an Operator. We aren't in the same chain of command, and I'm not on this team. This isn't high school."

Knuckles sat for a little bit, then said, "You don't want a job like Jennifer's? Wouldn't you like to do something more than just a support role?"

Carly considered the words, then said, "Yeah, I guess that would be cool, but I sure as shit wouldn't want to put up with the crap she did. I mean, my job's hard, but at least it's already seeded with females. I don't have to be the glass-ceiling breaker."

He turned to her and said, "And that's all it is? You don't want to try for something more because it's safer where you are?"

He saw her eyes squint, and he knew he'd overstepped. She said, "You think it's easy being a female case officer in the CIA? You think it was easy getting to where I am? Not everybody pines to be on a supersecret team. I work better alone. I like being the master of my own fate and don't need the dick measuring on a team to define my worth."

He smiled and held his hands up, saying, "I'm not looking for a fight; it's just that you won't get a shot if the command thinks I'm dating you. There can't be any skeletons in the closet that might interfere with the decision."

She said, "What do you mean, 'get a shot'?"

Pike entered the cabin, saying, "It looks like a split mission. Everyone on me."

Carly glared at Knuckles, but he unbuckled his seat belt, relieved. They gathered around one of the tables in the Rock Star bird, leaving Johan in the back chained to an eyebolt.

Pike said, "The Taskforce is still working through the ramifications of what we've sent them, trying to make connections, and we now have a change of mission."

Knuckles said, "So the Algeciras thing is a no-go?"

"No. It's still prime, but they continued digging into the bank account information, and one of the offshore accounts is tied to one in New York, and *that* account was used in Norfolk, Virginia. Right now, they don't know why. It's just a couple of lines on a bank transfer, but it's in Norfolk, and given the map we found, that's where we're headed."

Retro said, "Holy shit. The mother lode."

Pike grinned and said, "Yeah, I think so. There are still some posse comitatus issues with the Taskforce charter, but me, you, Veep, and Jennifer are headed back to DC now. Hopefully by the time we land they'll have something to give us for hunting."

Knuckles realized he was missing out. He said, "Wait, what? What am I doing?"

"You and Carly are headed to Algeciras. Find the guy with the phone and get information out of him. Find out what he knows. We don't have anything but a city at this point. We need something more."

He said, "She's not an Operator. I should be going with you."

The sentence, of course, made no sense, and Knuckles knew it. So did Carly, the insult sinking home. He saw her expression and said, "That's not what I meant. This Algeciras mission is a side note. Pike, you're going to need me on the X in Norfolk."

Jennifer said, "I'll go with her, if you want."

Pike said, "This isn't a democracy. Knuckles is going to Algeciras. I need experience there and you're it. We have Omega authority, and that's no small thing. I'll need your judgment. We'll overfly Algeciras and get a pinpoint. I expect a report of success by the time I land."

Knuckles nodded, not liking the answer. He glanced at Carly and saw nothing but venom. He said, "Maybe me and Jennifer should do it."

Pike said, "Nope. It's you and Carly. Let's see how that works out."

Knuckles saw exactly what he was doing. He said, "I'm not so sure this is smart."

Jennifer looked at Carly and said, "Why? I think it's perfect. It'll showcase her abilities on a live mission."

Carly said, "Why am I the only person who doesn't know what the state of play is? Why am I being tagged for a mission when I'm not even a member of the team?"

Pike said, "I might need everyone else. You want out, say the word, but you're now a member of the Taskforce. I use you as I see fit, just like I did with Creed in the Bahamas. You don't think you can handle it, I'll put Jennifer on it and go into my mission an Operator short. Your call."

Incensed, she said, "Who said I can't handle it?"

65

An hour later they were circling the city of Algeciras, Retro in the back working the technical kit for a pinpoint of the targeted phone. He said, "Got it. It's active."

The Taskforce information had placed the targeted handset in the cell network of Algeciras, but that was obviously too broad a target set to be of much use, so it was up to Retro to try to trick the handset into thinking their aircraft was a cell tower, then implant malware into the operating system of the phone that would allow him to manipulate its embedded GPS function.

Pike said, "Can you penetrate?"

If he couldn't, they'd have to locate the phone the old-fashioned way—by triangulating its signal, a technique that had been used against radio networks since World War II.

Retro said, "I think so. I'm talking to it now."

Five minutes later, he said, "It's in. I'm releasing the phone back to the network. I've got it slaved."

Pike directed the pilot to continue to the Jerez Airport, the closest commercial strip to the city, and Retro came forward carrying a laptop and what looked like a thick smartphone.

He set the laptop on the table and manipulated a mapping function, zooming in on a blue dot. He said, "According to Taskforce mapping data, it's sitting in a mosque right now."

Carly said, "That's good news. At least we know he's Muslim. How are we going to figure out if he's Moroccan, though? That could take some work."

Pike and Knuckles grinned, and she said, "What's so funny?"

Pike said, "If he looks Moroccan, we're taking him."

"But Kurt said . . ."

"Kurt knows what we're doing. Knuckles will make the call, but we're not going to spend five days developing this guy."

She glanced at Jennifer but said nothing else. Knuckles studied the map, saying, "How am I going to pinpoint his phone? There could be a hundred people inside praying."

Retro passed across the smartphone. "This is now slaved to his handset, so you can follow the marble until you sort out who has it. Let him go somewhere else, then take a snapshot of the people. Do that a few times, and you'll figure out who he is."

The pilot called for them to buckle up for the descent into Jerez, and ten minutes later they were on the ground. The aircraft taxied to the general aviation terminal; then the pilot killed the engines. Knuckles and Carly stood up, carrying nothing more than a backpack each. Pike said, "Make the call in one cycle of darkness. Either you get him or you decide to abort, but I want you headed back home tomorrow night at the latest. There's a rendition flight inbound right now. Whether it comes home with a terrorist or not, I want you on that aircraft."

Knuckles nodded, saying, "Don't do anything without me."

One and a half hours after landing, Knuckles and Carly were sitting in a rented Honda across the street from the mosque, having arrived later than they wanted. Luckily, the blue marble was still inside.

The airport ended up being about an hour outside of Algeciras, and Knuckles had exited the ramp of the plane like a condemned man, knowing he had to endure the entire drive next to Carly. He'd seen her talking to Jennifer and dreaded what he was about to experience, regretting what he'd said on the plane. He actually hoped that the man at the far end had some guns. Violence would be easier to face than Carly's wrath.

Thankfully, Carly had spent the first twenty minutes just navigating, giving him directions while he drove. It wasn't until they were on the long stretch of the A-381 highway that she finally tipped over the applecart.

She said, "Did you lie to me when we talked about me joining the Taskforce? Did you have some plan all along about me attending assessment and selection?"

Flustered, he said, "No. You were recruited by Kurt all on your own, for your actions in Greece. I don't factor in for support hires. That's someone else's job."

"That's not what I asked. I came to you to discuss it, as a friend. To get advice I trusted about leaving my career at the CIA to come work for your organization. Did you give me your honest opinion, or did you have some other plan?"

"Carly, we weren't even dating then. No, I had no other plan."

"But the invitation was rescinded when the Taskforce was put on stand-down after Greece. Nobody even knew if it was going to survive. During the stand-down we started dating, and then that action in Poland happened, with the Taskforce saving the day, and the president putting you guys back into operation. After that, I got the invitation again—and I came to talk to you. Again."

"I didn't really think about it."

She looked out of the window, playing with her hair. He knew he was in trouble. She said, "Jennifer believes you did. She told me you talked to her at length about her experiences. She didn't think it was idle curiosity."

He glanced at her but remained quiet. She said, "Well?"

He gripped the steering wheel harder than necessary and said, "Okay, okay. Maybe I did think about it. What's wrong with that?"

"But you said on the plane we couldn't have a relationship if I did that. So, I'm just wondering how this will work out. If you can't have both, which one do you want?"

Knuckles slapped the wheel and said, "Christ! Stop the grilling. I don't *know* what I want. Shit, I've never even *had* a true relationship before. Forget about it. It's probably a moot point anyway. Even if you wanted to go, Kurt won't allow it."

She said nothing. They rode in silence, Knuckles fuming in the cloud of confusion she'd generated. In truth, he hadn't really considered the fallout. Carly's choices were different from Jennifer's. Jennifer and Pike were civilians. He was active-duty Navy. But Carly wasn't even in the military. She was CIA. How was that fraternization?

Mercifully, they reached the outskirts of Algeciras, and Carly began to navigate to the blue marble on the phone. They hit a traffic circle, and halfway around it, Carly pointed and said, "That's the mosque."

Knuckles kept going, circling to the next exit. He took it, then did a U-turn so they were facing the building, with the traffic circle between them.

He said, "Doesn't look like a mosque. Looks like an auto-repair shop."

"Well, whatever it is, that's where the phone is located."

There were a few cars in the small parking lot out front, and upward of a dozen bicycles chained to a metal fence. Knuckles said, "Lot of bikes for a car shop. Could be something else."

The roll-up garage door began to rise, and Knuckles saw an open bay with rugs on the floor. Inside were about thirty men in the process of putting on their shoes from a rack on the left side, all Arabs.

Knuckles said, "Shouldn't have doubted Retro."

The men began to stream out, and Carly said, "Here we go."

66

Knuckles said, "We don't have to follow right behind the marble. Let's give it some breathing room, separate it from the pack."

Carly nodded, saying, "It's in front of the mosque right now."

Many of the men had already moved to bicycles or cars, with several already on the road, the pack breaking up. He waited a moment, then said, "Is it still there?"

She said, "Yes."

There were now only seven or eight men left, and the group was being whittled down by the second as people wandered off. Knuckles tried to keep track of each one breaking off, anticipating a movement call. Eventually, there were only three left, and Knuckles was afraid the equipment was failing.

"Still there?"

She glanced up and said, "Yep. No change."

"Well, it's either one of those three guys, or we're screwed."

Eventually, one man wearing a jumpsuit and a skullcap began moving toward a bike. He spent a second unlocking it, then pedaled away from the traffic circle, into a neighborhood of concrete-block houses.

He disappeared, and Carly said, "It's moving, it's moving."

"Which way?"

"North. It's going north."

That's our guy.

"Okay, let's follow him. Take the wheel."

"Why?"

"You never know when an opportunity will present itself."

Carly switched seats, muttering, "Here we go, flying by the seat of our pants."

Knuckles slid over to the passenger side, saying, "You didn't mind that seat-of-the-pants stuff when we first started dating. I remember a time at the Kennedy Center . . ."

She grinned, pulling into the circle. "There's a time and a place for everything."

They went through it, seeing the cyclist about two hundred meters ahead of them. Happy at the lightening of the tone, Knuckles said, "Let's hope this is the time and the place."

Carly followed, driving at a slow pace. Knuckles never gave a command, knowing this was her forte. As a CIA case officer, she had plenty of real-world experience conducting surveillance, and he trusted her instincts. This was one skill set where she was better than him.

The bike reached an intersection and took a right into a narrow lane, only one car wide. She reached it and kept going north. Knuckles said, "We're going to lose him."

Carly said, "Take a look around. This is his neighborhood. We're the outsiders. We go down that lane and we'll burn ourselves."

Knuckles knew she was right. He said, "We'd better pray this technology works."

She circled the block, then found a parking spot, saying, "What's he doing? Continuing on, or stopped?"

"It's stationary."

She said, "I'll bet that's the bed-down. He lives down that alley." She looked at him and said, "So, what now?"

Knuckles switched to Google Street View on the smartphone mapping app, studying the building the marble was in. He said, "It's a row of block houses all connected together. Each one has a roll-up door for a garage, and an entrance door to the right."

He rotated to the rear of the building, but the street view didn't travel down the back-alley footpath. He pulled a satellite image of the building, seeing an alley with garbage cans and a line of balconies on each house. He said, "Let's go on foot. You knock on the front door. I'll go around to the back. If he's got an escape plan, it will be through the rear."

She said, "If he answers the door, what do I do?"

"You speak fluent Spanish. Act like an official from the gas company or something, but get inside."

She said, "I don't speak Castilian like they do here."

He chuckled and said, "I don't think he'll know the difference. If anything, he'll barely speak Spanish at all."

"So, I knock on the door, and then, if he lets me in, I take him down?"

"Yeah. Get a gun on him and get him facedown."

She dug into her backpack, pulling out a Glock 27. She loaded a magazine, then racked a round. She looked skittish, and he said, "It's not that hard. He'll comply."

He followed her example, loading his own pistol, then studied the location on the map. He pinpointed his stopping point in the alley, memorizing what he could from the image, then said, "You good?"

She turned to him and said, "Tell me the truth: Is this a test for me? Would you do this differently if I weren't on the operation?"

Startled, Knuckles said, "No. No way. I would never

put someone in harm's way as a test. Jesus. This is a real-world operation. There are lives at stake. Is that what you think of me?"

She looked chagrined, then said, "I was just thinking about what Pike said when we left."

"Pike's looking for success. He's not looking for a test, and neither am I. Are you ready for this?"

She nodded. He looked into her eyes, saying, "I'm sending you to the front because he might react if he sees me. He won't suspect a woman. And because I trust you. Usually, I would only send an Operator on your mission, and as far as that goes, there's only one other woman on the planet I would give your tasking."

"Jennifer?"

He put in his Bluetooth earpiece, checked the connection, then opened the car door. He said, "Yep. But she's an Operator. Trust me, I would never test you."

He leaned back in and pecked her on the cheek, saying, "That'll come later."

She said, "What's that mean?" but he was trotting down the street.

Knuckles went around the block to the back alley, checking out the escape routes as he jogged. There was a back door to each unit, but it looked more like an entrance to a storage area than egress to the alley. Above each was a small balcony with an iron railing. He counted them, stopping when he was behind the target house. The balcony above had a rope attached to it, knots spaced every three feet. He keyed his Bluetooth and said, "Carly, Carly, I'm set."

She said, "I'm on the move."

He said, "Put your connection to speaker."

She did, and he heard the clicks of her steps and the

brushing of her arms against her top as she walked. Eventually, he heard, "I'm here. About to knock."

He said, "Be prepared for the unexpected. He's not a mastermind, but there's a rope back here, so he's put some thought into this."

She said, "Great," then he heard the knock. He heard a jumble of noises, then a man speaking broken Spanish. Carly said something back, and then he heard her whisper, "He's letting me in. He's letting me in."

"Get the door closed, then put him on the ground. I'm coming to the front."

He started running, then heard a gunshot, louder in his ear from the Bluetooth than on the street. Two more erupted in his earpiece. It was a damn gunfight. He stopped his movement, feeling dread. He said, "Carly, Carly, status."

He heard, "He's running! He's running! He's armed! He ran upstairs. I'm following."

He reversed course, streaking back down the alley, saying, "No. Let him go. I have him. Stay out of the line of fire. Let him think he's safe."

He saw a figure explode out onto the balcony, then flip onto the rope, scampering down it.

Halfway to the ground the man saw him coming down the alley. The man raised his pistol and got off one round, wide, just as Knuckles reached the tail end of the rope. He grabbed it and started violently swinging it left and right. The man dropped the pistol, clamping his hands onto the rope in an attempt to hold on. Knuckles ran with the rope sideways, then reversed back in the other direction, slamming the man's body into the brick wall. He fell at Knuckles's feet, the wind knocked out of him. He feebly tried to fight, raising his arms and gasping. Knuckles draped his arms around the man's neck and cut off the blood to his brain. The man slumped.

He called, "Carly, he's down. Get the vehicle. Meet me at the end of the alley."

"What about the house? Shouldn't we search it?"

She was right, but they had little time. He needed to carry this guy unconscious down the alley, and someone might have heard the gunshots. He said, "No time. Maybe we'll come back, but we need to get out of here, now."

She acknowledged, and he hoisted the man to his shoulders in a fireman's carry. He hoofed it up the narrow alley, reaching the end without incident. Then he saw a small girl looking at him through an upstairs window.

Nothing he could do about it.

Carly pulled up two minutes later, and he slid the man into the backseat. He jumped in the front and said, "Get out of here. Head back toward Jerez, but pull over once you're out of the city so I can tape this guy up."

She started driving, weaving through the city faster than necessary, the adrenaline coursing through her. Working his phone, he was thrown against the door on one turn. He said, "Whoa, whoa, slow it down. Slow is smooth and smooth is fast. We don't want to get pulled over."

She did so, and he contacted the Taskforce, saying he had a package for delivery. He hung up and said, "Well, that went okay."

She smiled hesitantly, and he asked, "What? Did I miss something?"

"I screwed that up, didn't I?"

"How? He's in the backseat."

"Yeah, but you expected me to take him down."

"I didn't 'expect' anything. That's what flying by the

seat of your pants means. You plan the best you can, and you react to the curveballs thrown your way."

"I should have followed him upstairs. If I had, you wouldn't have been exposed on the street, and we could have questioned him inside the house. I could have done it."

"No, you should have listened to me, and you did. Your life isn't worth chasing an armed man around an unknown floor plan. He lives there. He knew the terrain. You didn't, and after the gunshots, there was no way we were going to interrogate him there. You need to learn to leverage the team."

She nodded, unsure if he was just placating her. He said, "What happened, anyway?"

"He let me in, even turning his back to me. I followed him to the kitchen, and he opened a drawer, pulled a pistol, and took a shot. I fired back, and he took off running. That was about it."

Knuckles saw that there had been more to the action than she was telling. It had been close, and it had impacted her. It was a gunfight, and those were never easy. He said, "You did fine. There's no reason to be a hero unless it's called for. All we wanted was the target, and we got him."

She smiled, grateful, and he said, "But . . . you missed him?"

She gave him a sharp glare, and he said, "Now, *that's* something we'll have to work on."

67

Kurt's phone went off with the special ring. He rolled over in his bed and checked the time: two in the morning. Which meant it wasn't good news.

He shook the sleep out of his head and answered, saying, "Colonel Hale."

The duty officer for the Taskforce said, "Sir, we have an issue. Knuckles was successful, and he's conducted an interrogation. It's not good."

"What is it?"

"I really think you need to speak to him directly."

"Be there in ten. Tell him to stand by."

He threw on some jeans and a T-shirt, racing out of his high-rise next to the Clarendon Metro stop. He could have driven, but it would be just as quick to run the two blocks to Taskforce headquarters.

He entered through the underground parking garage, breathing more heavily than he wanted and thinking he needed to get back to the gym. He badged in to the elevator and exited on the third floor, seeing George Wolffe.

He said, "How on earth did you beat me here?"

George laughed and said, "I was still here fighting the bureaucracy, doing the stuff you don't have to worry about. Knuckles called jackpot, so I decided to wait and see what happened."

They walked down the hall to the command center, Kurt saying, "And what's he got?"

"Your call was good to go. He's got a Moroccan who planted a bomb on a boat from Algeciras. It's headed into Los Angeles as we speak."

They entered the command center and Kurt said, "Bring it up on the main screen."

The communications man said, "He's inbound right now on the rendition bird, so it may be choppy."

Kurt nodded, waiting. Eventually, the screen cleared, and Kurt saw Carly Ramirez. He said, "Carly, what's up? What do you have?"

"Sir, the guy has planted a bomb on a container ship headed to Los Angeles. He's working with the same cell. Jalal al-Khattabi—the guy we were chasing in Fez—helped him break security. It's the same crew, and it's planted on a boat called the *Al Salam II*."

"Where's the boat now?"

"The Taskforce is working that now, but that's not the biggest problem. The bomb has a cylinder of cobalt 60 inside. That's a radioactive material used for cancer treatment and food irradiation. It's deadly, and if it's exploded out, it will render the port inoperative."

Kurt held up a finger and turned away from the screen, saying, "Get me a CBRN guy, right now."

Two minutes later, George picked up the phone and said, "I got our CBRN officer on the line. Go easy. He thinks he's been awakened because it's the end of the world."

Kurt said, "It might be. Put him on speaker."

George punched a button, then nodded. Kurt said, "Hey, I don't have a lot of time here. You're the expert on chemical, biological, radiological, and nuclear events?"

He heard a nervous voice. "Yes, sir. I'm branched chemical in the Army. I have a degree—"

"Sorry. I don't give a shit. What I want to know is what the damage would be with a dirty bomb on a boat."

Now on firmer ground, the man said, "Well, that would depend on a ton of different variables. Wind speed, size of the explosive charge, how much radioactive material was involved, and blocking forces such as woods or mountains. If it were a bomb like Oklahoma City, it could do serious damage, spreading radiation over a vast distance. I'd have to know more than just 'dirty bomb.'"

"Say there was a bomb inside a CONEX on a boat, and it was laced with cobalt 60."

Kurt heard nothing, and waited. Eventually, the man said, "Cobalt 60 is pretty dangerous. We used to prepare for the 'doomsday bomb' back in the Cold War, when the old USSR talked about lacing their bombs with it. In a worldwide thermonuclear war, its half-life would render the entire earth uninhabitable. Hydrogen and neutron bombs were devastating, but they were designed to kill quickly, allowing the reclamation of the terrain. Their effects could be overcome. The fallout from a cobalt bomb would literally destroy the earth."

Kurt said, "I'm not talking about global thermonuclear war. What could happen with the scenario I'm giving?"

"If the cobalt was seeded into the explosives, it would depend on how big the explosive charge was. It's directly proportional to how far the explosive power could project the cobalt."

"Say half a CONEX. Say they had something the size of a Volkswagen Bug. What's the damage?"

"The explosion would be minimal. Not enough to even worry about as far as loss of life is concerned, but the spread of the cobalt would render everything in at least a quarter-mile radius as deadly. Of course, I say that assuming there aren't any weather vulnerabilities."

"What do you mean by that?"

"The cobalt will be thrown out from the explosion, so anything near that site would be deadly, but from then, it would depend on the atmosphere. If the cloud of radiation were spread by favorable winds, it could render an entire city uninhabitable."

"That bad?"

"Yes. Cobalt 60 was known as the doomsday bomb for a reason. It's that bad."

Taking that in, remaining calm, Kurt said, "Thank you."

George hung up the phone, and Kurt turned back to the screen. "Carly, you know for a fact he's telling the truth? The guy isn't just making shit up?"

"Sir, if he is, he's doing it with a healthy knowledge of cobalt 60. If it's fake, he's studied how to make it real. I think he's telling the truth."

Knuckles appeared from the back of the aircraft, crowding into the screen. He said, "You get the word, sir? This is no shit."

Kurt said, "I did, and I need your assessment. Is he telling the truth, or is he just playing you to get us to over-react?"

Knuckles looked at Carly, confused that Kurt was repeating the question. He said, "He's telling the truth. Carly's pretty good at interrogation, and she bled him dry. It's real, and it's on the way."

An analyst ran into the room and said, "Who asked for the itinerary of the *Al Salam* cargo ship?"

George said, "Here. Give it to me."

He looked at it, then said, "This stopped in Panama two days ago. Where's the end result?"

"Sir, apparently the ship's captain decided the new locks were unsafe. He transloaded his shipment by rail to several smaller feeder ships."

Kurt turned to the analyst, saying, "How many different ships? Who's got the cargo now?"

"Sir, there's no way to tell. The rail line drops it at the Balboa port, and it's like a standby thing. It wasn't planned, because the original ship was supposed to travel all the way through, so now those containers have been loaded wherever there's room."

"Jesus Christ, are you kidding me? We can't track the shipment?"

"We could with the actual container. It's sealed and has a manifest, but without knowing which one it is, it could be on any number of ships."

Kurt looked back at the screen and said, "Ask him what container it's in. Ask him to identify the container by company or however that works."

Knuckles flicked his head at Carly, and she disappeared from the screen, going back to the seat where the terrorist was chained.

Kurt said, "Get me Alexander Palmer on the phone."

George went to the back of the room, picking up a secure line. He began dialing, saying, "You know this is going to take a while."

"Meaning?"

"Get Hannister. Fuck working through the minions."

"I'm not there yet. Give Palmer a warning order, and let's keep working the problem."

Carly came back on the screen, saying, "He doesn't know the specific CONEX. He can name the shipper, but he says the firm shipped forty containers. He could identify the original one, but he wrecked it to introduce the cobalt, forcing them to manually transload from the bad container to a new one. He doesn't know the seal number on the new container. All he can really give us is the ship."

"Are you sure?"

Truculent, Carly said, "Yes, sir. I'm sure. This isn't my first rodeo. He did say the bomb is triggered by cell phone."

"Meaning there's someone that has to call it?"

"Yes."

"Does he have the number?"

"No. Only Jalal had that, the guy we missed in Fez."

George Wolffe said, "That's not a lot of help. If they can track the package, they can call from anywhere in the world."

Kurt nodded, saying, "It's some help. It gives us a way to prevent it."

George said, "How? Are you going to shut down the cell network of Los Angeles and the California coast for the next month? You know that ain't happening."

Kurt absorbed the enormity of what they were facing. He said, "Okay, okay. We're in crisis mode. Knuckles, get him back here to DC. Usual spot at Dulles."

"On the way. What's Pike doing?"

"He's here, begging to go to Norfolk, but I'm running up against the charter on this. I can't allow the Taskforce to operate on US soil. Anyway, I think that's a waste of time now. We finally got some clarity on the bank account, and it was tied to a credit card used at a water-sports shop at Virginia Beach. The FBI investigated and it checked out. The place exists, and has been there for years. It even has an outlet with MWR on Fort Lee. It wasn't terrorist related. We have one more purchase, but it's in Richmond, Virginia, hell and gone from Norfolk. Pike's sure he's on to something, but I'm thinking Norfolk was the miss, and it's LA."

Knuckles said, "If we're not doing anything anyway, can we head down there?"

Kurt said, "Why?"

"You know, take a few days off at Virginia Beach. Not as Taskforce. Just to take some leave before summer's totally gone."

Kurt smiled, knowing what he was asking. He said, "Who do you want to take? Does the entire team want a vacation? It'll be hard to sell that."

"How about just me and Carly, and Pike and Jennifer? Could you sell that?"

Kurt nodded, saying, "Yeah. That's plausible. Just don't get in any trouble. If you happen to stumble across anything, you back off immediately and feed it to me. Understood?"

"Roger that, sir. See you in a couple of hours."

George shouted from across the room, "I've got Palmer on the line."

Kurt picked it up, saying, "Sir, I have the attack, and it's not Norfolk. I need to speak to the president."

He heard, "What do you have?"

"It's Los Angeles, and it's on the way. I don't have time for a discussion. I need to talk to the president. He's got to interdict maritime traffic into Long Beach and Los Angeles."

He heard nothing for a moment, then, "Holy shit, man, you're talking about shutting down two of the largest ports in the United States. Are you sure?"

"Yes. I'm not saying shut them down. We have a pinpoint we can use. The bomb is radiological, which means we only need to slow down the traffic, getting the Coast Guard to check each and every boat from Panama with radiological detection devices outside the port zone."

"Okay, I'll take that forward. I need to talk to the secretary of commerce and transportation about the impact, and I'll need your analysis of how sure you are this will occur. We also need to approach this with an eye for the election before we do something rash—"

Kurt cut him off, saying, "Get me in touch with the president, right fucking now."

He heard nothing for a moment, then, "Colonel Hale, you do not dictate the response of the United States. There are people to consult. Ramifications you can't even begin to understand."

"With all due respect, that's horseshit. Get me the president, or I'll hang your ass with the deaths."

After a moment, he heard, "Stand by. I'll see what I can do. He's on a flight to North Carolina."

Kurt hung up the phone, seeing George do the same on the extension. George said, "That went well, I think. Maybe I should start looking into a welding school."

68

Tariq pulled into the driveway, amazed at the house he'd found for his band of killers. Located on the inland waterway of the Lafayette River, and only a stone's throw from a zoological park, it was an upper-middle-class neighborhood with wide, leafy roads. It was older, with most of the houses being built in the seventies or eighties, but it was certainly not a ghetto, like the places he'd found for Anwar. Unlike those rentals, this time he'd focused on access to the port instead of the ability to blend into the population.

He'd located a four-bedroom ranch house near a boat ramp called Haven Creek, the perfect location. From there, it was a short trip up the waterway to a multitude of shipping interests, both US military and Norfolk's international port terminal.

He pulled into the driveway, parking next to a trailer holding one Sea-Doo watercraft, large enough to carry three people.

Good.

He walked up to the front door and knocked. Nobody came. He rang the bell, then caught a shadow behind the drapes. The door opened, and he saw Jalal, furious.

Tariq said, "Hello, brother. It looks like everything is working out."

Jalal grabbed his arm, jerking him inside and closing the door. He said, "What the hell were you thinking?

Have you seen this neighborhood? We can't go anywhere without someone staring at us."

Tariq jerked his arm away and said, "It's not that big of a deal. I did the same thing before our attacks in 2001."

"This is *after* 2001, you jackass. I told you to find us something secure."

Indignant, Tariq said, "No, you told me to find something close to the port, with a boat ramp. I did that."

Jalal balled his fists and said, "Yes, yes, that was necessary, but not sufficient. You've put us in the heartland of suspicion. People look at us going to get groceries. We cannot last here."

Tariq said, "You don't have to. Even if the police come, they can't search anything without a warrant. All you need to do is be polite. Trust me."

Jalal shook his head, saying, "I'd rather be living in a ghetto in Tangier than here. It's nerve-wracking."

Tariq clapped him on the shoulder and said, "You'll be back there soon enough. How goes the preparation?"

Jalal said, "Follow me."

They went to the garage, and Tariq saw the two *shahid* completing the final work on their suicide vehicles. Two Sea-Doo performance watercraft with the front hatches open, wires and explosives crammed inside. He said, "Will this work?"

Jalal said, "Yes. They're basically building a torpedo. We studied explosive books from the Internet, and they've crafted what's called a shaped charge. When they ram the hull, instead of just exploding outward, it will drive a jet directly into the vessel, penetrating the hull. With both of them striking, it will sink a ship. It will cause the port to lock down."

Tariq nodded, saying, "Good, good. What is your target?"

"Really, it'll depend on the response from their port security. If they're quick and start chasing us, I'll have to commit early. I'd like to hit a cruise ship, but that terminal is farther along the waterway. Worst case, we'll hit one of the warships at the Navy base."

"That might make more of an impact than the cruise ship."

Jalal said, "What about the other vessel? The one in Los Angeles?"

"It should have arrived today, so this will be perfect."

"So you want us to attack tonight?"

"Yes. They'll feel Los Angeles, then get hit here, on the East Coast. It will shut down their entire port system. It will cripple them."

The two working on the watercraft stopped what they were doing. Tariq said, "You will be heroes. Martyrs that will live forever."

They both went back to work, not saying a word. Tariq gave Jalal a quizzical look, and he said, "They do what they do for Islam. Not for your cheering. They aren't some idiots recruited by the Islamic State."

Tariq nodded, saying, "I meant no insult. I understand the sacrifice."

"Do you?"

"Yes, I do. In fact, I'm on my own mission. I only came here to take the explosives for the third watercraft. The one that won't be used now."

"You? What are you going to do?"

"Not your concern. I just need the explosives."

Jalal gazed back to the work being conducted and said, "I'm taking the third watercraft. I'm going to use it."

"As a martyr?"

"Yes. It's my destiny. I can't ask my brothers to do what I would not."

Flustered at Jalal's statement, confused by the man's sudden willingness to die, Tariq said, "But . . . that won't work."

Jalal looked at him with contempt, saying, "You bought the supplies, but they're no longer yours. Your checkbook does not put you in charge. I will use them. I will lead the attack."

Torn, wanting to call his father for advice, Tariq said, "Jalal, there is another attack in planning. The final one. I need those explosives."

"Get more."

Tariq's phone vibrated, surprising him. He looked at the screen and saw it was his father. He held up a finger, saying, "One moment."

Jalal turned away, disgusted.

Tariq answered, saying, "Yes, Father?"

"I have a report from the shipping company. Every boat going into Los Angeles is being stopped and searched. I need you to alert the asset."

Tariq said, "What happened?"

"I have no idea. I'm in Morocco. All I know is that I've been notified about delays of shipping into Los Angeles. I did some investigation, and they're stopping every ship from Panama, boarding them, then conducting some type of search. They somehow suspect the plan. Alert the asset and have him blow the container."

"But that won't do any good. If it's at sea, it will do nothing."

"It will do more than allowing the container to be found. It's all we can hope for."

Tariq thought through the ramifications, then said, "Okay, okay. We still have the Norfolk attack. I'm here now, and it's going to work."

"That's not as important as your attack. Get the

sleeper cell moving to Charleston. Have him blow the container ship and leave. Right now."

"What if the ship is outside of cell phone range? Shouldn't we check where it's located?"

"It's stacked up in a bunch of ships outside the port. I have the report of delays. It's even on the news. They're searching each one, but it's in range. I don't know if they've already searched it and found the container, but every minute is a chance for it to be found. Call him."

"Okay, okay, I will, but Jalal is saying he wants to be a *shahid* now. He wants to martyr himself with the final explosives."

Jalal heard his name and stared at Tariq. Tariq held out a finger, waiting on the answer from his father.

"Give him the phone."

Tariq said, "He wants to talk to you."

Jalal took the phone, glaring at Tariq, amazed that he had to fight to give his life. Tariq watched the conversation, seeing Jalal shout, then mutter, then hand the phone back.

Tariq said, "Father?"

"He's willing. Don't ignore his sacrifice. Do the final attack. Don't let us down."

Tariq said, "I won't father. I won't."

He hung up, realizing the "sacrifice" his father had mentioned was the fact that Jalal wouldn't be allowed to kill himself. It was a world he had never fully understood, even as he leveraged it.

Jalal said, "You have an attack that will trump ours?"

"Maybe. Hopefully. It will be the capstone to all of our efforts."

"Will you be the *shahid* on this?"

"It's not a martyr attack, but I will give my life to make it happen, if necessary."

Jalal nodded, then pointed at a box in the corner of the garage. "The extra detonators and explosives are in there."

Tariq collected the box and turned to go. He reached the door and said, "Good luck tonight. May Allah be with you."

Jalal said, "Insh'Allah, we will succeed. May he be with you as well."

Tariq loaded the box in the trunk of his car, then sagged in the driver's seat, wondering for the hundredth time how they'd been discovered. He had no idea, and it worried him. He was in the land of the Great Satan, and if they knew about the ship in Los Angeles, they might know about him. Make no mistake, no matter what boasts he gave, there was no way on earth he was willing to be a martyr.

He pulled out his phone, initiated the Wickr application, then decided to skip it. The conversation was too complex to do over text messaging. Anwar needed to hear his voice and needed to understand the necessity of the action, both in conducting the attack and in getting to South Carolina as soon as possible.

He dialed the phone, hearing it ring. Eventually, a suspicious voice said, "Hello?"

"Anwar, this is Tariq. I have some instructions."

69

From the bridge, Mitchell Redwing could see Huntington Beach on the starboard side and could barely make out the gantry cranes of the port of Los Angeles past the bow, both because of the distance and because they were obscured by four other vessels waiting their turn to be searched. Off the port side he saw a much larger container ship bypass their conga line and continue to the port. He said, "How come the other ships are allowed in?"

Biggs, the first mate of the vessel, said, "It's something to do with the port of Panama. The other ships are from the Far East, so they're letting them in."

The closest ship to them had a US Coast Guard cutter alongside it, and Mitchell could see a group of men swarming around a container stack. He said, "How long are we supposed to wait here?"

"Until they're through with that ship. Then they'll come to us. They're here to run some sort of test or inspection on our containers."

"They're going to do each and every one?"

"Apparently so."

With the ship holding upward of three thousand containers, Mitch knew they might not make it into port tonight. He checked his phone for signal, then texted his girlfriend, letting her know he would probably miss their date.

Biggs said, "Call the captain. Looks like they're headed this way."

Mitchell put away his phone and saw a group of men in blue descend a ladder to the cutter. Twenty minutes later, they were pulling alongside, a small contingent from his ship ready to meet them, led by the captain of the vessel himself.

The first man up the ladder was a Coast Guard lieutenant commander named Marks, followed by a small platoon of men, some struggling under equipment bags. Mitchell noticed that at least five were civilians.

Marks stuck out his hand and said, "Captain, I'm sorry about the trouble, but we've received some information about a possible terrorist device being smuggled out of Panama. Before you can proceed, we need to inspect each container."

"That's physically impossible. There's absolutely no way to inspect each one without unloading. I can't even open the containers while they're stacked on my deck."

"Sir, I understand. The threat is radiological. We don't need to enter; we just need to get to the outside and test."

"Radiological? What do you mean?"

"Sir, I'm not at liberty to discuss the full parameters. I just need your help to get you on your way. Four of these men will go through your paperwork, and the six you see breaking out the detectors will go through your ship."

Mitchell saw each man powering up and testing what resembled a handheld spotlight, like a modified Q-beam, with an LCD display attached to the head and a pistol grip sprouting below it.

The captain nodded and said, "My first mate will

show you the paperwork. Mitchell here will guide you through the ship. Where would you like to start?"

"Wherever you think is best."

Two hours later, with the sun beginning its inevitable slide into the Pacific Ocean, Mitchell stood off to the side, watching the six engineers place their radiological detection devices against a container, take a reading, then move on. Some were tasked with climbing the stacks, the containers piled five high on the deck, forcing the use of ridiculous safety lines and climbing gear, which did nothing but slow the process down. He wished he could give his Filipino seamen a lesson on the device, then turn them free. It would take half the time.

His radio crackled from the first mate. "Mitchell, how's it going? Over."

"Slow and steady. We're about finished with the deck, but still need to do the hold, over."

"Okay. The captain is considering allowing nonessential crew to disembark. Anyone you want to nominate? Over."

"Martin. His mother is in the hospital, and we can risk losing him for the small duration we're out here, over."

"Don't think the captain will think highly of losing an engineer, but I'll ask, over."

Mitchell heard one of the survey technicians shout, pointing at the base container of the corner stack at the bow of the ship. He clicked the handheld and said, "Hang on. Something is happening, over."

One of the technicians ran up to him, saying, "We have a gamma emitter in that container. The survey equipment is saying it's a radioisotope consistent with cobalt 60."

Befuddled, Mitchell said, "What the hell does all of that mean?"

"It means you're carrying a dirty bomb, and we need to get this ship moving out to sea."

Mitchell said, "Dirty bomb? What are you talking about?"

He looked at the men on the bow of the ship, taking repeated readings of the base container. Before the technician could respond, the container turned into a ball of fire, the rear exploding out and shredding the circle of men.

Slack-jawed, Mitchell watched one scientist cut in half, his upper body clawing the deck, pulling himself forward and leaving a trail of intestines. Another, his body in flames, ran around screaming, then collapsed, his blackened face crusting with blood.

The base container, with smoke billowing out of it, began to collapse in on itself like a beer can being crushed by a giant, causing the four containers above, each weighing twenty tons, to heel over and hammer the next stack. The domino effect caused that stack to topple, hitting the one that Mitchell was standing next to. He shoved the technician forward, screaming, "Run!"

He made it five feet before the corner of a container drove him into the deck, the force of gravity slamming twenty tons of steel into his fragile body, turning it into an unrecognizable grease smear.

70

★★
★

I watched the man close the surf shop, knowing I was about to cross a line, but I liked it. The author H. L. Mencken once wrote, "Every normal man must be tempted, at times, to spit on his hands, hoist the black flag, and begin slitting throats."

And he was right. Well, except for the slitting-throats part. When your "normal" life included the ability to do such a thing, you had to rely on your own self-restraint, or lose the moral compass that separated an Operator from Blackbeard.

The man went to the rear parking lot, disappearing from view in the darkness. I heard Jennifer say, "Pike, Carly, this is Koko. He's unlocking a Volvo SUV. He's going to be on the move soon. Get ready."

I said, "Knuckles, you got a view?"

"No, but he can only leave one way. I'll shadow him, don't worry."

I said, "Roger that," and Jennifer came back on. "Pike, last chance to stop this juvenile thing."

We'd come down to Norfolk from DC in the early afternoon, ostensibly for a double date on leave to Virginia Beach, and I was a little surprised that Kurt had given Knuckles permission. The Taskforce was forbidden from working on US soil precisely because we were operating outside the supreme law of the land—the US Constitution. When the Taskforce had been formed,

Kurt had insisted on the CONUS restriction in the charter precisely to avoid turning into something like the DGST in Morocco, where anything could be justified to secure the peace. It looked like he was getting a little loose in his old age.

That was a joke, of course, because I knew why; it was because he trusted Knuckles and me. Nothing more than that. The rules were made for a framework devoid of individual character, and he knew we wouldn't take advantage of the freedom. He also wasn't convinced Los Angeles was the end of the threat.

The news reports were absolutely melting down about the strike earlier in the day, no pun intended; luckily, Knuckles and Carly's early warning had managed to avoid an unmitigated disaster. The ship itself had become a floating Hiroshima, with the loss of half the crew. Half who were immediately dead, anyway. It would have been a hell of a lot worse had that ship been allowed to reach port.

We'd left Kurt to work the Los Angeles problem and had traveled straight to the water-sports shop on Virginia Beach. The FBI had said there was no terrorist connection, but I'd learned that they hadn't even taken the time to go to the place. All they had done was check out the bona fides of the shop—and it, of course, had come up clean. They couldn't see any reason for a terrorist group to vacation at a surf shop, so they'd dropped it. Truthfully, I couldn't either, but it was worth investigating in person.

We'd gone in, asking about renting a few paddleboards. We couldn't flash a badge and start asking questions, so I'd told both Carly and Jennifer to try to find out about any unusual activity involving unknown Arab males. I figured we'd have to attack the problem from a hundred different angles, talking to more than one employee, but it turned out to be much easier than that.

While we were perusing the brochures with a twenty-something who was channeling Spicoli from *Fast Times at Ridgemont High,* a decidedly skeevy-looking guy came in, sporting dreadlocks, a T-shirt with more holes than fabric, and long, dirty toenails slammed into Nike shower shoes. The Spicoli look-alike took one look at him, then proved he was more than an airhead surfer. He walked over and firmly ran the guy out of the store.

He apologized, saying, "Sometimes that leech tries to steal stuff while I'm with customers, but it's not what the beach is really like."

Jennifer said, "I bet you deal with weirdos in this place all the time."

Out of the blue, he said, "Yeah, more than I like. Just a few days ago, I had these three guys from the Middle East come in who barely spoke English. They looked like they'd bought their beachwear at a Target store five minutes before showing up. But most of the folks are like you guys. Just people looking for a good time."

Carly said, "Were they Americans?"

"No way. They used passports as identification for the rentals. They were from Saudi Arabia."

"Well, maybe they don't get this kind of fun over there. What did they do?"

"Two days in a row they rented three Sea-Doo watercraft for two hours each day. A lot of money. All they wanted to do was ride around in circles or race each other."

He glanced at us conspiratorially and said, "I thought about reporting them, you know, because they were Arabs."

"Did they do anything wrong? Make you think they were up to something?"

"No. That's why I didn't. I don't want to be accused of racial profiling some prince from Saudi Arabia. All they did was run around in the water, like everyone else. Anyway, they had an address for a rental house here, so it seemed on the up-and-up."

I said, "What kind of Sea-Doo? That sounds more like something I'd want to do. Screw this paddleboard stuff."

He laughed, saying, "I hear you. They're a hell of a lot more fun."

He turned to the rack of brochures, and I leaned in to Jennifer, whispering, "When we fill out the forms, see where he puts them."

She nodded imperceptibly. He turned back around, showing us the packages, which included tours, dolphin sightings, or just plain running around on your own. I said, "We'll take the same package those Arab guys had."

"You want two hours? That's a long time to be out on the water."

"What do you recommend?"

"Take a half hour. If you want more, come on back. Those Arabs were out there like they were practicing for NASCAR or something. You'll probably be done in a half hour."

Knuckles glanced at me, and we were thinking the same thing: They weren't here for fun. I said, "We'll take the half hour."

We filled out the forms, showing identification and leaving an address and a deposit. I said, "So those Arabs put down a Saudi Arabian address?"

"No. They're apparently vacationing across the way, near the port."

That was all I needed to hear. We finished, and I kept the conversation going, distracting the guy while Jennifer got an eye from around the counter, seeing where he filed the paperwork.

We'd spent our thirty minutes on the machines, then retired back to our hotel, considering our next move.

I said, "I'm for cracking that place and getting the contracts. The odds are, they put down a fake address, but at least we'll have the passport information."

Carly said, "I'm with you. If they have an attack planned soon, they might have used their real address, not wanting to arouse suspicion with a fake one. They have no idea how those addresses would be checked out and might have worried about something like the DGST would have done in Morocco."

Knuckles said, "We can't do that. I promised Kurt. I need to call him before."

He had always been a little bit tighter with the rules than me, but in this case, it was his show. He'd gotten the permission, and it wasn't my word on the line.

I said, "I agree. You want to call, or do you want me to?"

He looked relieved, thinking I'd fight him. He said, "Let me do it."

Jennifer said, "But why on earth were they riding Jet Skis? It doesn't make any sense."

Carly said, "Maybe the Jet Skis were just what I said earlier. Maybe they've never gotten to do such a thing in Morocco. Remember, they're Berbers from the Rif. Maybe they just wanted to experience it before doing something heinous. They're human after all."

Knuckles said, "Maybe the Jet Skis are the weapon."

"Bingo," I said. "That's exactly what I'm thinking. Which is why we need to get in that place."

Jennifer said, "Wait, logically, that doesn't make any sense. They can't turn a rental into a weapon unless they stole it and rigged it with explosives somewhere else, and they didn't do that. Which means if they intend to do as you say, they must have their own already—and if they have their own Sea-Doo, why rent them at all and risk exposure?"

I said, "Too little information for an answer. But it's enough smoke to ask to be the fireman. Knuckles?"

He nodded, calling Kurt. Before the line answered, I hovered around him like a mother watching a stranger holding her baby. I said, "Don't make it sound like it's a big deal. We saw the security on the inside. Tell him it's an in and out. Easy pickings. Tell him—"

He cut me off with a finger, and I heard, "Sir, it's Knuckles. You told me to call if I found anything. Well, we found something."

He went through the sequence of events, describing what we wanted to do. There was a little bit of back-and-forth, and from Knuckles's end, I could tell it was centered on alerting the FBI or letting us do it. In the end, the timeline won Kurt over. The FBI wouldn't check out those receipts until they had a warrant, and that warrant wouldn't occur until we could wash the information of Taskforce fingerprints, which meant it would be serviced in three days, if we were lucky. Given the attack in LA, the map of Norfolk we found in Morocco, and the fact that three Arabs were here with Saudi Arabian passports, it was enough.

I knew Kurt was putting his ass on the line here, but I also understood he regarded the mission of saving lives as something sacrosanct. His career would always take a backseat.

I heard the conversation going our way, and then Knuckles surprised me, taking it one step further. He said, "Sir, we came down here without weapons."

He listened for a bit, then said, "Yeah, yeah, sir. I got

that. We aren't operational, but . . . we might be. I'm not asking for anything in the Taskforce arsenal. I'm just giving you a warning order that I might be reaching out to some friends around here."

He looked at me and grinned, listening to the phone. "Yes, sir. They would be friends at Little Creek."

And I understood what he was asking, given his SEAL pedigree. Naval Special Warfare Group 2, which was responsible for almost all East Coast SEAL teams, was within spitting distance of us.

He talked a little bit more, and hung up. I said, "We're good?"

"Yeah. He seems to trust me more than you for some reason."

I laughed, then said, "What was that about weapons?"

"He's not real happy about that, but he didn't tell me no. Sending us weapons would be admitting preplanned Taskforce involvement against our charter, but apparently letting me smooth talk some friends is okay."

I said, "Your issue was even bringing it up." Meaning I'd have just done it.

He said, "Yeah, well, I don't roll that way. I gave him my word."

I nodded. His instincts had kept me out of trouble more than once, so I wasn't going to fight him here. Hell, I wouldn't fight him at all, and he knew it.

I sent him on his way to the Little Creek naval base just down the road to use his SEAL undercover-brother connections. He'd set up a meeting with some master chief he'd called on the phone, and I'd taken Carly and Jennifer on a reconnaissance to determine our plan of attack.

71

We returned to the water-sports shop, this time looking for vulnerabilities on the outside, and found a single one. There was a shed to the side that housed all of the rental equipment, including the water-craft, and it was wired to the max, with cameras and a state-of-the-art alarm system. The main office was a two-story affair with wooden shingles, weathered wooden siding, and a faux lighthouse on the end.

Unlike the shed, it had a single camera inside and flimsy door and window contacts from an older alarm system—on every entrance except one. At the southern side, in between the office and the shed, there was a window that wasn't wired. It was eight feet off the ground, and small, most likely for a bathroom or storage closet. From its height and size, it must not have looked like a vulnerability, because only a child could get through it. Or a smaller woman, like Carly. She was only five feet three and would fit.

We returned to our hotel at twilight, meeting Knuckles in the parking lot. I said, "How'd it go?"

"Not so well." He opened the trunk, and inside I saw four beat-up AKM assault rifles, the wood stocks chipped and the bluing fading from the barrels.

I said, "What the hell are those?"

"War stocks taken from Afghanistan and Iraq, now used for foreign weapons training. They have a bunch of them stacked up, and they aren't really accounted for like US weapons. They're all just thrown into a footlocker and sealed. My buddy was willing to let those slip out for us to use, but he wasn't willing to give me any of the high-speed US weapons."

I conducted a functions check on one and said, "Jeez. What happened to the SEAL brotherhood?"

He loaded a magazine in one and said, "If we'd relied on your SF brotherhood, we'd be pointing our fingers as a weapon."

Touché.

He said, "What did you guys find?"

"Should be easy, as long as Carly doesn't get stuck in the window. Just have to wait for the shop to close."

Three hours later, I was listening to Jennifer make the calls, stationed in a vehicle adjacent to the back of the store. She said, "Truck's on the move, truck's on the move."

I looked over at Carly and said, "You ready to go?"

I could see she was nervous, but then again, any sane person who wasn't used to doing operations like this would be. She appeared to be channeling it well.

She nodded and said, "Yeah, yeah. I'm good. You'll give me early warning if anyone comes up, right?"

"I promise. Knuckles has the outer ring, Jennifer's got the inner, and I've got the bull's-eye. You get in, get the paperwork, and come right back out."

Knuckles came on the net. "I've got the eye. He's on the road, headed out, I'm fifty meters behind. You're clear."

She heard the call and said, "Okay. Let's do it."

We were parked at a dirt lot adjacent to a public path to the beach, a sandy berm with scrub on top separating us from the front of the shop. I called, "We're on the move," and we exited the vehicle, scrambling over the berm in the dark and scurrying low to the gap between the shed and the store.

We slapped up against the wall in a crouch, the window above us. I waited a beat, getting a read from Jennifer. She said, "No movement. You're good to go."

I said, "Knuckles?"

"Still moving north. No change."

Carly put a thin putty knife in her mouth and nodded. I said, "Looks like we *are* pirates."

She squinted her eyes in confusion. I said, "Nothing. Just a stray thought from earlier." I squatted down, my back to the wall and both of my hands held palm up at my shoulders.

She shook her head, but she *did* look like a pirate with the blade in her mouth. She put her right hand into my left, then her left foot onto my right palm. She hoisted herself up until she had both feet on my palms like a circus performer, leaning her body against the wall.

I said, "You ready to raise the black flag, pirate?"

She hesitated, and I thought she was going to step down, but she didn't. She pulled the putty knife out of her mouth, and said, "Let's go."

I stood up, sliding her body against the wall, then raised my arms, hoisting her to the level of the window. She worked the lock for what seemed like an eternity; then I heard the window slide open. She didn't say a word. All I felt was her feet leaving my hands.

I turned around and saw her struggling. The window was almost too small for her petite frame. Eventually, she slithered in, and I heard her bark out, "Inside," with a little bit of aggravation. I chuckled and said, "Remember that lone camera."

She said, "Got it. Moving."

I leaned against the wall and began the worst part of any mission where I wasn't the main effort: waiting.

That lasted all of five seconds. Knuckles came on and said, "Volvo's making a U-turn, I say again, Volvo is making a U-turn."

Did we trigger an alarm?

No way that would have happened. The police would have been alerted, not the guy in the truck.

I said, "Give me a time."

"Three minutes. Maybe less."

"Why?"

"Maybe he left his cell phone. I have no idea."

"Carly, you copy? Get out."

"I copy. I'll be in and out in less than that."

I expected, *On the way,* so was pleasantly surprised.

Two minutes went by, and I called again, "Carly, what's the status?"

"The file we identified is only today's rentals. I'm looking for past ones."

"Get out, now. Not enough time."

"No. I'm committed now."

That answer was not what I wanted to hear. Driving on with the mission was one thing, but when the team leader gives an order, it's followed. Especially if it comes from me.

I said, "Carly, get the fuck out, now."

I heard nothing. Jennifer called, "Got headlights."

I said, "Carly, you copy?"

Jennifer: "It's the owner. He's parking."

"Carly!"

Jennifer again: "He's moving to the front."

What the hell? I'm going to rip her head off.

I heard the window above me scrape open, and Carly

leaned out, saying, "Help me down," like she was sneaking out for a party in high school.

I slapped against the wall, holding my hands up, and she scraped herself through the window, feet first. She thumped around for a bit but found my hands. I lowered her to the ground. She was flushed with the mission, smiling. She held up a piece of paper and I pulled her face-to-face and said, "If I make a fucking call, you *follow* it, you understand?"

Shocked, expecting accolades, she bristled, saying, "I got the job done. I did what you couldn't. You can pull that bullshit team-leader crap on Jennifer, but don't bring it here."

Furious at the pushback, I spat out, "This isn't a game. We're professionals who act like it. You were endangering an organization I've spent a lifetime building. I'll give you that leeway in the future—*after* you've proven yourself. Now? No more lone-wolf shit. You follow orders."

She snarled, "I don't need to prove myself to you or anyone else. I've done just fine operating on my own."

I said, "You aren't on your own here. You're with a *team*. And you *listen* to the team leader. You got it?"

She bit her tongue and nodded.

I said, "Let's get the fuck out of here."

She handed me the rental agreement. I held it up and said, "Oh, by the way, good work."

She looked at me like I was a lunatic.

I smiled and said, "Hey, I can't argue with success. Only with you ignoring me."

I knelt down and began slinking back to the berm. She followed, and we scampered over it, reaching our car. I turned the dome light on and read the paperwork, seeing an address for here, in Norfolk. *Probably fake.*

I saw car headlights, then Knuckles and Jennifer coming over. I said, "Jennifer, get the computer out and find this address."

She took the paperwork and went back to her car. Knuckles said, "What do we have?"

"An address somewhere around here. The zip code fits. Other than that, nothing."

Knuckles said, "How'd it work out?"

Carly said, "I thought it was fine. Your asshole team leader thinks otherwise."

He scowled at me, and I said, "She did okay. She just needed some counseling after the fact."

He rolled his eyes, saying to her, "Let me guess, you didn't listen to him, yet he never listens to anyone. Story of my life."

He glanced at me, waiting on me to complete the joke, but I said, "This wasn't that. She really *didn't* listen, and it could have been mission failure." He heard my tone and understood the implications. She went back and forth between us like she was being dissected, which she was.

I saw her about to say something we'd both regret, and patted her on the knee. I said, "Hey, I'm not trying to hammer you. You did well in there. I'm not taking that away from you. Just learn from your mistakes."

She said, "I didn't see any mistakes."

Before I could answer, Jennifer came jogging back carrying a laptop. She turned the screen, saying, "It's a house across the Lafayette River. Here, in Norfolk."

I said, "Pull up street view."

She did, and I saw that the house was an older ranch style, but the neighborhood was definitely well-to-do. It looked like an old, established Virginia enclave. No way would terrorists have rented there. Jennifer said, "It's gotta be a fake."

Knuckles said, "Only one way to find out."

I nodded, saying, "I agree."

Jennifer said, "What are we going to do? Go barging in with our AKMs, demanding to see the lease?"

I said, "No. This is getting dangerous. Time to call in the big guns."

I dialed Kurt.

72

Jalal went into the den, seeing his two *shahid* praying on the carpet. They registered his presence, and he simply said, "Ready to go?"

They nodded, then went about gathering their things as if they were making a trip to the grocery store. Phones, keys, and, in Wasim's case, a pair of glasses. They turned back to him expectantly. He said, "Are you prepared, my brothers?"

They both nodded, and Jalal felt his eyes tear up. That caused the same reaction in Tanan and Wasim, and before he could prevent it, they were on the floor, crying together.

Eventually, the sobbing decreased. Jalal looked both of them in the eye and said, "It's time. May Allah welcome you into his embrace."

"What is the target? Did you decide where we should go?"

"You are the ones who determine that. Go where you can."

Wasim said, "Jalal, we've studied the bay. We have to make a choice. I know you wanted to attack the cruise ships, but that means we go left out of the river, into the ship channel. There's only one target there, and it's far away. If we go right, we have the largest naval base the United States has within our reach. It's right next to us."

"So you want me to pick a target? Is that it?"

Tanan said, "I've already picked it. If you'll let me."

Jalal smiled and said, "I am not the *shahid*. Please. What is it?"

"The USS *George Washington*. It is an aircraft carrier that has caused death in every Muslim enclave on earth. It is in port. Let us strike it."

Jalal shook his head and said, "No, no, no. We can't attack an aircraft carrier with our little watercraft. It will be like a bug striking a windshield."

"You're wrong. I've been researching, and it *will* damage the boat. Yes, it's large, but the size doesn't increase its strength. Remember the USS *Cole*, in Yemen in 2000? That was another large warship, and we came close to sinking it, killing many, many people. If I go first, I'll puncture the hull. Maybe not by much, but enough. If Wasim follows behind me and strikes the exact same point, it will be exponentially more effective. We won't sink the ship, I know, but we will render it inoperable. A glorious strike."

"But what will that do?"

"What will it do? Seriously? After Houston and Los Angeles? They'll have to shut down the ports all over the country. They won't be able to predict if there isn't another attack on the way. Every single attack has been different. Every blow has been unique. They'll make the connection between them, and then they'll have to make the ultimate decision to shut them down for fear of some other, unexpected attack. They have over three hundred major ports. They'll all be shut down. It will destroy their ability to trade. Everything from bananas to computers will be closed off. Isn't that the point of this anyway? Even if we fail to sink the carrier, the point is the attack. *That's* what will drive the economic destruction that Tariq has always preached."

Jalal paced a bit, considering, then said, "I believe you are right. It matters not what destruction we bring. Only the fact that we can. So be it. I like the final attack being against something that has slaughtered the *ummah* all over the earth."

Wasim and Tanan smiled, and an uncomfortable silence settled. Jalal broke it.

"Do you wish to do final prayers?"

Awkwardly, they both said, "We just completed them."

Jalal was unsure of how to deal with the tension in the room. He wasn't going to die, and felt like he should. It wasn't right. Tanan saw his face and said, "Brother, don't feel sorry for us. We'll be in paradise soon. Just get us to the boat ramp."

Jalal nodded but didn't feel assuaged. Resigned, he said, "Load up all of your things. I'll destroy them after you've left."

They both went to their room, coming out with the backpacks they'd had when they fled Morocco. He said, "You didn't leave anything in your room? The police will be here after we're done. Of that I'm sure."

"Does it matter?"

Jalal caught his eye, seeing the dedication, then said, "I suppose not."

They went out the front door to the pickup truck. Behind it was the trailer holding three Sea-Doo watercraft, one just as it was delivered, and two with the front hulls turned into explosive shaped charges.

Jalal loaded the knapsacks in the bed of the pickup, then said, "Well, this is it. In thirty minutes you will make the entire Khattabi clan proud. You will enter paradise. The boat ramp is only a mile away. Are you truly ready?"

Tanan said, "We have to fill up the watercraft. They have no fuel."

Jalal heard the words, dumbfounded at his oversight.

73

★★
★

Kurt answered the phone fairly tersely, saying, "Pike, you'd better not be calling to tell me you need bail."

I said, "Sir, no. But I do have a request. And it's going to hurt."

He said, "Seriously? Your actions as of late have caused a little bit of a stir back here. Specifically, how some Recce guy from South Africa crossed paths with a Taskforce asset, then both managed to find out about a ship headed to one of our largest ports with a dirty bomb."

I said, "That's what the Council cares about? Instead of cheering the fact that the architecture we created actually works, they want to nitpick the edges?"

"Yeah, that's what they want to do. Not for us, but they're circling the chum because of the South African. I've got him in holding, but I want to cut him free. Get him out of Taskforce control so I don't have to worry about the repercussions. If they want to question him officially, they can find him."

I realized Kurt was playing both sides against the middle, and I liked it. We were holding Johan without any due process or rights afforded by our judicial system, and he was asking me if he could let him go free, knowing that he could defend the decision by using the very arguments that were being thrown against the Taskforce as an extrajudicial force. In effect, doing what was correct by turning him loose into the real world of US justice, letting them conduct the due process.

He continued, "But I don't want to do that if he's got some information about terrorism. If he can prevent a death, I'll take the pain. I want your opinion."

I said, "Let him go. He's a white hat. It's been tarnished, but it's white."

"You sure?"

I didn't mention that I suspected he'd been the one to kill the source in the Bahamas. I suppose I should have, but I didn't. It would just complicate things, because Kurt couldn't ignore such information, but Johan had led us to the thread. In my mind, it canceled out. Harsh, I suppose, but there it was. He'd given me all the information he had, and he did it because he wanted to prevent further deaths, not because he was concerned about himself. And in my world, that was a cutline that meant something.

I said, "I'm sure. The guy has no other information on this thread, and he's not a threat. You want to cut him free, let the US Justice Department take up a case. You'll get no arguments with me."

I heard a sigh of relief; then he said, "Okay, what do you have?"

I took a deep breath, thinking what I'd say, then just let it out, "We did the B and E and got out clean. We have a potential safe house for the entire crew."

I ran down what we'd found, giving him the evidence of an attack coming in Norfolk and the fact that nobody had located the Tariq guy from Saudi Arabia. I ended with, "I can't take that house on my own. I've only got Knuckles and Jennifer. Carly isn't capable of an assault, and anyway, this isn't a Taskforce mission."

"What do you want?"

"I want the FBI Hostage Rescue Team. I want someone who can assault, and we need them right now."

"If you think it's that bad, call in the local SWAT team. Get the police on it. Let's flush it right now."

"No way. How the hell am I going to do that? Walk in and say I have a terrorist beehive to the local sheriff? That'll end up in a two-day clusterfuck. I want someone I trust. I've trained with them. I don't want some local-yokel team that shoots on the weekends. We're talking about a direct threat to the largest naval base on the continent. I *want* HRT."

"We don't have liaison with the Justice Department."

I knew that, but it didn't alter my request.

For some dumbass reason, when the Taskforce was created, and the president was deciding who would be on the Oversight Council, it was determined that including the attorney general would be hypocritical. Because we operated outside of US law, they decided that reading on the AG would be tantamount to giving him a coronary, or at least a conflict of interest, as he'd be responsible for sanctioning events that he was sworn to prevent. And so, I now had to beg for the one domestic agency that could help.

I said, "I got that, sir, but I *need* them. There is an attack coming, and it's going to happen soon. Possibly as early as tomorrow. If you've ever trusted me, do so now."

He said, "Okay, okay, I'll get them moving. You're lucky about the date, because they're on alert."

"Date? What do you mean?"

"It's September eleventh. Fifteenth anniversary. *Everyone's* on strip alert."

I looked at my watch and saw he was right. I said, "I didn't even realize it."

"Because you've been busy preventing the next one. What are you planning to do?"

"I'm going recce that house. Get eyes on and keep anyone from moving. I need someone to feed that intel to, or I'll end up assaulting the house myself."

I heard a sigh and realized he'd been awake for probably thirty-six hours. He said, "You'll get the team. I promise. Don't let them kill anyone else."

I said, "If it comes down to us, we'll stop them, but we've only got a bunch of AKMs from Iraq to do it with."

Before I hung up, I heard, "AKMs? What the hell are you talking about?"

74

We left our Virginia Beach hotel thirty minutes later, loading our rental with our cheap-ass Soviet weapons. Taking Highway 460, we went west across the Norfolk peninsula, crossing the Lafayette River and entering surface streets. Initially, we saw nothing but giant condominium farms, one after the other, but eventually, with Jennifer calling out directions, we began to pass through the neighborhoods I'd seen earlier on street view, at least as far as I could tell by the porch lights.

Jennifer said, "Another hundred meters and you'll get to a circle. Take the first right, and then your next left. The house will be at the end in a cul-de-sac."

I hit the circle, much larger than I would have expected in a neighborhood, with a copse of trees turning it into a mini-park. It had clearly been built in the days when land was cheap and space was prized. I took the first right, passing a Toyota Tundra pickup truck entering the circle. It wasn't until I was committed to the turn that I saw it was towing a trailer with three large Jet Ski–type watercraft—two parallel with each other and one in the front, perpendicular. I whipped my head around, trying to see who was driving, but it was hopeless.

Jennifer said, "What?"

"That truck is hauling Jet Skis."

"We're in a beach community. They're all over the place. You want to follow it?"

I was torn, but ultimately said, "No. Let's check out the house."

Jennifer nodded and said, "Next right."

"I'm going to drive straight past the road. Take a look down the street."

I did so, and she said, "Streetlights up front, three houses on the left, three houses on the right going down the street. Cul-de-sac is dark. Couldn't see anything."

I said, "Knuckles, you get anything?"

"Same. Too dark to see to the end."

To Jennifer, I said, "Check the map. Is there a road behind it? One we can stage on?"

She looked at her tablet and said, "Yes. Take the next right, then another right. It runs up against the river, and there's a park. We can stage there and penetrate on foot."

I followed her instructions, parking in front of a deserted basketball court, the Lafayette River beyond it, the dark water gently lapping the shore. Across the street was a line of trees protecting the backyards of the houses in the cul-de-sac.

I shut off the engine and called Kurt, giving him a SITREP. He told me the HRT team was inbound via helicopters.

I said, "Helicopters? Tell me they aren't going to fast-rope onto the site. Please tell me they're going to link up with me and do this with a little stealth. I haven't even gotten eyes on. The whole thing may be a bust."

He laughed and said, "They're flying to the airfield at the Norfolk Navy base. You wanted quick. That's what you got."

"What's the timeline?"

"Should be there in under thirty minutes. Figure they'll have to sort out and cross-load into vehicles on Norfolk, they should be at your location in an hour."

"How are they going to get to the target from the airfield?"

"I have no idea, but they have a plan."

I said, "This oughta work out swell." I gave him our location, telling him to relay the link-up location to the team. He said he'd do so, and I hung up.

I turned to the team and said, "Okay, Knuckles and I are going to enter those trees and get a look-see. I'll figure out a vantage point for surveillance while we wait on the FBI to arrive. You two will coordinate with them. They're coming to this location. Call when they arrive, and we'll pull back and brief them, then turn the crisis site over."

Knuckles broke out his nifty Taliban gun, and I did the same. We slipped out of the car, weaving between the illumination of the streetlights. We entered the tree line directly behind the house and took a knee on the outskirts of the backyard.

The house was dark. It looked deserted. I waited a bit, getting a feel for the area and listening for any signs that someone had seen us. I heard none. After about five minutes, I said, "I think this place is empty. You go left; I'll go right. See if you can find any activity. Meet back here no later than ten minutes from now."

Knuckles looked at his watch, nodded, then slipped into the darkness like a wraith. I followed suit, going the opposite direction, sticking to the tree line to hide my movement.

I scuttled up under a window then slowly rose, seeing nothing, the house pitch-black. Not even a digital light from a clock or microwave. I continued on, hitting the driveway. It was empty. I took a risk and peeked into the window of the garage door, the faint illumination from a streetlight showing me that it, too, was empty. I circled back to the link-up point, finding Knuckles already there.

I said, "You see anything at all?"

"No. I think it's a dry hole."

I looked at my watch. The FBI were still at least thirty to forty-five minutes behind, and if the terrorists were gone, we were losing the edge. I called Jennifer. "Koko, Koko, come forward with Carly. Tell her to bring a lock-pick kit."

"Say again?"

"Come forward with a lockpick kit. You bring an AKM. We're cracking this thing."

All I heard was "Roger." Three minutes later, they were next to us. I said, "We think it's empty, but we're not sure, so here's how this will go: Carly will crack the lock. Knuckles and I will pull security on the door. Jennifer, you pull security to the rear. We'll enter, clear the first room we find, then repeat the procedure for each door that's closed. We're not blowing through this. No violence of action. It's going to be slow and stealthy until we find a threat. Then, it's game on. No threat, no noise."

I went to each, saying, "Understand?"

They nodded, and I pointed to the back of the house, to a door next to the concrete patio. "Carly, that's your target. You can pick a lock pretty well, right? That's something they teach at the farm?"

She nodded, saying, "I could have taught that weak crap at the farm."

I looked at Knuckles, and, apologetically, he said, "She didn't have a stellar upbringing. She can crack just about anything."

To Carly, I said, "Glad to hear it, but you listen to me,

understand? You do what I say. No more lone-wolf shit. It's not only your life in the balance."

She nodded, and Knuckles and I slipped out of cover, closing on the door, him on the left and me on the right. We waited a few seconds, and when there was no reaction, I called Carly and Jennifer forward. Carly slid up beneath the knob and Jennifer rotated to the rear, finding a patch of shadow to conceal herself.

Three minutes later, Carly slowly rotated the doorknob, then turned and nodded to me. I nodded back, and she opened the door, letting it swing inward. Knuckles entered at a crouch, his weapon at the ready. I followed behind, entering a den. We took up points of dominance, then surveyed the area on a knee, finding nothing.

We continued through the house, repeating the Carly procedure at each closed door. Eventually, the house was clear, and it was most definitely empty.

I ceased the stealth, saying, "Get the lights on. Search this place. Knuckles, Carly, take the bedrooms. Jennifer, you get the den. I'll check out the garage."

Everyone scattered, and I went to the garage, flipping on a light. The place was clearly a rental, because there were no shelves, bikes, lawn tools, or anything else. I saw a small pile in the corner and went to investigate, finding snippets of wire, some electrical connections, and discarded paint cans, one three-gallon, another five. I picked one up and looked inside, finding a residue that wasn't paint.

I scraped the edge and held it up to my nose, recognizing the scent. It was explosive residue. And the cans could mean only one thing.

My phone vibrated, and I answered, hearing Kurt exasperated. "The team is at your location, but the only thing there is an empty car."

"Tell them to come to the target. We've cleared it. It's empty."

He said, "You did *what*?"

I said, "I'll tell you the specifics later, but it was a good call. I'm in the garage now, and it looks like whoever was here was building shaped charges. They're gone, which means they're on the hunt."

"Shit. You mean tonight?"

"Yeah. Worst case, that's what's going to happen."

"Any idea of the target?"

"None. We need to get whoever runs the security here on high alert. Coast Guard, port authority, Navy, whoever. Get them moving. Get boats in the water."

I heard Knuckles calling and said, "Stand by. Knuckles has found something."

I ran back inside, and he said, "The place is pristine. Nothing but rental furniture. We found one thing in the trash."

He held out a receipt, and I said, "What is it?"

"Bill of sale for three Sea-Doo watercraft and a trailer."

I said, "From Richmond?"

"Yep."

I put the phone to my ear and said, "Okay, sir, we figured out what that 'random' purchase was in Richmond. They bought Jet Skis using that bank account, which means they've turned them into manned torpedoes. Get a response going, right now. They're on the move."

He said, "Already working it. What do you have to go on?"

"Nothing. We passed a truck carrying three Jet Skis on the way in, and I'm thinking that's them. Give the analysts our location and tell them to pinpoint every single boat ramp within a ten-mile radius. We're going to have to go fishing."

He said, "Got it. Link up with the FBI and give them the information. They have a maritime team as well. Maybe they can help."

Resigned, I said, "Roger all, sir."

He said, "That didn't sound too confident."

I hesitated, then said, "Sir, I think we're too late. I should have ignored this house and hit that truck with the Jet Skis. I think I fucked up."

"You haven't yet. Work the problem. I'll give you whatever you need."

75

Jalal was learning the hard way that backing a trailer into a boat ramp wasn't as easy as backing a car into a garage. Every time he turned the wheel, the damn trailer went the opposite direction. To make matters worse, the boat ramp wasn't a wide, flat expanse, but a narrow ramp dropping down into the water between two concrete walls, barely wider than the trailer.

He bashed the end into the left side, tearing off the brake light. Tanan said, "Stop, stop! You're going to jam it into the concrete and we won't be able to get the watercraft off at all."

Jalal cursed, pulling forward yet again. Hampering him further was the fact that there were no lights at the ramp, specifically because it was closed from dusk to dawn. He was beginning to think they should have spent more time driving the trailer around than they had the Jet Skis. Even lining up the watercraft with the gas pump had been a chore.

He stopped yet again, saying, "Both of you get out and guide me in. This is getting ridiculous. We've wasted an hour and a half. At this rate, we'll attack in daylight."

The two exited, wading into the water on either side of the trailer. Jalal pulled forward again, then began slowly backing up. Tanan pointed him to go to the right, and he thought he did, but the reverse view from the mirror, coupled with the trailer doing exactly what he didn't want, caused him to overcorrect. Tannan began waving his arms to the right, trying to push him aside with body language. Jalal spun the wheel and the trailer jackknifed, forcing Wasim to dive out of the way.

Jalal scraped the trailer on the concrete, snapping the ribs that protected the sides of the watercraft and jamming the frame into the wall. He cursed and put the truck into drive, only to find that it wouldn't move.

He rolled down the window, saying, "Wasim, something is holding it. See what it is."

Wasim waded through the water, then climbed onto the trailer. He used a flashlight to peer into the murky depths. Jalal saw the light shut off and said, "Well?"

"I think you bent the axle. The wheel is twisted out of line."

Jalal looked to the heavens, wondering what else could go wrong. He thought a moment, then said, "We'll take them off here. I'll unhook the trailer and leave it after you're gone."

Tanan said, "They're still a foot above the water."

"I know. We'll have to muscle them off." He went to the first watercraft and began pushing to the rear, saying, "Come on. The longer we stay here, the greater the risk of being discovered."

After twenty minutes, the first Sea-Doo was floating in the water. Tanan held the front anchor point, saying, "We can't let it float free. If it runs into the wall with the nose, it's liable to go off."

"Hold it still. Wassim and I can get the other one. Once it's off, you two leave immediately. Remember, no wake until you hit the ship channel. Take it nice and slow up the river. I don't want anyone alerted. This launch has been disaster enough."

*　　*　　*

The commander of the HRT team was a special agent who introduced himself as Brock. Knuckles took one look at him and smiled, shaking his hand. I said, "You guys know each other?"

"Yeah. Brock's the guy I worked with in Paris, when I took that shrapnel in my ass."

I knew then that Brock had lost some men. Four HRT guys had been shredded in a diabolical trap laid by some Irish terrorists. Knuckles had barely escaped with his life.

I shook his hand and said, "Knuckles told me about you. Sorry for the guys you lost."

He said, "Yeah. Me too, me too. Sometimes you bite the bear; sometimes the bear bites you. I'd like to be the one doing the biting tonight. I've been told not to ask who you are or why you're here, so I won't. What do you have?"

I said, "Carly, you got that survey of the ship channel?"

Earlier, I'd put her CIA analytical skills to use, telling her to find the most likely targets in the area.

She said, "Yes," and came over with a laptop. To Brock I said, "What we have is a cell of terrorists who have created manned torpedoes using shaped charges in the noses of Sea-Doo watercraft. They were in this house, and I'm sure we missed them by minutes. They're moving to the hunt, and we have little time to stop them."

Carly pulled up the screen and said, "From here the Lafayette River hits the channel to the north after about three kilometers. At that point, the targets open up both left and right. To the left are a multitude of shipping concerns, to include tanker and chemical docks, but the most likely target would be the Half Moone Cruise terminal. There are two ships in dock right now from Carnival and Norwegian. To the right, and much closer, is the international Norfolk port terminal for container ships and the piers for the Norfolk naval base."

I nodded, then said to Brock, "You guys have antimateriel sniper systems?"

"You mean fifty-cals? Yeah, we got a couple."

"Anyone here that shoots them for a living? You have a sniper team?"

"One." He turned and said, "Marcus, get in here."

A tall, swarthy man came into the den, saying, "What's up?"

I said, "What antimateriel sniper systems do you have?"

"A Barrett M107 and an Accuracy International AX50."

I looked at Knuckles. "Which one do you want?"

"The Barrett. It's not as accurate, but it's semiauto."

Brock said, "What are you talking about?"

I said, "Send your sniper team to the cruise terminal." I pointed at the map, saying, "The entrance to the Elizabeth River is a chokepoint. Get 'em up high, and tell them to kill any Jet Ski–type watercraft on the river."

He said, "I . . . I can't order a kill mission without knowing the target."

I said, "The target is a Jet Ski with a bomb strapped to the front." I turned to the sniper and said, "You hit the front of the vehicle. If it's our target, it will explode. If not, you've just killed a Jet Ski."

He looked at Brock, and Brock nodded. "Go ahead. Use the power of your badge, and get up there."

The man raced out of the room, shouting another agent's name.

I said, "Knuckles, you get to Norfolk."

Brock waved a hand, saying, "Wait a minute. I can get another man to shoot."

"You said you only had one team."

"Only one *sniper* team, but we're all trained. I'll send another team to Norfolk."

I said, "No way. Knuckles is the best shot I know. He's going."

Brock became indignant, saying, "Hold on here. This is an FBI operation. I can't let some . . . military cell operate on US soil. I don't even know who you guys are."

I turned to him quickly, snatching him up by the collar and leaning him back. I said, ever so slowly, "He's a SEAL-trained sniper that's taken lives behind the scope. I don't have time for the dick measuring. He's going."

Brock nodded rapidly, and I knew the mantle of command had just been passed to me. I said, "Give me a man to send with him."

Jennifer came running up with another computer, saying, "We've received the boat ramp information."

I said, "What're we looking at?"

"The closest one is the Haven Creek Boat Ramp. It's literally a mile away. The next is in the opposite direction, across the bridge on the other side of the Lafayette River. There are two more on the peninsula, but they're both private marinas. I don't think they'll use them."

"Okay, Brock, you take the one across the river. Give me two men, and I'll take the one close by. We passed a Toyota Tundra truck, gray, hauling Jet Skis on the way in, and I think that was them. They're probably already in the water, but if they're not, take them out."

He said, "I'm running out of men. I can't send someone with Knuckles *and* cover all the bases."

"I need your authority to get Knuckles onto the Norfolk naval base and give him a spotter for his shots."

"If you want an assault element, I can't spare someone. Either you lose the men you want, or he does."

I considered, then said, "You still have someone on the airfield?"

"Yeah, yeah. I have the pilots, but they're all HRT special agents as well."

"Get them to the piers. Tell them to tell whoever's in charge of security that an FBI sniper team is on the way."

I looked at Jennifer and said, "You're going with Knuckles. You've done enough long-range work that you know what he needs."

She nodded, then turned to Knuckles, saying, "You work just like Pike? Same calls?"

"Yeah. That'll do nicely."

Carly watched the exchange, slightly amazed, finally understanding where Jennifer stood.

A man came running in toting a weapon that looked like an assault rifle that was on steroids, with an enormous scope and a muzzle brake that you could cook a steak on. The Barrett fired the same caliber as a heavy machine gun, could reach out to two thousand yards, and was designed to take out vehicles, bunkers, and other hard targets. The Barrett was not as accurate as other sniper systems designed to kill humans, but it would get the job done.

Knuckles said, "You have tracer rounds for that thing?"

"We have marking rounds, but they aren't match grade. They aren't nearly as accurate."

"I'm going to be shooting into the black of the ocean. I need them for my spotter. Load me up with two mags."

The man raced out of the room and Knuckles said, "Jenn, let's go hunting."

They left the room at a trot, and I said, "Where are my men? We're losing precious time."

Brock called the remainder of his team into the room and began giving orders, telling them the mission and the suspected vehicle. He finished with, "Dingler, Jesus, you're with Pike here. Take his orders as you would with me."

Dingler and Jesus didn't look too happy, but they came over to me, waiting on a command. I said, "Tell me Dingler is a callsign."

He scowled, and I said, "Sorry. Load up in the Hyundai rental that you found when you got here."

Carly said, "What do you want me to do?"

I pointed at the weapon Knuckles had left behind and said, "Can you shoot that AKM?"

"Yeah, yeah, I'm weapons trained from the farm." She saw my expression and held up a hand, saying, "Knuckles has already told me how disgusted you guys are with my people saying that, but at the very least, I can get a sight picture and make this weapon fire."

She removed the magazine, jacked the round out, did a functions check, then reloaded, putting the weapon on safe. I nodded and said, "You're coming with me."

76

The final contingent of HRT assaulters and my small team raced through the backyard to the basketball court, the HRT guys loading up in a high-speed Suburban worthy of their body armor, weapons, and night vision goggles. Carly and I loaded into our Hyundai Sonata, worthy of our Taliban AKs. Jesus and Dingler looked absolutely disgusted at their direction in life.

I said, "You two in the back, no seat belts. Get ready to get some, because these guys are killers. I've already had a firefight with them once."

They loaded and Dingler said, "Where was that?"

"Morocco."

They took that in and realized the weapons and the car weren't indicative of the skill. I started rolling, and without a command, Carly started navigating.

Good. She's learning.

Jennifer had said the boat ramp was only a mile away, and that may have been so as the crow flies, but the drive was one left and right after another. Eventually we hit a two-lane highway that wasn't in the heart of a neighborhood, and I floored it.

Carly said, "It's a half mile ahead. Be careful. If you don't make the exit, you'll be on the bridge and have to travel all the way across before you can turn around."

I said, "Give me a countdown."

"A thousand meters . . ."

"Eight hundred . . ."

"Six hundred . . ."

I asked, "Right exit or left?"

"Left. Four hundred . . ."

I was doing eighty miles an hour on the small highway when headlights passed me. In the blink of an eye, I recognized a Toyota Tundra truck, gray. But without a trailer.

I slammed on the brakes to slow down enough to maintain control, then yanked up the emergency brake handle and jerked the wheel, sending the car into a classic *Rockford Files* J-turn and throwing everyone into the windows. I immediately floored the vehicle, now headed the other way.

From the back, Dingler shouted, "What the fuck are you doing?"

"The truck just passed us. Get ready to assault. I'm going to PIT him. When he spins out, you two deploy and lock down the driver."

Incredulous, he said, "How the fuck do you know it's the truck? You don't even have a license plate. You can't just ram a civilian because you *think* it's a bad guy."

I gained on the truck, now back to eighty miles an hour. I said, "Yes, I can."

Carly just held on, unsure of how she should respond. Support her new organization, or support what she'd been told her entire life was the way things worked? She opted for silence.

Thankfully, the road was deserted, and I gained on the truck rapidly. When I came within fifty yards, the driver goosed the accelerator, and I saw him throw something out of the window. I knew I was right.

I pulled into the left lane and jammed the gas pedal to the firewall, hearing the engine scream in protest. I slowly gained on him, until my right axle was just behind his left rear tire.

I said, "Get ready. When he spins out, I'm slamming the brakes. Get on him."

I torqued the wheel to the right, hammering my front end into the rear of the truck. Because of the empty pickup bed, the vehicle was front heavy, and it didn't take much.

I ground against the truck like a NASCAR driver trying to put someone into the wall, and Carly, on the passenger side, practically crawled into my seat to get away from the impact. I kept pushing, and we raced down the road locked together. Suddenly, the truck's rear tires broke traction, and he spun completely around, sliding through the shoulder and throwing up gravel and smoke.

I regained control of my vehicle and looked in the rearview, seeing the truck in a ditch, nose in, the rear wheels spinning in the mud, the driver struggling to get back on the asphalt.

I slammed on the breaks and shouted, "Out, out, out!"

I flung open my door and leapt to the pavement. The FBI guys beat me to the punch, impressing me. By the time I was on the street, they were running toward the truck with their guns up.

I sprinted behind them with my pathetic AK raised. I saw the driver kick the door open and fall into the road, then jump up, raising a pistol.

No!

Before I could say anything, both of the FBI men fired, shredding the body with multiple rounds. I had to give it to them, they could shoot, but that guy dead was the *last* thing I wanted.

Dingler kicked the terrorist's weapon away while Jesus provided cover; then they began searching him. I entered the cab, ripping through it but finding nothing. I went to the bed and saw three backpacks. I hollered at Carly, saying, "Get this stuff into our trunk. We don't have time to search it now."

She began unloading and I ran to the FBI team. They finished searching the body, Dingler standing up with a passport and wallet. I said, "I wanted him alive."

Defensively, Dingler said, "He had a weapon."

I sighed and said, "I know. I know. You made the right call. But I *still* wanted him alive."

Dingler passed what they'd found, and I said, "No cell phone? Where's his phone?"

"He doesn't have one on his body. Maybe it's in the truck."

I remembered the driver throwing something out the window and realized it was the handset. He knew it was the end game and that his phone would break open whatever cell was still operational. I said, "No. It's in the bushes somewhere back there. We don't have time to look for it."

Carly came forward carrying the rucks and I said, "We need to move."

We ran back to our car, loaded the rucksacks, and then went flying back to the dock. Carly gave me directions again, and I broke at the exit, circling around and seeing a narrow lane dropping down into the river. A trailer was jammed sideways right where the water started lapping the concrete. On top of it was a single Sea-Doo.

I slammed the brakes and leapt out, running to the trailer. I stood for a moment, then said, "They're on the loose."

Jesus said, "We need to call this in. Let Brock know we have the launch point."

I nodded and said, "Do it." I looked at Carly and said, "Tell Knuckles on our net."

I went to the Sea-Doo and opened the hatch at the front, expecting to see four shaped charges wired to explode. I saw an empty container. And got an idea.

"Carly, how long is this river?"

"Three kilometers. Maybe more, given the bends."

I shouted at the FBI guys, "Help me get this in the water."

They ran over, manhandling the watercraft until we finally had it floating. Dingler said, "What are you doing?"

I said, "Chasing them. Get on."

He balked, saying, "Whoa, no way."

"Jesus, get on here."

He looked at Dingler, and Dingler said, "We aren't boarding that with you. You're a target once you go. You'll get killed by friendly fire."

I had no time to argue with him. Every second we waited, the enemy was getting closer to the kill. And truthfully, I was growing tired of his shit.

"Carly, get your weapon."

She grabbed her AKM and waded into the water, then slid onto the back, no questions at all. Dingler looked embarrassed. I said, "Give me your NODs."

He handed over his night vision goggles and I said, "Jesus's too."

Jesus passed them across, and I gave them to Carly. Dingler said, "What do you want us to do?"

I tossed him the keys to the rental, saying, "Do your FBI shit with the guy dead on the highway. Search the bags. Find the phone. Do whatever it is you do at a crime scene."

He said, "What are you going to do?"

I fired up the watercraft, secretly glad for the practice the day before, and said, "What I do best. Kill terrorists."

77

I'd considered letting Carly drive, leaving me to do the shooting, but Carly had never been on one of these before yesterday, and had certainly not operated any vehicle under night vision. I decided that the driving would be the more difficult task, and that proved correct as soon as we started moving.

Initially, I drove slowly, getting a feel for controlling the watercraft with my NODs. It was tricky, because the houses on the shore were all illuminated, with most having some sort of vapor lamp next to a dock that caused the NODs to white out. I found that if I stuck to the center and looked straight ahead, I could manage it.

I said, "How are you doing back there?"

"I'm okay. It took a second to get these goggles on right."

"Can you use your weapon?"

She said, "Yes, if you don't throw me off."

"Okay, hang on. We're going as fast as this thing can move."

I felt the AKM pressed into my back as she wrapped her arms around me, and I punched the throttle—and boy, could that thing move. Much more powerful than the ones we had rented, the acceleration startled me. The bow flew up high, and the watercraft began skipping across the river so quickly I had to throttle back or risk missing a bend in the river and running straight into a bank.

I found a happy medium and settled into a rhythm of gunning the engine for a short time, assessing what was ahead, then gunning again. I had just finished a run and was preparing to scoot forward yet again, when I caught something dark on the water about a hundred meters ahead. Maybe a log, or a boat that had drifted loose. I puttered forward, staring intently, and it passed by a light from shore. It was moving under power.

I said, "Carly, I think I have one to my front."

I felt her shift, leaning back and bringing her weapon up. She said, "What are we going to do?"

I goosed the engine ever so slightly and began to close in on whatever it was. Under the NODs, I could see a figure turning around. It wasn't a night fisherman in a johnboat. It was a Jet Ski.

I released the throttle, letting the watercraft drift forward, and could now hear the one to my front. He'd probably done the same thing, hearing me, but he couldn't see in the dark.

I said, "I'm going to race right up to him full throttle, then let up just as we get to him. When we drift by him, you blast him with the AKM. Hit the man, not the Sea-Doo. Don't wait for our Jet Ski to stop, because he's going to react."

She said, "Uhhh . . . okay."

I said, "Just put that baby on auto and let it rip."

"Which side?"

"Right side. You ready?"

I heard nothing but felt her moving, adjusting her seating position and bringing her weapon up. She said, "I need to rest the muzzle on your leg."

"Do it. Just don't pull the trigger."

I felt the barrel slide up my leg, then her left arm wrap around my waist and her head tuck into my back. She said, "If this isn't flying by the seat of our pants, someone needs to define that for me."

I said, "Here we go," and punched the throttle. The bow rose and we closed the distance in the span of seconds. Twenty feet back, I released, and we sank back into the water, sliding past the target. In the green image of the NODs I saw the startled expression on the man's face. Carly rotated to the right, raised the weapon, and began firing. The noise was deafening right next to my ear. I leaned to get away from the muzzle blast and saw the rounds stitching the water in front of the target.

I screamed, "You're to the front! You're to the front!" She let off the trigger, adjusted her aim, and the target hammered his throttle, getting out of the kill zone.

Shit. Weapons training my ass.

I shouted, "Hang on," and gave chase. I felt Carly wildly grabbing with her left hand, and I worried that she'd dropped the weapon, but then the hand released and the barrel appeared next to my shoulder. I got right behind the target, seeing the second Jet Ski ahead of it, now also at full throttle.

I settled into the sweet spot of flat water in his wake, and we closed the distance. I got about twenty meters behind him, the spray from his machine splashing both of us and making it hard to see with the NODs.

Carly started firing again, this time single rounds. On the third squeeze of the trigger the Jet Ski jerked hard right, flinging the driver off. I raced over to it, circling, and saw the man in the water trying to swim with one arm.

I said, "Finish him. The other one's getting away."

Carly aimed the weapon but didn't fire. I said again, "*Finish* him." Nothing happened. I jerked the rifle out of her hands, pointed it at the guy's skull, and broke the trigger. His head snapped back, and he rolled over in the water, facedown. I handed the weapon back to her and said, "Get ready. We're going after number two the same way."

I waited until I felt her left hand on my waist, then gave the Jet Ski the entire throttle. We began going so fast we were airborne as much as we were in the water, skipping across the wavelets in the river like a flat stone tossed by a child.

The target to our front was now easy to make out under the night vision, because he, too, was going as fast as he could, and the wake stood out like chalk on a blackboard.

I thought there was no way we were going to catch him, but we inexorably closed the distance, and I realized it was because he was driving blind. He didn't have the advantage of night vision and couldn't maximize the velocity of the watercraft.

The river began to widen, and I knew we were close to the ship channel. I came within seventy meters and shouted, "Start shooting!"

I heard, "What?"

"Start shooting! He's going to get away!"

If he made it to the channel, I'd have to break off, because as far as I knew—hoped—there was an armed flotilla on the lookout for two Jet Skis. I knew for a fact that there were at least two snipers doing that.

Even as I gave the command to fire, I saw it was a waste of time. The greatest shooter on earth couldn't make this shot, hitting a moving target, in the dark, from a platform that was both hurtling forward and slamming up and down. The only way to kill him would be to close the gap as much as possible, then slow down.

I felt the barrel slide off my leg and shouted, "Never mind, never mind."

She cinched back onto me, and I valiantly tried to catch him. He reached the outskirts of the channel, leaving behind the houses and entering the industrial port areas. The open water and lighting gave him confidence, and he increased his speed. He reached the head of the estuary and went right, now at full throttle.

I pulled up short, sliding in the water with the engine on idle.

Carly said, "What are we doing?"

"I can't follow him into the channel; that's just asking to get shot. We look like the terrorists."

I put in my Bluetooth, turned on the encryption in my cell phone, and said, "Knuckles, Knuckles, this is Pike, you copy?"

"This is Knuckles. Go."

"One down, one still coming. He went right. He's coming to you."

"Roger all." That was it. Nothing more. The voice was calm and robotic, filling me with confidence. There were very few people on earth who could do what Knuckles was about to attempt, but he was one of them.

I pulled off my goggles, turned around to Carly, and saw that she was as white as a sheet. I didn't know if it was from the cold water or fear. I said, "You okay?"

She nodded hesitantly, then said, "I'm sorry I didn't . . . take the shot."

I said, "Don't sweat it. It was a lot to put on you. I didn't grab the weapon because I was angry. I did it to spare you. Shooting a man who's trying to kill you is one thing, but that was different. I understand it's not easy."

I saw relief float across her face and realized she thought the terrorist had escaped because of her hesitation. She said, "Thank you."

I said, "You did fine; don't worry about the other guy. That's Knuckles's problem now."

She nodded again, but without a lot of confidence, and I wondered if she was second-guessing what I had done. I said, "You understand why I took the shot, right?"

Her voice became firm, "Yes, yes. It was the only choice with the other man getting away. The man I hit was still mobile, and the weapon was still running. I just . . . I mean . . . I couldn't . . ."

She trailed off and I said, "I know. I've been there."

We sat in silence a moment; then she said, "Can we go back at a normal speed?"

I chuckled and said, "Sure," then noticed her goggles were missing from her head. I asked, "What happened to your NODs?"

"I threw them into the river."

"What?"

"I've never fired a weapon using night vision. When I tried to shoot the first time, I couldn't even see the sights. I was spraying blind. That's why I missed. I ripped the NODs off and started shooting single shots using the sights."

I'd never even thought to ask if she could shoot wearing NODs. To me, saying you were weapons qualified and not being able to do that was like saying you were a naval aviator and not being able to land on a carrier. Even so, I was slightly impressed. "You hit that guy in the dark?"

She smiled and said, "I aimed at the jet of water coming out of the tail, then just raised it an inch. Trust me, it was luck."

I turned the Sea-Doo around and started heading back to the boat ramp. I said, "First rule of the

Taskforce—there is no such thing as good luck. It's always your incredible skill. If something goes wrong, however, there is certainly such a thing as bad luck."

She laughed and I said, "I'd start working on that bad-luck thing when you tell Dingler you lost his four-thousand-dollar government-issued night vision goggles."

78

Knuckles tapped Jennifer's leg with his foot, getting her attention. She pulled out a foam earplug from her right ear and he said, "One target remaining, and it's headed our way. Get eyes out."

She picked up a ten-power combination range finder/binocular, scanning from the tip of the international port down to where they lay. Knuckles did the same through the scope on the Barrett, seating the weapon into his shoulder. The two seamen behind them shifted uncomfortably, unsure if they were supposed to do anything.

They'd met the FBI pilots at gate three, right off of Interstate 564, and were surprised to learn that they'd already coordinated to get them on the bridge of an aircraft carrier. The FBI had whisked them to pier five, the berth of the gigantic USS *George Washington* aircraft carrier. They'd jogged down the pier toward the gangway and were stopped by a master-at-arms petty officer and two seamen acting as shore patrol.

The petty officer said, "I need to see your badges before letting you on board the ship."

The special agent showed his, prompting the petty officer to look at Knuckles and Jennifer expectantly. Knuckles showed his US Navy CAC card, and the petty officer said, "That's not going to get you on board. What about her?"

Frustrated that the idiot was asking for badges while

Knuckles was standing in front of him holding what amounted to a semiautomatic bazooka, he said, "Look, she's with me, and we're going to the bridge. If we wanted to do anything harmful to this ship, I'd just shoot all three of you right now."

The petty officer's eyes went wide, and he began to bluster. Knuckles said, "Get out of the way."

The petty officer put his hand on the butt of his pistol, and Knuckles said, "You draw that thing, and you'll reap the consequences."

The petty officer backed down but said, "These two will accompany you at all times."

Knuckles said, "Fine by me," then pushed him out of the way. The seamen followed with a smirk, apparently liking what Knuckles had done. Halfway up the gangway, Knuckles turned and said, "You guys know the quickest way to the bridge?"

The first seaman nodded, and Knuckles said, "Take the lead."

Eight minutes later they were on a platform on top of the bridge, the flat top of the aircraft carrier landing deck far below. Knuckles extended the bipod of the Barrett, getting it into position, and Jennifer began to range target reference points from the Lafayette River to their location.

Knuckles finished establishing his firing position, satisfied, and asked, "What do you have?"

Jennifer showed him a crude drawing she'd made, saying, "TRP 1 is the last gantry crane of the first set on the international port. Distance 2,935 meters. TRP 2 is the first gantry crane of the second set at the international port. Distance 1,956 meters. TRP 3 is the final pier of the international port, the boundary one with the Navy base. Distance 1,030 meters."

Knuckles smiled and said, "Very good, commando. Let me see the reticle you're using." She passed the binoculars over, saying, "It's got night vision, so I'll probably be the one who sees him first."

Knuckles brought the binos up to his eyes, seeing an MRAD reticle just like the one in his scope, with hash lines that could be used to measure distance for windage and drop of the bullet, as well as guide him into the target from her calls.

He handed it back to her, looked over his shoulder at the two seamen, and said, "You guys have any ear protection?"

"We work on a carrier. I think we can handle it."

Knuckles said, "Suit yourself." He didn't mention that the Barrett was about the loudest rifle he'd ever fired, with the muzzle brake actually providing a small concussive shock wave.

He went behind the scope, making sure he could find the TRPs without the aid of night vision. He ranged each with the scope, getting a point of focus for rapid acquisition, then settled in to wait, feeling the breeze off the ocean.

Every thirty seconds, he and Jennifer alternated scanning the river, looking for signs of a Jet Ski. Knuckles realized it would be hard to locate the target early enough if the attack was at the international port. They'd be on an attack run before he could engage, and if they hit the first section of gantry cranes, his weapon didn't even have the range to reach. Luckily, there were no ships berthed at the first section, and the odds were that they wouldn't simply attack the port cranes. He was hoping they would be drawn in by the mighty United States Navy.

An hour into the overwatch, Pike's call had come in.

Knuckles alerted Jennifer, removed his Bluetooth, and put in an earplug, willing his heart rate to slow. He began scanning the dark water, looking for any sign of a wake, breathing like a metronome. In—out—in—out, methodically getting into a hypnotic rhythm he wouldn't break until the mission was done, his pulse rate dropping with each breath.

He reached the end of his search zone and returned the scope to the far side, starting over in a methodical sector scan, clearing each bit of water. Next to him, louder than necessary, Jennifer said, "Target! TRP 2, up nine, right seven."

He swiveled to TRP 2, put his reticle on the center, and scanned the distance she'd called. He found the target. Robotically, he said, "Target acquired. Ready, ready."

She said, "Send it," and the rifle boomed, a blast that rippled the air around them, the buttstock slamming into his shoulder. He heard the two seaman shout but ignored them, waiting on his spotter. She said, "Up three, right two."

He'd failed the lead and the elevation. The bullet had landed behind the Sea-Doo. He adjusted his aim point, then said, "Ready, ready."

"Send it."

BOOM.

"Up one, right one. He's inside a thousand."

BOOM.

"Elevation good, left one. Knuckles, he's coming right at us. We're his target."

Knuckles ignored the stray chatter, focusing on the reticle and her call.

BOOM.

"Hit!"

The Sea-Doo continued driving straight at them. Jennifer said, "He's still coming. That was a hit, but he's still coming."

Knuckles said nothing, breathing out, focusing all his energy into not having any energy, turning his body to stone. He broke the trigger one more time.

The night sky was blistered by an explosion, the Sea-Doo disappearing in a fireball that caused Jennifer to duck her head.

When she looked up again, she saw the water on fire, less than four hundred meters from the ship.

Knuckles dropped the buttstock, looked at her deadpan, and said, "Target down."

She grinned at him, then punched him in the arm, saying, "Were you just trying to scare me? Waiting until I wet my pants?"

He smiled, his teeth white in the darkness. "That was good spotting, Koko. Might need to upgrade your callsign."

She took the compliment, then said, "That was some *phenomenal* shooting."

He stood up, saying, "Yeah, you'll never see Pike make that shot."

She gathered up the range finder and stood with him, saying, "I've seen him do something better."

He said, "What? Rome? Bosnia?"

She grinned and said, "No. Not on an operation."

He folded up the bipod legs, knowing that she was ribbing him because of his pushback in the past about their relationship. He rolled his eyes and picked up the weapon, saying, "I *do not* want to hear it."

She laughed and turned around, seeing the two

seamen cowering in the corner with their hands over their ears.

Knuckles said, "Thanks for the help."

The first seaman nodded. When he made no attempt to rise, Knuckles glanced at Jennifer, then said, "We can find our own way down."

79

Dawn was slowly arriving, with the Norfolk Navy base security lights blinking out one by one from the illumination of the rising sun. The area around pier five was a nuthouse, with enough police cars spinning their lights to make someone think Charles Manson was on the loose.

I'd told my team to hang back in the shadows and let the FBI take the lead, and they were more than happy to do so. All of them were currently sitting in our rental car, the radio on some random pop station. I could see Jennifer and Knuckles slumped over, asleep. Carly was still awake, probably running our last action through her head over and over again.

I would love to have joined them, but I was waiting on Brock to finish whatever he was doing with the gaggle of vehicles from about fourteen different agencies. They were probably all arguing over who had jurisdiction.

Carly and I had returned to the dock, skipping right by the Sea-Doo and the body, and had then sat around waiting on an FBI explosive ordnance disposal team. In the meantime, Dingler had asked me to retrieve the body, and I'd said, "Not my job. I just kill them."

As far as I was concerned, he could go get it himself. He did, dragging the body back with our Sea-Doo. We'd searched it, finding another passport and a cell phone. A waterlogged, worthless cell phone.

Eventually, EOD had arrived, and I'd hauled one of them back to the floating bomb. When we got there, he said, "I can't work on it out over the water."

"Okay. Get on it and drive it back."

He looked at me like I was crazy, and I said, "It's not going to go off. I chased that thing at full throttle, watching it bounce up and down."

He stared at it for a moment, and I said, "Let me guess. You want *me* to drive it back, but only after you're clear of the area."

He shook his head and said, "No. It's just that I've never driven one of those things."

I said, "I'll do it."

"No, you won't. I'm not letting anyone get near that thing but me. Show me how it works."

That was more like what I thought he'd say. EOD guys weren't in the business of being afraid of a bomb. I gave him a quick class, and off we went, puttering back to the boat ramp. By the time we got there, Brock was on station, asking me to come back to the Norfolk naval base. I got my rental keys from Dingler and tossed them to Carly, telling her to follow us because I had to do some gentle persuasion with Brock.

We started driving, and he said, "You pulled it off. That was some good shooting, and Dingler says you're border-line psychotic for going after them with the last Jet Ski."

I said, "No. *Dingler's* borderline psychotic. And it was *your* sniper who took the shot."

"What?"

"We were never here. You take the credit from the moment you 'found' the safe house until you stopped the attack."

"No way. I'm not taking credit for something I didn't do."

"Yes, you are. We had nothing to do with this. Frame it however you want. Make it vague, I don't care, like 'elements of the FBI blah-blah-blah,' or 'a combined effort with multiple federal agencies discovered, blah-blah-blah,' but under no circumstances will you mention the females or what Knuckles and I did."

"The press is going to want to know. They're going to start tearing this apart."

"Come on. They'll take whatever you give them, especially when you answer every damn question with, 'I can't comment on an ongoing investigation.'"

He looked at me and said, "This isn't right. I can't take the accolades for something I didn't do."

"Unfortunately, it's exactly right. Trust me."

"Dingler refused to get on with you. Now I'm going to say *he* was the one who took out the Sea-Doo?"

I said, "I'm way ahead of you. I figured you'd need some proof, so I left his night vision goggles at the bottom of the river."

"You did what?"

"Don't you see? Of *course* he was there; how else would his NODs get there?"

"You dumped his NODs in the river? Do you have any idea how sensitive those things are? They're a controlled item, for God's sake."

I looked shocked and said, "Me? Talk to your man. *He's* the one who left them."

He quit talking to me, spending the rest of the drive to the Navy base muttering to himself. When we arrived at the pier he saw the cluster of cars and must have immediately assumed someone was trying to take over, or maybe it was SOP for anyone in a three-letter agency to get sucked into a meeting to compare badges, because he took off running to the scrum. Either way, I'd been waiting ever since. I'd let the others try to catch some rack time but was afraid to do so myself. You never know what you're going to miss by taking a nap.

I saw Knuckles sit up in the passenger seat and walked over to the car. Jennifer was asleep in the back, and I was glad to see that Carly had also finally closed her eyes.

Knuckles rolled down the window and pointed behind me, saying, "Looks like the meeting's over."

I turned around to see Brock headed my way. I said, "About time."

Knuckles exited the vehicle, and Carly woke up. She followed, gently closing the door so as not to wake Jennifer. Brock reached us and said, "Okay, I think I've sold your plan. September eleventh is helping us out. The story is about the past and how we've gotten our act together for the future. Thank God we stopped it. They're going to have a press conference in an hour. DHS will take the lead, then let the port authority speak, then me, then the sheriff's department, and probably the Navy as well. DHS wanted to know what the hell happened, and I told them the basics of where the action had taken place but said I haven't finished talking to my men. They bought it."

I said, "I appreciate it. What did you come up with as far as further evidence? Any actionable intelligence?"

"Not really. The backpacks are just full of clothes and sundry items. We can use it to determine where they've been, but it's no use for future actions. We found one cell phone on the guy you killed, but it was in his pocket, and it's waterlogged. We have our tech guys working it, but that'll take some time. The other cell phone is still in the woods somewhere, if that's even what you saw him throw. We have the passport information, and we're working that for cross-links."

I pulled out the one we'd found on the guy with the truck and said, "Did you get this information?"

He said, "Yeah. Dingler passed it to me, but I could use the actual, if you don't mind."

Carly said, "Let me see that."

I handed the passport to her and said, "Yeah, you can have it as long as I can access it with a phone call."

"That won't be an issue."

I pulled out the dead guy's wallet and said, "You can have this too. Nothing in it but money, but you might be able to get something from the leather or the dye or whatever CSI stuff you guys do."

He took it, then said, "You think this attack was it?"

"We should all keep looking, but this one had the most infrastructure behind it, and, given the date and the target, I think this was the big finale of the fireworks show."

Someone shouted from the scrum of authorities, and Brock said, "I have to get back to work. I appreciate the help." He saw Carly still going through the passport and was polite enough not to demand it right then. He said, "Don't lose any of the evidence."

I said, "I won't. I appreciate you keeping us out of it." I shook his hand, and he jogged away.

Carly went through the passport page by page. She said, "This thing is brand-new. Only place it's been used is to get to the United States."

Knuckles said, "So?"

"They left from Morocco, but there's no entry stamp for that country. They had to have received the passport there. How do some Berbers get a Saudi Arabian passport in Morocco?"

She flipped to the last page, and a card fluttered to the ground. She picked it up and said, "That's how."

80

She handed the card to me, and all I saw was a typical business card, with print in both Arabic and English. I said, "Okay? What did you find?"

She smiled and said, "You're the smart one. Read the fine print. Read the name."

The English at the bottom said Tariq bin Abdul-Aziz, the guy who we believed was the financier. *Holy shit*.

I said, "All right, lone wolf! That's what I wanted to see."

She smiled and said, "That's not the best part. Flip it over."

I did so and saw Arabic writing in blue ink.

I looked up at her, and she said, "Lone Wolf did good."

I broke into a grin and said, "Oh yeah, Lone Wolf did very good." I called the Taskforce intel cell.

They answered with some stupid cover organization like, "Pete's Flowers," and I said, "Go encrypted."

They did, and I said, "This is Pike." I handed the card to Knuckles and said, "I'm about to send you a picture of Arabic writing. I want an answer of what it is while I wait."

Knuckles pulled out his phone, took a photo, then gave me a thumbs-up. I said, "It's on the way."

A minute later, the analyst came back. "It's an address. The Cottages at Patriots Point, in Mount Pleasant, South Carolina."

Jesus Christ.

"Does it have a number? A cottage number?"

"Nope, not from what I can see."

"Get me Colonel Hale."

"He's in an O&I update with the teams. I'll have him call you as soon as he's done."

"Get me Colonel Hale right fucking now. This is a Prairie Fire."

Prairie Fire was the code word for an Operator or team in dire straights and about to be overrun, which caused the entire Taskforce to stop whatever they were doing to help. I was misusing it here, but I knew it would get me Kurt.

He said, "Roger that. Stand by."

Knuckles looked at me with a question. I said, "It's an address for vacation cottages in Mount Pleasant, South Carolina. They're still on the hunt."

Kurt came on the line, using his command voice. He said, "Pike, what's the Prairie Fire? Earlier you said everything went damn near perfect."

"Sir, we found a business card with an address scribbled in Arabic for rental cottages in Mount Pleasant, South Carolina."

"So? What's the emergency?"

I realized he didn't see the significance. I wouldn't have either, except I lived there. "It's the town across the Cooper River from the Charleston peninsula. The business card is from Tariq bin Abdul-Aziz. This isn't done yet. They're going to attack the Port of Charleston."

"Whoa. Wait a minute. Mount Pleasant is actually Charleston?"

"Yes, sir. As far as the port is concerned, it is."

"Where'd you find the card?"

"On the body of a dead terrorist."

"But you think they might still be operational without him?"

"I do. At the least, we should act like they are."

"Okay, okay, well, you live there. What's your assessment for an attack?" Before I could answer, he said, "Hang on," then yelled down the hall. Five seconds later, the phone gave an audible click, and Kurt said, "I've got an analyst on speaker. Go ahead."

I said, "The port is actually separated, with a cruise and shipping terminal on the Charleston side of the river, and another shipping terminal on the Mount P side, at the end of Long Point Road. There is no shortage of targets, but I don't think this is going to be another suicide cell. I think it's going to be something like the others, where the ship is the missile, like in Houston and Los Angeles. Get the intel cell working on any connections between the tanker that went off and the container ship that had the dirty bomb, then cross-reference that with anything coming into the port."

I heard an unknown voice say, "We're already working that. We have some connections with a Saudi Arabian company, and we can run that against the Port of Charleston shipping schedule. All of that is available."

Kurt said, "I'll get the word out to the port, getting all responsible authorities on high alert for an attack."

I said, "This is exactly why they've targeted the ports. They've got a thousand different agencies in charge, from the civilian company contracted for security to DHS on the federal side mucking up everything with layers of bureaucracy. In between, there's the Coast Guard, individual port authority, Army Corps of Engineers, and God knows who else. They'll never be able to coordinate."

"They've done fine since 9/11."

"Seriously? They've done fine because *nobody's* attacked them. Sir, we've had three separate attacks, and if it hadn't been for us, all three would have succeeded. What scares me is that every one has been different. The terrorists aren't stupid. They saw what happened after 9/11. They know we react to a specific attack, putting a Band-Aid on to prevent the same event from succeeding, but go no further. Tell the authorities to think outside the box for threats. These guys started with a conventional attack, and they've amped up the imagination with each strike."

"I understand, Pike. I get it. When will you be back? The intel cell could use your team's input. You know more about these guys than anyone, and if we're going to find that vulnerability you're afraid of, it'll probably come from you."

The statement confused me, and I let him know it. "Back there? Sir, I'm not coming back. Send me the Rock Star bird with my team, and get the hacking cell to explore those cottage rentals. Tell them to look for anything out of the ordinary for a recent rental—Arabic names, foreign persons, paid in cash, *anything*—and give me the information when we land. I'm going hunting."

I heard a sigh, then, "Pike, I can't authorize an official Taskforce action on US soil. I've already stretched it with your 'vacation.' You have the FBI HRT sitting right there. I'll use them. It's their jurisdiction. We'll point the way, but they'll do the arrests."

I squeezed my hands into fists, almost crushing the phone, but waited before I answered in anger. When I did, it was with a calm voice. "Sir, you just told me my team knows more about these guys than anyone else, and on top of that, it's in my hometown. I know that area inside and out. Shit, I even know the floor plan of the cottages because I've stayed there with Jennifer. It makes no sense to try to turn the FBI onto this. They'll spend the next forty-eight hours getting warrants and planning."

"That's the way the world works, Pike. I don't like it either."

"Sir, don't make me say the obvious."

He paused; then I heard, "You're telling me there may be a hit before then, and we could have prevented it."

"Yes. Like we did the *last* two."

He paused again, and I knew I was playing dirty pool by pulling on his sense of mission. His reason for existence. But it was the only card I had. He said, "Okay, I'll send the bird, and the team, but you hit the ground and do nothing. I'm going to have to clear this with the president himself."

"Roger all, sir."

"Pike, I mean it."

"Sir, I understand. I won't do anything without talking to you first. Just get that port on alert and see if you can find some connections between the previous ship attacks. Maybe none of this will be necessary."

"Will do. And you might be right about that. Best case you wiped out the cell planning the attack. The guy with the card was probably the one who was executing the plan, and you killed him."

"Maybe, but maybe not. Tariq is more than a financier. I think he's an operational planner, and he's the one that got them the passports, explosives, and everything else. And that asshole Anwar is still on the loose, and he was the one who set off the Houston attack."

81

Tariq heard the alarm go off and rolled over, hitting the snooze button. He put his head back into the pillow and tried to go back to sleep. It had been a long night, and they still had a couple of hours before they needed to leave for the mission.

Sleep eluded him. All he could think about was the failed mission in Norfolk, and the final one to come. He was nervous. The longer he lay in bed, the more the sweat built under his arms. Somehow the Great Satan had managed to thwart each of the two port attacks. He had no idea how but still felt confident that it had nothing to do with him. He was convinced the Moroccan cell had been penetrated, and that had led to their deaths.

Anwar was a clean break, as was he.

He got out of bed, seeing it was eight o'clock in the morning. He thought about waking Anwar but decided to let him sleep. He'd been working all night, and Tariq needed him to be sharp. He was the only one who could work the drone.

Tariq had picked up Anwar on the last flight from Atlanta to Charleston, then driven him straight to the cottage safe house. The flight from Los Angeles had been a risk, given that Anwar's face was plastered all over the place as a domestic terrorist, but he was traveling on a passport from Saudi Arabia, and he was flying first class. Very few airlines were willing to question s who'd paid full fare, and the enormous security bureau-cracy of the United States was something Tariq lever-aged. Just as he had in 2001.

When Anwar had arrived, he was not what Tariq ex-pected. Tall and lanky, dressed in sweatpants and T-shirt, he didn't look the part of a mastermind terrorist.

Tariq shook his hand, saying, "It's good to finally meet. You have no clothes?"

"I checked them."

They went to baggage claim and stood around like everyone else, waiting on the luggage. Eventually, Anwar removed a backpack and said, "Where'd you park?"

Tariq said, "That's all you have? Why didn't you carry it on?"

"I have something that couldn't go through the X-ray machine."

Tariq nodded, wondering what on earth he could have that would cause an issue with airport security. They walked across the loading zone to the parking ga-rage, and as soon as the doors to the car closed, Anwar asked, "You got the drone? The one I asked for?"

"Yes. It should be at the cottage now."

"What's it called?"

Tariq realized Anwar was testing him. He said, "The ICON? Aeronavics ICON? That thing was expensive."

Anwar leaned back in the seat and said, "Yes, but it will do everything we want. Much better than a cheap Chinese drone you can buy at Brookstone, like the one I used before."

"I don't see why it matters. You killed the man in Nevada with that cheap drone."

"We aren't trying to kill an unsuspecting man. This one will have protection. There are countermeasures they can employ. Make no mistake, they'll have ways to prevent our attack. Using the drone is unique, but such a threat hasn't escaped notice. I've been doing research, and I've developed a way to defeat the countermeasures."

They left Interstate 26 and crossed the Ravenel Bridge, giving them a full view of the Charleston Harbor. Reaching the top, Tariq said, "There's the target. That big ship out there with the lights."

Anwar put his head to the window and said, "Why there?"

"Who knows? I guess it's patriotic for these heathens. You'd know more than me. But that's where the man will be. They're dumb enough to put it on the web. He starts talking at ten A.M."

"Did you find a spot to launch? A place where I can control the drone without interference?"

"Yes. I'll show you."

They exited on the right side of the bridge, onto Coleman Boulevard. Tariq took the first right, next to a large sign.

Anwar read it and said, "Patriots Point? That's what this place is called?"

Tariq grinned and said, "Yes. I found that ironic as well."

"Perfect."

Tariq wound past baseball fields and Shriner temples, then reached the parking lot for the ship they'd seen on the bridge. He said, "That's it. The USS *Yorktown*. An aircraft carrier from World War Two, now a museum. He'll be on the deck tomorrow at ten."

Anwar surveyed the area, saying, "It's ideal. A large, flat area with nothing to interfere. No power lines, light poles, or anything else. It'll be easier than Nevada."

Tariq put the car in drive and said, "Good, good. That's what I wanted to hear."

He went through a traffic circle and took the third road, heading to the Patriots Point golf course.

Anwar said, "Have you thought about what I asked for? After this is done?"

Tariq looked at him in the dim glow of the dash lights. In truth, he hadn't given Anwar's request a minute's thought, but that didn't mean he couldn't pretend he had. After all, the request was fairly simple and required nothing from him.

"Yes, I have. I've talked to my father, and you can use that passport for whatever you would like. If you accomplish this mission, I will give you enough money to go to Somalia."

Looking out the windshield, Anwar smiled. He said, "They will accept me as a hero. I won't be just another foreign fighter. I'll be the man who struck a great blow."

Tariq nodded, knowing Anwar would get killed in his first week in the bloodbath between Al Shabaab and the African Union forces. Anwar had technical skill, but he had no warrior instincts to protect him in a hellhole like Somalia. He didn't say that, of course.

"But first, you must accomplish this mission. Remain focused on the task at hand."

"Yes, yes. Of course. I have to prove myself first. I've been studying on the Internet. I won't fail you."

Tariq saw a historical marker and pulled over to the side of the road, the darkness cloaking them. He pointed to an opening next to the marker and said, "You see that trail?"

"Yes."

"It goes through the forest to the water. At the end of it is a wooden sightseeing platform, surrounded by trees. Nobody comes out here. We will use that platform to launch the drone. Straight above the trees, the way we came, is the target. You said to find something within a thousand meters, and that's it."

"I'd like to see it tomorrow. Practice with the drone before we execute."

Tariq put the car in drive and circled back, saying, "Of course."

They went back through the traffic circle, taking a different road. They passed a hotel, then pulled into the secluded section of the cottages. Tariq tossed a key to Anwar and said, "We have to walk from here. Unfortunately, we have the cottage in the back. I wanted to stay away from the street."

Anwar looked at the first cottage in front of them, seeing a house that was better than anything he'd ever slept in. He grabbed his small backpack and said, "I'd walk a mile to sleep in something like that."

Tariq laughed, and they entered the property, walking through the trees on a bike path to their cottage. He was glad it was near midnight, as Anwar's appearance would draw attention in this affluent area. A young black man wearing grubby sweats, with his hair in cornrows—it wouldn't do for him to be seen.

They circled around a lake with a fountain, the shrubs around it making it look like something out of Disney World, finally reaching the farthest cottage.

On the front porch was a large box. Tariq said, "That's your baby."

Tariq unlocked the door, and Anwar was torn between running into the house to see the splendor and tearing into the box. Tariq said, "Get settled first. I'll bring the drone in."

A childlike smile on his face, Anwar ran inside, seeing the sunken den and the ceiling fans. He whooped and ran to a bedroom, coming out seconds later. He said, "Sorry. I see that one's taken. Where's my room?"

Tariq smiled and said, "The next one over. It's just as good, only a little smaller."

Anwar ran into it, and Tariq waited. When he didn't come back out, Tariq went to the room, finding Anwar working the jets on the bathtub.

He said, "You can use that after the work is done. We have a lot to do."

Anwar nodded, refocusing on the mission. He said, "You have the explosives?"

"Yes. In the closet."

Anwar went back into the den and opened the box. He pulled out the pieces to a quadcopter drone, much larger than the pathetic one he'd used in Nevada. Able to carry close to a fifteen-pound payload, it was made for surveying power lines and industrial facilities and making Hollywood movies. With a user-defined software capability and a dual control panel that allowed simultaneous manipulation of the camera and the drone, it was state of the art.

Something Anwar could only dream of. The closest he'd ever come were pictures on the Internet.

He said, "Did you get the laptop as well?"

"Yes. It's on the kitchen table. But why do you want to manipulate the software? From what I've seen on the brochure, you can't make this thing fly any better."

Anwar went to the laptop and said, "We have Wi-Fi?"

"Yes, I paid for that, as you asked. Why?"

Anwar booted up the system and said, "Our drone is powerful, but it has a weakness. I can send it on a GPS track, which requires the drone to receive a GPS signal, or I can fly it with my control panel, which requires the drone to receive my radio signal. Both of those are vulnerabilities that the government has worked to over-come. Make no mistake, when this thing is seen, it will be targeted. They will try to block both signals. So, what we need is a third way to fly the drone."

He started typing on the computer, pulling up one weird website after another.

Tariq said, "What third way?"

"Facial recognition. There are a bunch of PhD students here in the US who have developed facial recognition software, trying to get drones to follow a certain person by his facial features alone. Some of the software algorithms are good; others are a waste of time. They're students, after all, but the good thing is they want to brag about what they've done, so they put the software on the net. I found one open-source experiment called, appropriately enough, *Predator*. And I want to load that into the drone."

"Wait, you want to load the man's face into the drone? And it will chase him?"

Anwar laughed and said, "No. We aren't at the Skynet level yet. Most of these are built on certain characteristics that have to remain, like a hand in a pocket or a specific vehicle. Hard things that don't change."

He typed on the computer, and Tariq said, "What 'hard thing' are you looking for?"

Anwar turned the computer around and said, "This. I get the software installed, and it will fly to this at sixty kilometers an hour."

On the screen, Tariq saw the Great Seal of the United States.

82

We reached the crest of the Ravenel Bridge and I could see activity at the *Yorktown*. A ton of people milling around the parking lot, probably here for some sort of conference. Built in World War II, it was actually the second carrier to bear that name, the first being sunk at the Battle of Midway. It now housed a Medal of Honor museum as well as all sorts of naval aviation artifacts, and was rented out for conferences and other events. Jennifer and I had been to it a couple of times, when we were spending a lazy Saturday looking for something to do.

Jennifer took a right off Coleman Boulevard onto Patriots Point Road and began to wind down toward the end, where the cottages were located. I knew Kurt said not to do anything, but just driving by wasn't something I'd call "operational."

We passed the College of Charleston sports fields, then a sign proclaiming helicopter rides, one of the few things I hadn't done in Charleston.

It was one of those rinky-dink three-seater helicopters that looked like it had been built with toy parts and flew damn near every day, going back and forth giving tours of the harbor for about fifty bucks, and landing literally in a patch of grass next to the parking lot for the *Yorktown*.

We went through the first traffic circle and ran into a phalanx of security at the lot's entrance. At first, I thought it was the "high alert" call that Kurt had made, and that they were taking no chances about anyone trying to harm the carrier, but as we drove by I saw it was something else. There were too many people running around with suits and earpieces. Not something I would expect from port security.

They'd created an open lane for folks like us just trying to drive by, and had a uniformed policeman controlling traffic. We went by the mess of security and returned to the quiet, tree-lined drive.

My phone rang, and I saw it was Kurt. I told Jennifer to pull over, then to call Knuckles behind us, telling him the same.

"Hey, sir, give me some good news."

"Are you on the ground? Right now?"

I lied, "Yes, I'm headed to my office just up the road from the cottages on Coleman Boulevard."

"Pike, it's not good news. Not good at all. I just hung up the phone with the president—"

I cut him off, saying, "He didn't authorize the operation? After everything I've done to save his ass?"

"Quit interrupting!"

The comment was sharp, and uncharacteristic of him. I said, "Yes, sir," and shut up. He said, "Yes, he authorized the operation. What's not good is that he's on the campaign trail, and he's giving a speech on the *Yorktown* today."

That explains the security.

He continued, "We don't know if this was just a coincidence with what you discovered in Norfolk, but we found no connections between the Saudi shipping firm and anything coming to the Port of Charleston. It's too dangerous to ignore. I have to call him back right now, because the secret service is spinning up the counterassault team."

"You have the location?"

"Yes. Tariq rented it under his true name. It was

child's play for Creed to get into their database. It's cottage number nine, in the back. Can you hit it?"

"In about five minutes. Don't let the CAT launch. We have control of the target. The last thing I want is a friendly-fire incident."

"Will do. I have to get back to the president. He's on the ground as well and is due to speak in thirty minutes."

"Got it, sir. Call you in a few."

I said, "Everyone in Knuckles's van, now. Jennifer, bring the tablet."

Jennifer, Veep, and I ran back to Knuckles's rental van and crammed inside. In as brief a time as I could, I explained the situation, ending with, "We're hitting it right now. Jennifer, bring up the satellite view of the cottages. Veep, get out a notebook and hand it to Jennifer."

She did as I asked, then gave me the tablet. I said, "Sketch out the floor plan of the cottage we stayed in."

I pulled up the satellite image, showing a line of cottages with a view of the harbor, then the rental office, then three more cottages surrounding a small lake with a fountain. Number nine was the farthest away and butted up against woods behind it. To the east was some sort of bike trail or service drive running right up to the side of the target cottage.

I said, "Okay, we park up high, away from the rental office, and use this service road, going in on foot. We'll breach the back of the house. Jennifer and Carly, you're squirter control. Take pistols only. Jennifer, you lock down the front, facing the lake. Carly, you lock down the back, just in case someone jumps out a window after we enter."

Carly said, "What am I supposed to do?"

"Prevent anyone from escaping, using lethal force if you have to. Can you do that?"

"Yes."

She looked confident, so I didn't press. I said, "Okay, plan's changed from what we discussed on the plane down. No more explosive breach. We do that, and we'll get a response immediately from the clusterfuck of security for the president. We go mechanical. Veep, you have the Bam-Bam. Order of march is Knuckles, me, Retro, then Veep." I paused and said, "Jennifer, you done?"

She handed me her sketch, and I laid it on the seat. "All of the cottages are the same; the only differences are the decorations and trim." I pointed, "A central den, an open kitchen off of it, and two bedrooms. We go in, clear the den and kitchen, then hit the bedrooms, two men each, first come, first served. No stealth here, boys. I want speed and violence. Remember, it's a daylight hit, so we don't spend any time getting set. We get within the sphere of observation of the house, and we assume we've been compromised. Any questions?"

Veep said, "Weapons? I don't really want to do this with a Glock."

I laughed and said, "Me either. We'll use the .300 Blackout, but we go in concealed, which means a jacket."

The .300 was an integrally suppressed short-barreled rifle built on the AR platform that fired subsonic ammunition, making it extremely quiet when used. It had a stock that folded over at the charging handle, making it pretty compact, but not invisible. We had harnesses that would allow it to be concealed in the armpit, but it required something to cover it, which would look mildly strange in the Charleston heat.

The system wasn't designed to be something that could infiltrate a security force looking for a threat—more like concealing the fact that you had a weapon from someone across the street, at night—but it beat trying to walk down that service road with our rifles at port arms.

I said, "Kit up. I want to be moving in less than five minutes. We'll travel in a single vehicle."

Three minutes later, we were rolling. Jennifer went through a traffic circle, then pulled over, bouncing up on the sidewalk. To our left was the service drive, a broken strip of asphalt leading through the trees. I said, "Everyone ready?"

I got a thumbs-up, and we exited the van, quickly getting into the tree line. We moved at a rapid clip, in a wedge formation with Knuckles on point. I knew everyone wanted to bring out their weapons—because I did—but the lake to our right gave an unobstructed view from the other cottages.

We reached the fountain at the head of the lake, and I could see the front porch of the cottage across. Knuckles held up a fist, and we stopped. He said, "This is last covered and concealed."

I nodded and said, "Carly, Jennifer, get in position. Call when you're set. Keep the guns out of sight unless you need them."

They began walking together, but about fifty meters up, I saw them split, Carly going to the left, and Jennifer to the right.

We waited, then heard, "Koko set," followed by "Carly set." Off the radio, I said, "We really need to give her a callsign." On the net, I said, "Roger, here we come."

We broke out our rifles, snapping the stocks in place, then waited a beat while Veep opened up the handles of the Bam-Bam.

A miniature battering ram, it looked like a twelve-inch section of a wooden six-by-six but was made of steel, with folding handles on top.

He slung his weapon across his chest and got both hands on the handles. I said, "Knuckles, on your command."

83

Knuckles nodded, and we began walking forward with our weapons at the ready. The minute Knuckles caught a glimpse of a window from the target, he assumed that anyone on the other side could see him, and broke into a sprint. We followed directly behind him.

Knuckles turned the corner of the cottage and sprang up the steps two at a time, locking down the back door with his rifle. I came up behind him, putting a barrel on the window to his right. Retro did the same to the window on the left. Veep was last.

He shattered the deadbolt with the battering ram, splintering the doorjamb and flinging the door open.

Knuckles sprinted in, barrel high, with me right behind him. He went left, and I went right. I heard Veep and Retro following behind. The den was empty, and so was the kitchen. We raced to the bedrooms, me and Veep on the first one, Knuckles and Retro on the second. It wasn't planned, but we kicked the doors in like synchronized swimmers.

They were empty.

My bedroom had a cheap backpack and some clothes, but nothing else. Knuckles's had another suitcase, with additional clothes that were clearly more expensive.

We returned to the den, and I saw a box next to the couch. I went to it and realized it was a FedEx delivery container. Inside was a smaller box, for an industrial-strength personal drone.

Knuckles said, "Pike, over here."

I went to the kitchen and saw him holding up wires and a silver tube about the size of a cigarette. I said, "Is that what I think it is?"

"Yep. It's a blasting cap."

I said, "Veep, go through that box and get the manual for the drone. I need to know its specs—specifically, how much can it carry, how long can it fly, and what's its operational distance from the controller."

I called Kurt. He answered on the first ring.

"What did you find?"

"Sir, it's a dry hole, but they were here. We must have missed them by minutes. There's a box for a commercial drone, and we found evidence of explosives. He's built another flying bomb."

"My God."

"Tell the president to cancel the speech."

Kurt said, "It's going to start in about five minutes. Stand by."

He hung up, and I said, "Veep, what do you have?"

"It's pretty robust. With a ten-pound payload, it can stay aloft for twenty minutes. The more weight you add, the less time of flight. Its max payload is fifteen pounds. Its radius of flight is a little over a thousand meters."

My phone rang again, "Pike, he's not leaving the stage."

"What? Whose stupid idea is that? Call him yourself. Someone is looking at this with campaign optics instead of national security."

"That was from him. He said that, as the president, he wouldn't flee the scene, leaving the crowd in danger."

"Then get the fucking crowd off the boat."

"Impossible. They're packed in like cattle, and the only ways off the ship are narrow, one-person stairwells. Even if we got them off, they have a hundred-meter walk down the pier to the parking lot. The president thinks that if he leaves, they'll become a target of opportunity that his secret service detail can't possibly protect. If he stays, he'll be the target. Best case, the secret service can protect him. Worst case, only he and his detail will take the attack."

"Sir, that's very courageous of him. Not to be callous, but losing the president of the United States is a hell of a lot worse than losing some of his supporters."

"Pike, it's not my call. Find them and make the whole thing a moot point."

"Sir, I have nothing to go on. They could be anywhere." Then I thought of the range of the drone and some other unique vulnerabilities.

I said, "Sir, there's a helicopter that's flying tours just outside the parking lot for the *Yorktown*. I need the most senior agent you can find for the secret service detail. Tell him to meet me there right now. If anyone gives you pushback, tell the president to order it."

He said, "That didn't take long. What did you figure out?"

"Nothing just yet, but I have an idea. Get the agent there, or I'm going to have to use a gun."

"He's on the way as soon as I hang up."

I pocketed the phone and said, "Everyone back to the van, now."

We collapsed and stowed our weapons on the run, reaching the van in seconds. I said, "Veep, you drive. Go to that helicopter launchpad."

He slid behind the wheel and I said, "Carly, Jennifer, you're going up in the helo. The drone has a range just outside of a kilometer, and it has to fly from an open space. They won't be launching it from inside the forest. Take some binos and go spot him. Do a cloverleaf until you're either out of gas or the damn drone has struck."

Knuckles said, "Pike, with a klick range they could be launching from the other side of the river, on the Charleston peninsula."

"Yeah, they could, but if they were going to do that, why get a cottage on this side? No, I think they're close. Probably at one of the soccer or softball fields up the road. Jennifer, find some boundaries on the map that you can ID from the air. Go no further than fifteen hundred meters."

I returned to Knuckles. "When they find the target, you guys are going to launch to interdict."

"What are you going to do?"

"See what sort of security the secret service has for drones. Do whatever I can to increase the odds of stopping it."

Veep pulled up to the little shed advertising the tours, and I saw at least two families with children, and one guy wearing a suit with an earpiece cable running down the collar of his shirt.

I jumped out with Carly and Jennifer following. I said, "Secret service?"

He nodded, looking at me warily. He said, "They told me you were, too."

"I'm the *super*secret service. I need to use your badge to commandeer that helicopter."

"What?"

"You heard about the possible threat against the president?" He nodded, and I said, "I need aerial observation to find it, so unless you have a helicopter jammed up your ass, get your badge out."

Jennifer elbowed me in the side, but it worked. He pulled out his badge and handed it to me. I said, "Follow me out, and make sure they can see that earpiece."

I turned and cut through the line, saying, "I apologize, folks. I'm from the FAA, and we've had complaints that this helicopter hasn't made its required maintenance. I can't let you get on it until we do a test flight."

That was enough for the mothers. The thing looked dangerous enough as it was, and there was no way a mother would let her children get on it with the FAA saying it's not airworthy. The person booking the tours jumped up and said, "That's bullshit!"

I reached the helicopter, and the pilot said, "What are you doing? Those people are in front of you."

I flashed the badge and said, "Secret service. We need to use your helicopter to find a threat against the president of the United States. I can't order you to do it, but I'm hoping you'll want to do it out of patriotism. You'll be paid for the time lost."

A huge grin spread across his face, and I thought he was going to start weeping with joy. He said, "Get in, get in!"

Next to him were only two seats. I said, "These women are secret service; they'll be doing the spotting." I was thinking, *No damn way will I get in this death trap.*

His grin became wider, if that was possible. "Well, come on, gals!"

Thirty seconds later, the rotors were turning, and they were off. I went back out to the van and said, "Stage on the exit for the *Yorktown* parking lot so you can react quickly both north and south. If they find something, no mercy. If you can capture one of them alive, that would be great, but you won't hear me crying if you're forced to pop both of them."

Knuckles said, "You got it," and slid the van door closed. Veep pulled away, and I turned to the secret service agent. "What tools do you have to defend against a commercial drone attack?"

84

Tariq saw the woods open up ahead of him and felt relief. He didn't want to show it, but he found the tangle of brush and trees to be a little claustrophobic. Even though their car was only about a hundred meters behind them, and they were on a gravel trail, he was afraid of getting lost.

They reached a small opening, that, strangely enough, had three rows of benches facing the trees, as if they were used for some type of performance, but there was no stage. Just more woods. Tariq couldn't fathom a reason for them to be there. He swatted a mosquito, cursing the infernal bugs; then he heard Anwar say, "Is that it?"

Tariq looked up and saw a wooden ramp leading to a platform with rails. Beyond it was the water of the Charleston Harbor. "Yes, that's it." *Finally.*

They climbed up the ramp, and Tariq saw that the platform wasn't on the water's edge, but set back, with about seventy meters of salt marsh between the viewing stand and the water.

Anwar placed the drone on the platform and opened up the control box, a plastic briefcase like something out of James Bond. Both the lid and the casing housed a video screen, with the lower screen having two joysticks to the left and right at the base, and various switches and dials on either side.

Tariq opened a cheap canvas beach bag, saying, "You want the bomb?"

"No. I want to test it first. Make sure the software I installed works. You got the sign I made in the bag?"

Tariq pulled out a section of cardboard that Anwar had cut from the shipping box. In the center of it he'd drawn a black anarchy symbol with thick permanent marker.

Anwar began manipulating the controller, going through his preflight routine, powering up the processor. He began tapping things on the touch screen as fast as a bartender at happy hour.

Tariq grew bored watching and checked his Wickr account yet again. He'd expected Jalal to contact him by now and was beginning to worry that he, too, had been lost in Norfolk. He heard the whopping of the blades from the tour helicopter and joked, "Don't run into that thing. It'll be back overhead in ten minutes."

Anwar missed the humor, saying, "They won't let that anywhere near the US president."

Tariq didn't bother to say he was kidding, returning to his phone. Minutes later, he was startled when the blades of the drone began spinning. Anwar did something with the controls, and the drone shot up in the air. Tariq watched it flit left and right and saw the childlike grin on Anwar's face. He made the drone fly low and fast over the ocean, then abruptly sent it to the right, then left.

He said, "This thing turns on a dime. Much, much better than that drone I had in Nevada."

He released the controls and said, "Time to test the GPS guidance."

The drone rose to treetop height and skated through

the air directly at them, flying faster than Tariq would have thought possible.

It reached a point ten feet above their heads and hovered, the blades creating a downdraft of wind. Anwar said, "So, manual controls are fine. GPS is fine. Let's check out the recognition software."

He sent the drone back out over the water, then said, "Hold up the sign high, over your head."

Tariq did, and Anwar used the onboard camera to find it, zooming in until the sign filled his upper screen. He went to the lower touch screen and tapped it once, twice, three times. He said, "Ready?"

Tariq nodded, and Anwar tapped the screen a final time. The drone began streaking toward their location just as it had before, but this time at an angle, headed straight for the sign.

Tariq said, "Will it stop?" When he didn't receive an answer, his voice became shrill. "Anwar!"

At the last second, he dove to the ground, hearing Anwar laugh. He looked up, and the drone was hovering five feet off of the deck.

Tariq stood, brushing himself off, and Anwar landed the drone, saying, "I had a five-foot buffer for the test. For the real thing, I'll set the buffer to zero."

Tariq said, "I didn't find that amusing. Quit acting like a child."

Anwar nodded and said, "Hand me the bomb now."

Tariq pulled out the contraption Anwar had built, full of plungers and silver tubes sticking out of a ball of mud-colored explosive mix. Anwar began seating it in the secondary platform next to the camera, saying, "It's too bad we have to have the camera for the recognition software. It prevented me from packing this thing with nails and screws."

"Why?"

"Too much weight. Everything's a trade-off."

When he was done, the ball rested below the housing of the drone and was about the same size. Anwar said, "Perfect," and Tariq said, "Shhh!"

"What?"

"Someone's coming."

Anwar became quiet. Tariq heard two people talking, coming closer. He saw Anwar reach behind his back and pull out a large revolver.

Tariq hissed, "Where did you get that?"

"I bought it on the streets of LA, in that dump of a neighborhood you left me in."

"What are you doing?"

"They can't be allowed to see us. After this, there will be a manhunt like no other, and if they give our description, we won't make it out of the city."

A man and a woman appeared at the base of the ramp, pushing mountain bikes. They leaned them against a tree, then turned to the ramp, only noticing the two on the platform when they were halfway up.

The man said, "Hello?"

Anwar shot him in the chest. The woman screamed and began running down the trail. Anwar gave chase, leaving Tariq behind, frozen. The man on the deck said, "Help me"; then bloody froth came out of his mouth. A second shot rang out, causing Tariq to jump, startled.

Anwar came running back to the platform, jogging up out of breath. He reached the wounded man and fired another round, this one into his head. Tariq was shocked at the violence.

Anwar stepped over the man, and Tariq shouted, "What are you doing?"

Surprised, Anwar said, "Allah's will. Killing infidels wherever I find them. Isn't that what this is all about?"

Tariq knew then there was a difference between the men he facilitated and himself. He'd engineered the attacks but never really understood the carnage because he'd never seen it up close.

Anwar said, "What time is it? Can I launch? Someone may have heard those shots."

Tariq looked at his watch and saw it was a quarter past ten. The president would be speaking now. "Yes. Let's do it and get out of here."

Anwar launched the drone into the air, and Tariq followed it with his eyes until it was lost over the trees.

85

Knuckles heard the faint popping of the rotor blades change pitch and knew the helicopter was making another pass. He had just about given up hope. Jennifer and Carly had overflown every square inch of open terrain, circling the multitude of soccer and baseball fields, overflying the tennis courts, and then had surveyed anything that could be used as a launch point, going so far as to travel across the Ravenel Bridge to Waterfront Park just on the other side.

They'd found nothing.

Now they were starting a grid search of the golf course, trying to find a drone operator among the numerous pedestrians playing on the course. It was a futile endeavor.

He heard the blades pitch again, signaling a course change, and his earpiece came to life.

"Knuckles, Knuckles, this is Koko. Jackpot. I say again, jackpot."

Everybody in the van bolted upright at the call. Knuckles said, "Give me a lock-on."

"They're on a viewing platform at the edge of the water, through the woods. It's too hard to explain, but I know it. Pike and I have run that trail before."

Off the radio, he said, "Start the van. Kit up."

To her, he said, "Give me something."

"Go to the golf course. It's your first right through the traffic circle."

"Then what?"

"Then I'll meet you."

Knuckles thought, *Huh?* But he said, "Go, go, go!"

Veep raced down the asphalt, hitting the traffic circle at a high rate of speed, skidding through it and bouncing the right two tires over the curb. He cranked the wheel hard and lined back up, and Knuckles saw the helicopter in the middle of the road, rotors turning. Veep pulled outside the danger zone of the rotors and stopped. Knuckles slid open the van door and saw a car farther down on the shoulder. He ran around the front of the van, seeing the pilot grinning stupidly and holding a thumbs-up. It was probably more excitement than he'd ever experienced in his life.

Jennifer and Carly came scurrying around the nose, hunched over until they were clear, then sprinted toward him. Knuckles said, "Where do we go?"

She pointed at a historical marker and said, "There's a gravel trail right next to that sign. It threads through the woods for about a hundred meters, ending at a viewing platform for the harbor. Two guys were on that platform, and there was a drone out over the water. We missed them initially because it looks like a wood line."

"How will I know I'm close? Is there anything that I can use to determine that? I don't want to be just as surprised as they are."

"You want me to lead? I can stop fifty meters out. I remember the trail drops down and turns right."

"Yeah, but don't fuck it up. We have the big guns, and I don't want to answer to Pike if you get hurt."

She smiled and said, "You know better than that. You ready?"

"Yeah, one second." He turned to Carly and said, "See that car down the road? I want you to check it out.

If it's locked, break the glass. I'm betting it's theirs. If it's not, tough shit."

She said, "Whew. Yeah, I can do that. I thought you were going to ask me to be a decoy to draw their fire or something."

Knuckles smiled and said, "You haven't aggravated me enough for that yet, unlike Jennifer." He looked at his team and said, "Guns up. Let's go hunting."

Before they took a step, they heard a crack reverberate through the woods. Knuckles said, "That sounded like . . ."

Ten seconds later, they heard another crack, this one closer. Knuckles said, "That's from the trail. Jennifer, go. If you see anything, and I mean *anything*, you drop flat behind cover, and we'll deal with it."

She nodded but pulled her Glock out anyway, then began jogging across the grass toward the historical marker. She squatted down, peering into the tree line, waiting on the team to coalesce around her. Knuckles took a knee beside her and looked down the trail. He could see only about ten meters before it went hard to the left. He said, "What are the odds we could just go straight in? Skip the path and flank them?"

"Well, you can't get lost, because you'd eventually hit the water, but it would be noisy. The brush around here is part swamp, part jungle. If we had the time, I'd say do it, but to do it right, you'd spend the next hour sneaking up on them, or sound like a herd of water buffalo."

Knuckles nodded and said, "Okay, looks like you're it." He nudged her forward, saying, "Lead me to them, Koko."

They took off down the trail like a band of Indians on the warpath, slinking low but moving fast, using the shadows of the trees to mask their advance.

Forty meters in, Knuckles caught a flash of color ahead of them. He hissed, and Jennifer stopped. He motioned her to the back of the formation and raised his weapon. He looked over his shoulder, seeing Retro on the right. He told him with hand and arm signals to take a firing point to cover his advance. Retro slid off into the brush, then clicked his radio twice.

Knuckles went forward slowly, Veep to his left, scanning the thicket for a threat. Knuckles rounded a bend in the trail and sank next to a tree, staring through his optics.

It was a human body, lying in the grass off the trail, the upper torso hidden in the undergrowth. He scanned down the body and saw smooth legs and biking shoes. He stood up and raced down the hill, Veep following.

The head was facedown, but it did nothing to hide the damage to the skull. It was shattered, with the blood congealing in the mulch of the forest. Knuckles clicked his radio and whispered, "Koko, how far from this point?"

"Maybe forty meters. Just ahead is a bend, and it drops into a bowl leading to the platform. Once you leave the crest of the bowl, you're very close."

"What's the platform like?"

"It's above the ground by about ten feet, but the only clear shot they'll have is down the ramp. The rest is overgrown with woods."

He was now faced with a choice. Sneak, or assault. From what Jennifer said, sneaking would work until they dropped down; then it would be an assault anyway.

He said, "All elements, all elements, this is the LCC. Retro, go right. Stand by for my call to move. We're going straight in, and when they focus on us, you flank them. Veep, you follow right behind me. They'll hear us coming, but I think they'll believe we're another group of tourists. They'll want to ambush, but they won't get that chance. As soon as you have a shot, take it."

Retro said, "Roger. Standing by."

He looked at Veep and said, "Ready?"

Veep nodded, and Knuckles stood up, raised his weapon, and started running down the path. He reached the drop and said, "Retro, move now."

He continued on, running by a bunch of wooden benches. He saw the ramp, and another body lying on it, bleeding out. He circled left around the ramp, looking for a shot, and saw two people up high, one bending over a box, the other shouting and pointing at their advance. He squeezed off a round, smacking the standing man in the shoulder.

The one on the box jumped up and raised a pistol, cracking a round at him, the bullet snapping by Knuckles's head, causing him to dive into the muck. He rolled under the ramp and heard Veep fire, followed by two more booms from the pistol. Then he saw Retro behind the platform, taking aim. The muzzle pulsed a subsonic round, and he heard, "Shooter down. One more still up there, crouched low. I don't have a shot. Don't know if he's armed."

Knuckles rolled out, saying, "Veep, cover me. If he stands up, smoke him."

He raced up the ramp and heard, "He's jumping over, he's jumping over."

Knuckles made it to the top and saw the man running toward the water. He turned to the other one, seeing a body barely older than a teenager, dressed like a derelict, his head misshapen by the round embedded in the back of it. He went to the box on the floor and saw a video image of the USS *Yorktown*, the president speaking in the center of the screen.

Veep came up and pointed, saying, "He's getting away."

Knuckles said, "Trust me, that Arab isn't going to escape through the water. I'll deal with him in a minute. Fly this thing away from the boat."

He called Pike and gave a SITREP, saying the mission was accomplished and telling him the drone was under their control.

Veep bent down to the suitcase, and Knuckles hoisted himself over the side of the platform, going after the man struggling in the waist-deep marsh, the pluff mud sucking him down with every step.

He was about to drop to the ground when he heard Veep say, "It's not listening to the radio signals. They've been cut somehow."

86

The secret service agent—Snelling—gave me a pin to place on my shirt that said I was one of the good guys, then used his authority to get me to the top of the carrier. I immediately saw what Kurt had told me. Every stairwell was a narrow, one-person-only affair, and there weren't that many of them. It might not have been a problem when the ship was operational, but it would definitely hamper getting five hundred civilians off quickly.

We went through the bridge, complete with mannequins acting as if they were fighting World War II, and entered the flight deck, which was absolutely jam-packed with people, all the way to the back of the deck, behind the historical aircraft where they couldn't even see the president talking.

On the way up, jogging the metal stairs, the echo of his feet bouncing off the steel of the ship, Snelling had said, "We have four DroneDefenders on top. Do you have any idea what direction it's coming from?"

I said, "I don't. What's a DroneDefender?"

"It's a focused jammer mounted on a rifle stock. Basically, it cuts the drone's ability to receive GPS or radio signals and causes it to either fall out of the sky or return to base, depending on the type of drone. It defeats the ability of anyone to control it."

"What's the range?"

"About four hundred meters."

"Do you have radar? Something to find the drones to get the weapons on target?"

"Yeah, but we only have one. That's why I asked the direction. Face it the wrong way, and it's worthless."

We reached the deck and he said, "How serious is this threat?"

"It's serious. If I were going to call it, I'd say that fucking thing is in the air and headed this way. It'll be an explosive charge, probably kinetic in action and not triggered by remote. They'll want to fly it straight into where the president is speaking, so aim the radar away from him. Where's his podium? Does he have a backdrop?"

"Yes. The stage is in the middle of the ship, just in front of the tower for the bridge. He's speaking toward the bow, although they've got video monitors for all the folks behind him."

"Then it'll be coming from the bow."

We pushed through the crowd, and I saw President Hannister take the podium, showing not a whit of concern that he was being hunted. He cracked a few jokes and then went into his campaign speech. I have to admit, it was pretty impressive. He was on four or five giant monitors, and I didn't see him scanning the sky, looking for his doom.

We reached the edge of the bow and two different agents ran up, holding what looked like AR-15s with a couple of boom mikes for barrels. Snelling said, "Where should we put them?"

"On each corner. Put the other two at the rear in case the drone flies by them. And get a guy up high, on top of the bridge, with binos. Where do we stand with the radar?"

"That's actually on top of the bridge right now. He's

scanning the bow and has about a forty-five-degree spread, which means he can see anything to the left and right of the bow in a cone that extends about a hundred meters both ways."

"Good. How long is the president going to talk?"

"Believe it or not, over thirty minutes. Probably closer to forty-five."

I shook my head, then heard my radio earpiece go off with Jennifer calling Knuckles. I felt my first bit of hope, because I sure as hell didn't trust all of this technological bullshit.

That hope was drowned five seconds later, when Snelling said, "They have one, they have one."

He went to his radio, and I heard him say, "Spike leaders, Spike leaders, we have a UAV inbound." He paused, then read off a grid reference that meant nothing to me, but hopefully meant something to the guys with the DroneDefenders.

I caught my end of the radio traffic with Knuckles, just bits and pieces, but it was enough to tell me they'd found the hornets' nest. Maybe they'd "cut the control" by killing that sorry son of a bitch.

Snelling was scanning the sky. He pointed and said, "There!" He immediately went to his radio and began giving commands, bringing the aft DroneDefenders forward to the bow.

I looked at where he was pointing and saw a speck in the distance, coming closer. It closed on the deck, and the DroneDefenders all aimed at it, unleashing an overwhelming barrage of electronic interference.

Knuckles called, giving me a quick SITREP and saying they had control, and I didn't have the sense to tell the secret service to quit what they were doing. Of course, I also didn't know that the guy who'd built the weapon was a nascent genius and that our actions were playing into the terrorist's hands.

The DroneDefenders stopped the UAV in its tracks, so to speak, causing it to hover about seventy-five meters in front of the bow, only thirty feet above the deck. It remained stationary, and Knuckles called saying, "We're looking at the screen, and we have no control. We can't fly it away. I don't know why."

I exhaled and said, "We got it. We got it. The secret service has an antidrone gun."

Knuckles said, "The camera is zooming in on the president."

I ignored the call and said to Snelling, "What now? Just let it hover until it runs out of juice?"

"Honestly, I don't know. This is the first time we've ever dealt with this type of threat."

I said, "You see that crap hanging below it? That's a bomb. If it runs out of juice, it's going to hit the water like concrete, and it's going to go off."

I heard the president droning on in the background, the people cheering everything he said. Snelling wiped his upper lip and said, "I don't know what else we can do."

Knuckles said, "Pike, that thing is doing something strange. We aren't touching anything, and it's zooming in on the president."

I clicked on and said, "It's the electromagnetic interference. These guys are torching it."

He said, "I don't think so. It's stable and controlled. It's not like it's freaking out and going batshit. It's looking for something."

I took that in and said, "Keep me abreast of what you see."

To Snelling, I said, "Shoot that fucking thing down, right now."

"What? We can't start firing during a presidential speech. We have it contained."

Knuckles came on, "Pike, for some reason, the camera has gone from the president and is now scanning left and right."

I said, "Snelling, that thing has some program to defeat your weapons. I have a man that's looking at the feed right now. It's doing strange shit, and your DroneDefenders aren't interfering."

"Pike, I can't just start blazing away during a presidential speech. I get you operate under different rules— I saw that with the helo—but that drone has lost control from the source."

I said, "I *know* it's lost control from the source, because my men just slaughtered the guys controlling it. They're now telling me it's doing stuff on its own."

Knuckles said, "Pike, it's found something it's interested in. It's zooming in on the seal attached to the president's podium."

My mind went into overdrive, assessing everything I knew about the problem, and realized we'd lost control because we were blasting the drone. I had men who owned the hardware, and I was preventing them from executing.

I said, "Turn off the DroneDefenders. Turn them off, right now."

"No way. That's the only thing keeping it away."

"Snelling, turn them off. My men have the control box, but they can't do anything because you've cut the signal. That fucking thing is on some secondary protocol, like you said before, where sometimes it flies back to base. You made it blind, and instead of flying back to base, it's started searching."

He looked at me hesitantly, and I understood the

pressure he was under. The president's life hung in the balance, but I knew I was right.

Knuckles said, "The screen is now nothing but the seal. What's going on?"

I said, "I don't know," and the drone began to move. Slowly at first, but then it picked up speed. The men with the DroneDefenders tracked it, hosing it down with electrical jamming, but it did no good.

I shouted, "Turn them off!" And the drone began streaking toward us at an incredible speed. I ripped off my jacket and exposed my weapon. Snelling saw the rifle and immediately reacted as if I was a threat, his nascent suspicions of me causing his secret service instincts to take over. He jumped toward me and I hammered him with the barrel, right on the forehead, splitting the skin. He dropped to the deck, and out of the corner of my eye I saw other secret service agents reacting to my display.

The drone reached the deck going forty miles an hour and began to descend. I snapped my stock in place, thinking, *Please, dear God, let me hit it before they hit me.*

I raised the weapon and began firing controlled pairs, each one missing. The drone dropped lower, now directly to my front. I saw an agent shouting at me, his weapon drawn, and knew I was going to die. He aimed, and I broke the trigger.

The air above us turned into a fireball, the shock wave driving everyone within thirty yards into the deck. I hammered hard and rolled over, disoriented. I heard screaming, the trampling of feet, and saw a flaming bit of the drone to my left, but I didn't move.

I just lay there, taking one sweet breath after another.

87

Knuckles opened the fridge and pulled out another beer. I said, "You going to chip in for all those longnecks?"

He said, "I'm an employee of Grolier Recovery Services, and as such, I consider this part of my salary."

He twisted off the cap and hummed it toward the garbage can. I watched it ricochet off both walls in the corner, then hit the bucket.

He said, "Actually, come to think of it, this is about all that you ever pay me."

I said, "Nice shot."

Jennifer and Carly came from the back of our office, Jennifer saying, "And that's about all there is to see. It's pretty Spartan, but it does the trick. We're incorporated as an LLC, have a DUNS number, and all the other stuff, so it's a solid cover as far as the Taskforce goes. And occasionally, Pike and I go on real archeological digs, which are pretty fun."

Jennifer took a seat on the couch next to me, and Carly pulled the chair from around my desk, rolling over by Knuckles. She said, "Can't ask for a better view."

Our office was smack-dab on Shem Creek, an inlet that went out to the Charleston Harbor on the left side of Patriots Point. Built in the late seventies, it housed a bank, then a real estate office, then a few retail shops, and finally us. It was a little shabby, but that didn't bother me.

The rent was cheap, and Carly was right; the view of the marsh out of every window was spectacular. Not to mention two of my favorite bars were within walking distance.

Jennifer said, "What time is Kurt supposed to arrive?"

"Any minute. I think he was just turning around the Rock Star bird in DC and coming straight in. He's supposed to meet the president on Air Force One before he flies to his next event, then come over here."

I'd sent Retro and Veep back to DC with the Rock Star bird, escorting one Tariq bin Abdul-Aziz. I'd kept Knuckles with me—as my second in command—for any cleanup that might be needed, and Carly, as a CIA case officer, for any interagency coordination that might occur. Which is to say, we were going to sit on the back deck of my office and drink beer, watching the dolphins swim in Shem Creek. Rank has its privileges.

After giving me the readout from the drone camera and making sure I was alive, Knuckles had dropped down into the muck and stalked out to Tariq, who had managed to get all of fifty meters in the pluff mud. Knuckles hadn't even brought a weapon. Tariq had seen him approaching and had begun crying, with his arms over his head and blood running down one biceps. Knuckles had peeled his arms off, then slugged him hard enough to knock him out. He'd grabbed a leg and dragged Tariq back to the platform through the mud.

The team had carried him back to the van, meeting Carly. She'd told them she'd found a rental agreement for Tariq in the car, and Knuckles had searched his body, finding the keys. He'd tossed them to Carly and told her to follow. They'd come to the office on Shem Creek and locked him up.

After they were clear, Knuckles had called 911 from a decrepit pay phone at a gas station and hysterically screamed about hearing gunshots at the trail, and then had hung up. From the news, the authorities believed that Anwar had acted alone, which allowed Tariq to disappear into Taskforce control.

As for me, I was unceremoniously arrested by the secret service. They knew I'd saved the president's life but had no idea why or who I was. All they knew was that I had whipped out a pretty sophisticated weapon and started shooting within a stone's throw of the man they were charged with protecting. They'd defaulted to holding me under guard until the chaos of the *Yorktown* could be sorted out.

Eventually, President Hannister—at some unknown location he'd been whisked to—had heard the story of what had happened, and he'd put two and two together. After five hours of sitting under the watchful eye of a secret service counterassault team member, outfitted in stylish ninja black with Velcro accents, I'd been released. No questions asked. The CAT member had simply handed me back all of my equipment, including my weapon, and asked me where I wanted to go.

I said, "I think I left my car on the sidewalk past the parking lot."

He'd driven me there, then had said, "You've got some powerful friends."

I said, "You have no idea."

I'd exited, and he'd leaned over, saying, "Nobody official will say this, but thanks."

Like I'd just given his car a jump start, I'd said, "No problem. It was my pleasure."

I'd met the team at the office, and we'd coordinated exfil. Twenty-four hours later, it was like nothing had happened.

I pulled my own beer from the fridge and said, "Kurt

had better hurry the hell up. I'm not wasting the day sitting in my office."

Knuckles laughed and said, "Life of a commando. Hurry up and wait."

Like magic, as soon as he said the words, there was a knock on the door. I opened it to find both Kurt and George on my stoop.

I said, "I feel honored that both of you gentlemen would travel so far from the seat of power to visit."

Kurt pushed in and said, "Got any more of those?"

Knuckles opened the fridge, pulled out two bottles, and tossed them to the pair.

Kurt opened his and took a swig. I said, "Well, don't keep us in suspense. How do we look?"

George said, "Good. Not perfect, but good. There's a little bit of cleanup to do, and a few threads that some-one can find, but if we're lucky, it'll just be a conspiracy theory in ten years."

"Is Tariq talking?"

Kurt said, "Yeah. He's singing. We're getting all sorts of information, and not just with this operation, but deep-dive stuff on terrorist financing around the world going back to 9/11. Tariq had more shell accounts than you could shake a stick at."

The comment brought a question I'd been wondering about. "What did you guys do with Johan? Do you still have him?"

"Nope. I took your advice and let him go."

"Did the FBI pick him up?"

"Not yet. Right now, they're digging into Icarus Solutions and his boss. There are serious indicators that Dexter Worthington may have helped finance 9/11. In-advertently, but he helped all the same, and if he knew Tariq was bad after the fact, he never said anything."

"I hope they fry his ass."

"They're building a case, but it'll take time."

"Where's Johan now? Do you know?"

"No idea. Probably back in South Africa. That's where I would have gone after all of this."

I shook my head and said, "I don't know about that. He didn't strike me as a runner."

88

Dexter Worthington hung up the phone, poured himself two fingers of bourbon, and drained the whole thing. Now the FBI wanted him to travel to their Florida office to answer more questions. Apparently, that scourge of Dexter's life—Tariq bin Abdul-Aziz—was suspected of financing terrorism worldwide, including the latest attacks on US soil, and he was running loose in America.

Ostensibly, it was just a follow-up to close out the questions they'd had about Dexter's offshore accounts with the Saudi, and he wasn't under any cloud of suspicion, but Dexter was beginning to believe that he was also the target of the probe.

The door to his office swung open, and Dexter found himself looking into the ice-blue eyes of Johan van Rensburg.

Startled, Dexter said, "Where the hell have you been? I've been trying to contact you for days. The FBI has been here. They're going crazy over those offshore accounts you found. How'd they get them?"

Johan said, "I don't have a lot of time, which means you don't either. I have some questions, and I want you to answer me honestly."

"What? Why?"

"You knew that your money financed the terror attacks in 2001. My question is, did you know before, or find out after?"

"I . . . I don't know what you're talking about."

Johan turned around and closed the door, saying, "Dexter, please. We're beyond the guilt phase. I just left the custody of one of your intelligence units, and they showed me what Tariq bin Abdul-Aziz has been doing with his accounts around the world. You told me you didn't know who he was. That was a lie. His name is in the 9/11 congressional report, and I saw you reading it when it was finally released."

"Intelligence unit? What were you doing with them?"

Johan snarled, "Stopping a terrorist attack funded from a bank account with your name on it."

Dexter held up his hands, leaning back. He said, "Okay, okay, I did see the report, but it wasn't proof of anything. Even the congressional committee concluded it wasn't proof of anything."

Johan walked around the desk, circling behind Dexter's chair. He said, "Because you didn't give them the proof. Why didn't you tell them what you knew about the bank accounts after the attacks? Was it money? The original contract in Saudi Arabia? Or did Tariq pay to keep you quiet?"

Dexter craned his head around, saying, "No! He never paid me anything. I never even spoke to him again after that."

Johan said, "Do you know how many people are dead because of him?"

"I have nothing to do with whatever he's done!"

Johan looped a cotton rope around Dexter's neck and pulled back hard enough to lift Dexter in the air, but not enough to choke him. Dexter's arms flailed about, his head bent backward over the top of the chair.

Johan looked down into his eyes and said, "If you had told what you knew, those people might still be alive.

The US might have been able to crack open the entire financial network, preventing any number of attacks. So, yes, you did have something to do with it, even if by omission."

Dexter croaked, "Please. I didn't mean to hurt anyone."

Johan said, "Do you like the television show *Happy Days*?"

The words settled in Dexter's brain, but he was sure he'd misheard. Or maybe Johan was insane. He remained quiet, trembling in fear, the rope biting deeper and deeper.

Johan said, "I met a boy who loved that show. Loved to watch what he believed was the true America. He learned English from the series. Can you believe that dedication? But because of you, he's now dead. I'd like you to tell him something for me, when you see him."

What?

Johan cinched the rope tightly, and Dexter felt his windpipe crush. He began to fight for his life, his vision tunneling down to a soda straw. Before it went black completely, he heard Johan say, "Tell him I'm sorry."

89

I got Kurt another beer and said, "So, Tariq is taking a trip to the Cloud? He's ours? He probably has a ton of information in his head we can use."

Kurt took a swig and said, "Unfortunately, no. He's being turned over to the FBI for prosecution. The president wants to make an example of him to others who might be financing terrorism."

"Sir, they do that, and he'll get a lawyer and clam up. We won't get anything more out of him."

"Yeah, but there's a greater goal here. Most of the Islamic terrorist groups around the world are funded by wealthy Gulf Arabs. Their countries do little to stop it, other than give us platitudes about taking it seriously. The president wants to show that if they won't do anything on their own, we will. We'd like to go after the father as well, since he's truly the money flow, but unless we can entice him to fly to the US from Morocco, he's out of reach."

"Morocco? That's where he is?"

"Yes."

"When is the transfer?"

"Tomorrow. We get one more day with him."

"Can you hold him longer?"

"Not unless you have some specific vein of intelligence you want to mine. I can't block the transfer without cause."

"I don't have any questions, but if you hand him over, it'll make the news, and we'll miss your really big fish.

Tariq's father will flee to Saudi Arabia, and they'll never extradite him."

"Neither will Morocco."

"Don't be so sure. Can you build me a concise case against him, proving he funded the port attacks?"

"Yeah, it's airtight, but why?"

I pulled out my phone and dialed a long number. As it rang, I said, "By the way, I'm billing the Taskforce for these international calls."

While I waited for it to connect, I said, "Oh, and you'll have to pay for the helicopter we used yesterday. And I wrecked a rental car in Norfolk."

Kurt rolled his eyes, and I said, "I also lost a set of FBI night vision goggles. I'm afraid that's a big-ticket item I'll be claiming on my travel voucher."

That caused his eyebrows to shoot up. He said, "You lost *what*?"

I heard the phone connect and held up a finger. Ahmed al-Raffiki answered, saying, "Pike? Are you back in Morocco? I thought they only allowed one trip a year for Islamophobes."

I laughed and said, "No, I'm in the US. How's the arm?"

"It's coming along nicely. I see you had some close calls in the United States and that the perpetrators were Moroccans. Anything to do with what we worked on?"

"Everything. Your help thwarted that attack against the Navy ship. I appreciate it."

He said, "You're welcome. Is that why you called?"

"No. Were you serious about arresting those who kill in the name of Islam?"

"Yes, of course."

"All of the Moroccans had passports from Saudi

Arabia, and we've tracked the financing to a Saudi billionaire. We have his son, but we want the father."

"How does this involve me? You think because I'm an Arab I can order Saudi Arabia to do something?"

"No. The father is in Morocco. We're set to announce the son's arrest, but as soon as we do, the father will flee home. We want to prevent that. We want you to arrest him, then extradite him to us."

I heard him exhale; then he said, "That is asking a lot. There will be enormous pressure brought to bear from the Saudi royal family."

"I know. I want to do it quickly, before Saudi Arabia can protest. Before they can lean on the monarch to prevent it. Tomorrow I will give you the official investigation with all of the evidence against him. It is ironclad. It will protect your king and leave Saudi Arabia protesting to us."

"You have this evidence?"

"Yes, and it's not just suspicion. It's hard facts that tie him not only to these current attacks, but into the original attacks on 9/11."

"Send it to me."

I hung up the phone and said to Kurt, "You hold that guy for three more days, and you're going to get the mother lode."

Kurt said, "I had no idea you were so good at cross-cultural communication."

Jennifer laughed and said, "He's not good at that at all. If anything, Ahmed is cooperating because of me."

Carly interjected, saying, "When I saw him in the cell, he was all fuzzy and warm. He looked like he was trying to get Ahmed to empathize."

I said, "That was just my cover. Screw cross-cultural communication."

Knuckles said, "Yeah, that's probably Pike's weakest skill."

I sat back down and patted Jennifer's knee, saying, "Speaking of skill, Jennifer tells me you think you're a better shot because of that Hollywood mission on the carrier."

Knuckles flicked his eyes to her, wondering what pillow talk had occurred. He said, "I think I proved that the other night."

"Really? Let's review the bidding here. You shot a Sea-Doo driving on the water in two dimensions, using *my* spotter, the one I taught. Anybody could have done that with her calling the shots."

I took a swig of my beer and said, "Try hitting a drone that's flying in three dimensions and going forty miles an hour. Now, *that* is some shooting."

Knuckles said, "From what I heard, it was so damn close to you, you could have thrown a rock at it. A child could have hit it."

Carly said, "You guys are incorrigible."

I said, "Sir, what do you think? Drone or Jet Ski?"

He said, "Don't drag me into this."

I said, "Okay, how about this, Knuckles? The true measure is not how well *you* can shoot, but how well you can teach others."

Confused, Knuckles said, "So?"

"Well, Carly showed some real skill with me a few days ago. She has innate Operator qualities, but truth be told, she's pathetic with a weapon."

I saw her expression go from pleased to indignant. To Knuckles, I said, "Maybe when you're through training your own spotter, we can have them do a shoot-off. Kurt can be the judge."

I looked at Carly, then at Kurt, and said, "After she's been through selection."

ACKNOWLEDGMENTS

Since this is the "acknowledgments" page, I guess I should acknowledge that I came close to biting off more than I could chew with this plot. It sounded fairly simple at first—explore the possible state sponsorship of the tragedy of 9/11, and have the group attempt to duplicate a spectacular attack in the modern day, on the fifteenth anniversary. I picked the ports within our waters because it is a unique vulnerability that's never really been exploited, but the more research I did, the harder it became to thread the needle between the attacks and the Taskforce's assets. It was almost unmanageable in scope, and I found myself wanting to kick my own ass on more than one occasion during the writing process for creating the plot. Which leads to a thank-you for my wife and family for putting up with my cranky self for the past six months.

I'm indebted to some anonymous folks for letting me pick their brains on the port infrastructure, and for pointing the way to further research into the esoteric laws and security considerations surrounding the international shipping industry. It's safe to say that the ports of the United States are vulnerable to all manner of exploitation, from human trafficking to drugs to terrorism, but I was pleasantly surprised to learn that attacking one wasn't nearly as easy as I thought it would be. We have a strong wall of infrastructure in place to defeat such attempts, and while it isn't perfect—and never will be—it's a hell of a lot better than I thought it was. This caused some sleepless nights and significantly amped-up research to make such an attack realistic.

Tariq is based on a real person from Saudi Arabia who did indeed flee Florida just before 9/11 and had some nefarious potential ties to some of the 9/11 hijackers. A special thanks to Dan Christensen, the editor of the *Florida Bulldog*, for providing me with a copy of one of the FBI reports into the investigation, which they obtained through a FOIA request. The *Florida Bulldog* (formerly the *Broward Bulldog*, now FloridaBulldog.org) did an enormous amount of work on the potential link between the family and the attacks, which was picked up by news agencies all over the world. It's worth a Google search to read their investigative report, because there certainly is an enormous amount of smoke—especially given the now-unclassified pages from the intelligence committee reports on potential Saudi complicity.

The Panama Papers are, of course, real, and are also worth a little reading, if just to see the machinations of the sordid world of offshore banking. The revelations have already brought down at least one political leader (the prime minister of Iceland) and caused an investigation into a host of others, but of course, my use of them was complete literary license.

A special thanks to Mint Tea Tours, a Morocco tour company who created a custom tour package to facilitate my research. When I told them what I wanted to do and why, they accommodated my every whim, traveling at a blistering pace to conduct research in all of the cities I needed to hit, traversing the breadth of the country. Along with the simple mechanics of travel, they also provided some interesting insights into the different perspectives of Islam in their own country. A lot of the conversations in this manuscript were real. Morocco itself is a beautiful country and—contrary to what would be conventional wisdom to most in the United States—is completely safe and well worth the visit. The only strange occurrence was getting questioned as I left the ferry in Tangier. I'd put down "writer" on my immigration paperwork, and the official—after not caring what I said—ran me down off the ferry, wanting to know if I was a reporter for a newspaper or magazine. I got the impression someone had talked to him, and they wanted to control whatever came out in the press. He was satisfied when I told him I wrote books (of course, in no way did I tell them what kind of books, or what I was researching . . .).

Gibraltar was a "Jennifer" stop. Since we were driving all over Spain and on our way to the port of Algeciras, my wife said, "We're already here. Let's go check it out." We did, and on a cable car to the top of the Rock, playing tourist, I asked the guy running the car what the giant dock was down below. He said it was the biggest dry dock repair facility in the Med, and the one place that could repair the giant tankers and container ships that plied the sea. At that point, the stop became integral to the plot and is a prime example of what on-the-ground research gets me, as I usually stumble into something without even looking. That and the cool monkeys at the top of the Rock, of course.

A special thanks to my daughter's boyfriend, Ben, for showing me the ins and outs of Pokémon Go. Originally, I was just going to use the zero-day vulnerability the app has when signing in with Gmail, but after learning how it worked, and reading some ridiculous stories of mishaps while playing the game, I decided to use it for real. Yes, I downloaded it, then went about my neighborhood with my daughter looking for a gym . . .

The commercial drone attacks in this plot have

thankfully not happened as of yet, but it's only a matter of time, and something about which the Department of Defense is keenly aware. The proliferation of small UAVs and the exponential growth in technology has created a poor-man's targeting system that is very real, and because of it, has sparked a cottage industry of anti-drone technology companies. Some are good, and others are just hype, but rest assured, we're going to see an attack using a "toy" drone sooner rather than later. When that happens, defense systems will get serious in a hurry.

As always, a huge thanks to my agent, John Talbot, and the entire Dutton Taskforce crew. Ben, Jess, Liza, and Elina—this one took a little longer, but your efforts to sharpen the edges paid off (in more ways than one—as fate would have it, both Jess and Liza went to Granada at the same time I was writing this manuscript, and while I spent some time there, it was in a regular hotel. If you want to know how I found out about the "cave apartments," thank Liza. Team effort!). Thanks for all that you do!

TURN THE PAGE FOR AN EXCERPT

Pike Logan and his team are tracking an American arms dealer in Tel Aviv who may—or may not—be attempting to sell sensitive nuclear weapons components to the highest bidder. When Pike's team breaks up an attempt to kill a friend and former Mossad direct action team member, they stumble upon much more than they expected—a concerted conspiracy to topple a democratic African country.

DUTTON | Penguin Random House

1

Being a spy is a lot like being a bank robber. In espionage—as in crime—it's always the little things that get you. You can plan for an entire operation, allowing for one contingency after another, foreseeing when and where things might go wrong, but you inevitably miss the little things. A drop of sweat on a doorknob, drywall shavings left behind after the installation of a bug, a nick in the brass plate of a lock from a tension wrench. Small things with huge impacts.

In this case, the little thing happened before Aaron Bergmann had even left Israel, when a travel voucher routed through Mossad headquarters included a man who had been specifically excluded from the mission read-on. For a specific reason. And that little thing would prove devastating for Aaron and his neophyte apprentice.

Casually tapping the tablet in front of him, Aaron said, "Alex, turn just a tad bit to the right. I'm missing the man on the left side of the table."

Across the table from him Alexandra Levy shifted slightly, her face aglow. She said, "This is so exiting! Straight out of a James Bond movie."

He chuckled, then said, "Right there. Good." He hit record on the tablet.

Alex stiffened a little bit, as if she were posing for a photographer, holding her angle. She whispered, "That thing will really read their lips? Tell us what they're saying?"

Aaron said, "Yep. If you can keep the camera on them, but don't look so rigid. Relax a little. I'll tell you if it shifts off."

Aaron continued manipulating a piece of software in his tablet, something that was highly classified and usually reserved for active Mossad agents. A simple button camera in Alexandra's blouse was tied by Bluetooth to his tablet and seemed to be something out of a 007 movie, but in truth, both were commercially available to anyone who wanted one. The secret was the software churning through what the camera sent it.

Artificial intelligence for facial recognition had grown by leaps and bounds in recent years, and the Mossad had taken that in a different direction, focusing on the spoken word. They'd replicated the human act of lip reading into the cyber world, designing a software suite that could decipher what was being said without hearing sound.

Alex relaxed her body a bit, contrition floating across her face. "Sorry. This isn't my expertise. You should be doing the camera work."

He laid the tablet on the table and took a sip of beer, saying, "You're doing fine. This beats working in the diamond exchange, right? Keep up the talent and I might recruit you for my firm."

She grinned and said, "No, no, this is enough excitement. I enjoy being able to help—I've never even been to Africa—but I'll stick with my boring job."

There was no fear in the statement. No realization of the risk. It was like she thought they were executing a high school senior prank. She had no idea of the threat level.

That would come later.

She glanced over the balcony toward their target and said, "Besides, I don't think your partner would agree to that. I think she hates me."

Three people sat at the table they were filming: two white and one black. Their target was a man of about thirty-five and, unlike the rest of the patrons in the restaurant, was dressed in a suit as if he were still working in his office in Israel. The other white man looked like he was about to head out on a safari, wearing cargo pants and a shirt that had more pockets than a photographer's vest. He had shaggy blond hair, ice blue eyes, and a feral quality. Aaron had seen his type plenty of times before, but only in a war zone. It intrigued him.

The final man was tall, with a thin mustache and coal black skin. He was dressed like a local but didn't act like one. Ramrod straight, he showed not a whit of humor. Had they held the meeting at a café in downtown Johannesburg—where the target was staying—they would have attracted attention by their very disparate appearances, but they didn't here. Which explained why Aaron's target had chosen this restaurant. The one thing remaining was to find out why the meeting was occurring.

The only man Aaron recognized was the one the Mossad had asked him to track—an employee of a diamond broker in Tel Aviv. The other two were a mystery, but he'd know about them soon enough when they reviewed the footage later.

The primary problem with the lipreading software was choosing a language—try to lipread German when the target was speaking Chinese and you'd get gibberish. Here, in the township of Soweto, just outside the city center of Johannesburg, South Africa, he was sure they were speaking English. There was no way the black man spoke Hebrew, and he would be astounded if his target from Israel spoke something like Swahili or Afrikaans. No, they'd be speaking English, and the fact that his method of recording the conversation came through in visual rather than auditory means was a plus in the current environment.

The outdoor balcony they were on belonged to a restaurant called Sakhumzi, as did the patio holding the target's table. Just a stone's throw from the historical houses of Nelson Mandela and Bishop Tutu, in the section of Soweto known as Orlando West, the restaurant hosted a smorgasbord of local food and native performers and was a permanent stop for tour groups large and small traveling to see the ghetto made famous in the uprising against apartheid. Because of it, there was a constant drumbeat of laughter and clapping—something that had no effect on the lipreading software. As long as Aaron could keep a line of sight with whoever was talking.

Aaron focused on the computer, tapping icons and ensuring three computer-generated squares remained over the mouths. He said, "Position is good. Keep that." When he hadn't responded to Alex's statement, she repeated, "Your partner doesn't care for me at all. I thought she was going to throw me out of your house."

Aaron looked up from the tablet and said, "Shoshana? She doesn't hate you. She's just mad because I brought you instead of her. She was aggravated at me for the decision. It's nothing personal."

Making sure not to disrupt the camera angle, she said, "I don't think so. When you left the room, she was . . . a little scary."

Aaron laughed and returned to the tablet, offhandedly saying, "You need to get to know her. She's not all knives and death threats. She just acts that way. She understands that she didn't have the knowledge base for this mission. When we fly back tomorrow, I'll take you to dinner. The three of us."

Alex smiled and said, "I'd like that. I think she thought . . ."

Aaron looked up from the tablet and said, "Thought what?"

"That we . . . I mean, you and me . . . might . . ."

Aaron scoffed and said, "You're twenty years younger than me."

She said, "Yeah, but it was the Mossad that asked me . . . *you* asked me . . . I mean, they wouldn't do that unless it was for a reason."

Aaron realized she thought she really *was* in a movie. And realized she was hitting on him. A twenty-something *sabra* that worked inside the Israeli diamond exchange, she was no doubt attractive. Brown hair, brown eyes, liquid skin, and a quiet intelligence surrounded by an innocence he no longer possessed, he would have hunted her like a wolf a decade ago, but no longer. She deserved to live in her innocence. His entire existence was ensuring people like her could do so. He decided to put an end to the fantasy.

"Alex, I picked you because you understand the diamond market. Yes, you're attractive, which meant I could use you to blend in, but I need your knowledge. Period. You listen to the tape, you tell me what they're talking about within the diamond world, and I write an assessment. That's it. This isn't a complex thing. We're not here to save Israel from Blofeld. We're here to save Israel from embarrassment. That's all. It's a simple mission."

Turning red, she tilted forward and whispered, "What does that mean? I wasn't suggesting anything."

He said, "You're screwing with the camera angle. Lean back."

The target at the table answered a cell phone.

Aaron said, "Shit. Lean back—now."

Alex did so abruptly, causing the camera to sway wildly. Aaron said, "Stay still."

The man turned away from them, still on the phone.

Aaron said, "We need to move. *You* need to move. Stand up and go to the bathroom. Walk by the table and get me a shot of his face as long as you can. Stop and ask the table for directions, but not to him. Let him keep talking on the phone."

Hesitantly, Alex stood. More forcefully than he wanted, Aaron said, "Go."

She did, sidling between the throngs of tour bus patrons and locals, threading between the tables and down the stairs, the picture on Aaron's tablet jumping left and right. She reached the patio and it stabilized. She walked toward the restrooms, then stopped at the table, asking directions. He recorded about a fifteen-second snippet of the phone conversation, unsure if the software would be able to utilize the footage because the target's face was partially obscured by his smartphone.

He glanced over the balcony to see the interaction, and she broke contact, doing a passable job of being a tourist. He saw no outward interest in the interruption.

Aaron ignored the rest of the feed, wondering if Alex would be smart enough to cut it off if she really chose to use the bathroom. She did. Or maybe the Bluetooth simply lost contact because of distance. He grinned and took a sip of his beer, surreptitiously giving the target table a side-eye.

The target was asking a waitress for the check. He immediately picked up his phone and called Alex, telling her to return.

The men tossed some rand on the table, preparing to

leave, and he saw her coming across the patio. She mounted the stairs to the balcony and he stood, saying, "Hopefully they take the same car. If they split up, we'll stick to the target."

Hidden by the balcony railing, they let the group exit the restaurant, then followed, getting to the parking lot just as they were loading a single car. While he had made the comment earlier about one vehicle, a part of him spiked at the action, since they'd arrived in two separate cars.

He should have listened to his sixth sense. Lulled by the minimal threat of his mission, he thought he had his bases covered but had forgotten a hard truth he had learned in the past: In warfare, the enemy gets a vote.

2

Crossing the lobby to the Las Vegas Venetian casino, another gaggle of bearded men went by, all wearing cargo pants and baseball caps with Velcro patches. Half of them toted some form of corduroy nylon backpack, which also sported a variety of gun-porn patches, like *ISIS Hunter* or a *Punisher* skull.

I said, "I have never seen this many super-commando 'operators' in one place in my life."

Knuckles laughed and said, "Yeah, this event brings 'em out of the woodwork, no doubt. But make no mistake, the real deal's running around in here as well. In fact, keep your eyes peeled. The odds of us running into someone we know are pretty high, so be prepared to run the cover story."

Working in cover was the worst when you did it in an area where the locals potentially knew you. Whenever that happened, the nastiest thing that could occur— besides getting your fingernails pulled out by the enemy—was running into someone who knows who you are in real life. It was the surest way to blow the hell out of what you were pretending. An FBI agent infiltrating an outlaw motorcycle gang would be in dire straights if he bumped into a friend from law school.

In this case, Knuckles was still active duty Navy and I was retired Army. In the world of the Taskforce, when we were out in the Badlands earning our *ISIS Hunter* patches for real, he was a civilian employee of my company, but if another SEAL from his past saw him here, they'd know that was bullshit, so we'd created a story that was plausible should that happen to either of us.

It was my first trip to the fabled SHOT Show in Las Vegas, the largest gun show on earth, and the interior of the Sands convention center was literally stuffed with booth after booth selling various weapons, accessories, and outdoor gear. It was Mecca to people like me, and the Taskforce sent a contingent every year to prowl the halls looking for anything new that we could incorporate into our mission. Back when I was on active duty, as the team leader, I'd always let a junior member of the team make the trip, and Knuckles, my 2IC, had been a few times before.

Given how he was dressed, I'm surprised they let him in.

In contrast to the bearded ones, he looked like he had come to protest the convention, with his long hippy hair, Che Guevara T-shirt, and lack of any tacticool paraphernalia. He was even wearing a leather necklace with a bronze peace sign the size of a fifty-cent piece—either as irony or a challenge. With him it was hard to tell, but if someone took it as a challenge, they'd be sorely wishing they hadn't. Unlike a lot of the posers at the convention, he was most definitely an Operator.

While the trip *was* a little bit of a boondoggle, we did have a specific mission. We'd just come from a booth manned by a company called ZEV Technologies—a maker of high-end aftermarket components and custom frame/slide work for Glock pistols—and had sealed a deal to test some pistols for our specific applications.

Although we already had our own armorer support that we used to hone our combat weapons, Kurt

Hale—the commander of the Taskforce—was wondering if we weren't just reinventing the wheel and wanted to see if it would be better to simply farm out the work. After talking to ZEV, I was beginning to believe he was right, only our wheels were something from a Conestoga wagon while ZEV was racing around on run-flats.

We pushed through the crowd and entered the cavernous Venetian casino, working our way to Las Vegas Boulevard. We exited into the sunshine, leaving the commandos and gamblers only to be hit by Guatemalan refugees trying to hand me cards with hookers offering their services. One of the strangest things about Vegas.

Knuckles said, "What did you think?"

"Seriously? I think we should have flown here with the entire team's Glocks. No question they can do better than our internal armorers. Nothing against them, but did you work the one they had on display? Better trigger than ours by far."

Knuckles took a left toward Caesars Palace, passing the gigantic Venetian hotel, saying, "So forget about any other vendors?"

He had a point. While we didn't fall under any official DoD rules about contracts, it would be stupid to latch on to the first one we found. We had a list of potential companies that could meet our goals, and it wouldn't be right not to at least check them out. But I was pretty sure where I would end up on my recommendation to Kurt.

I said, "Naw, we should hit 'em up as well, but we only get two days out here, and I want some Vegas time. I'll send Retro and Jennifer to go hunt them down."

"Retro isn't going to like that, and Jennifer's not exactly an expert."

Retro had been a teammate of mine since Jesus was wearing diapers, but all things come to a close sooner or later. He was set to retire from the military at the end of the month and had truly come out here as a complete vacation. Kurt knew he wasn't needed but had let him come along as a little retirement gift. Unbeknownst to me, in all our time together, I learned he absolutely loved playing craps, and his wife frowned on gambling. He had planned on spending his entire time in the casinos betting away his per diem like a drunken sailor.

As we were planning to leave for the trip, he'd begged to come along, getting a seat through Kurt, then had turned around and told his wife he was desperately needed for national security, which she bought. As they say, "What happens in Vegas . . ."

I said, "It's not going to kill him to take a break for a few hours, and as far as Jennifer goes, she could learn something."

Jennifer was my partner in Grolier Recovery Services—our company—and, outside of some serious weapons training I'd given her, had no military experience. She wasn't qualified to judge whether a vendor was worthy, and wasn't needed on this trip either, but I'd paid for her to come along out of my own pocket because, well, she was a partner in more ways than one. She'd planned on spending her time at the pool—or if the weather was too cold, in the spa.

I felt my phone vibrate and saw it was her. I said, "Speak of the devil."

I answered, "Hey, we're on Vegas Boulevard headed home. What's up?"

"Kurt wants to talk on the VPN. Secure."

"About what?"

"Apparently, about a mission. In Vegas."

BRAD TAYLOR

"Readers of novels set in the world
of Special Forces have many choices,
but Taylor is one of the best."
—*Booklist*

For a complete list of titles,
please visit prh.com/bradtaylor.